Lament

Elsie Park

Published by Elsie Park, 2024.

LAMENT

First edition. November 25, 2024.

ISBN: 979-8227417640

Written by Elsie Park.

·

Chapter 1: A Storm in the Heart

The wind howled like a banshee, tugging at my clothes as I braced myself against the tempest. Each gust seemed to carry whispers of secrets long buried beneath the roiling waters of Lake Glimmer. My heart raced, not just from the adrenaline of the storm, but from the weight of the truth I sought. Generations of my family had been swallowed by this lake—lost to the depths without a trace. As I squinted through the sheets of rain, I could almost feel their cold fingers brushing against my skin, urging me forward.

Lightning split the sky, illuminating the shoreline for a brief moment. That's when I saw him—a silhouette against the chaos, tall and broad, exuding an energy that crackled in the air like static. He stood there, a defiant figure clad in dark clothing, his hair slicked back and wet, eyes glowing with an intensity that sent shivers down my spine. It was absurd to think that in the midst of this violent storm, I would feel anything but fear, yet here I was, inexplicably drawn to him.

"Step away from the water!" His voice boomed over the tumult, sharp and commanding. I could feel the weight of authority in his words, yet there was an undeniable hint of urgency that piqued my curiosity. "This isn't a place for you."

"Is that your official line?" I shouted back, irritation bubbling beneath my skin. "I'm not here for a swim. I'm here for answers—answers you clearly don't want anyone to find."

He took a step closer, the rain plastering his shirt to his body, revealing muscles that seemed chiseled from stone. "This is not just a mystery; it's dangerous. You have no idea what you're tampering with."

"Oh, I have an inkling," I retorted, taking a bold step toward him. "But I'm not about to let some suit dictate what I can and cannot do. This lake holds the key to my family's past, and I refuse to back down because of some bureaucratic agent who thinks he can control the storm."

His lips curved into a half-smirk, and in that moment, the storm felt almost like a backdrop to our burgeoning conflict, electric and alive. "You have spirit, I'll give you that. But it's misplaced. You think this is about you, but it's so much bigger than that."

I scoffed, rain mingling with the stubborn tears that clung to my lashes. "Bigger? Like what? Ghost stories? My family's folklore? I've spent my life digging into the past, and all I've found are dead ends. But I refuse to let it end here."

The ground trembled beneath us, and for a fleeting moment, our argument was overshadowed by something far more ominous. The earth shivered as if it were awakening from a deep slumber, and the storm intensified, wind shrieking like a wild animal. The air grew thick with anticipation, charged with an energy that felt alive. I glanced toward the lake, and in the distance, I could see it—the faint glow, pulsing like a heartbeat beneath the churning surface.

"What is that?" I asked, my voice barely a whisper against the fury of the storm.

He hesitated, his fiery gaze shifting from me to the lake. "That's what I'm trying to protect you from. It's... something ancient. Something that shouldn't be disturbed."

"Disturbed?" I echoed incredulously. "It's been here long before either of us, and if my family's history is any indication, it won't stop until it has what it wants."

As if in response to my words, a crack of thunder erupted overhead, and the ground bucked violently. I stumbled, but before I could regain my balance, he reached out and steadied me, his hand warm against the cold, wet fabric of my shirt. The connection sent an unexpected jolt of electricity through me, startling and confusing.

"Listen to me," he urged, his voice dropping an octave, laced with urgency. "You're not safe here. Whatever lies beneath that water is more powerful than you can comprehend. If you're here to uncover the truth, you need to be careful about what you wish for."

I pulled away from his grip, irritated by the vulnerability that threatened to seep into my resolve. "And you think I'll just take your word for it? You don't know me, or my family. We've fought for the truth, and I won't let you—or anyone—stand in my way."

"Then you're a fool," he shot back, his voice rough with emotion. "A fool who doesn't understand the consequences of digging too deep. I didn't come here to fight you; I came to protect you."

A moment of silence passed between us, tension thick enough to slice through the downpour. The pulsing glow from the lake intensified, shimmering like a beacon in the night, as if it were calling out to us, beckoning. My heart thrummed in time with the glow, a rhythm that seemed to promise secrets and revelations, but also danger.

"Protect me?" I said, incredulous. "You're just here to enforce rules. You don't care about my family or their legacy."

His expression shifted, and for a fleeting moment, the mask of authority slipped, revealing a glimmer of understanding—or perhaps empathy. "It's not just rules. It's the lives at stake. People have gone missing for a reason, and I won't let you become another victim."

With those words hanging between us, the storm unleashed its fury anew, and I realized that this tempest was not just a natural phenomenon. It was a reflection of the chaos swirling within me—a storm of my own, ignited by the fiery stranger and the dark secrets that lay in wait beneath the lake's surface.

We stood, two souls at odds, yet strangely connected, as the glow from the depths pulsed once more, promising both peril and revelation. In that electric moment, I knew that the storm was only just beginning.

The storm intensified, swirling around us like a malevolent specter, and I felt an intoxicating mix of fear and exhilaration coursing through my veins. He was still standing there, drenched yet unyielding, a fierce protector in the midst of chaos. The connection between us crackled with an energy I couldn't quite place, like static in the air before a storm, and I fought against the pull of it even as I felt my own resolve wavering.

"Let me guess," he said, his voice cutting through the cacophony with an edge of sarcasm that momentarily surprised me. "You think you're going to wade in there, wrestle the secrets of Lake Glimmer from its depths, and come out the other side with a heartwarming family reunion?"

I shot him a glare, the rain stinging my cheeks like angry bees. "If anyone's going to reunite with the past, it's me. You're just here to throw around your authority and make sure I don't find what I'm looking for."

"Authority? Hardly. I'd call it more of a public service." He shifted his weight, bracing himself against the relentless wind, and I couldn't help but notice how his presence seemed to anchor me amidst the storm. "Look, I get it. Family legacies are important. But this isn't just about ghosts. It's about something far more dangerous."

The glow from the lake pulsed again, a beacon in the dark, and it was as if the very water was listening to our argument, the ancient power beneath it simmering with anticipation. I took a step closer, drawn by an instinct I didn't fully understand. "What do you know about it? Why are you really here?"

For a heartbeat, he hesitated, the rain running down his face like molten silver. "You wouldn't believe me if I told you."

"Try me." I crossed my arms defiantly, refusing to back down. "I've lived in the shadow of this lake my entire life. I'm not going to let some agent with a bad attitude intimidate me into turning back now."

A flicker of amusement danced in his eyes, and he let out a low chuckle that almost drowned in the storm. "You're like a wildflower in a hurricane, you know that? Stubborn and beautiful, but so very out of place."

"Thanks for the compliment, but I'm not the one lost out here." I stepped closer, intrigued by the fire in his gaze. "Tell me what you're hiding. There's something more going on here, and I won't just walk away because you ask me to."

"Fine," he relented, his voice dropping to a more serious tone. "But you need to understand the stakes. This lake is more than just water and secrets; it's a gateway. The disappearances are connected to something that was sealed away a long time ago. There are forces at play that neither of us can fully comprehend."

The revelation hung between us, heavy and palpable, and I felt my heart race with a mix of fear and curiosity. "What kind of forces?"

"Ones that thrive in the dark," he said, glancing over his shoulder as if expecting shadows to spring to life. "Things that want to reclaim what was lost, and they're not shy about using anyone who gets in their way."

"Are you saying my family was... involved?" The words tasted bitter in my mouth. "That my ancestors had something to do with this?"

He met my gaze, the fire in his eyes dimming momentarily as he processed my words. "I don't know. But the way you're drawn to this place, the way your family's history is intertwined with it—it all points to something deeper. You're not just an innocent bystander in this."

I took a step back, the implications of his words sinking in like a stone in my stomach. "So what? I'm supposed to turn my back on the very thing that defines me? I can't just walk away."

"I'm not asking you to walk away. I'm asking you to be careful." His voice softened, a thread of concern woven into his words. "I don't want to see you get hurt. Not because of this lake, or the past, or whatever else is lurking in the shadows."

Before I could respond, another tremor rocked the ground, and the glow from the lake pulsed violently. A crack of thunder shattered the moment, and for a brief instant, the world around us seemed to still, suspended in a fragile balance between chaos and clarity.

Then, with a roar, the water surged upwards, and I stumbled forward, caught off guard by the force of it. "What the hell is happening?" I shouted, my voice barely piercing the din.

"Get back!" he yelled, reaching for my arm. But before I could react, the glow erupted, and from the depths, something rose—an iridescent shape that seemed to shimmer and shift like liquid glass. It hovered just above the surface, defying gravity, pulsating with an otherworldly light that illuminated the darkened shoreline.

"Stay away from it!" he warned, his grip tightening around my arm as we both took a cautious step back. The air crackled with energy, electric and alive, and I felt the overwhelming pull of the lake, as if it were whispering promises of answers and secrets long hidden.

"What is that?" I breathed, captivated despite the danger that loomed.

"I don't know," he replied, his tone grave. "But it's not friendly. Whatever it is, it's awakened."

The glow danced like a heartbeat, and I could feel my own pulse quickening in response. It was beautiful and terrifying all at once, an echo of the mysteries that lay just beyond my reach. "We need to find out what it wants," I said, adrenaline flooding my senses. "This is what I came for!"

"Are you insane?" He shook his head, disbelief mingling with concern. "You can't just wade into the unknown like that!"

"But if it's connected to my family—"

"Your family's legacy is precisely why you should keep your distance!" he countered, his voice fierce. "You have no idea what you're dealing with!"

Yet, as I stared at the luminescent shape before us, the world around us faded, leaving only the pulsating glow that seemed to call out to me, beckoning me forward. The air thickened, charged with an energy that surged through me, igniting a fire I had never felt before.

"Watch me," I said defiantly, adrenaline and determination propelling me toward the shimmering light, even as he shouted my name, desperation lacing his voice. In that moment, I was no longer just a seeker of truth; I was on the brink of uncovering something that could change everything. The storm raged on, but I had chosen my path, and the heart of the storm awaited.

I stepped forward, heart pounding, the shimmering light before me igniting a flicker of hope and danger in equal measure. The agent's protest echoed in my mind, but my curiosity overpowered his caution. With each step I took toward the glowing shape, the air thickened, buzzing with an energy that felt both intoxicating and treacherous. I barely registered his frantic attempts to pull me back; my focus was consumed by the ethereal light that beckoned like a siren's call.

"Don't be an idiot!" he shouted, his voice strained with urgency. But his words faded into the background as the glow pulsed, illuminating the rain-slicked rocks beneath my feet, making them glisten like jewels. "You have no idea what you're doing!"

"Neither do you!" I shot back, a twinge of defiance edging my voice. "But I can't just ignore this. Not now." I felt an inexplicable pull, as if the lake was whispering my name, urging me to unravel its secrets.

I had been searching for answers for so long, digging through dusty archives and piecing together fragmented stories. And now, standing at the precipice of something far larger than myself, I was not about to turn away. The water glimmered with an almost sentient energy, and I could feel it humming beneath my skin, resonating with my very core.

As I approached the edge of the water, the glow intensified, swirling in mesmerizing patterns that danced like tendrils of smoke. "Stop!" he shouted again, desperation coloring his tone, but I was already too far gone, my heart racing in tandem with the pulsing light.

The moment my fingers grazed the surface of the water, it felt as if time itself had stopped. A shockwave of cold rippled through me, and images flooded my mind—flashes of my ancestors, faces blurred by time, their eyes wide with fear, their voices a chorus of warnings. They were trapped, their stories intertwined with the lake, held captive by something dark and ancient.

"Get away from there!" he roared, panic lacing his words as he lunged forward, but it was too late. The water surged, and a wave shot up, enveloping me in its cool embrace, pulling me into the depths. The world above faded, swallowed by darkness as I plunged into the lake's depths.

Air escaped my lungs in a gasp, the cold wrapping around me like a shroud. For a heartbeat, I flailed, disoriented and afraid. But then I felt it—a current, gentle yet insistent, guiding me deeper. I let go of my panic and surrendered to the pull, trusting it would lead me to the truth.

Surrounded by shadows, I felt weightless, suspended in time. Images flashed before my eyes, memories not my own, weaving a tapestry of history—children laughing by the shore, families gathered for festivities, faces that morphed into expressions of sorrow and loss. I could sense the pain that seeped from the depths of the lake, the echoes of countless lives intertwined with my own.

Then came a voice, soft yet resonant, as if it originated from the very fabric of the water. "Help us." It was a plea, an urgency wrapped in a longing that resonated through the darkness. "You are one of us. Break the cycle."

A rush of clarity washed over me, filling the void of fear. This was not just a search for answers; it was an invitation to embrace my heritage, to confront the shadows that had plagued my family for generations. But how? How could I possibly help when I didn't even know what was being asked of me?

Suddenly, I was pulled upward, the water swirling around me in a frantic rush, and I broke the surface with a gasp, the storm still raging above. I blinked against the downpour, my heart racing as I found myself face-to-face with him again, his expression a mix of relief and fury.

"You're insane!" he shouted, rage and concern battling in his tone. "You could have drowned! What were you thinking?"

"I was thinking..." My voice trembled as I struggled to find the words. "I was thinking there's something down there. Something that needs to be uncovered."

"Or something that wants to keep you there!" he shot back, anger boiling over. "You have to stop this obsession. It's not just your past. It's dangerous!"

The words stung, and for a moment, I felt the weight of his fear pressing against me, but beneath that was something else—something raw and protective. "You don't understand," I replied, shaking my head, water spraying everywhere. "It's all connected. My family, the lake, the disappearances... They're calling for me."

"Calling for you?" His tone was incredulous, but beneath the bluster, I sensed a flicker of curiosity. "What do you mean?"

Before I could respond, a thunderous crack echoed overhead, and the ground shook once more, sending tremors rippling through my feet. We both stumbled, and I could feel the lake responding, the water swirling violently as if the depths themselves were awakening.

And then it happened—a great, dark shape emerged from the center of the lake, rising like a specter from a forgotten nightmare. A mass of shadows and light twisted together, forming a visage that was both hauntingly beautiful and terrifying. It loomed above us, an embodiment of all the fear that had plagued my family for generations.

"What is that?" I breathed, fear clawing at my throat as the creature surged toward us, a tempest of power and ancient sorrow.

He grabbed my arm, his grip firm yet protective, and we both took a step back. "I don't know, but we need to get out of here!"

"No! We can't run from it," I insisted, pulling away. "This is what I've been searching for! I need to confront it!"

"Are you out of your mind?" he shouted, his voice rising above the storm. "You don't know what it wants!"

The creature twisted, a swirling mass of shadows that shimmered with an iridescent glow, and I felt it reaching out, the energy crackling in the air between us. I couldn't turn away; my heart pounded in rhythm with the glow, an unbreakable bond forming between us.

"Help us," it echoed, the plea resonating through me, binding me to the very essence of the lake. In that moment, I realized it wasn't just a voice but a chorus of the lost, yearning for release.

The agent's hand tightened around my wrist, his fear palpable. "Don't! You don't know what it's capable of!"

But as the creature surged closer, drawing me in with its magnetic energy, I knew I had crossed a threshold. The weight of my family's past pressed upon my shoulders, demanding resolution. This was my moment—whether I was ready for it or not.

As the world around us faded into darkness, I felt the boundaries of reality blurring, caught between the safety of the shore and the depth of the unknown. With the storm raging overhead and the creature looming before us, I took a step forward, ready to embrace the darkness, when suddenly the ground erupted beneath us.

The last thing I heard was his voice, sharp with desperation, cutting through the chaos as the world collapsed into chaos. "No, don't! It's not safe!"

And then, in an instant, the darkness enveloped me completely, swallowing the storm and the light, leaving only silence in its wake.

Chapter 2: Shadows on the Lake

The sun dipped below the horizon, painting the sky in hues of violet and gold, casting elongated shadows that danced across the water's surface. I sat at the old oak table on the porch, the rough wood cool against my palms as I fanned open the yellowed pages of my family's journals. Each crinkled leaf whispered tales of my ancestors and their ties to the lake, its depths cradling their secrets like a mother. Legends of creatures lurking beneath the surface flitted through my mind, evoking both dread and intrigue. The air was thick with the scent of pine and damp earth, a heady blend that reminded me of summer storms.

As I read, the shadows lengthened, and I felt a shiver of awareness slide down my spine. Isaac was close. The hairs on my arms prickled, not from the chill in the evening air, but from the electric tension that always simmered between us. He emerged from the woods, his figure half-illuminated by the last rays of sunlight, a silhouette framed by the towering trees. The moment our eyes met, an unspoken challenge crackled in the space between us, the lingering effects of past arguments coiling like smoke.

"Still digging through the family dirt?" he asked, his tone teasing but edged with seriousness. I couldn't help but notice how the fading light caught the angles of his jaw, sharp and unyielding, a mask that hinted at the complexities buried beneath. He stepped closer, and I could see the glint of something—fear?—in his hazel eyes.

"Just trying to understand what I'm up against," I shot back, unable to hide the defiance in my voice. My heart raced, both at his presence and the memory of the last time we clashed. It had been months, but that night at the lake, with the water lapping against the shore like a restless child, still haunted me.

"Some things are better left alone," he insisted, folding his arms across his chest, a barrier that both intrigued and frustrated me.

"This place isn't what you think. It's cursed. The journals just give it a romantic spin." His words hung between us, heavy with foreboding.

"Cursed?" I repeated, incredulous. "That sounds like the plot of a bad horror movie. Do you actually believe that?" I could feel my pulse quickening, not entirely from fear but from the thrill of confrontation.

He stepped closer, his expression darkening. "You don't know what you're playing with, Emily. These stories... they're not just tales to scare children. My grandfather disappeared here, and my mother never spoke of it. I've seen things—"

"What, like ghosts? Is that what you're trying to tell me?" I interjected, unable to resist the sarcastic edge creeping into my voice. "Come on, Isaac. You can't seriously believe in all of this. We're not living in a fairy tale."

"Fairy tales?" He laughed, the sound rich and bitter. "Maybe they're the only way to make sense of this place. You're here because you think you're uncovering family history, but what if you're just digging up nightmares? You're too curious for your own good."

"And you're too stubborn to see what's right in front of you," I shot back, refusing to back down. The tension between us crackled like the distant thunder I could feel rumbling through the air, threatening a storm. "You think I'm going to turn tail and run just because you say so? You don't know me."

"I know enough," he replied, his voice low, the challenge in his eyes igniting something deep within me. "I know this lake is dangerous. You're too smart to risk it. Leave while you still can."

The challenge was palpable, a dance between defiance and desire that kept me anchored to the spot. I wanted to dismiss him, to shove aside the doubts creeping into my mind, but there was something in his voice—an urgency that resonated with the anxious beat of my heart.

"Is that what you want?" I asked, my voice dropping to a whisper. "For me to just walk away? To forget this place and all its mysteries?"

"Of course not," he replied, his voice softening. "I want you to be safe. But the more you delve into this, the more it pulls you under. You think I'm being dramatic? This lake... it doesn't let go easily. And neither do its secrets."

The words hung between us, a precarious balance of fear and yearning. I took a breath, letting the weight of his warning settle into the space around us. The lake, with its inky depths, felt like a living entity, watching, waiting, and I was determined to unveil whatever lay hidden beneath its surface.

As the first drops of rain began to fall, splattering against the porch like whispered secrets, I looked into Isaac's eyes and saw something shift. It was as if the shadows around us thickened, merging with the gloom that lingered at the edge of the lake, and I knew then that our confrontation was only the beginning.

The rain picked up, a gentle patter at first, then a steady rhythm that echoed like a heartbeat against the wooden porch. I took a step back from the railing, the splintered wood pressing into my palm as I pondered Isaac's warning. He stood there, shadows cloaking him, a steadfast guardian to the secrets he clearly believed were better left undisturbed. I could feel the weight of his gaze, a mixture of concern and something more elusive, something that made my pulse quicken.

"Maybe you're right," I conceded, my voice cutting through the drumming rain. "But what if I'm not just chasing shadows? What if I'm meant to uncover the truth?" My heart thrummed with a strange mix of fear and excitement, the allure of the lake tugging at me like an unseen tide.

He stepped closer, the space between us charged with unspoken tension. "The truth isn't always what we want it to be," he said, his voice barely above a whisper, as if afraid the shadows might overhear. "Sometimes it's darker than we expect."

The air crackled, and for a moment, the only sound was the steady drumming of the rain and the distant rustle of leaves. My thoughts raced, battling with the pull of his words. The thought of abandoning this quest felt like letting go of a lifeline, the very essence of who I was. I needed to know what lay beneath the surface—not just of the lake, but of everything that had brought me back here.

"Are you going to stand there and play the reluctant hero?" I shot back, challenging him as the rain soaked into my clothes. "Or are you going to help me?"

Isaac's jaw tightened, the muscles flexing as he processed my words. "I'm not your hero, Emily," he replied, a flash of vulnerability breaking through his guarded demeanor. "But maybe I'm not ready to let you dive into this alone, either."

The revelation landed softly, wrapping around us like the mist rolling off the lake. It was a twist I hadn't expected, a crack in the armor he always wore. "So you want to keep me safe by sticking around? I appreciate the gesture, but I can handle myself."

"Is that so?" he shot back, a smirk tugging at the corners of his mouth, the storm in his eyes softening momentarily. "You think those ancient legends will bend to your will just because you've got a brave heart?"

The challenge in his tone ignited something within me, a flame I had long buried under layers of practicality. "I've faced tougher things than legends. You have no idea what I've dealt with."

"I know more than you think," he replied, stepping even closer, the intensity between us palpable. "I've seen how the lake can twist even the strongest wills. It doesn't care who you are or how brave you feel."

As his words settled in, I felt a flicker of doubt, a momentary crack in my bravado. Perhaps he was right; maybe I was standing on the edge of something vast and unknowable, teetering on the brink of disaster. But the thought of turning back now was unthinkable. I had come too far, unearthed too many echoes of the past, to retreat now.

"I'm not afraid of what lies beneath," I insisted, a conviction igniting in my chest. "But I could use someone who understands this place."

Isaac studied me, the rain pooling around our feet, mirroring the depths of the lake. "Then let's make a deal," he said, a hint of mischief returning to his eyes. "I'll help you with your search, but if things start to get weird—and they will—you promise to listen to me."

I couldn't help but laugh at the absurdity of it all. "Fine. But only if you promise not to treat me like a damsel in distress. I can handle myself, remember?"

He chuckled, the tension easing just a bit. "Deal. Just don't expect me to be your knight in shining armor every time you decide to poke the beast."

The moment hung, our laughter mingling with the sound of the rain as it transformed into a gentle shower. It was unexpected, this alliance born from shared determination and reluctant camaraderie. The shadows around us seemed to shift, as if the lake itself was watching, intrigued by our fragile bond.

"Let's check the boathouse," I suggested, a spark of excitement igniting my spirit. "If there's anything left behind from the last time someone tried to explore these waters, it might be there."

Isaac nodded, the glimmer of adventure lighting up his face. "Lead the way, then. But remember, if you hear anything strange, you run, got it?"

"Or I could just stand and engage in a witty banter," I replied with a smirk. "What's a little supernatural creature compared to my razor-sharp wit?"

He groaned dramatically, the corners of his mouth twitching upwards. "I'm not sure if your humor is a blessing or a curse."

We moved towards the boathouse, the rain forming a curtain that blurred the world beyond. The path was slick with mud, but my heart raced with the thrill of exploration. The boathouse loomed ahead, its silhouette framed by the trees, a forgotten relic of summers past. I pushed open the creaky door, the scent of damp wood and nostalgia wrapping around me like a familiar cloak.

Inside, the light was dim, filtering through the cobwebbed windows. Dust motes danced in the faint illumination, and I felt as if I had stepped back in time. Old fishing gear hung on the walls, nets twisted like forgotten dreams. I moved deeper into the space, curiosity guiding my steps.

"This is it," I murmured, scanning the cluttered interior. "If there's anything of value, it has to be here."

Isaac joined me, his presence warm and grounding. "What are we looking for, exactly?"

"Anything—journal entries, old maps, even personal items that could hint at what happened here," I replied, my fingers grazing the surface of a weathered table, feeling the stories embedded in the wood. "This place is a treasure trove of history. It just needs a little digging."

He smiled, a mixture of admiration and apprehension flickering in his eyes. "Just promise me that when the shadows start whispering, you'll remember this is no ordinary treasure hunt."

"Deal," I said, my heart swelling with a sense of purpose. Together, we began to sift through the remnants of the past, unaware of the depths of the mysteries we were about to unearth.

The boathouse was a time capsule, holding the scent of wet wood and the weight of forgotten memories. Dust motes swirled in the air like tiny phantoms, and I could almost hear the echoes of laughter and splashes from summers long past. As I rummaged through the clutter, I felt a blend of anticipation and dread, a sense that something vital lingered just out of reach, hidden among the remnants of this old place.

Isaac joined me in exploring the shadowy corners, his fingers brushing over the rusted tools and frayed fishing nets, a frown etched on his brow. "Do you ever get the feeling that some things should just stay buried?" he mused, casting a sidelong glance at me.

I shot him a playful smirk. "Are you suggesting we let the lake keep its secrets? That would be a real buzzkill, don't you think? We came all this way for a little mystery, didn't we?"

"Sure, but there's a fine line between intrigue and insanity," he replied, his voice laced with concern. "You seem hell-bent on crossing it."

I couldn't resist rolling my eyes. "Oh please, I've danced with insanity before. Besides, what's life without a bit of risk? Think of it as an adventure. A very, very damp adventure."

He chuckled, but I noticed a flicker of worry in his gaze. "Just promise me if you find something weird—like an ancient curse or, I don't know, a cursed heirloom—you'll tell me before you start chanting incantations."

"Noted," I said, flipping through an old tackle box, its once-bright orange lid now faded and grimy. A collection of rusted hooks and tangled lines greeted me, each a testament to the passage of time. "But if I find a magic wand, I'm using it."

"Of course you are," he replied dryly. "Can't let practicality ruin the fun."

The banter helped ease the tension, but it didn't quiet the nagging sense of unease that had settled in my stomach. I could almost feel the lake breathing, a living entity that sensed our presence, urging us to discover what lay beneath its still surface.

As we rummaged deeper, I stumbled upon an old trunk, half-hidden beneath a dusty tarp. The wood was cracked, but it held a promise of discovery. "Hey, look at this!" I called, excitement bubbling in my voice as I knelt beside it. "This could be the jackpot."

Isaac leaned over, his curiosity piqued. "What do you think is in there? The last remains of a summer camp gone wrong?"

"Only one way to find out," I replied, my heart racing as I pried open the lid. It creaked ominously, and I hesitated for a moment, the weight of anticipation pressing down on me. The trunk revealed a jumble of items: faded photographs, an old compass, and a set of journals that looked just as ancient as the ones I'd already been through.

"Bingo!" I exclaimed, carefully pulling out the journals and flipping through them. The pages were filled with neat, swirling script that seemed to beckon me closer. I caught snippets of stories—campfire tales about the lake, adventures of young love, and hints of darker undercurrents that sent a shiver down my spine.

"Let me see," Isaac said, his eyes lighting up as he leaned closer. "Anything worth sharing, or are they just love letters to the lake?"

I chuckled, but my laughter faded as I read deeper. "Some of these are... unsettling. There are references to people disappearing and strange lights on the water at night. It's like the lake was calling them."

Isaac's expression grew serious. "See? This is what I was talking about. You can't just ignore this. If it's all true..."

"Then what?" I challenged, my pulse quickening. "We let it scare us into submission? No way. If there's something lurking here, I want to know what it is."

He opened his mouth to respond, but suddenly, a loud crash echoed from outside, cutting our argument short. The sound reverberated through the boathouse, and instinctively, we both froze, hearts racing in sync.

"What was that?" I whispered, a chill running down my spine.

"I have no idea," Isaac replied, his brow furrowing as he glanced toward the door. "But it didn't sound like something good."

We exchanged a look, and I could see the uncertainty mirrored in his eyes. Without speaking, we crept toward the entrance, the old wood creaking beneath our feet. The rain had intensified, drumming against the roof like an urgent heartbeat, and I felt the weight of something looming just beyond the threshold.

As we reached the door, I hesitated, my hand hovering over the latch. "What if it's just a branch?" I asked, trying to quell the rising dread within me.

"Or something much worse," Isaac murmured, his tone serious.

Taking a deep breath, I swung the door open, the hinges protesting loudly. The world outside was a blur of rain and shadows, the lake glimmering ominously in the muted light. My eyes scanned the landscape, heart racing as I searched for the source of the noise.

Then I saw it—something glinting in the water, just beyond the dock, illuminated by flashes of lightning that danced across the sky. My breath caught in my throat. It was a shape, darker than the water, and it moved with an unsettling grace, cutting through the surface as if it were alive.

"Emily, we need to go," Isaac urged, his voice tense.

But I couldn't move. Something compelled me to stay, to stare deeper into the depths of the lake, where the shape twisted and turned, beckoning. A primal instinct surged within me, pulling me closer, even as every rational thought screamed to run.

"Wait," I breathed, unable to tear my gaze away. "Do you see that?"

Isaac stepped closer, his hand gripping my arm, urgency radiating from him. "It's not safe. We should—"

And then, as if in response to my unspoken question, the shape surged upward, breaking the water's surface with a sudden ferocity, a cascade of droplets scattering like diamonds in the stormy air. The moment was breathtaking, filled with raw beauty and terror, and as the figure emerged, my heart plummeted into my stomach.

It was a face, hauntingly familiar yet entirely otherworldly, eyes reflecting the storm, a visage of longing and sorrow. My heart raced as recognition hit me like a bolt of lightning.

"Isaac, I think I know what it is," I whispered, fear and wonder intermingling.

But before I could finish, the figure dipped back below the surface, disappearing into the depths with a grace that belied the chaos swirling around us.

"Emily!" Isaac's voice broke through the haze, filled with panic. "We need to go—now!"

But as I turned to him, the world around us seemed to shift, shadows elongating and twisting, the lake roaring with a voice of its own, drowning out reason as I was drawn toward the water's edge, compelled to dive into the depths of my family's legacy, unaware of the darkness that awaited.

Chapter 3: Under the Glimmer Moon

The night air wraps around me like a silken shawl, cool and crisp, each breath I take infused with the earthy scent of damp leaves and lingering wildflowers. The moon hangs low in the sky, a luminous orb spilling silver light across the surface of the lake, transforming the familiar landscape into something ethereal. My heart pounds with an electric rhythm as I slip through the tall grass, each step a delicate dance between exhilaration and trepidation.

"Stop right there!" Isaac's voice slices through the tranquility, sharp as a knife. He emerges from the shadows like a storm cloud, his face taut with frustration, eyes gleaming under the moonlight. "You can't be serious about going to the water. You know what they say about the lake at night."

"Of course I know what they say," I reply, my tone light, attempting to pierce the tension. "That it calls to the lonely, lures them in with sweet whispers." I can't resist the playful flicker in my heart, even as dread curls in my stomach. "But I'm not lonely, Isaac. Just curious."

He steps closer, hands shoved deep in his pockets, the tension in his stance betraying his worry. "Curiosity doesn't matter when it comes to the lake. It's not just water, you know. It has a way of—"

"Claiming people?" I interject, mimicking the local folklore that has seeped into our conversations like the fog rolling in from the water's edge. "I thought you didn't believe in fairy tales."

"Not fairy tales. Facts." He shakes his head, dark hair falling into his eyes, and for a moment, I want to reach up and tuck it back, to smooth the creases of concern etched on his brow. "People have gone missing, Mia. The lake isn't just a pretty face."

The moonlight catches the water in a sparkling array, and for a heartbeat, I'm mesmerized. It's as if the surface is alive, pulsating with a rhythm all its own, echoing the quickening of my heart. "Maybe it's time someone defied the legends," I whisper, half to myself, half to the boy who seems to understand me more than anyone else.

"Maybe it's time someone listened to reason," he replies, voice laced with urgency. But his words fade as I feel that inexplicable pull, a magnetic force that beckons me closer to the shoreline. I can't shake the sensation that the water knows me, that it remembers every secret I've whispered into the wind, every wish I've cast beneath the stars.

"Please, Mia," he implores, stepping forward, his expression softening. "Don't do this. I can't lose you to whatever the lake wants."

His earnestness strikes a chord within me, a melody of friendship woven with something deeper, a tether that pulls at my heart. I look up at him, seeing not just the boy I've known forever but the man he's becoming—protective, fierce, unyielding. "You won't lose me. I promise. I just need to see for myself."

As if the universe decides to test our resolve, a sudden gust of wind rushes past, causing the water to ripple and sway, distorting the reflection of the moon into a thousand dancing shards of light. The haunting stillness is broken by a distant echo, a voice drifting on the breeze—a sweet, sorrowful lament that sends shivers down my spine.

"What was that?" Isaac's eyes widen, a mix of disbelief and growing concern. I can see the struggle on his face, the part of him that wants to pull me away, and the part that wants to discover the truth alongside me.

"Maybe it's the lake's siren call," I tease lightly, trying to mask my own unease. But deep down, that voice weaves a spell around my heart, compelling me forward with each haunting note. "Maybe it's trying to tell us something."

"No, it's trying to lure you in!" His tone sharpens, the fear clear in his eyes as he grips my arm, a lifeline tethering me to reality. "We need to leave now. This isn't a game."

Yet the urge to step into the water swells within me, like a tide rising against the shore, pulling me into its depths. "But what if it's beautiful?" I murmur, almost to myself. "What if it's something we've both been longing for?"

"Stop it!" His voice is a mixture of anger and desperation, but I can see the battle waging in his heart. "You don't know what you're saying. Don't let it play tricks on you."

With a surge of determination, I pull free from his grasp, taking a step toward the water, its surface glimmering like a blanket of stars waiting to embrace me. "Isaac, I have to know."

Before I can take another step, the water erupts, a shimmering cascade of moonlight revealing a figure emerging from the depths. It's a woman—no, a creature—with hair that flows like liquid silver, skin glistening with the sheen of the lake. She sings, her voice echoing like the sweetest of dreams, a siren's call that feels oddly familiar.

"Mia!" Isaac's voice breaks through the fog, but I'm entranced, the woman's eyes locking onto mine, pulling me closer to the water's edge as if we're two pieces of a puzzle, fated to fit together. My heart races, caught in the riptide of emotion that surges through me, a longing that transcends the physical.

"Come," she whispers, her voice a gentle caress, inviting me to leave the shore behind. "You're meant for this."

In that moment, with the moon watching overhead like a celestial guardian, I stand on the precipice of decision, torn between the safety of the known and the allure of the unknown, with Isaac's fierce grip my only anchor.

The air thickens with tension, a charged silence wrapping around us as the figure in the water beckons. Her voice, melodic and haunting, drips with an enticing allure that feels like it could slip through my fingers if I dared to grasp it too tightly. I watch, transfixed, as her iridescent skin shimmers under the moonlight, casting ethereal reflections across the lake. It's as if she were born from the water itself, a creature of dreams and secrets.

"Mia, don't!" Isaac's voice cuts through my reverie, tinged with urgency, but the words are merely a whisper against the swell of desire that surges within me. The woman's gaze is magnetic, drawing me closer, every ounce of reason battling against an instinctual longing to join her in that crystalline embrace.

"What if she knows something?" I counter, my voice barely above a murmur. "What if she can show us something we've never seen?" The wild side of me, the part that craves adventure and the thrill of the unknown, pulses through my veins like wildfire, fanning the flames of curiosity that have always lingered in the corners of my mind.

"She's not here to help," Isaac insists, his grip tightening around my arm, an anchor in the swirling sea of my thoughts. "Look at her, Mia! She's... she's not human."

"Neither are we, really," I shoot back, a challenge in my tone as I meet his gaze, the intensity sparking like a live wire between us. "What do we even know about ourselves?"

His frustration flares, the tension in the air palpable. "That's not the point!" He takes a step forward, trying to shield me from her haunting presence. "She's dangerous. You don't get to decide if she's friendly or not."

The woman tilts her head, a faint smile playing on her lips, and for a fleeting moment, I see understanding in her gaze—a shared secret that spans the gap between our worlds. I feel my heartbeat quicken, resonating with the strange rhythm of the water, a pulse that sings in time with the notes of her song. "Come to me," she croons, a silky invitation that sends a thrill through my body. "I can show you wonders beyond your imagination."

"Don't listen to her!" Isaac's voice is strained, rising over the gentle lapping of the waves against the shore. I can see the battle of emotions play out on his face: fear, frustration, and something deeper, a flicker of longing that makes my chest tighten.

"What if it's true?" I whisper, letting the words slip out before I can reconsider. "What if she can take us somewhere—somewhere that we belong?"

"Belong?" His scoff is sharp, echoing in the night air. "What if she wants to drown you instead? You don't even know what that means!"

The moon casts a silver path on the water, and I feel it calling to me, wrapping around my senses like a lover's embrace. "But what if she shows me who I really am?" I murmur, more to myself than to him, my heart racing with possibilities.

Suddenly, the surface of the lake ripples violently, the spell of the moment shattering as if reality has snapped back into focus. The woman's expression shifts, a flash of annoyance crossing her features, and before I can process it, the water churns around her, swirling into a vortex. The serene night morphs into chaos, and I stumble backward, drawn away from the shore by an unseen force.

"Run!" Isaac yells, pulling me back with all his strength, but the pull of the water is relentless. The air thrums with energy, a pulse that syncs with the frantic beat of my heart. It's intoxicating and terrifying all at once, and the woman's voice transforms, twisting into a cacophony of sound, rising in a desperate crescendo that threatens to swallow us whole.

"No!" I shout, shaking off his grip as adrenaline surges through me, a reckless defiance igniting my every nerve. "I have to know!"

In an impulsive leap, I dart forward, breaking free from Isaac's grasp, plunging my feet into the cool embrace of the water. It envelops me, wrapping around my ankles, pulling me deeper, and the world above blurs as I venture further into the depths. The surface gleams like a curtain of stars, and I feel the weight of the night pressing down on me, urging me onward.

"Mia, don't!" Isaac's voice is distant now, a fading echo as I push against the current, the woman's song enveloping me in a cocoon of sound. Every note seems to resonate with my soul, each word weaving through me like a thread of silver. It's beautiful and terrifying, and for a moment, I surrender completely.

Then, I break the surface with a gasp, the moonlight shimmering around me, illuminating the path to the woman. "Show me!" I cry out, my voice filled with a fervent desperation, the water swirling around my waist, beckoning me closer. I see her now, a figure not just of myth but of flesh and spirit, and something deep within me stirs—a flicker of recognition, of understanding that's been buried under years of uncertainty.

But just as I'm about to take another step, the water explodes around me, sending a spray of droplets into the air like fireworks. The woman's expression shifts once more, darkening with a fierce intensity that makes my heart stutter. "You wish to know?" she calls, voice now a commanding echo that reverberates through the night. "Then you must pay the price."

Isaac's shout pierces through my thoughts, snapping me back to reality. "Mia! Come back!" His desperation cuts through the enchantment, and suddenly the weight of his fear crashes into me, drowning out the siren's song. The lake, once so inviting, now feels like a maw, eager to consume what it cannot understand.

"Wait!" I plead, feeling the tug of the water, the seductive promise of knowledge and belonging fighting against the instinct to retreat. "What do you mean by 'price'?"

The woman's lips curve into a smile that lacks warmth, her eyes glittering with a knowing glint. "To uncover the truth, dear one, you must first relinquish what you hold most dear. Only then will the waters reveal the secrets they guard."

I freeze, the implications of her words striking me like a cold wave. The air around us shifts, crackling with tension, and in that moment, everything becomes painfully clear. My dreams, my desires, my very sense of self—how much am I willing to risk for the truth? And at what cost?

"Mia!" Isaac's frantic voice jolts me further, the bond between us a tether I hadn't fully appreciated until now. I glance back at him, his face pale and drawn, fear etched in every line. The realization washes over me: the lake may promise revelations, but it threatens to drown everything I hold dear in its depths.

As I waver on the brink of decision, I'm torn between the allure of the unknown and the safety of what I've always known. The water's seductive pull is undeniable, but as I meet Isaac's desperate gaze, I realize the true depth of what I risk losing—the connection we share, the friendship forged through laughter and trials.

"Maybe some truths are not meant to be uncovered," I murmur, stepping back from the water's edge, the chill of its embrace receding. As the woman's expression hardens, I feel a flicker of defiance ignite within me, stronger than the call of the lake. "I choose my own path."

Isaac's relief washes over me like a warm wave, his presence anchoring me to reality as I turn away from the lake, my heart racing with the weight of my choice. The moon's light bathes us in a silver glow as I take one last glance at the figure in the water, who now stares back with a mixture of disappointment and wrath. A low rumble echoes beneath the surface, a reminder that some doors, once opened, cannot be closed again.

Together, we retreat from the water's edge, hearts pounding in unison as the night envelops us, our bond fortified in the face of the unknown. The lake may hold its secrets, but I've chosen my truth—and with Isaac by my side, I know I can face whatever darkness lies ahead.

The moment hangs between us, the tension thick as fog swirling over the lake. I feel Isaac's heartbeat echoing in the grip of his hands around my arms, his warmth a fierce contrast to the cool night air.

But as I wrestle with the pull of the water and the weight of his concern, the woman's voice still lingers in the recesses of my mind, her haunting melody a reminder of the possibilities that lie just beyond the shore.

"I can't believe you almost went in there," he breathes, finally releasing me, though the urgency in his gaze doesn't waver. "You really don't understand the danger, do you?"

"Danger?" I scoff lightly, but there's an edge of vulnerability in my voice. "Or just something we don't understand? Maybe that's what makes it dangerous. The unknown." The words tumble out, propelled by an impulsive curiosity, a reckless desire to chase the whispers that tease at my soul.

"I get it," he snaps, frustration flaring again. "But this isn't about a thrill. It's about life and death."

"Is it?" My tone sharpens, the heat of our argument igniting something deep within me. "What if life is about taking risks? Maybe you're the one afraid of what lies beyond the edge, Isaac. Maybe you're afraid of what we could find."

His jaw clenches, and I can see the internal battle raging behind his eyes. "I'm afraid of losing you."

The sincerity in his voice catches me off guard. I've always known Isaac as the fearless protector, the one who took the lead in our adventures, but here he stands, vulnerable, the walls he built around himself cracking under the weight of concern. "You won't lose me," I reply, softer now, my heart aching with the shared intensity of the moment. "I'm not going anywhere. I just want to know what's calling to me. To us."

He glances back at the lake, the surface now calm, betraying none of the chaos that had erupted moments before. "You want to know? Then let's go back home. We can look it up—figure it out without risking everything."

I shake my head, the frustration bubbling within me like a kettle on the verge of boiling over. "You're not listening. It's not just about knowing. It's about feeling. Don't you ever feel like you're meant for something more than this? More than this town, this life?"

His eyes search mine, and for a brief second, I see the flicker of understanding—an acknowledgment of the restlessness that has been our silent companion all these years. But then, the fear rushes back in, extinguishing that spark. "You're right. I want more. But not at the cost of your life."

"Isaac, I—" I start, but before I can finish, the atmosphere shifts once more. A breeze sweeps across the water, stirring it to life, and with it comes a ripple of unease that crawls under my skin. The woman resurfaces, her eyes glowing with an otherworldly light that pierces through the shadows, locking onto mine with a fierce intensity.

"I know your name, child of the land," she calls, her voice now a blend of challenge and temptation. "You wish to know the truth of your heart? Then come."

"See?" I whisper, excitement bubbling within me, mingled with fear. "She's waiting for me."

"Mia, no!" Isaac's grip tightens as I take an involuntary step forward. "This isn't a game. Don't let her pull you in."

I look back at him, uncertainty creeping in. "What if this is our chance? What if she has the answers we've been searching for?"

"Or what if she leads you into darkness?" he counters, his voice urgent, filled with the weight of a thousand warnings.

The water begins to swirl again, the rhythm matching the frantic beat of my heart. It feels alive, breathing in sync with my yearning. "If I'm going to find out who I really am, I can't keep holding back," I insist, the conviction in my voice rising despite the fear creeping into my mind. "I need to know."

With a final surge of determination, I break free from Isaac's grasp, stepping into the water, the cold sending shivers up my spine as it embraces my legs, pulling me deeper into its depths. "Mia!" he shouts, panic straining his voice. I turn to him, the uncertainty in his eyes cutting through me like a dagger, but my resolve hardens.

The woman extends a hand, her fingers glistening like silver under the moonlight, beckoning me closer. "You are more than you know," she whispers, and with that, I feel a deep connection to her—a bond that transcends reality, tying my fate to the lake's. The waves swirl around my waist, almost lifting me off my feet, and I feel as though I'm standing on the edge of two worlds, teetering between what I've always known and what I could become.

"Don't let her trick you!" Isaac's voice pierces through the cacophony, filled with a desperate edge. But there's a growing thrill in my chest, an intoxicating rush that comes from the thrill of the unknown. "This is my choice!"

I look into the woman's eyes, and for the first time, I see a glimmer of truth shining beneath the surface—a promise of understanding, of something that has eluded me for so long. "I want to know!" I shout, more to the lake than to Isaac, my voice mingling with the rhythm of the water. "Show me!"

As I plunge deeper, the world around me shifts, transforming from the moonlit night to a swirling abyss, colors merging and bending around me. I'm enveloped in an embrace of darkness and light, the water caressing my skin like silk, drawing me further into its depths.

Suddenly, the sensation shifts, and I'm no longer alone. Shadows emerge from the depths, swirling around me like specters caught in a dance, whispering secrets I can almost comprehend. They flicker like candle flames, darting in and out of my vision, but they feel familiar, somehow known. "You wanted the truth," the woman's voice echoes through the currents, echoing the shadows. "Now you must face it."

The whirlpool of sensations surges around me, the current pulling me in every direction, and I catch glimpses of fragmented memories swirling through the chaos—images of laughter, tears, and unspoken wishes. I see myself as a child, running through sunlit fields, my laughter mingling with the wind, a time when the world felt limitless. But those images fade, replaced by darker shadows—moments of loss and longing, of dreams deferred, a tapestry woven with both joy and sorrow.

"Let go of what you thought you knew," the woman urges, her voice a lullaby woven with strength. "Embrace who you are meant to be."

The shadows loom closer, a cacophony of whispers swirling in my mind, and suddenly the world tilts beneath me. I grasp at the water, heart pounding, fear and excitement wrestling for dominance. "No! I won't let you take me!" I scream, but the current pulls tighter, threatening to swallow me whole.

And then, just as I feel the weight of inevitability pressing in, a blinding light flashes, illuminating the depths around me, illuminating the shadows that have haunted my dreams. My breath catches in my throat, and I realize I'm on the brink of discovering something monumental, something that could change everything I've ever known.

But as the light grows brighter, illuminating the truth I've yearned for, the woman's form shifts once more, her expression darkening, a fierce tempest brewing in her gaze. "You dare challenge the waters?" she bellows, the calm of the lake shattering into chaos.

In an instant, the grip of the current tightens, pulling me down into the depths, and the light winks out, plunging me into an abyss of darkness. My heart races, panic surging through my veins as I realize I've crossed a threshold from which there may be no return. Just as I'm about to succumb to the cold embrace of the water, I hear Isaac's voice, distant yet desperate, breaking through the chaos.

"Mia!"

And then, everything goes dark.

Chapter 4: The Pact Unspoken

Dawn broke over the town of Willow Creek with a deceptive calmness, the kind that felt like a prelude to chaos. The sun spilled golden light across the cobblestone streets, illuminating the faded storefronts that lined Main Street. Mrs. Whitmore's bakery, always the first to wake, filled the air with the sweet scent of fresh bread, a tempting promise of warmth that belied the tension buzzing just beneath the surface. Yet, as I stepped outside, I felt that familiar chill wrap around me, a whisper of unease riding the brisk morning air.

Another disappearance had stolen the night, and I was all too aware that this was not just a trivial event; it was a reminder of the shadows lurking in our idyllic little town. I strolled down the street, absorbing the murmurs of my neighbors—those furtive glances exchanged over coffee cups, the anxious pacing of familiar faces. Each person I passed seemed tethered to a secret they dared not voice, their eyes darting away as if the very mention of the vanished could summon some dark specter.

My heart raced as I approached Isaac's shop, the old apothecary that had been in his family for generations. The door creaked open with a familiar groan, echoing the quiet resignation I felt. Inside, the air was thick with the scent of herbs and spices, a soothing balm for my frayed nerves. Isaac stood behind the counter, his back turned to me, methodically arranging jars filled with curious concoctions. The moment he sensed my presence, he paused, a stillness enveloping the room that made the hairs on my arms stand on end.

"Morning, Sarah," he said without turning, his voice a low rumble that seemed to resonate with unspoken thoughts. "You hear about the Johnsons?"

The mention of the family whose son had gone missing two nights ago pulled me deeper into the maelstrom of fear swirling within me. "Of course I did. It's all anyone can talk about." I stepped closer, lowering my voice. "What's really going on, Isaac? This can't keep happening. There has to be a reason."

At last, he turned to face me, and the weight of his gaze held a mixture of concern and something darker, a shadow of knowledge he hadn't yet chosen to share. "It's not just random, you know. There's a pattern here. You should be careful."

I crossed my arms defiantly, refusing to let his warning penetrate my resolve. "I'm not afraid of ghosts or whatever old legends you believe in. I need to know the truth."

He sighed, a deep exhale that spoke of burdens too heavy to bear alone. "You're part of this too, Sarah. Your family—there was a pact. One that binds us to this place in ways you can't even begin to understand."

My breath caught in my throat, the words hitting me like a physical blow. "What do you mean? What kind of pact?"

"It's complicated," he replied, rubbing the back of his neck as if the very thought of explaining it pained him. "It goes back generations. There are things in these woods—things we agreed to protect and, in return, we were meant to be safe. But the balance is tipping, and now..." He hesitated, the fear in his eyes tightening my chest. "Now people are paying the price."

The room seemed to grow smaller, the shelves of herbs looming like sentinels over our conversation. I couldn't help but feel a flicker of dread—a connection I hadn't wanted to acknowledge. "Why didn't anyone tell me?" My voice cracked slightly, the betrayal stinging. "Why am I just finding this out now?"

"Because some truths are meant to stay buried." Isaac stepped closer, his eyes intense, pleading for me to understand. "Your family, they tried to break free from it. They didn't want to be part of the pact anymore, and that's why they left. But you—" He pointed an accusing finger at me, though his tone was softening. "You're tied to this place, Sarah. You always have been. The lake calls to you."

The lake. The very heart of Willow Creek, where the water shimmered like glass under the moonlight. It had always felt like a siren, whispering secrets I was too afraid to explore. I could feel the weight of its history pressing down on me, a reminder of the stories woven into the fabric of my family's past.

"And what does that mean?" I asked, though part of me dreaded the answer. "What happens if I refuse to accept it? If I just—ignore it?"

Isaac shook his head, a grim smile flickering across his lips. "That's not an option, Sarah. Ignoring it only invites more trouble. You're already part of this narrative whether you like it or not. You need to understand what you're up against, and fast. We can't afford to lose anyone else."

The gravity of his words settled around us, a shared understanding that perhaps there was more at stake than I had ever realized. I felt the invisible thread binding us tighten, an unspoken pact forged not by choice but by circumstance.

As I turned to leave, determination coursing through my veins, a sudden chill crept in, a premonition that something was coming. The wind howled outside, rattling the windows, and I couldn't shake the feeling that it carried with it the echoes of the past—whispers of those who had vanished, forever intertwined with the lake that dominated our lives. The town, with all its quaint charm, was a façade masking a darker truth, and I was more entwined in its secrets than I had ever dared to imagine.

Isaac's voice pulled me from my thoughts, sharp and urgent. "You can't face this alone, Sarah. We need to work together."

I met his gaze, my heart racing with uncertainty and a flicker of something else—hope. "Then we'll uncover the truth. Together." The words hung in the air, a fragile promise that tethered us in a world laden with shadows, each step forward a step deeper into the unknown.

The following days in Willow Creek felt like a slow burn, the tension simmering just beneath the surface, turning the air thick with unspoken fears and unanswered questions. I moved through my routines with a distracted sort of grace, the sights and sounds of the town blending into a dull backdrop as I grappled with Isaac's revelation. Each morning, the sun rose reluctantly, casting long shadows that felt too familiar, too ominous.

I found myself wandering towards the lake more often than not, drawn to its surface that gleamed like a silver coin tossed into a well, filled with wishes and warnings alike. It was the kind of place where whispers of secrets hung in the air, lingering just out of reach, like the mist that crept across the water at dawn. My heart raced at the thought of uncovering the truths buried there, yet fear wrapped its icy fingers around my resolve. What if the lake held not just memories but something far more sinister?

"Are you going to stand there all day, or do you plan to join me on this side of the dock?" Isaac's voice sliced through my reverie, pulling me back to the present. I blinked, realizing I had drifted to the water's edge without even noticing.

He leaned against a weathered wooden post, his dark hair tousled by the wind, eyes glimmering with an uncharacteristic spark of mischief. "If you're waiting for the fish to jump out and hand you the answers, I think you'll be waiting a while."

"Very funny," I retorted, but a smile crept onto my lips. "What makes you think I'd trust fish for information?"

"Because you're running out of options," he replied, pushing off the post and stepping closer, his expression serious once more. "We need to dig deeper, Sarah. If there's a pact, there must be a way to find out what it is—and how it can be broken."

The gravity of his words settled between us, and I nodded, the smile fading as the reality of our situation sank in. "But where do we even start? How do we find answers about something that's been hidden for years?"

"Some things are buried deep, but the town has its history," he said, gesturing towards the old library that loomed on the corner of Main Street, its façade a charming relic of a bygone era. "Let's start with the records. There might be something in the archives that can give us a clue."

I hesitated, the weight of dread creeping in again. "What if we uncover something we're not ready to face?"

"Then we'll face it together," he said, his voice steady, offering me a lifeline I desperately needed.

With that, we made our way to the library, the crisp autumn leaves crunching beneath our feet, a sound both comforting and unnerving. Inside, the musty scent of old books wrapped around us, and the soft light filtering through stained glass cast a kaleidoscope of colors across the wooden floor. It was a place steeped in stories, yet filled with an eerie quiet that made the hairs on my arms stand on end.

"Welcome to the past," I muttered, half to myself, half to Isaac as I led the way to the local history section. The shelves were packed with tomes of every shape and size, each one a gateway to a different time, a different world.

Isaac started browsing, his fingers dancing over spines as he searched for anything that might hint at our inquiry. I joined him, skimming the titles, the names of long-dead residents and events that had shaped the town.

"Here," Isaac called, pulling a heavy leather-bound volume from the shelf. Dust motes swirled in the light as he opened it, pages yellowed with age. "The History of Willow Creek. It's got to have something."

He flipped through the pages with a fevered intensity, and I leaned closer, my curiosity piqued. "What are you looking for?"

"Anything that mentions your family or the lake," he replied, eyes darting over the text. "We need to find a link, something that ties everything together."

Minutes turned into an hour as we scoured the book, surrounded by the quiet whispers of the past. There was something thrilling about uncovering our town's history, even as the creeping sense of dread gnawed at my insides. As Isaac read, I couldn't shake the feeling that we were treading dangerously close to a truth that could shatter our world.

"Wait," Isaac said suddenly, his finger stopping on a passage. "Here it is—something about a gathering at the lake. A council of families, each one promising to protect the land and its secrets." He looked up, excitement mingling with caution. "Your family was part of it, Sarah. They were involved in something much bigger than just... being here."

"What does it say?" My heart pounded as I leaned closer, desperate for clarity.

"It mentions an oath, a pact that was made to guard the lake's treasures and mysteries. But if that's true, then what happened? Why would your family leave?" His voice was low, a mix of awe and concern.

I swallowed hard, the weight of my own family's choices crashing down upon me. "I don't know. My parents always avoided the topic. They'd mention Willow Creek like it was just a place to live, never anything more."

"Maybe they were trying to protect you," he mused, brow furrowing. "But now it's your turn to find out what that protection cost."

My chest tightened as the reality of our situation loomed before us like a storm cloud, dark and ominous. "And what if we don't like what we find?"

"Then we deal with it. Together." Isaac's determination was palpable, a steadfast anchor amid the rising tide of uncertainty.

Just as I opened my mouth to respond, a sudden crash from the back of the library interrupted us, the sound echoing through the aisles like a gunshot. We both froze, eyes wide, the quiet broken by the rustling of pages and the pounding of our hearts.

"Did you hear that?" I whispered, a mix of fear and curiosity flooding my veins.

"Stay here," Isaac commanded softly, his eyes narrowing. But as he moved towards the sound, I felt an instinctual pull to follow, to face whatever darkness awaited us together.

The two of us ventured towards the back, the air thickening with tension, and as we rounded the corner, I caught a glimpse of movement—a shadow darting just out of sight. My breath caught as the realization hit: whatever secrets lay buried in Willow Creek, they were not going to stay hidden for long.

The shadow darting at the back of the library moved like a wisp of smoke, almost too swift to grasp. I exchanged a glance with Isaac, whose expression mirrored my apprehension. There was an electricity in the air, a palpable tension that clung to us like cobwebs in the corners of the room. "We should check it out," I said, my voice barely above a whisper. "Together."

"Together," he echoed, though I could see the hesitance etched in his features. We stepped cautiously, our footsteps muffled by the thick carpet, hearts drumming a nervous rhythm as we approached the source of the disturbance.

The library was a maze of bookshelves, each row crammed with volumes holding the whispers of history and lore. I felt as if we were intruders in a sacred space, and yet there was no turning back now. Just as we rounded the corner, a figure slipped behind a towering shelf, and I stopped short, a rush of adrenaline flooding my system.

"Hello?" I called, my voice firm despite the tremor beneath it. "Is anyone there?"

The only answer was silence, thick and heavy, punctuated by the sound of Isaac's quiet intake of breath beside me. He moved slightly ahead, eyes scanning the dimly lit area, the flickering overhead lights casting eerie shadows that danced along the walls.

Suddenly, a loud crash echoed from the shelves, sending a cascade of books tumbling to the floor. Isaac's instinct kicked in; he lunged forward, grabbing my wrist. "Stay close," he warned, urgency lining his voice.

I nodded, adrenaline coursing through me. Whatever was lurking in the library felt like a specter from the past, perhaps tied to the very secrets we were trying to uncover. We crept further, and as we rounded the next corner, the culprit revealed itself—a young woman, her hair wild and her clothes torn, eyes wide with panic.

"What are you doing here?" she gasped, breathless and frantic. "You have to leave! They're coming!"

I blinked, trying to process the urgency of her words. "Who's coming?" I demanded, sensing the danger in the air. "And who are you?"

"Names don't matter right now," she replied, her gaze darting around as if expecting shadows to leap from the books. "But if you're here, it means you've found something. You've tapped into the pact, haven't you?"

Isaac and I exchanged glances, the tension mounting. "What do you know about it?" Isaac pressed, his tone commanding.

The woman took a step back, her eyes narrowing. "I know too much," she said, a hint of bitterness in her voice. "My family has been trying to escape it for years. The pact binds us to the lake, to the very essence of this town. But it's all a lie—a trap set by those who wield the power of the water."

"Wait," I interjected, trying to piece together the fragments of information. "What do you mean a lie? How do we break it?"

"They won't let you leave, not without a price," she said, her voice dropping to a whisper. "They'll take what they want, and they're hungry. If you've felt the call of the lake, if it's pulling at you, then you're already marked."

I felt a chill slide down my spine as her words sank in, resonating with the fear I'd carried since Isaac's warning. "Marked?" I repeated, confusion and concern battling within me.

"It's not just the disappearances," she continued, her tone urgent. "People are drawn to the lake, like moths to a flame. But once you go in, once you give in to its pull, it demands a sacrifice. It thrives on fear, on despair. You have to find a way to confront it before it consumes you."

Isaac stepped closer, his voice steady but low. "How do we confront it? What do we need to do?"

"The lake's heart is where the truth lies," she said, her gaze distant. "But beware the guardians. They'll stop at nothing to protect their secrets."

Before I could ask for more, the air shifted, an unearthly chill seeping into the library. I shivered, glancing over my shoulder. "What guardians?"

Suddenly, the lights flickered violently, plunging us into shadows. The woman's eyes widened in terror. "They're here!" she shrieked, and I felt the panic rise in my throat as I turned to see something dark and formless creeping from the corners of the library, moving with unnatural speed.

"Run!" Isaac shouted, pulling me toward the exit as a shape loomed larger, emerging from the darkness with a menacing presence. My heart raced, and instinct kicked in. We darted towards the front of the library, the sound of footsteps echoing behind us, relentless and insistent.

"Where are we going?" I gasped, my lungs burning as we sprinted for the door.

"The lake!" Isaac yelled, his grip firm on my wrist. "We need to confront whatever is waiting for us there. It's our only chance!"

The woman hesitated, glancing back as if caught between her own fear and the need to escape. "I can't go back! You have to understand!"

"Then stay!" I shouted as we burst through the front door, the crisp air hitting us like a wave of reality. But the moment we stepped outside, the atmosphere shifted again; the sun was nearly gone, replaced by an ominous twilight that enveloped the town like a shroud.

Isaac and I dashed towards the lake, its surface reflecting the deepening indigo of the sky. "What if we can't face it?" I asked, glancing back at the library, its windows now dark, a hollow shell of knowledge hiding untold truths.

"We don't have a choice," Isaac replied, determination etched on his face. "We're already part of this. We have to break the cycle."

The wind picked up, howling through the trees as we reached the water's edge, and I felt the air thrum with energy, a force pulling us closer to the shore. The lake, so serene by day, now writhed with a sinister allure, the water swirling as if responding to our fear.

Just then, a figure emerged from the depths, a silhouette rising from the water, the lake's heart revealing itself—a guardian, perhaps. My heart raced as it drew nearer, its features obscured by the darkness, yet its presence loomed larger than life.

"Sarah," it whispered, the voice both familiar and haunting. "You cannot escape your fate."

In that moment, everything felt suspended in time, the world narrowing down to the beating of my heart and the glint of something sharp and wickedly beautiful in the guardian's hand. A rush of adrenaline surged through me, mingling with fear, and I realized, perhaps too late, that the moment of confrontation had arrived, and the pact unspoken was about to be spoken at last, with consequences I could scarcely imagine.

Chapter 5: Echoes of the Past

The air in the town hall was thick with dust and old paper, the scent of aged wood mingling with the stale remnants of forgotten history. Each step I took echoed off the faded blue walls, the sound a lonely companion to my search. I had buried my fingers in the archives, sifting through yellowed documents and brittle newspaper clippings that chronicled years of despair and superstition. The more I dug, the more I felt the weight of the past pressing down on me, a tangible force pulling at the edges of my consciousness.

There was talk of a pact, a sinister agreement woven into the fabric of this town's existence, hidden within the currents of the very lake that had drawn me back. The townsfolk spoke in hushed tones, their eyes darting to the water as if it were alive, as if it watched and waited. I stumbled upon stories of a bloodline cursed—a lineage entwined with the lake's power. The whispers of a woman in white haunted these pages, described as a spectral figure who emerged from the depths, shrouded in mystery and vengeance, claiming what was promised with a chilling certainty.

I could almost see her, a silhouette against the rippling water, her long hair streaming behind her like a veil of shadows. The idea of a curse felt ludicrous, yet the more I read, the more I understood: this town had crafted its own mythology, a narrative as rich and deep as the lake itself. And here I was, an unwilling participant in a story written long before I took my first breath, a thread woven into the fabric of this town's legacy. The realization clawed at me; I could no longer stand on the periphery of this tale. I was bound to it.

As I leaned closer, the dusty light from the grimy windows illuminated a fragment of an old letter, the ink faded but still legible. It spoke of a promise made beneath the moonlight, a transaction steeped in desperation. The last line, however, sent a shiver down my spine: "The waters will not forget." A flicker of movement caught my eye, and I turned, my heart racing, expecting to see Isaac lurking in the shadows. But the hall was empty, save for the relics of a time that had long since passed.

My mind raced, tangled in threads of fear and fascination, as I left the hall. The weight of the discoveries pulled me toward the lake, its presence a siren call I could not resist. I felt drawn to the water, as if the depths held the answers I sought. I could almost hear the echoes of the past whispering secrets just beneath the surface, begging to be unearthed.

As I stepped onto the rocky shoreline, the lake spread before me like a shimmering expanse of glass, reflecting the late afternoon sun. I crouched down, my fingers trailing through the cool water, and for a moment, I felt as though the lake was alive, breathing with an ancient rhythm. A chill ran up my spine, and I shivered, recalling the tales of the woman in white. Was she watching? Waiting? The very thought sent tendrils of apprehension curling around my heart.

Just then, the undercurrent of the moment shifted, and I sensed a presence behind me. I turned to find Isaac standing there, his brow furrowed and his expression fierce, as if he had just emerged from a tempest. His dark hair tousled by the wind, he looked like a man caught between duty and desire, his intensity both comforting and unsettling.

"What are you doing here?" he demanded, his voice low and laced with urgency.

"I'm looking for answers," I replied, defiance dancing in my tone. "You can't just sweep this under the rug. The town's history is tied to this lake, and if there's a chance that understanding it can change what's happening, I need to know."

He took a step closer, and the air between us crackled with tension. "You don't understand what you're dealing with, Olivia. You think these stories are just legends, but they're rooted in something real and dangerous. You're putting yourself at risk."

I met his gaze, a mixture of determination and disbelief swirling within me. "You think I'm afraid? I've been afraid for too long, Isaac. It's time I confront this—whatever it is."

He hesitated, his jaw tightening as he struggled with his emotions. "And what if confronting it changes everything? What if it leads to more danger?"

"Then I'll face it," I said, the resolve in my voice surprising even myself. "I'm already caught up in this. Running won't solve anything."

He sighed, a sound heavy with resignation and something deeper. "I wish you wouldn't dig into this. I wish I could protect you by keeping you away from it."

"Protect me?" I scoffed, unable to hide the bitterness in my voice. "You mean shelter me from the truth? That's not protection, Isaac. That's a prison."

His expression softened momentarily, revealing the layers beneath his tough exterior. "You don't know what you're asking for. There are forces at play that you can't comprehend, and I've been sent here to keep you safe."

My heart raced at his admission, the implications swirling in my mind. "Sent? By whom?"

He opened his mouth to respond, but the words seemed trapped, swirling in a storm of unspoken truths. "It's not what you think. There's so much more at stake here, and it's not just about you or me. It's about the legacy of this town and the price that's been paid over generations."

The gravity of his words pressed against me, and I felt the walls closing in, as if the lake itself had risen, ready to engulf us both. Yet, despite the fear, a spark of understanding ignited within me. "You care," I said softly, the realization dawning. "You care about what happens to me."

He looked away, the vulnerability in his gaze flashing like lightning. "It's complicated, Olivia. You need to understand that my role isn't just about protecting you. It's about a promise made long ago, one that ties us together in ways you can't even imagine."

And in that moment, I knew that whatever curse lay beneath the surface of the lake, it would intertwine our fates, pulling us deeper into the mystery, deeper into the heart of the very thing that sought to claim us both.

The sun dipped low, casting long shadows across the lake's surface as I stood there, my heart racing. Isaac's revelation hung in the air like a promise unfulfilled, a truth barely grasped but fraught with consequence. I could see it in his eyes, the way they darkened with unspoken fears and a guarded longing. It was a delicate dance between duty and desire, and I found myself wanting to step closer, to understand the depths of his commitment and the weight of his secrets.

"You keep saying it's complicated," I challenged, folding my arms defiantly. "But you're not giving me the chance to see what that complexity is. How can I trust you when you won't share the full story?"

He stepped back, creating distance as if the air itself crackled with unspent energy. "Trust is earned, not given freely, Olivia. There are things about my past, about this place, that—"

"Are you really going to keep playing the mystery man?" I interrupted, frustration simmering just below the surface. "Because I'm tired of cryptic warnings and veiled threats. If you're here to protect me, then maybe you should let me in on the 'why.'"

He hesitated, the internal struggle evident as he raked a hand through his hair. "It's not just my choice. There are forces that don't want you to know. They will do anything to keep the past buried." His voice softened, his tone almost pleading. "And I can't let that happen. Not to you."

I took a breath, feeling the weight of the world shift slightly on my shoulders. "Then help me understand. If this curse is real, then what's the point of hiding it? Knowledge is power, right? I can't fight something I don't understand."

Isaac looked away, his jaw tight. The water rippled behind him, mirroring the turmoil within. "It's not about fighting. It's about survival." He paused, the vulnerability creeping back into his gaze. "I was sent to protect you, yes, but I also... I have my own reasons for being here. I'm tied to this legacy just as much as you are."

"What do you mean?" I pressed, desperate to peel back the layers of his guarded heart. "What's your connection?"

"Because," he said slowly, as if each word was a stone dropped into the depths of the lake, "I'm part of that bloodline too."

A silence enveloped us, thick and heavy. My mind reeled, struggling to grasp the implication of his words. The curse was not just a story passed down through generations; it was a reality that bound us both. "So you're saying you're... cursed as well?"

He nodded, the tension in his shoulders evident. "There's a reason I'm here. The same reason you're being pulled into this. We're both part of something much larger, something dark and entwined. And if we don't figure it out, we're both at risk."

The implications crashed over me like a wave, the cool water of understanding washing away some of the uncertainty. "What are we supposed to do then? Just sit around waiting for a ghost to rise from the lake and claim us?"

His lips quirked, a ghost of a smile breaking through his seriousness. "You're not far off. But if we can uncover the truth together, maybe we can find a way to break the cycle."

Before I could respond, a low growl emanated from the nearby tree line, pulling our attention from the depths of our conversation. A dark shape moved through the underbrush, and my heart leapt into my throat. Isaac tensed, his protective instincts kicking in as he stepped in front of me, his posture shifting to one of readiness.

"Stay behind me," he commanded, his voice low and firm.

I peered around him, the shadows stretching ominously, and squinted into the fading light. Then I saw it: a scruffy, fur-covered creature, more shadow than substance, poking its head out. "Is that a dog?"

Isaac relaxed slightly, but his eyes remained vigilant. "It's a stray. They've been appearing more often, but I haven't figured out why. Just be cautious."

As if sensing our tension, the creature advanced, wagging its tail, dirty and bedraggled but with a spark of curiosity in its eyes. It was a little scruffball, one ear flopped over and a tongue lolling out as it approached. "Oh come on," I said, bending down to offer my hand. "Don't be shy. You're not going to bite me, are you?"

The dog sniffed at my fingers, its tail wagging furiously, and I felt a rush of warmth. "See, Isaac? Not all creatures are here to haunt us."

He chuckled softly, albeit still wary. "Just be careful. We don't know if it's just a friendly stray or if it has a dark secret of its own."

With a playful swat, I replied, "Oh please, as if I'd let a scrappy mutt intimidate me." I scratched behind its ear, earning a soft growl of contentment. "What do you want to call him? Ghost? Or maybe Specter?"

Isaac rolled his eyes, amusement flickering in his gaze. "How about just 'Dog' for now? Keep it simple."

"Dog it is," I declared, straightening up. "But you know, you have to admit, there's something charming about this little guy. Just look at him!"

And as if on cue, Dog let out a loud bark, as if to affirm my point, and I laughed. It was a small moment, but it felt like an anchor amidst the swirling chaos of our lives.

Isaac's expression shifted again, the heaviness of our earlier conversation settling back in. "We can't ignore the truth for long. Whatever is tied to that lake, it's not going away. And neither are we."

"Then let's get to work," I replied, my voice steady. "Together. We're in this mess together, Isaac."

As we turned back toward the shoreline, the sun kissed the horizon, painting the sky in hues of orange and violet, illuminating the dark waters ahead. The echoes of the past resonated around us, and with every step, I felt a surge of purpose. Whatever secrets lay beneath the surface, I was ready to face them, ready to delve deeper into the mysteries that surrounded me. It was time to unravel the threads of our fates, to confront the curse that had bound us together.

With Dog bounding ahead of us, I felt a strange blend of fear and exhilaration. The journey ahead would be fraught with danger, but I was no longer alone. I had Isaac, and together, we would unearth the truths hidden in the depths of our shared history.

The air hummed with an unsettling energy as we made our way back to the town, Dog trotting happily ahead, oblivious to the tension that wove through the atmosphere. Each step felt heavy with the weight of revelations and the gravity of the curse that loomed over us like a dark cloud. I caught Isaac stealing glances at me, as if he were weighing my resolve against the gravity of our situation. With each sideways look, I felt the flicker of a connection—a bond forged in uncertainty and shadows.

"So what's the plan?" I asked, breaking the silence. "If we're supposed to unravel this curse together, we should probably start by figuring out what exactly it is that binds us to this lake."

He nodded, his expression serious. "We need to dig deeper into your family history. The archives only scratched the surface. There may be something more in the local library, records that go beyond the gossip and folklore."

"The library?" I mused, a grin breaking through the tension. "Great. I've always wanted to be trapped in a musty building with a potentially cursed book. It's like a romance novel waiting to happen."

"Don't get too excited," he replied, a hint of a smile playing on his lips. "This is serious business. And I doubt the library has much in the way of charm or romance."

"Sure, but think of it this way—if the library has all the drama of a gothic novel, I'll need to bring popcorn," I shot back, trying to lighten the mood.

His smile widened, and for a moment, the weight of the world slipped away. I savored the brief respite, grateful for the small victory. We made our way through the town, the streets familiar yet foreign, the echo of footsteps stirring memories I couldn't quite grasp.

As we approached the library, I couldn't shake the feeling that we were walking into a trap—a web spun from the very fabric of this town's history. The library loomed before us, its stone facade an imposing reminder of the past, each brick a testimony to the stories hidden within. I pushed the door open, the hinges creaking like the whispers of long-forgotten tales.

Inside, the smell of old books wrapped around us like a warm blanket, dust motes swirling in the sunlight that streamed through the tall windows. The silence was profound, a reverent hush that invited us to explore the secrets that lay dormant on the shelves.

"Where do we start?" I asked, glancing around. The rows of books seemed endless, a labyrinth of knowledge waiting to be uncovered.

"Let's look for anything on local history, particularly around the lake," he suggested, moving toward a section labeled 'Local Lore.'

I followed, curiosity piqued. As I began pulling books from the shelves, I noticed one in particular that seemed out of place. It was bound in deep green leather, its spine cracked and worn. I reached for it, a shiver of anticipation racing through me as I flipped it open.

The pages were filled with delicate sketches of the town and the lake, accompanied by handwritten notes that danced across the pages. But it was the faded inscription on the front page that caught my breath: "To those who seek the truth, may the waters reveal what lies beneath."

Isaac leaned closer, his breath hitching as he read over my shoulder. "That sounds ominously poetic."

"Or like a warning," I murmured, tracing the letters with my fingertip. The more I read, the more I felt the presence of the past wrapping around me. Each word resonated with a haunting familiarity, stirring something deep within me.

"Look at this," I said, flipping to a page that depicted a drawing of the woman in white—a figure ethereal and ghostly, her flowing gown rippling like water. "It's her. The woman from the stories."

"Legend has it she comes to reclaim what was lost," Isaac said, a serious note in his voice. "But what does that mean for us?"

Just then, a loud crash echoed through the library, the sound of something heavy hitting the ground. Our heads snapped toward the source of the noise, and my heart raced as we rushed toward the sound. We found a large, dusty book lying open on the floor, its pages fluttering wildly as if caught in a storm.

"Did you see that?" I whispered, my skin prickling. "It just fell open like someone wanted us to find it."

Isaac knelt beside it, scanning the text. "It's a journal—likely from someone who was here during the time of the original pact." His brow furrowed as he read. "They describe rituals performed by the lake, sacrifices made to appease something ancient. This isn't just folklore; it's a warning."

"Great," I said, sarcasm slipping through my lips despite the seriousness of the situation. "I love how every small town seems to have its own version of creepy rituals."

He didn't smile, his expression grave as he continued reading. "This person believed that breaking the pact would unleash something terrible. They mentioned a blood moon and a gathering at the lake. If we're tied to this in any way—"

"Then we might be running out of time," I finished, the weight of his words settling in my stomach like a stone.

Suddenly, the lights flickered, plunging the library into near darkness. I gasped, instinctively reaching for Isaac's arm, my heart pounding in my chest. "What was that?"

"I don't know," he said, his voice steady but his eyes scanning the room, alert. "But we need to find the rest of this journal and get out of here."

As if responding to his words, the lights flickered back on, and in that brief moment of illumination, I caught a glimpse of something—movement in the corner of my eye. I turned, heart racing, and my breath caught in my throat.

There, standing among the shelves, was the unmistakable outline of a woman in white, her figure shimmering with an otherworldly glow. She gazed at us with hollow eyes, a sorrowful expression etched across her delicate features, before she vanished into the shadows.

"Olivia!" Isaac's voice pierced through the haze of shock. "Did you see that?"

"I... I did," I stammered, my voice barely a whisper. "What does she want?"

Before Isaac could answer, a deep rumble echoed from outside, shaking the ground beneath us. The windows rattled, and the shadows seemed to stretch, reaching for us as the room filled with an eerie silence, punctuated only by the sound of our racing hearts.

The air grew heavy, the weight of the lake's power pressing in around us, and I felt the unmistakable pull of destiny drawing us closer to the truth. Just as I was about to speak, the lights flickered again, plunging us into darkness once more.

This time, there was no flickering back to normal. The room was swallowed in an impenetrable blackness, and a chilling voice whispered through the air, cold and ancient, reverberating against the walls: "The time has come to pay the price."

With that, the ground trembled violently, and I felt myself slipping, losing my footing as chaos erupted around us, the world spiraling into the abyss.

Chapter 6: Flames in the Mist

The fog hung thick over the lake, swirling and curling around me like a reluctant lover. Each step I took was accompanied by the soft crunch of gravel beneath my boots, a sound that felt lost in the vast silence surrounding me. The air was cool, a stark contrast to the heat I could feel radiating from the other side of the water. It was as if the lake itself was breathing, each exhalation heavy with the scent of damp earth and something more primal—a hint of smoke, perhaps, or something sinister that sent shivers down my spine.

Isaac's silhouette emerged from the gloom, a dark figure outlined against the flickering flames that danced wildly in the distance. The fire licked the night sky, casting an orange glow that painted his features in sharp relief, accentuating the furrow of his brow and the determined set of his jaw. My heart quickened at the sight of him, that familiar tug of affection mixing uneasily with the dread that had settled over me since the tales of the Naiad resurfaced.

"Eva," he called, his voice cutting through the fog like a blade. The urgency in his tone urged me forward, through the curling tendrils of mist that clung to my skin like a second layer. I reached him just as a gust of wind sent sparks shooting into the air, illuminating the shadows that loomed beyond the flames. The fear in my chest tightened as I grasped his hand, seeking comfort in the warmth of his skin. It was a small gesture, but in that moment, it felt monumental—an unspoken pact between us, that we would face whatever darkness awaited together.

"What did you find?" I asked, forcing my voice to steady despite the quiver of fear that threaded through my words. I was not just a witness to this horror; I was a part of it now, entangled in the fate of our town, the weight of its secrets resting heavily on my shoulders.

Isaac turned his gaze to the flickering fire, where the shadows moved with a life of their own, twisting and writhing as if they were alive. "It's real," he said, his voice low, almost reverent. "The stories... they weren't just folklore. There's something in the lake—something we've awakened."

My breath caught in my throat as I stepped closer, peering through the haze to where the flames devoured the darkness. "What is it? What do we do?" I could hear the tremor in my own voice, a blend of dread and fascination. It was maddening how fear could ignite a curiosity I never wanted to indulge.

"There's a creature—a Naiad," he said, his eyes reflecting the firelight as he turned to me, a mixture of fear and resolve swirling within them. "They're guardians of the water, but if they feel threatened..." He trailed off, the implication hanging in the air between us.

"Threatened how?" I pressed, my heart racing. "What could we possibly have done to provoke it?"

He hesitated, glancing back at the fire. "The lake's curse—it's tied to our ancestors, to the pact they made. When we started digging near the shore, the disturbance must have awakened something that was meant to stay buried."

A cold shiver crept down my spine as I remembered the excavation site we had stumbled upon last week, the unearthed relics that hinted at a forgotten time. I had brushed it off as mere history, something to be cataloged and studied. The weight of our ignorance felt unbearable now, a burden of responsibility I never sought.

As if in answer to our fears, a low, haunting sound resonated from the depths of the lake—a mournful song that seemed to rise from the very heart of the water. It twisted around us, wrapping its icy tendrils around my heart. The flames flickered violently, as if in response, and I could see it then—a shape, glistening and elusive, moving beneath the surface, a figure so ethereal it almost seemed to glow.

"Look," I whispered, my voice barely a breath. "What is that?"

Isaac's grip tightened on my hand, his eyes wide as the shape emerged from the depths, water cascading off it like jewels. It was beautiful and terrifying, a creature of the lake adorned with shimmering scales that caught the firelight. But its eyes—those haunting, deep-set eyes—were filled with an ancient sorrow that struck me to the core.

"It's here," he said, his voice barely above a whisper. "We need to understand why it's returned."

My heart raced as I watched the Naiad's graceful movements, so fluid and captivating, yet laced with an undeniable anger. I couldn't shake the feeling that we were intruders in its domain, unwelcome guests in a story far older than us.

"What if it wants revenge?" I murmured, my voice trembling with a mix of awe and fear. "What if it blames us for waking it?"

Isaac's brow furrowed, and I could see the wheels turning in his mind. "Then we need to find a way to communicate—to learn what it wants."

The urgency of his words resonated deep within me, a call to action that pulled me from my fear. The Naiad's song grew louder, filling the air with a haunting melody that danced around us like a wisp of smoke. It felt like a challenge, a plea, and beneath the fear, I felt a flicker of determination ignite within my chest.

"Together," I whispered, squeezing his hand tighter. "We'll figure this out. We have to."

Isaac nodded, the resolve in his gaze matching my own. As we stood there, hand in hand, the fog swirling around us like a cloak of uncertainty, I knew one thing for certain: we were about to uncover a truth that could change everything.

The Naiad's ethereal figure shimmered like a mirage as it hovered just below the surface, its luminescent skin catching the firelight in a dazzling display. I could feel Isaac's heart thumping through our clasped hands, echoing the rising tension in the air. The creature's mournful song wound around us, a bittersweet melody that stirred something deep within my chest—a longing I couldn't quite name.

"What do you think it's trying to say?" I asked, straining to catch every nuance of that haunting voice. Each note seemed to wrap around my thoughts, weaving in and out of my consciousness like a forgotten memory trying to resurface. "Is it warning us, or is it pleading for something?"

Isaac's brow furrowed as he leaned closer to the lake, his eyes locked on the Naiad's luminous gaze. "Maybe it's both. The lake holds secrets, and we've disturbed its peace." His voice was steady, but I could hear the tension beneath it, the unspoken fear that curled at the edges of our determination.

The fire crackled between us, casting long shadows that danced along the shore like ghostly figures. The mist thickened, swirling ominously, and I could almost feel the weight of the town's collective fears pressing down upon us. I had heard the stories whispered in hushed tones, tales of a beautiful water spirit luring the unwary into the depths. But the creature before us seemed more complex than any storybook villain. There was a sadness in its eyes, a depth of emotion that spoke to something greater than mere vengeance.

"Look," I said, drawing closer to the water's edge, the heat of the flames mingling with the cool dampness of the fog. "It's not attacking. It's... it's communicating." I could see its features soften, the sharp edges of its form becoming more fluid, like the water it emerged from. There was something almost human in the sorrowful tilt of its head, a vulnerability that sparked a fierce protectiveness within me.

"Communicating how?" Isaac asked, his voice barely above a whisper. "We don't even speak the same language."

"Maybe we don't need to," I replied, stepping closer. "Sometimes, silence speaks louder than words." As the Naiad's gaze locked onto mine, I felt an electric pulse of understanding pass between us. It was as if the very fabric of the world had thinned, connecting me to the creature in a way I couldn't explain.

The Naiad began to weave through the water, its movements both graceful and fluid, like a dancer performing in the embrace of a gentle breeze. The flames crackled, and for a moment, it felt as though the very elements were conspiring to bring us together. I could hear the whispers of the lake, the stories it held locked away, and I felt a fierce longing to uncover them.

"Wait here," I said to Isaac, my voice steady despite the uncertainty roiling in my stomach. Before he could protest, I stepped into the shallows, feeling the cool water wrap around my ankles. The Naiad paused, tilting its head as if assessing my intent.

"Can you understand me?" I asked, the words escaping my lips like a prayer. The creature studied me with eyes like deep pools, reflecting the flickering flames and the shadows that clung to the shore. I reached out a hand, palm up, as though offering a gesture of peace. "I'm not here to hurt you. We're here to listen."

For a heartbeat, time stood still. The fog swirled, and the night held its breath. The Naiad swam closer, its skin glistening with water droplets that sparkled like stars caught in its wake. My heart raced, a wild drumbeat echoing through my veins. I could sense Isaac's eyes on me, a mix of concern and awe that urged me to retreat. But I was rooted to the spot, caught in the web of the moment.

In an unexpected flash, the Naiad dove beneath the surface, the water shimmering in its wake, and my heart sank with a sudden dread. Just as I feared it had vanished for good, it resurfaced a few feet away, clutching something small and glimmering in its hand—an object half-submerged, cradled like a precious jewel.

"What is that?" Isaac shouted from the shore, his voice breaking through the thick air.

"I don't know!" I called back, my focus solely on the Naiad. The creature extended its hand, the object glinting in the firelight—a pendant, intricately carved with swirling designs that mirrored the patterns of the water's surface. It was beautiful, and yet, it held a weight of history that felt almost tangible.

The Naiad held it aloft, a silent offering that transcended language. I could feel the intensity of its gaze, urging me to take the pendant, to understand its significance. "What do you want me to do?" I whispered, the weight of the moment pressing down upon me.

The water bubbled as the Naiad spoke again, its voice flowing like the current, soft yet urgent. "Return it," it seemed to say, the sound wrapping around me like a warm embrace. "To where it belongs."

I glanced back at Isaac, whose eyes were wide with realization. "The pendant—it must have been part of the curse. It's the key to understanding what's happening!"

With a determined nod, I reached out, fingers trembling as I accepted the pendant from the Naiad. Its warmth radiated through me, a pulse that felt alive, full of stories begging to be told. The moment my fingers brushed against the smooth surface, I saw a flash—a vision of the lake, vibrant and alive, before it had been shrouded in mist and fear. I saw a time when people gathered along its shores, laughing and singing, free from the burdens of the past.

But then darkness flooded my mind, images of storms and betrayal swirling like a tempest. The laughter turned to cries of fear, the joyous gatherings replaced by shadows of sorrow. The necklace was not just an artifact; it was a memory, a tether to the past that had been lost, forgotten.

"Eva, be careful!" Isaac's voice broke through my reverie, and I looked up to see the Naiad watching me intently, its expression shifting from hope to something darker, more urgent. The flames flickered wildly, casting long shadows as the fog thickened around us once more.

"Tell me what I need to do!" I called out, feeling the weight of the pendant in my palm, a pulse of energy that resonated with my own heartbeat. I could sense the Naiad's frustration, the urgency of its quest for redemption clashing against my own desire for answers.

With one final, piercing gaze, the Naiad disappeared beneath the water, leaving behind a ripple of uncertainty that echoed in the silence. I stood there, pendant in hand, my heart racing with a mixture of fear and exhilaration. The path ahead was shrouded in fog, but I knew one thing: whatever lay ahead, I would face it head-on, with Isaac by my side. Together, we would unravel the mysteries of the lake and confront the curse that had haunted our town for far too long.

The pendant felt alive in my hand, a conduit to the past, pulsing with the urgency of unspoken histories. I turned to Isaac, who stood rooted on the shore, his brow furrowed with concern, the shadows of the trees dancing around him like anxious sentinels. "What now?" he asked, his voice a low murmur, the firelight flickering across his features, highlighting the resolve beneath the fear.

"I think... I think we have to return it to the lake," I replied, the words tumbling from my lips before I could second-guess myself. The vision of laughter and joy I had glimpsed was seared into my memory, and I felt a compulsion to restore what had been lost. "The Naiad—it wanted this back. It's part of the curse, part of what binds this place to its dark history."

Isaac's eyes widened, and I could see him grappling with the implications. "You mean, toss it back in? Just like that?" His skepticism was palpable, but beneath it, I detected a flicker of intrigue. "What if that doesn't work? What if it makes everything worse?"

"It's a risk we have to take," I insisted, my heart racing at the thought. "What choice do we have? The curse is already haunting our town. If we don't try to break it, we're only letting it grow stronger."

He hesitated, glancing back at the flickering flames, their warmth beckoning us like a siren's call. "Fine," he said finally, determination hardening his expression. "But if the Naiad tries to drag you under, I'm diving in after you."

A rush of warmth spread through me at his words, a fierce sense of solidarity that steeled my resolve. "Then let's do this together." I took a deep breath, feeling the weight of the pendant anchor me, as if it were a lifeline connecting me to the Naiad and to the history of the lake itself.

We approached the water's edge, where the mist curled and swirled like a living entity. The cold water lapped at my ankles, sending chills up my spine, but I pressed forward, stepping deeper until it kissed my knees. I could feel the lake's pulse beneath the surface, a heartbeat that synchronized with my own.

"Are you ready?" Isaac called out, standing just behind me, a protective presence that anchored me against the uncertainty swirling around us.

"Ready as I'll ever be," I replied, my voice steadying as I held the pendant up to the flickering light of the fire. The intricate carvings gleamed, and for a moment, I imagined the people who had once worn it, their laughter mingling with the water's gentle whispers.

With a final glance at Isaac, I threw the pendant into the depths of the lake, the glimmering object cutting through the water like a comet through the night sky. The moment it hit the surface, the air crackled with energy, a ripple of magic that spread outwards, distorting the mist in wild patterns. The water bubbled violently, and I stumbled back, heart racing as the surface began to churn.

"What did we just do?" Isaac's voice cracked slightly, but there was no time for fear now; the Naiad's song rose to a fever pitch, wrapping around us in an overwhelming wave of sound and sensation.

The water erupted, shooting up in a brilliant fountain of light, and from its depths, the Naiad emerged, more radiant and fearsome than before. Its body shimmered with a spectrum of colors, reflecting the flames as it rose higher, and for a brief moment, it looked almost divine.

But then, that beauty twisted into something darker. The Naiad's eyes, once filled with sadness, now blazed with a fury that sent a jolt of fear through my veins. "You dare disturb the balance?" it roared, its voice echoing across the water, reverberating through my bones.

The flames flickered violently, and I felt Isaac tense behind me, ready to spring into action. "We didn't mean any harm!" I shouted, my voice rising above the chaos. "We're trying to help!"

"Help?" The Naiad's laughter was a chilling sound, sharp and full of disdain. "You think a trinket can reverse the ages of betrayal? You've awakened me, but you do not understand the consequences of your actions!"

A wave crashed against the shore, soaking my clothes and tugging at my feet like a riptide, and I struggled to maintain my balance. The flames sputtered, dimming as the wind howled, snatching the heat from the air and replacing it with a bitter chill.

"What consequences?" I cried out, desperation rising in my throat. "We just want to know why the curse exists, why you're bound to this lake!"

The Naiad paused, its expression shifting momentarily from anger to something akin to sorrow. "You seek knowledge, yet you tread upon the bones of your ancestors. They created this curse, not I! They were the ones who betrayed the sacred bond between land and water, and their sins now fall upon your shoulders."

Isaac moved closer to me, his presence a reassuring force as I tried to process the weight of those words. "What do you mean?" he asked, his voice steady despite the chaos around us. "What was the bond?"

"The bond was of love," the Naiad said, its voice softening, but there was an edge of warning that remained. "A love that twisted into greed and desire, leading to betrayal. And now, your town is cursed to repeat the cycle until the balance is restored. You are the descendants of those who wronged me."

"Then how do we break the cycle?" I asked, urgency filling my voice. "Tell us what to do!"

The Naiad tilted its head, studying me with a gaze that felt like it pierced straight to my soul. "You must seek the truth buried beneath the surface. Only then can you confront the sins of your forebears and restore what has been lost."

Before I could respond, the ground beneath me trembled, the water swirling violently as if it were alive. The flames sputtered, struggling against the rising tide, and in that instant, I understood—I had awakened something greater than myself, a force of nature that demanded reckoning.

"Isaac!" I shouted, feeling the world around us spiral out of control. "We need to get back!"

As I turned to flee, the water surged, reaching for us with desperate fingers. The Naiad's voice rose above the chaos, its words a final warning that echoed in the depths of my mind: "Only when the truth is unearthed can you hope to be free."

I grasped Isaac's hand, and together we stumbled back from the water's edge, hearts pounding as the fog thickened around us, cloaking the world in uncertainty. Just as we turned to escape, a shadowy figure emerged from the mist, a silhouette more monstrous than the Naiad itself, its intentions cloaked in darkness. My heart sank as I realized that whatever truth awaited us was far more terrifying than I had ever imagined.

Chapter 7: Bound by Secrets

The moon hung low over Lake Windermere, casting a silvery glow across its rippling surface. The night air was thick with the scent of pine and damp earth, a fragrant reminder of the rain that had washed over the region just hours before. Each breath I took filled my lungs with the crispness of the forest, an intoxicating mix of adventure and fear, as I crept through the underbrush behind Isaac. He was a shadow, moving with a grace that belied the turmoil lurking beneath his calm exterior.

"Why do you have to be so stubborn?" I whispered, the words barely escaping my lips as I stepped on a twig, the sharp crack echoing like a gunshot in the stillness. I froze, heart pounding, but Isaac didn't turn around. He continued to walk, his silhouette framed by the ghostly light of the moon, oblivious or perhaps intentionally ignoring my presence.

I was in too deep, yes, but my instincts pulled me forward. The truth was a siren call, and no matter how hard Isaac tried to push me away, I could feel the gravitational pull of his secrets dragging me closer. My thoughts raced back to the moments we shared—each encounter layered with unspoken words and glances that lingered a heartbeat too long. There was something in him, a depth that mirrored my own sense of loss, and the more I discovered about him, the more tangled our fates seemed to become.

Isaac paused by the edge of the lake, the water lapping softly at the shore, as if the very essence of the lake sought to comfort him. It was dark, nearly pitch black except for the stars reflecting like scattered diamonds upon the surface. I stepped closer, allowing the damp grass to cool my bare feet, my heart racing as I caught a glimpse of his expression. There was a flicker of something—vulnerability, perhaps—but it vanished as quickly as it appeared, replaced by that familiar stoicism.

"Why are you here?" he asked, his voice low, a mix of irritation and concern that made my stomach twist. He didn't even bother to look at me, his gaze fixed on the water, as if it held all the answers to questions he couldn't bear to face.

"Because you're hiding something, and I'm tired of living in the shadows," I replied, my tone sharper than I intended. "I deserve to know the truth, especially when it involves my family. You can't keep pushing me away just because it's easier."

The silence stretched between us, thick and uncomfortable, punctuated only by the distant call of a night bird. I watched as his jaw clenched, the muscles twitching under the tension. He turned to me then, and the intensity of his gaze sent a shiver up my spine. "Some truths are dangerous, and some ghosts are better left buried."

"Or they'll haunt us forever," I shot back, my breath catching in my throat. I had struck a chord, and for a moment, it seemed as if I had broken through the walls he had built so carefully around himself. "I'm not afraid of ghosts, Isaac. I'm afraid of not knowing. Of living a lie."

"Lies are often more comfortable than the truth," he replied, the weariness in his voice cutting deeper than any accusation. "You don't know what you're asking for."

"Then help me understand," I implored, stepping closer, the tension crackling in the air between us like a live wire. "Please. You don't have to do this alone."

For a moment, he hesitated, his expression wavering as if he were caught in the undertow of his own fears. "You really want to know?" he asked, his voice a low murmur, almost lost in the whispering wind. "What if I told you my past is filled with darkness? That the lake is not just beautiful, but also a graveyard of secrets?"

"Then I would tell you that I'm willing to face that darkness with you," I said, my heart racing. "Because it's better than being alone in the light."

A flicker of something—hope, perhaps?—crossed his face, but it was quickly masked by his guarded nature. He took a deep breath, as if steeling himself against the tide of memories threatening to surge forth. "My family's past is tangled with yours, you know. The day your mother vanished, the town whispered about a curse. But the truth is more complicated than that."

"Tell me," I urged, unable to suppress the longing in my voice. "We can't keep dancing around it. I want to know about my mother and whatever part your family played in it."

He closed his eyes, the weight of the world pressing down on him. "All right," he said finally, the words emerging like a confession. "But once I tell you, there's no turning back. You'll see me for who I really am, and it may change everything."

"I'd rather know than be left in the dark," I insisted, feeling a rush of determination. "I'd rather face whatever it is than let it fester between us."

He opened his eyes, searching mine as if looking for some sign of bravery. "Okay," he breathed. "But remember, you asked for this."

As he began to speak, the stars above twinkled like the bright eyes of long-lost friends, and the water continued its gentle murmur, cradling our secrets in its depths. The truth was unfurling before me like a delicate flower, and even as the darkness threatened to overwhelm us, there was a sense of purpose in the air, a promise of understanding, and perhaps even connection, that I had longed for.

The tension between us crackled like a live wire, but as Isaac took a deep breath, the air shifted, thickening with the weight of the secrets he was about to unveil. I leaned in closer, the cool breeze teasing my hair and heightening my senses. I had never felt so alive, hanging on the precipice of something monumental, yet terrifying.

"There's a story," he began, his voice barely above a whisper, as if the trees surrounding us might be eavesdropping. "A long time ago, when our families were still on speaking terms, your mother was involved in something... unusual. It was a summer filled with rumors and hushed conversations, the kind that flourish in small towns where everyone knows everyone else's business but never dares to ask the right questions."

I nodded, heart pounding in anticipation. "Go on," I urged, my palms clammy as I wrapped my arms around myself. "What happened?"

He sighed, a sound laden with regret. "It started with an old journal, one that belonged to your grandmother. She was an unconventional woman, an herbalist, a healer. The town respected her, but they also feared her because she dabbled in the unknown. One evening, during a particularly intense storm, she went missing. That's when your mother found the journal. She thought it held the key to finding her."

"Is that how she disappeared?" I asked, my voice a mere breath. "Did she go looking for your grandmother?"

Isaac's gaze flickered to the lake, the moonlight dancing on the water's surface like fleeting memories. "Not exactly. She found something in that journal—something she wasn't supposed to. It spoke of rituals, of powers meant to remain untouched. Your mother believed it could bring her back, that she could summon her from wherever she had gone."

I could hardly breathe. The pieces began to shift and slide into place, forming a picture I wasn't sure I wanted to see. "And then what? Did she try to perform one of those rituals?"

Isaac hesitated, his brow furrowing as if the thought alone pained him. "Yes. She was desperate, and desperation can drive people to do irrational things. That night, she went to the lake, the last place anyone saw your grandmother. The storm was raging, and..." He paused again, searching for the right words. "She never came back."

"Just like that?" I pressed, feeling a mix of anger and sorrow for the woman I had lost long before I'd ever known her. "She just vanished into thin air?"

"Pretty much," Isaac replied, his voice heavy with unspoken sorrow. "When the storm passed, the search parties scoured the area, but it was like she was swallowed whole. There were whispers about curses and dark forces at play. The townsfolk turned against my family, believing that our bloodline was cursed, that we had driven your family to madness."

"Madness?" I echoed, disbelief surging through me. "You mean they thought your family was responsible for my mother's disappearance?"

"Not just thought," he said, frustration creeping into his tone. "They were convinced. It didn't help that my great-grandfather had been rumored to practice dark magic, or that my family had a reputation for being secretive. We were branded as pariahs, and your family... well, your family carried the weight of tragedy. The connection forged by loss became a chasm filled with blame and fear."

A heavy silence settled between us, punctuated only by the soft lapping of the water against the shore. The weight of Isaac's words hung in the air, a potent mix of grief and resentment. "So, all this time, my mother's disappearance has been shrouded in shadows because of your family?" I asked, trying to wrap my mind around the implications.

"It's more complicated than that," he replied, rubbing the back of his neck as if trying to relieve the tension that had taken residence there. "There were whispers of a curse on both sides. Each family felt the other was at fault, and that blame twisted into something dangerous, something that still lingers. We're caught in this web of secrets and silence."

I could see the pain in his eyes, the burden of his family's history weighing heavily on him. "And what about you?" I questioned, a sudden realization dawning upon me. "What do you believe? Do you think you're cursed too?"

Isaac shook his head, a humorless laugh escaping his lips. "I don't know what I believe anymore. I grew up hearing stories, watching the townsfolk side-eye us. I've spent years trying to distance myself from the darkness they attributed to my blood. But here I am, drawn back to this place, tangled in a legacy I didn't choose."

There was a vulnerability in him that I hadn't seen before, a fracture in the walls he had built. "You're not defined by your family's past," I said softly, stepping closer, my heart aching for him. "We can choose our paths."

He looked at me, searching my expression for something he needed, a glimmer of hope, perhaps. "And what if I'm too far gone? What if this darkness isn't just a tale spun by fearful minds, but something I can't escape?"

"We all have darkness within us," I replied, my voice steady. "But we also have the power to face it. You're not alone in this, Isaac. Whatever happened, it doesn't have to dictate our future."

The air around us crackled with unspoken promises, and as the moonlight shimmered on the lake, I reached out, daring to bridge the distance between us. Our fingers brushed, a simple connection that sent a jolt of warmth coursing through me. In that moment, I felt the weight of our shared grief and the flicker of understanding.

Before he could respond, a rustling in the trees drew my attention, a shadow darting across the path behind us. I turned, my heart racing, instinctively taking a step back. "What was that?" I whispered, suddenly aware that our fragile moment had been interrupted by the unknown.

Isaac's expression shifted from contemplation to alertness. "I don't know, but we should be careful," he said, his voice now a tense whisper. The atmosphere shifted again, the air thick with apprehension as we exchanged glances, both acutely aware that the past wasn't finished with us yet.

Whatever had haunted our families was still lurking, waiting for the right moment to reveal itself. And as we stood at the edge of that darkened lake, I knew we were only beginning to uncover the truth—a truth that would challenge everything we believed about ourselves and each other.

The sound of rustling leaves sent a shiver down my spine, a reminder that we were not alone in the quiet embrace of the night. I turned sharply, scanning the trees for any sign of movement. My heart raced, the adrenaline coursing through me as I felt the electric pulse of fear and curiosity entwine. Isaac stood beside me, his body tense, ready for whatever might emerge from the darkness.

"Stay close," he whispered, his voice low but firm, a command wrapped in concern. I nodded, a silent agreement passing between us as we both braced for whatever threat lurked in the shadows. The moonlight painted our surroundings in shades of silver and blue, the beauty of the night stark against the rising tension.

Just then, a figure stepped out from behind a tree, emerging like a ghost from the very fabric of the night. My breath hitched, heart leaping into my throat. It was just a girl, maybe a few years younger than me, with wild curls framing her freckled face and eyes that gleamed like emeralds in the low light. She looked just as startled as we were.

"Who are you?" Isaac demanded, his tone protective as he positioned himself slightly in front of me, a shield against the unexpected intrusion.

"I'm just... looking for something," she stammered, glancing nervously between us. "I didn't mean to scare you. I thought I heard voices."

"Are you from around here?" I asked, trying to ease the tension. The girl was just a kid, after all.

"Sort of," she said, wringing her hands together. "I'm Holly. I come here sometimes, but I've never seen you before. Are you guys okay? You look a bit... intense."

Isaac relaxed his stance, the suspicion ebbing away as he studied her. "We're fine. Just having a conversation." His gaze softened as he noticed the unease in her expression. "What are you looking for?"

Holly's shoulders slumped, and she hesitated. "A... thing. It's a necklace, one my grandmother gave me. I think I dropped it when I was exploring by the lake."

My instinct was to reassure her, to show her the kindness that had been lacking in my own life lately. "We can help you look for it," I offered, feeling a sudden bond forming in the shared search for something lost. "The lake's not that big."

"Are you sure? I don't want to impose," Holly said, her eyes wide with a mixture of gratitude and disbelief.

"Not at all," Isaac interjected, a hint of warmth returning to his voice. "If it's here, we'll find it."

We began to comb the area, our small group now an unexpected trio united by a common goal. As we moved closer to the water's edge, I couldn't shake the feeling that there was more to Holly than she let on. She seemed oddly familiar with the surroundings, as if she had more than a casual connection to the lake.

"Do you come here often?" I asked, trying to keep the conversation light.

"Yeah," she replied, glancing at the water with an intensity that made my skin prickle. "I love the stories. My family has lived here for generations, and there are tales—old tales about the lake." She paused, her voice dropping to a conspiratorial whisper. "About how it can reveal secrets, sometimes in ways you least expect."

"Secrets?" Isaac repeated, his curiosity piqued. "What kind of secrets?"

Holly bit her lip, her eyes darting between us. "The kind that can change everything. My grandmother used to say that the lake remembers. It remembers the people who've come and gone, the promises made, and the mistakes that haunt the living. If you listen closely, it'll tell you."

I felt a chill crawl down my spine, the weight of her words settling heavily in the air. "What do you mean? Like... how does it tell you?"

Holly shrugged, a flicker of something mischievous dancing in her gaze. "People say it whispers in the night, if you're brave enough to listen. Sometimes, you see shadows, figures in the water. They're the ones who couldn't let go."

Isaac exchanged a glance with me, a mixture of intrigue and caution in his eyes. "You really believe that?"

"I don't know," she admitted, her voice softening. "But I've seen things. Strange things. My grandmother was... different. She taught me to be open to the impossible. She believed the lake had its own spirit."

The breeze rustled through the trees, and for a moment, it felt as though the forest was alive, leaning in to hear more. "Have you ever seen one of those figures?" I asked, my curiosity overriding my apprehension.

Holly nodded, her expression turning serious. "Once. On a stormy night, just like this one. I swear I saw my grandmother in the water, reaching out to me. I thought it was just a trick of the light, but it felt so real." She shivered, wrapping her arms around herself. "I've been trying to find that necklace ever since. I thought it might help me understand what I saw."

We continued our search, the atmosphere thickening with tension as the night wore on. I couldn't shake the feeling that we had crossed a threshold into a realm where the past and present converged. The air felt electric, charged with secrets yet to be uncovered.

As I knelt by the water's edge, my fingers grazing the surface, I caught a glimpse of something sparkling beneath the moonlit water. My heart raced as I leaned closer, brushing my hand through the cool liquid. "Holly, is this what you're looking for?" I called out, my voice cutting through the heavy silence.

But before she could respond, the water shifted, rippling as if something unseen was stirring beneath. The moment hung suspended in time, an unspoken warning echoing in my mind. I pulled back, confusion swirling within me. "What just happened?"

Isaac's expression morphed into one of alarm. "Get away from the water!"

Before I could react, a sudden gust of wind swept across the lake, sending a chilling wave splashing against my legs. The surface churned violently, and shadows began to swirl beneath, dark shapes twisting and coiling in an otherworldly dance. Holly stumbled back, her eyes wide with fear as she gasped, "What is that?"

I felt the ground tremble beneath us, the whispers of the lake intensifying into a cacophony of voices, rising and falling like the tide. Panic surged within me, but beneath it all, there was an undeniable pull, a call to the secrets buried in the depths. Something was awakening, and I could feel it reaching out for me.

"What do we do?" I yelled over the roar of the water, heart racing as I turned to Isaac. But he was frozen, eyes locked on the lake, a mixture of fear and recognition etched on his face.

"I don't know," he admitted, his voice barely audible. "But we need to leave. Now!"

As we turned to run, the shadows beneath the surface surged, erupting into a wave of darkness that roared like a tempest. It was then that I realized the truth: the lake was not just a place of beauty and serenity; it was a keeper of secrets that could no longer remain silent.

And as we fled, I knew deep down that whatever had been awakened that night would not let us go so easily. The past had finally come to reclaim its due, and we were caught in the storm, poised at the edge of a truth we were not yet ready to face.

Chapter 8: The Kiss of Fate

The town grows colder, a chill that seeps into bones and memories. Each evening as dusk swallows the horizon, a gray veil settles over the landscape, muffling the world in an eerie quiet. The leaves, once vibrant in their autumn splendor, have surrendered to the inevitable, their colors fading to brittle browns, as if the trees themselves are grieving. I wander the cobblestone streets of Greystone, my breath forming tiny clouds in the air, the scent of damp earth and fallen leaves swirling around me like an old, bittersweet song.

As I stroll, my feet lead me towards the lake, its surface reflecting the moody sky, a mirror of turmoil and longing. The water glimmers with an unsettling beauty, inviting yet ominous, as if it knows secrets I have yet to uncover. It calls to me like a forgotten lullaby, tugging at the edges of my mind and wrapping around my heart. Isaac walks beside me, his presence a comforting weight, but even he cannot quell the growing pull of the water. I glance at him, his brow furrowed in concern, and I wonder if he feels it too—the way the air thickens when we approach the shore, the way the world feels suspended, as if holding its breath.

"Are you sure you want to go back?" he asks, his voice low, almost lost in the wind. There's an edge of worry in his tone, a hint of something deeper lurking beneath the surface. It makes my heart flutter, a mix of gratitude and unease. Isaac has been my anchor, my steadfast companion through the storms of life, yet this moment feels different, electric with unspoken words and what-ifs.

"I don't know," I admit, my voice barely above a whisper. The lake whispers my name in a voice I don't recognize, a voice that sounds like my mother's, pulling me closer. Memories of her dance just out of reach, ephemeral like the mist that rises off the water at dawn. I take a step toward the lake, drawn by an unseen force, but Isaac catches my arm gently, his touch grounding me.

"Let's not get too close," he says, his eyes searching mine, trying to decipher the turmoil swirling within me. His worry feels familiar, yet I see something more—an urgency, perhaps, that matches the tempest brewing in my heart.

The tension between us snaps like a taut string, and suddenly, I'm overwhelmed by an impulse I can't ignore. I lean into him, craving the heat of his body, the steadiness of his spirit. Our lips meet, and the kiss is fierce and desperate, an explosion of emotions that ignites every fiber of my being. The world fades, the chill of the air replaced by the warmth radiating from him. For a brief moment, it feels like we're defying the fate that looms over us both, escaping into a bubble of intimacy that shields us from the chaos outside.

But it's fleeting, like a spark that fizzles out just as quickly as it ignites. The lake calls again, louder this time, its voice insistent and haunting. I pull back, breathless, my heart racing not just from the kiss but from the overwhelming need to understand what's happening. The water ripples, its surface disturbed by unseen currents, mirroring the storm inside me.

"What was that?" Isaac asks, his voice a mix of surprise and longing, as if he's just now awakening to the depths of his own feelings. The question hangs in the air, heavy and laden with possibilities, yet I don't have an answer. Instead, I turn back to the lake, my gaze drawn to its depths, searching for clarity, for answers that elude me like shadows at dusk.

"I don't know," I say, shaking my head, frustration bubbling up within me. "It's like the lake has a mind of its own. I can't explain it, but I feel... I feel drawn to it. Like it wants something from me."

His expression shifts, a mix of understanding and caution. "What do you mean? Drawn to it how?"

"It's hard to describe," I reply, my voice trembling. "It feels like... like it knows me, like it has a connection to my past. Every time I come here, it pulls me in deeper, as if it holds the key to something I've lost."

Isaac steps closer, the space between us narrowing as he leans in, his breath warm against my cheek. "Maybe we can figure it out together," he says softly, his gaze unwavering. "You don't have to face this alone."

His words wrap around me like a balm, soothing the frayed edges of my heart. Yet, the lake's pull remains relentless, an unseen hand reaching into my very soul, beckoning me closer. The memory of my mother flits at the edges of my consciousness, a specter of love and loss that complicates everything. What did she leave behind? What pieces of her linger in the depths of this water?

Just then, a sudden gust of wind sweeps across the shore, sending a chill racing through me. It carries with it the scent of pine and something else—something sweet and familiar, yet distant. I shiver involuntarily, the hairs on the back of my neck standing on end. "What if it's more than just memories?" I say, voicing the fear that clings to me. "What if the lake is trying to tell me something, something I'm not ready to hear?"

Isaac's brow furrows, his concern deepening. "We'll face it together, whatever it is," he promises, his eyes shining with determination. "You're not alone in this. I won't let you go."

As he speaks, I feel a spark of hope ignite within me, battling the shadows that threaten to engulf my spirit. Perhaps he's right; perhaps this time I don't have to face the unknown alone. But the kiss, the warmth of his lips on mine, lingers like a ghost, reminding me that even as I yearn for answers, I'm tethered to a bond that could change everything.

In that moment, under the brooding sky and the watchful gaze of the lake, I realize I stand at the precipice of a choice—between diving into the depths of my past or retreating to the safety of the present. The lake's call grows louder, insistent, promising revelations wrapped in the shrouds of fate. And I know, deep down, that whatever path I choose, it will alter the course of my life and perhaps even our fragile connection. The air crackles with possibility, and I find myself holding my breath, teetering on the edge of everything I've ever known.

The kiss lingers in the air between us, heavy with the unspoken words we've danced around for weeks. I can still feel the warmth of Isaac's lips on mine, an ember in the growing chill of the evening. It's a moment suspended in time, both electrifying and terrifying, a thin veil pulled back to reveal the deeper currents swirling beneath the surface of our friendship. Yet the weight of the lake looms large, a silent sentinel watching over us, demanding my attention. I pull back slightly, still caught in the lingering heat of his gaze, trying to shake off the allure of the water's siren song.

"Okay, maybe that was a bit impulsive," I manage, the corners of my mouth twitching into a half-smile despite the nervous flutter in my stomach. It feels good to lighten the moment, but my heart races at the thought of what's to come. I've spent so long building walls around my heart, and yet here I am, ready to leap into the unknown with him, a daring move for someone like me.

Isaac's expression shifts, a playful glint in his eyes. "A bit? That was more like an Olympic-level dive into impulsivity. Who knew you had it in you?"

I laugh, a soft sound that mingles with the evening breeze. "Well, let's just say it's a side effect of the lake's influence. It seems to have a way of bringing out the reckless part of me."

"Reckless, huh?" He steps closer, the warmth radiating from his body making me forget about the biting cold surrounding us. "Then I'd suggest we stay away from the water. No more impulsive decisions until we know what's going on."

"Agreed," I say, my heart still racing from both the kiss and the thrill of his words. But even as I say it, a part of me knows the pull of the lake is too strong to ignore for long. I cast a glance over my shoulder, the water glimmering under the fading light, a captivating canvas that seems to change with each passing moment.

Just then, a sudden rustle in the nearby trees catches my attention, snapping me out of my reverie. My heart races anew, anxiety flaring at the sudden shift in atmosphere. "Did you hear that?" I ask, my voice barely above a whisper.

Isaac nods, his brow furrowing in concern. "Yeah, it sounded like something—or someone—moving through the underbrush."

A shiver runs down my spine, and I glance towards the thickening shadows where the trees stand guard, ancient sentinels wrapped in the embrace of dusk. "We should probably check it out," I suggest, the spirit of adventure mixing with the fear knotting in my stomach.

"Are you serious?" he asks, a half-smile playing on his lips, though there's a hint of wariness in his eyes. "You just kissed me, and now you want to play detective? What are you, a daredevil on a mission?"

"Or maybe just someone who's curious about what the lake might be hiding," I counter, my voice gaining strength. "Besides, if it's nothing, we'll have a great story to tell later, right?"

"Or we'll become a local legend about the foolish kids who disappeared at the haunted lake," he quips, but I see the spark of excitement igniting in his eyes.

"Then let's not become legends just yet." I lead the way, my heart pounding not just from the fear of the unknown but from the thrill of having Isaac by my side. With every step I take toward the trees, I feel the bond between us tightening, and the uncertainty that's haunted me fades, replaced by a rush of adrenaline.

As we approach the edge of the treeline, the sounds grow louder, distinct now—a soft crunch of leaves, a gentle splash, like something disturbing the stillness of the water. I take a deep breath, the crisp air filling my lungs, and push aside the creeping doubt. "What if it's just an animal?"

"Or a ghost?" he replies, a teasing smile playing on his lips, but his voice trembles with anticipation.

"Stop it! You're making me nervous," I shoot back, playfully nudging him with my shoulder.

Isaac glances back at me, his expression shifting from playful to serious. "Okay, on three." He counts down, and I nod, my heart racing in sync with his words. "One... Two..."

"Three!"

We burst through the underbrush, and there, in a clearing illuminated by the dim light of the moon, we find not a ghost, but a young girl, no older than twelve, crouched by the water's edge. She's staring into the lake, her silhouette framed by the silver glow of the moon. The sight of her sends a wave of unease crashing over me, a feeling I can't quite place.

"Hey! Are you okay?" I call out, trying to keep my voice steady. The girl jumps at the sound, turning to face us, her wide eyes reflecting a mixture of surprise and something darker—fear, perhaps.

"Leave me alone!" she snaps, her voice sharp like shattered glass.

Isaac takes a cautious step forward. "We're not here to hurt you. We just want to help."

"Help?" She scoffs, the word dripping with sarcasm. "You can't help me. No one can."

Her despair sends a shiver down my spine. Something about her resonates with the feelings I've been wrestling with—the weight of loss, the search for answers, the unyielding tug of the lake. "What do you mean?" I ask softly, my heart aching for this girl who seems so lost.

The girl's gaze flickers back to the water, a flicker of desperation flashing in her eyes. "It's calling to me. I can't ignore it. You don't understand."

"Maybe we do," I say, stepping closer. "The lake has been calling to us too."

Her eyes narrow, and for a moment, I see the walls she's built around her heart. "You don't know what it's like. It's not just a call; it's a promise."

"What kind of promise?" Isaac asks, his voice steady, filled with an urgency I can feel thrumming in the air.

"A promise of something more," she whispers, her words hanging heavy in the air between us. "Something I lost."

A wave of recognition crashes over me, the girl's anguish echoing my own. I glance at Isaac, the gravity of the moment settling around us. The lake has secrets, dark and deep, and now it seems the veil has lifted, exposing us to its mysteries. The tension builds, the air crackling with energy, and I know that whatever lies ahead will change everything.

"Something I lost." The girl's voice trembles as she stares into the depths of the lake, her expression a mixture of longing and despair. I feel an unshakable connection to her words, the same hollow ache resonating deep within me. It's as if she holds the key to a mystery I've been chasing, a reflection of my own hidden fears.

"Lost?" I echo, inching closer, desperate to understand. "What did you lose? Maybe we can help you find it."

Her gaze flickers to me, then back to the water, and for a moment, I think she might actually open up, that the ice surrounding her heart might thaw just enough for us to connect. "You can't help me," she says, her voice quiet yet resolute, as if she's repeated this mantra to herself a thousand times. "You don't know what it's like to be so close to something you can't have."

"Try us," Isaac interjects, stepping forward with an encouraging smile. "You'd be surprised what we know about loss."

She snorts, a sound laden with bitterness. "Yeah, right. You're both so...normal."

"Normal is overrated," I say, sharing a look with Isaac that says we're in this together. "What if we're not as normal as you think? What if we have our own lake-induced issues?"

The girl arches an eyebrow, curiosity peeking through her defenses. "Like what?"

Isaac crosses his arms, feigning contemplation. "I may or may not have a secret collection of rubber ducks that I hoard for good luck. It's very serious."

"Right," she scoffs, but I catch the hint of a smile tugging at her lips. "Rubber ducks? That's your big secret?"

I chime in, "And I once tried to build a raft to sail across the lake. It didn't end well. Let's just say I've had my fair share of encounters with the water."

The corners of her mouth twitch upward, and for a fleeting moment, it seems we've cracked her armor. "That's just ridiculous," she says, shaking her head. "I thought I was the only one around here who was weird."

"Welcome to the club," Isaac says, extending his hand as if offering her an invitation. "Membership comes with unlimited awkward moments and questionable decisions."

The girl looks at his hand, then back at us, the glimmer of hope battling with the shadows in her eyes. "Why would you want to be friends with me?"

"Because we're all a little lost," I reply, my voice steady. "And sometimes it helps to have company on the way to finding what we need. We're not here to judge you. We just want to help."

For a moment, silence stretches between us, the weight of unspoken fears and shared uncertainties hanging in the air. I can feel the lake watching, listening, as if it knows we're on the cusp of something important.

The girl takes a hesitant step forward, her gaze locked on mine. "Okay, but you have to promise you won't give up if it gets scary."

"I promise," I say, and I mean it. There's something about this moment that feels pivotal, a turning point that might lead us to truths we've both been running from.

"Let's go back to the water," she suggests, her voice now barely above a whisper. "Maybe if we talk to it, it will listen."

"What do you mean?" Isaac asks, his brow furrowed in confusion, but I can sense the intrigue in his voice.

"I don't know," she admits, her vulnerability raw and real. "It sounds crazy, but I've heard it calling me, and sometimes, when I speak to it, I can almost hear responses."

"Then let's try," I say, a mix of excitement and dread thrumming in my veins. We move as one, drawn to the water's edge, the atmosphere thick with anticipation.

As we stand there, the moonlight casting silver ripples across the lake, I can feel the air shifting, charged with energy. "What do we say?" I ask, feeling both ridiculous and brave.

"Just...ask for what you need," the girl replies, her voice steadying. "It might know something we don't."

I take a deep breath, the cool air filling my lungs as I step closer to the water. "Okay," I say, my heart pounding. "Here goes nothing." I lean slightly over the edge, the surface shimmering like liquid glass. "We're here," I call out, my voice echoing in the stillness. "We want to understand. Please, help us."

For a moment, nothing happens. The only sound is the gentle lapping of the waves against the shore, the rustling of leaves overhead as a breeze sweeps through the trees. I exchange a glance with Isaac, uncertainty creeping in, but before I can voice my doubt, the lake stirs.

The water begins to bubble and churn, swirling in patterns that defy logic. My breath catches in my throat as a low hum vibrates through the air, resonating deep within me. The girl's eyes widen in fear and wonder, her earlier bravado slipping away.

"What's happening?" she breathes, gripping my arm.

"I don't know," I whisper, transfixed by the scene unfolding before us. The surface of the lake glows faintly, casting eerie shadows that dance like phantoms beneath the water. "Is this...normal?"

"I don't think so," Isaac replies, his voice low, almost reverent.

Suddenly, a voice, soft yet powerful, echoes around us, a symphony of sound that seems to come from the very depths of the lake. It's a language I can't understand, but it washes over me, stirring emotions long buried, igniting a spark of recognition.

"Can you hear that?" I ask, my heart racing.

"Yes," the girl murmurs, her eyes wide, fixed on the mesmerizing display. "It's...talking to us."

"Then let it," Isaac urges, stepping closer, his hand brushing against mine. "This is what we came for, isn't it? To find the answers?"

The voice crescendos, swirling around us like a tempest, and I can feel the energy crackling in the air. It beckons me, drawing me closer to the water's edge, and for a moment, I'm caught between fear and fascination.

But just as I reach the precipice of understanding, a sudden silence falls, like a curtain drawn abruptly on a stage. The water calms, the glow fading, leaving us breathless and bewildered.

"What...what just happened?" I stammer, my heart racing.

"I think we just touched something," the girl breathes, her voice trembling with excitement and fear.

Before I can respond, the ground beneath us shudders, a low rumble echoing through the trees. The lake ripples violently, sending waves crashing against the shore.

"What is happening?" Isaac shouts, his eyes wide with panic.

The girl stumbles back, fear etched across her face. "It doesn't want us here!"

Just as the words leave her lips, a dark shape rises from the depths of the lake, looming and shadowy, sending an icy chill down my spine. I can't look away, frozen in place as it surfaces, revealing a form both magnificent and terrifying. The air crackles with a sense of impending doom, and I realize, too late, that we may have awakened something that was better left undisturbed.

"Run!" Isaac yells, grabbing my hand, but my feet remain rooted, drawn by the mystery and danger that now stands before us. The girl's scream pierces the night, and the world around us blurs into chaos as we stand on the brink of a truth that could shatter everything we thought we knew.

Chapter 9: The Phantom Below

The lake lay before us like a vast, blue mirror, its surface glimmering in the early morning light, an illusion of serenity that belied the chaos lurking beneath. I stood at the water's edge, the cool, damp earth sinking beneath my bare feet, a reminder of the unseen weight waiting for us in those depths. The memories of my dreams clung to me like the chill in the air, a haunting echo of hands reaching for me, pulling me down into a world I didn't fully understand. I felt as if the lake itself was alive, whispering secrets just beyond my grasp, calling me home.

Isaac stood beside me, his brow furrowed in concern, the shadows of my dreams etched into his striking features. His dark hair, tousled by the wind, framed a face that was both handsome and troubled. The deep blue of his eyes mirrored the lake's depths, a tempest brewing just beneath the surface. "We shouldn't do this," he said, his voice barely above a whisper, filled with urgency. "You don't know what's down there."

I turned to him, a smile dancing on my lips, but it didn't reach my heart. "And you do?" I challenged, tilting my head, my gaze locking onto his. "Do you think we'll find the answers on land? Or in the whispers of the wind? No, Isaac. The truth lies beneath."

His eyes flashed with a mix of fear and something else—an understanding that we were both ensnared by the same force. I knew he felt it too, the call of the lake, a pull that intertwined our fates. The air around us crackled with unspoken words, heavy with the tension of things left unsaid, and it filled me with a thrill that was equal parts fear and exhilaration.

"Fine," he said finally, the fight leaving his voice, surrendering to the inevitable. "But if we do this, we do it together."

We stepped into the water, and the cold enveloped me like an icy embrace. Each step felt like an initiation, the liquid wrapping around my legs, pulling me deeper into its embrace. My breath caught in my throat as we waded further, the world above slowly fading into a muted haze of light and sound. The surface shimmered like a distant memory, and I could feel the heartbeat of the lake resonating beneath us, a pulse that thrummed in time with my own.

"Are you ready?" I asked, glancing back at him, our faces illuminated by the scattered sunlight breaking through the surface. The determination etched in his features reassured me. We were two souls diving into the unknown, propelled by a force we could neither comprehend nor resist.

"Always," he replied, his voice steadier now.

And then we plunged beneath the surface, a world of liquid shadows enveloping us, the cool water closing over our heads like a dark shroud. I felt the pressure building in my ears, but I ignored it, focusing instead on the thrill of the descent. I kicked my legs, feeling the weightlessness of the water around me, and caught a glimpse of Isaac beside me, his eyes wide with wonder and fear.

It was dark down here, a strange kind of darkness that felt alive, as if the water had swallowed not just light but time itself. The colors faded into shades of deep blue and green, a palette of ancient secrets hidden in the depths. My heart raced as I kicked harder, and suddenly, the lake opened up before us, revealing an underwater world that seemed to shimmer with a life of its own.

Beneath the surface, I saw shapes darting in and out of view, shadows flickering like memories just beyond reach. The sensation of being watched enveloped me, prickling at my skin and sending a shiver down my spine. I wanted to reach out, to touch the delicate ferns swaying with the current, to explore the otherworldly beauty of the submerged realm. But there was an urgency tugging at me, a need to uncover what lay hidden below, a treasure buried within the lake's mysterious embrace.

As we descended further, I could sense something stirring, an ancient presence that echoed through the water. It felt familiar, yet foreign, an entity that was both welcoming and menacing. My thoughts drifted back to my dreams, to the hands that had reached for me, and I wondered if this was the source of that pull. I glanced at Isaac, his expression mirroring my own mix of awe and apprehension.

A sudden rush of cold surrounded us, an otherworldly chill that cut through the water like a knife. My instincts screamed at me to turn back, but a voice, deep and resonant, called out to us, threading through the water like a whisper. "Stay..." it beckoned, wrapping around us like a comforting embrace. The promise of revelations and truths lingered just out of reach, tantalizing and terrifying all at once.

Isaac took my hand, squeezing it tightly. His grip was warm, a stark contrast to the icy water swirling around us, and I drew strength from it. "We can't stay too long," he said, though I could sense the reluctance in his voice. "We need to find a way back."

But before I could respond, the world around us shifted. A flash of movement caught my eye—something darted just out of reach, shimmering like a pearl in the murky water. My heart raced with a mix of curiosity and dread as I felt the entity's presence intensify, a current that seemed to guide us deeper into the unknown.

"We need to go!" Isaac urged, pulling me back, but I could feel the magnetic draw of the depths. There was something waiting for us, a truth hidden in the shadows, and I could almost taste it on my tongue—a promise of revelations that would change everything. I took a deep breath, the air burning in my lungs, and looked into Isaac's eyes, searching for a sign, a reason to turn back.

But I saw only determination, and in that moment, I knew we were bound together, not just by love but by an unbreakable connection to the lake itself. As the darkness closed in, I felt a surge of adrenaline, a fierce resolve igniting within me. Whatever lay ahead, I was ready to face it, to dive into the depths and uncover the mysteries that awaited us.

The darkness enveloped us, thick and oppressive, yet beneath it lurked a pulse, a rhythm that echoed like a heartbeat. The further we descended, the more the shadows began to dance, illuminating shapes and forms that glimmered just beyond the edges of perception. It was mesmerizing and terrifying, a kaleidoscope of colors that played tricks on my mind, teasing me with the promise of secrets hidden beneath the lake's surface.

Isaac's hand tightened around mine, our fingers intertwined like vines clinging to life. "We need to focus," he said, his voice steady despite the chaos around us. "Whatever's down here, we're not alone." I nodded, the gravity of his words settling heavily in the waterlogged air between us. It was true. An energy thrummed through the depths, pulling us deeper into the unknown.

As I kicked through the water, my heart raced with anticipation. I could almost hear whispers, soft and melodic, as if the lake itself were singing to us, drawing us toward the unseen. It was intoxicating, and I yearned to surrender to it, to let go of my fears and follow the song that beckoned me deeper into its embrace.

"Do you hear that?" I asked, my voice muffled by the water, but I could see Isaac nodding, his eyes wide with a mixture of wonder and apprehension.

"It's beautiful," he murmured, awe transforming his expression. "But it feels...wrong, doesn't it?"

"Yes," I agreed, feeling the weight of his concern. It was beautiful, yes, but it also felt like a trap, like honey laced with poison. The desire to uncover the truth battled with an instinctual need to escape, to swim back to the surface where sunlight and safety awaited us. Yet here, in this dark realm, we were drawn into a web woven from forgotten memories and ancient promises.

Suddenly, a flicker of movement caught my eye. A shadow darted past us, sleek and graceful, gliding through the water with an elegance that was almost surreal. My heart raced; there was something distinctly unearthly about it, a creature that seemed to embody both grace and danger. It vanished into the darkness before I could make sense of what I had seen, but its presence lingered in the water like a cold shiver against my skin.

"I think we should—" Isaac started, but before he could finish, the water around us shifted, swirling like a tempest. The current picked up, tugging us along with a ferocity that left me gasping for breath, my lungs screaming for air. The whispers grew louder, drowning out my thoughts, a cacophony of voices that beckoned me closer, deeper.

"Hold on!" I yelled, clinging to Isaac as the world spun around us. The shadows twisted, forming shapes that felt almost familiar—faces emerging from the darkness, eyes glimmering with a knowing light. They reached for us, their hands like shadows stretching across the water, beckoning us into their depths.

"Who are they?" Isaac shouted, his voice barely audible over the rush of water.

"Souls of the lake?" I ventured, my heart racing. "Or perhaps just our imaginations?"

"Either way, we need to find a way back!" He pulled me against him, his warmth contrasting with the chill that enveloped us. I could see the determination etched into his features, and I felt a flicker of resolve igniting within me.

Just then, a loud crack echoed through the water, a sound that resonated deep within my chest. The lake shuddered, and the shadows twisted violently, transforming the once-serene environment into something chaotic and tumultuous. My heart raced, and panic clawed at the edges of my mind as I realized we were caught in something far beyond our understanding.

"Swim!" Isaac shouted, his voice cutting through the chaos. We kicked against the current, our bodies moving in tandem, fueled by adrenaline and the instinct to survive. The pull of the darkness was still strong, but together we fought against it, pushing toward the flickering light that seemed to beckon us from the surface.

As we swam, I could feel the water grow warmer, the oppressive darkness lifting like a curtain drawn back to reveal the stage of our existence. But just as hope began to blossom, I felt a tug on my leg, a strong force pulling me back down into the abyss. My breath hitched in my throat as I looked back, dread pooling in my stomach.

Isaac was still beside me, but the shadows had thickened, swirling around us like a living entity. "Don't let go!" he yelled, his voice strained, filled with urgency. "Whatever it is, we can't let it take us!"

With every ounce of strength I had, I kicked harder, fighting against the current that sought to drag me back. The creature—whatever it was—pulled me deeper, wrapping around my legs like chains forged from the lake's darkest secrets. I could feel it, a whisper against my skin, a promise that echoed in my mind. "Stay... come to us..."

"No!" I shouted, defiance coursing through me. "I won't!"

Summoning every bit of willpower, I broke free from its grasp, swimming alongside Isaac as we clawed our way toward the surface. Each stroke felt like an eternity, and as the light above us grew brighter, a surge of hope washed over me. We were close, so close, but the pull of the darkness still lurked behind, a reminder of the chaos that sought to reclaim us.

With one final push, we broke through the surface, gasping for air as sunlight pierced through the water, shimmering like diamonds scattered on the waves. I could hardly process the relief flooding through me, the warmth of the sun kissing my skin as I clung to Isaac, our breaths mingling with the crisp air around us.

"We made it," I breathed, disbelief washing over me as I looked into his eyes, wild and bright with the adrenaline of survival. But as I caught my breath, a cold shiver ran down my spine. I turned to look at the water, the once-inviting surface now hiding its mysteries once more. What lay beneath was a question we hadn't yet answered, and I could feel the shadows lurking, watching, waiting for our return.

The sun cast shimmering reflections across the lake's surface, but beneath the glittering facade, shadows shifted and flickered like ghosts, taunting us with their elusive nature. I pulled myself from the depths of the water, gasping as the cool air filled my lungs. Isaac was beside me, his hair plastered to his forehead, droplets of water cascading down his sun-kissed skin like tiny jewels. His eyes, normally filled with warmth, now sparkled with a wild mix of fear and exhilaration that sent a thrill coursing through me.

"What was that?" he asked, shaking his head as if to clear the remnants of the abyss we had just escaped. I shivered at the thought, the memory of that dark entity pulling at my leg still vivid in my mind.

"Something ancient," I replied, my voice still thick with the weight of the water. "Something that wants us to stay." I glanced back at the lake, where ripples distorted the once-calm surface, and an uneasy feeling settled in my stomach. "But I don't know why."

Isaac's expression turned serious, his brow furrowing as he surveyed the water. "We can't go back. Not yet. Whatever that was, it's not just a figment of our imagination." He took a step closer, his voice dropping to a conspiratorial whisper. "You felt it too, didn't you? The way it called to you?"

"I did," I admitted, a shiver running through me that had nothing to do with the cold. "But I can't explain it. It felt... familiar, as if I've been tied to it my whole life." The realization sent a jolt of fear through me.

Isaac's gaze pierced through the hazy light, searching my eyes as if trying to uncover the secrets hidden there. "Then we need to find out what it is. And what it wants from us."

I nodded, but doubt nagged at the back of my mind. "But how? We barely made it back from the last dive."

His determination shone like a beacon. "We research. We learn. There has to be something about this place, something in the town's history."

"Research? You mean dive into dusty old books?" I scoffed, half-teasing, but my heart raced at the thought of what we might uncover. "I suppose that's better than returning to the water without a plan."

"Dusty old books have saved us before," he shot back with a grin, the tension easing slightly between us. "Besides, it'll give us a chance to talk more about what happened. Maybe there are other people who've felt this connection. Or better yet, a way to break it."

He stepped back, giving me space to breathe, but my thoughts were swirling like the water we had just escaped. "Okay, let's find some books," I conceded, "but let's also avoid any more unscheduled swims, shall we?"

With a shared glance of determination, we headed toward the small library nestled at the edge of town. Its facade was charmingly antiquated, a stark contrast to the sleek modernity that surrounded it. A heavy wooden door creaked open, revealing a dimly lit space lined with towering shelves filled with books that smelled of must and history. Dust motes danced in the golden rays filtering through the windows, and I felt a familiar comfort wash over me. This was where stories lived—where mysteries begged to be unraveled.

Isaac moved to the history section, his fingers tracing the spines of books with reverent care. "Let's see if we can find anything about the lake," he murmured. I joined him, scanning titles as if they held the key to our salvation.

"Look at this!" I exclaimed, pulling a tattered volume from the shelf. The cover was embossed with gold lettering that had long lost its luster. "Local Legends: Myths and Mysteries of Riverton."

Isaac raised an eyebrow, a smile teasing the corners of his mouth. "Now that sounds promising. Lead the way."

As I flipped through the pages, we stumbled upon a chapter dedicated to the lake, its words rich with folklore and cautionary tales. "It says here that the lake was once a sacred site for an ancient tribe," I read aloud, my voice hushed in the reverent silence of the library. "They believed it to be a gateway to the spirit world, a place where the line between life and death blurred."

Isaac leaned closer, his breath warm against my ear. "What else does it say?"

"Listen to this," I continued, heart pounding as I read the next passage. "Legend has it that those who ventured too far into the depths could be lost forever, ensnared by the spirits of the water. It was said that they could call out to their loved ones, drawing them in with promises of eternal connection."

The words hung heavy in the air between us, their meaning resonating with the experience we had just endured. "That sounds exactly like what we felt," Isaac whispered, eyes wide with understanding. "It's not just a legend—it's a warning."

As I turned the page, something slipped out, fluttering to the ground like a fallen leaf. I bent to pick it up, a delicate, yellowed photograph that had once been tucked neatly between the pages. The image was faded but unmistakable—a group of people standing by the lake, their expressions solemn, almost mournful. But it was the figure at the forefront that sent a chill down my spine.

"Isaac..." I breathed, my voice barely a whisper. The woman in the photograph looked strikingly familiar, her features echoing mine in a way that sent shivers coursing through my veins. "Who is she?"

He leaned closer, a frown knitting his brow. "I don't know, but she looks like she belongs to a different time. Do you think…?"

"What?" I urged, holding my breath as he studied the picture.

"What if she's one of the ones who got lost?" he suggested, the gravity of his words sinking in like a stone. "What if we're connected to her somehow?"

The thought sent a thrill of dread coursing through me. I stared at the photograph, searching for answers, but the woman's gaze remained distant, inscrutable. Just then, the door to the library creaked open, and a chill swept through the room as a figure stepped inside.

A tall woman with sharp features and striking silver hair emerged from the shadows, her eyes glinting like shards of glass. She moved with an otherworldly grace, a knowing smile playing on her lips. "You've found her, haven't you?" she asked, her voice smooth and haunting.

My pulse quickened as she stepped closer, and an unsettling sense of familiarity washed over me. "What do you know about her?" I demanded, clutching the photograph tightly as if it were a lifeline.

The woman's smile widened, revealing a depth of knowledge that sent shivers down my spine. "More than you can imagine. The lake remembers, and so do its lost souls."

Before I could respond, she reached out, her fingers brushing against my wrist, and in that instant, I was overwhelmed by a flood of memories—visions of the lake, of hands reaching, of eyes watching from the depths. "You must come back," she urged, her voice a hypnotic melody, pulling me toward her.

Just as quickly as the connection sparked, it vanished, leaving me breathless and disoriented. I staggered back, heart pounding, and met Isaac's wide gaze, his expression a mix of confusion and concern.

"What did she do?" he asked, voice low and tense.

"I don't know," I whispered, my voice trembling. "But whatever it is, we're not finished yet."

As the woman began to speak again, her words tangled in the air like smoke, I felt the room darken, shadows creeping in from the corners. I glanced at the photograph, the woman's gaze now feeling more like a call than an answer, and suddenly, the weight of my connection to the lake crashed down around me like an impending storm.

"What do you mean?" I demanded, but before she could respond, the lights flickered overhead, plunging us into momentary darkness. Panic surged through me as the shadows twisted and churned, swallowing the light, and I could feel the cold presence of the lake creeping back into my thoughts.

The woman's voice, now a distant echo, reached out to us. "You must choose, or be consumed by the depths."

And just like that, the world spun, the ground beneath us trembling with a force that felt both alive and malevolent. A chilling realization coursed through me; the lake was not just a place. It was a living entity, and it was hungry.

Chapter 10: Whispers in the Depths

The air was thick with humidity, the kind that clung to my skin like a second layer, and as I stepped out onto the creaking dock, the wood groaned beneath my feet, as if the old boards were reluctant to bear my weight. The lake stretched before me, its surface shimmering like a thousand scattered diamonds under the moonlight. I could almost hear it beckoning, a soft, siren song that called to the very marrow of my bones. Isaac's presence beside me felt both comforting and intrusive, a warm hand on my back that both anchored me and made me painfully aware of the choice I was constantly forced to confront.

"Are you sure you want to do this again?" Isaac asked, his voice low and heavy with concern. He shifted, casting a shadow over my sun-kissed skin, and I could feel the warmth radiating from him, grounding me in reality. Yet, the reality he represented felt so mundane compared to the enchanting pull of the lake. I turned my gaze from him, fixing it instead on the dark water that seemed to pulse with life.

"I have to," I replied, my voice barely above a whisper. Each word seemed to evaporate into the air, lost to the night like a prayer. I had tried to explain this to him before, the way the lake called to me in a language that felt ancient, like a lover whispering sweet nothings in the dark. "You wouldn't understand." It was a truth wrapped in a layer of tenderness; how could he comprehend the bond I felt with something so wild, so untamed?

He huffed softly, frustration bubbling just beneath the surface. "Try me. I might surprise you." There was a spark in his eyes, a challenge in the way he straightened his shoulders, but all I could think about was the figure that haunted my dreams—the woman in the mist who whispered my name with a voice that was both familiar and foreign. She was becoming a part of me, an entity entwined with my very being, and every night that I resisted her call felt like tearing apart a fragile thread that connected me to my own soul.

"I can't leave her," I murmured, though I didn't fully understand who I meant. The line between the woman and the lake blurred in my mind. In the days that followed, I tried to piece together her identity, but she remained elusive, like smoke slipping through my fingers. Each night, I stepped closer to the water's edge, compelled to discover the truth hidden beneath its shimmering facade.

Isaac exhaled sharply, his breath visible in the cool evening air. "This isn't safe. I can't keep watching you do this to yourself." His words hung in the air like the damp fog rolling off the lake, thick and suffocating. I could see the desperation etching deeper lines into his face, the crease in his brow deepening with every moment I lingered by the water.

"Don't you see?" I snapped, irritation bubbling to the surface. "It's not about safety. It's about understanding. What if she's trying to tell me something? What if I'm meant to help her?" I whirled around to face him, the tension between us crackling like a live wire. "You don't get to decide what I do with my life, Isaac. I need to find out why I'm being drawn to her."

Isaac stepped back, the hurt flashing in his eyes like a flare against the darkening sky. "And what if it's a trap? What if she's not trying to help you, but to pull you under?" The sincerity of his concern broke through my stubbornness, and I could see how my fixation on the lake was fracturing our fragile reality. The whispers in my mind intensified, swirling into a cacophony that drowned out his pleas.

I closed my eyes, blocking out the world around me, focusing on the sounds that seemed to call out from the depths. A splash, a gentle ripple, and then—a name. "Serena." It was soft and sweet, like the promise of spring after a long winter. I gasped, my eyes shooting open, locking onto Isaac's bewildered expression. "That's it! That's her name."

"Who?" His tone shifted, the frustration morphing into an almost frantic curiosity.

"The woman in the lake—she's called Serena. I know it. I can feel it." I had crossed a threshold, breaking free from the fear that had kept me tethered to the shore. The name echoed in my mind, reverberating through me like a forgotten melody finally recalled.

Isaac stepped forward, his brows furrowing. "And what does she want from you?"

"Maybe she wants me to find her," I said, my heart racing with the possibility. Each beat felt synchronized with the rhythm of the waves, and in that moment, I was torn between two worlds—the one I knew with Isaac, with its warmth and safety, and the one that shimmered just beyond my reach, shrouded in mystery and promise.

"Are you really willing to risk everything for a voice in your head?" His words dripped with disbelief, but there was a flicker of understanding lurking behind them. The tension coiled tighter around us, as if the very air was charged with the weight of our choices.

"Sometimes, the things we can't see are worth the risk." I took a deep breath, stepping toward the edge, the moonlight dancing on the water's surface, inviting me to plunge deeper into the unknown. It felt like a moment suspended in time, the past and future colliding in a single breath as I balanced on the precipice of two lives.

The lake surged with an energy I could no longer resist, and I knew that whatever lay ahead would demand everything from me—my heart, my trust, and perhaps even my very soul. But standing there, gazing into the depths, I couldn't help but wonder if maybe, just maybe, I could unravel the mystery of Serena without losing myself in the process.

The moon hung low in the sky, a pale guardian casting silver beams that danced across the lake's surface, illuminating the dark ripples that beckoned me closer. Each night felt like a clandestine meeting with an old friend I had yet to fully understand, a rendezvous fraught with secrets and half-formed memories. Isaac lingered a few paces back, a shadow painted in concern, his eyes wide and searching, as if he could physically reel me back from the water's edge with sheer will alone.

"Serena," I whispered, the name tasting foreign on my tongue, yet somehow right. The air thickened with tension, and I could feel Isaac's gaze boring into me, a mix of worry and frustration that made me want to laugh and cry all at once. "What if she needs me? What if I'm the only one who can help her?"

"Help her? She's not just some lost puppy in the woods, Rowan." His voice was low, but the edge of panic was unmistakable. "She's a ghost. A whisper. You don't even know what she wants." He stepped closer, the warmth of his body contrasting sharply with the chill creeping from the lake. "And you think you're equipped to deal with whatever darkness that might bring?"

I turned my back to the shimmering expanse, facing him fully now. "It's not just darkness, Isaac. It's… it's an invitation." My voice trembled slightly, but I pressed on. "You wouldn't understand. She feels real to me, more real than any of this." I gestured toward the town looming behind us, its lights twinkling like a distant promise, a safe harbor that now felt suffocating.

Isaac's brow furrowed, the concern deepening into something akin to hurt. "Rowan, you're not in the right headspace. This place has a way of messing with people. You have to let it go." His words hung in the air, weighty and unyielding, but my heart thudded in my chest, a rebellious drumbeat urging me to leap.

"I can't just walk away!" The words escaped me before I could stop them, fueled by a frustration I hadn't realized had been simmering just below the surface. I took a breath, trying to steady myself. "I won't."

A silence enveloped us, thick as the mist that hovered just above the water, and I could see the struggle in his eyes. He opened his mouth, perhaps to argue further, but I cut him off with a wave of my hand, the movement filled with a sudden clarity. "I need to know who she is. I need to know why she's calling me."

Before he could respond, I turned my back on him again and stepped toward the water. I could feel the cool breeze wrapping around my legs like an embrace, the surface shimmering invitingly. It was as if the lake itself were a living entity, waiting patiently for my next move. My heart raced as I stepped closer, my reflection rippling and distorting with each gentle wave. I closed my eyes, letting the soft sounds of the lake wash over me, soothing my frayed nerves.

"Rowan, wait!" Isaac's voice sliced through the tranquility, pulling me back momentarily from the edge. I turned to see him stepping forward, his expression a blend of desperation and determination. "You can't just dive in without knowing what you're getting into. We need to think this through."

I felt a pang of guilt shoot through me; he cared deeply, but it felt so impossibly distant, like a thread fraying as I stretched further from the shore. "What if I don't want to think anymore?" I said, and my tone was sharper than I intended. "What if I'm tired of feeling lost? What if I want to find out where this leads?"

He moved closer, the distance between us narrowing to mere inches, the air crackling with unspoken words and emotions. "Then you'll drag me down with you," he said, his voice a low murmur. "I don't want to lose you, Rowan."

My resolve wavered as I looked into his eyes, dark and earnest, reflecting the fear that lived just beneath the surface. I could feel the weight of his words pressing against me, but the siren call of the water was insistent, weaving through my thoughts like a silken thread. "I don't want to lose you either," I confessed, my voice softening. "But I have to do this. I have to try."

Before he could argue, I took a step closer to the edge, the water lapping eagerly at my feet, sending a delightful chill up my spine. In that moment, everything around me fell away—the town, the worries, the fears—until there was only the lake, a dark abyss filled with possibility.

I closed my eyes once more, willing myself to listen. "Serena," I whispered, letting the name roll off my tongue like a spell. "What do you need from me?" The water began to ripple violently, responding as if it were alive, a sudden rush of energy surging through my veins. I felt my heart race in tandem with the lake's pulse, a connection forging itself in the depths of my soul.

And then, as if the lake itself were answering, the surface broke.

A flash of pale, shimmering light erupted from beneath the water, spiraling upward like a dancer emerging from the depths. My breath caught in my throat as I stumbled back, splashing water onto Isaac's shoes, but I couldn't look away. The figure materialized—a ghostly silhouette that slowly took shape, a woman cloaked in ethereal mist, her features indistinct yet hauntingly familiar.

"Rowan..." she breathed, her voice echoing softly across the stillness of the night, wrapping around me like a tender embrace. "I've been waiting for you."

The world shifted beneath my feet, the lake roiling with unspoken secrets and desires. I felt Isaac stiffen beside me, his hand reaching out instinctively, but I was entranced, lost in the depths of Serena's gaze. This was it, the moment I had been searching for, the tether between my mundane existence and the magical unknown. I took a breath, half a step forward, feeling the urge to dive in deeper—to unravel the mystery that lay before me.

The air around us shimmered with electricity, a storm brewing just below the surface. But it wasn't just the lake that was changing; it was me. The whispers had become a roar, and in that moment, I knew—whatever this was, it was only the beginning.

The woman's voice, soft yet commanding, hung in the air, weaving around me like a silky thread. "Rowan..." she called, her tone both familiar and distant, echoing the very essence of my name. I stood frozen, mesmerized, the rippling water sparkling under her ethereal glow, and I felt as if the ground beneath my feet had turned to mist. Every fiber of my being tingled with the thrill of the unknown, the exhilaration of finally making contact with the elusive specter who had haunted my dreams.

Isaac's grip on my arm tightened, grounding me in reality, his breath quickening beside me. "What are you doing? This isn't safe!" His urgency was palpable, but it only pushed me further toward the water, drawn by an invisible force that blurred the lines between fear and desire.

"Don't you feel it?" I turned to him, desperation lacing my words. "It's not just a ghost. It's a connection. I need to know what she wants." I could see the panic in his eyes, reflecting my own turmoil, but this was my moment, a chance to discover a part of myself that had been lost in the shadows.

The figure shimmered again, the mist swirling around her like a storm. "Rowan, I have waited for so long," she breathed, her voice both a melody and a plea. "You must come to me. Only you can break the cycle."

"Break the cycle?" I echoed, the words echoing in my mind like the faintest of chimes. "What do you mean?" The urgency in her tone wrapped around me, igniting a spark of determination. Isaac's hand tightened as he pulled me back, but the movement felt futile, as though the water itself were conspiring to pull me in.

"You're bound to this place," Serena continued, her eyes piercing through the mist, shimmering with a depth of sorrow and longing. "But you have the power to change it. To set me free."

"Free from what?" I demanded, a mix of fear and curiosity swirling within me. I wanted to dive into the depths of her story, to piece together the fragments of the past that had woven us together in such a mysterious way.

"A curse," she replied, her voice quivering like the gentle ripples on the lake. "One that has trapped me here, and one that threatens to pull you under as well. You must listen. You are not just a witness to this history; you are a part of it."

Isaac stepped closer, his expression now a mix of determination and confusion. "Rowan, please. This isn't just some fantasy. You don't know what's waiting for you down there."

"Do you really think I'd let something happen to you?" I shot back, frustration igniting within me. "If she's telling the truth, then I can't turn my back on her. Not now."

Serena's presence radiated a warmth that contrasted sharply with the cool night air. "Trust me," she whispered, and I felt the weight of her gaze settle on my heart, urging me to take that final step into the unknown.

Without warning, the surface of the lake erupted. A fierce wind whipped around us, carrying with it a chill that made my skin prick with goosebumps. Water splashed up, and for a moment, I was lost in the chaos, my heart pounding in my chest like a drum. Serena's form flickered, wavering like a candle caught in a storm. "You must decide now!"

With a gasp, I turned to Isaac, desperation etched across his features. "What if she's right?" I implored, my voice trembling. "What if this is my chance to change everything?"

"Rowan, no!" His voice rose, filled with a fierce urgency that echoed through the night. "This could be a trap! You can't just—"

But before he could finish, the water surged, wrapping around my ankles, pulling me toward the edge. I gasped as I felt the lake's cold fingers envelop me, a sensation both alarming and thrilling. I fought against the current, but it was as if the lake had a will of its own, a hunger for what it had lost.

"Rowan!" Isaac's shout was desperate, his hand reaching for me, but I was transfixed, caught in the dance of shadows and whispers that filled the air around us. The world narrowed to a single point: Serena's gaze, filled with hope and an undeniable urgency.

"Come with me," she urged, extending a hand that shimmered like moonlight. The space between us shrank, and in that moment, I felt an undeniable pull. The water whispered promises of freedom, of revelations that could change everything, and yet, I could still feel Isaac's fear wrapping around me like chains.

"Please," I whispered, torn between two worlds. "I don't know what to choose."

And just like that, the surface erupted again, a massive wave crashing against the dock, sending splintered wood flying and knocking Isaac off balance. "Rowan!" His voice was swallowed by the roar of the water, panic coloring his tone as he struggled to maintain his footing.

Time seemed to slow as I stood at the brink, the mist swirling around Serena, her outstretched hand shimmering with promise and danger. My heart pounded in my ears, drowning out all rational thought as I felt the energy shift, the very essence of the lake pulsating with urgency.

Then came a jarring realization—a choice that held the weight of my entire existence. Could I truly dive into this unknown world, risking everything I held dear? Or would I let fear bind me to the shore, forever haunted by the whispers that would never let me go?

With one final glance at Isaac, I felt the world tilt, the air thick with magic and the promise of revelation. I stepped forward, ready to embrace the unknown, but as I did, the lake roared in protest, and the mist enveloped me completely.

In that moment, everything fell silent. The world around me faded to black, and I felt myself slipping, the sensation of falling through a void of nothingness. And just before the darkness consumed me, I caught a glimpse of Isaac's horrified face, his outstretched hand reaching for me, desperate and unwilling to let go.

The last thing I heard was the faint whisper of my name, carried on the wind—"Rowan..."—before the world dissolved into silence.

Chapter 11: The Hidden Covenant

The storm unfurled around us like a shroud, heavy clouds bruising the horizon as I stepped cautiously through the twisted remains of what once was a chapel. Its stone walls, now draped in a cascade of vines, whispered secrets of forgotten prayers and lost souls. Each step I took on the damp earth felt like a descent into history, where the air was thick with the scent of moss and decay, and the taste of impending rain lingered on my lips. Isaac led the way, his silhouette framed against the tumultuous sky, and I couldn't help but admire the quiet determination etched on his face, a blend of fear and resolve that echoed my own internal storm.

"I found it," he said, his voice barely audible above the growing roar of the wind. He turned back to me, eyes glinting with a mix of urgency and something softer, more vulnerable. "I think it holds the answers we've been searching for."

I stepped closer, the crumbling stones cool against my fingertips. The chapel had stood here for centuries, a sentinel over the lake's restless waters, and I wondered what tales it could tell if only it could speak. A flicker of lightning illuminated the cryptic inscriptions carved into the stone, casting shadows that danced like specters around us. I squinted at the markings, trying to make sense of the elegant script that twisted and turned, each letter a brushstroke in a grand, unholy artwork.

"Do you think it's true?" I asked, my heart racing. "What they say about the lake? That it's cursed?"

Isaac stepped closer, his breath warm against the cool air. "It's not just a curse, Ava. It's more complex than that. I believe it's a prison."

The word sent a chill racing down my spine, its implications swirling around us like the storm above. My mind was a maelstrom of thoughts—images of the lake's surface, deceptively calm yet hiding unfathomable depths beneath, haunted me. What could be locked away beneath those waters? And why were our families tied to it?

I caught Isaac's gaze, searching for answers. "What do you mean? A prison for what?"

His expression darkened, shadows playing across his handsome features. "For something—or someone. The inscriptions talk about a covenant, a promise made generations ago to keep whatever it is contained." He traced a finger over the stone, revealing words that seemed to shimmer with a life of their own. "Our families...they're part of this. Bound by blood to guard the lake's secret."

As the wind howled around us, the weight of his words pressed down like an iron shackle, and I could feel the ground shift beneath my feet. "What does that mean for us?" I whispered, feeling the very air between us crackle with tension. It was as if the storm itself anticipated the answer, holding its breath in rapt attention.

Isaac hesitated, his brow furrowing as if grappling with a truth that was almost too heavy to bear. "I don't know. But it changes everything." His voice was steady, yet I could sense the tremor beneath. "If our families are intertwined in this covenant, it could put us in danger. We might be caught in the crossfire of a conflict we never asked for."

The ground felt more unstable now, and I pulled my cardigan tighter around my shoulders, fighting against the chill that seeped into my bones. "What if...what if the lake isn't just a prison?" I proposed, uncertainty lacing my words. "What if it holds something powerful that others want to control?"

Isaac's eyes widened, the storm outside echoing the tempest of thoughts raging within us. "That's a possibility we can't ignore." His fingers brushed against mine, a fleeting connection that sent a jolt of warmth through the cold air. "And if that's true, then we need to find out what it is before someone else does."

The storm outside intensified, the rain crashing against the stone walls like a drumroll heralding something monumental. I felt it then, the pulse of history thrumming beneath our feet, the echoes of our ancestors urging us to act. This chapel had witnessed sacrifices, had borne witness to the choices made to protect the lake's secret. Now, it was our turn to unravel that mystery, to uncover the truth buried within our families' pasts.

"What do we do?" I asked, my voice steadier than I felt. "Where do we start?"

"Here," Isaac said, a glimmer of determination sparking in his eyes. "We decipher these inscriptions. They'll guide us to what we need to know."

As he stepped closer to the wall, I joined him, peering at the ancient text that seemed to writhe under our scrutiny. The markings told a story of a bond forged in desperation, a pact made to contain darkness, to seal away a force that could shatter lives if unleashed. The realization settled over me, heavy as the storm clouds, that we were not merely investigating a family secret; we were entangled in a legacy of guardianship that demanded sacrifice.

"Look," Isaac said suddenly, his voice a low whisper, drawing my attention to a specific carving that depicted a figure bound in chains, gazing longingly at the surface of a tranquil lake. "It's like they knew what they were keeping locked away, but also how dangerous it could be if it ever escaped."

"What if it's already been released?" I mused, dread curling in my stomach like a coiling serpent. The thought of whatever lurked beneath the water, free to roam, sent a wave of nausea crashing over me.

Isaac turned to face me, his expression fierce and unwavering. "Then we have to be ready. We can't let fear dictate our actions. We need to confront this together."

In that moment, amidst the roaring storm and the weight of our families' legacy, I knew we were no longer just two people caught in a whirlwind of secrets. We were allies, bound by an unbreakable thread woven from shared purpose and the palpable tension crackling between us. The lake's mysteries beckoned, and together, we would plunge into the depths of its history, ready to face whatever lay beneath.

The air crackled with tension, a palpable energy that twisted around us like the tendrils of ivy clinging to the chapel's walls. As Isaac and I stood shoulder to shoulder, our breaths mingled in the cool, damp air, a blend of trepidation and determination simmering just beneath the surface. The storm's fury outside mirrored the chaos brewing within me. Each flash of lightning illuminated the inscriptions, revealing layers of meaning that seemed to pulse with a life of their own. The words were more than mere symbols; they felt like warnings, secrets kept by the stones themselves.

"Okay, let's see what we're really up against," Isaac said, squinting at the intricate carvings. "If this is a prison, we need to know who—or what—is locked inside." His voice carried a hint of bravado, but I could see the flicker of uncertainty behind his bravado, a candle struggling against a gale.

I leaned in, tracing my fingers over the delicate lines of a serpent entwined with a key, its eyes gleaming as though aware of our scrutiny. "What do you think it means? The key and the serpent?" I asked, my curiosity igniting a spark of courage within me.

He chuckled softly, the sound warm despite the chill that clung to the stone. "Well, I suppose we could start by taking a guess. Keys usually unlock things, and serpents... well, they often symbolize knowledge, temptation, or danger." His eyes danced with mischief, the storm outside doing nothing to dampen the flicker of humor that always seemed to surface between us. "I'd say we're in for a little of all three."

I rolled my eyes, but my heart raced at his teasing. "You're not helping."

"Just trying to lighten the mood," he replied, a smirk breaking through the tension. "But you're right. This is serious. We need to dig deeper."

We spent what felt like hours poring over the inscriptions, our hands brushing against the cool stone as we traced the contours of the symbols, piecing together a tapestry of history woven from pain and protection. Each carving seemed to whisper secrets, and the deeper we delved, the more I felt a connection to the generations that had come before us—people who had fought against unseen threats to safeguard their loved ones and the land they cherished.

But as I deciphered the cryptic phrases, unease seeped into the back of my mind. "What if this prison isn't just about keeping something locked away?" I asked, my voice low, almost a whisper. "What if it's about control? What if it's meant to keep the power of the lake from falling into the wrong hands?"

Isaac's expression turned serious, and he nodded slowly. "You're onto something. If our families have been guarding this secret, it must be for a reason. But what if someone wants to exploit it?"

The thought sent shivers racing down my spine. The lake, once a serene backdrop to my childhood, now loomed as a dark force, a place of hidden dangers and ancient grudges. "So we're not just uncovering family secrets. We're standing on the edge of a potential catastrophe."

"Exactly," Isaac replied, his brow furrowing. "And we need to be careful. If there's someone out there looking for whatever's contained in that lake, we can't let them find it first."

As if to punctuate his words, the chapel shuddered under a powerful gust of wind, rattling the shutters and causing dust to rain down like forgotten memories. I glanced around, half-expecting a ghostly figure to materialize among the shadows, but nothing stirred.

It was just us, two souls bound by fate, standing at the crossroads of destiny.

Suddenly, the stone beneath my fingers shifted, a loose fragment giving way to reveal a hidden compartment. I gasped, my heart leaping as I pulled away a few scattered stones, exposing a small, weathered box engraved with the same serpent design. "Isaac, look!" I exclaimed, my excitement cutting through the tension like a knife.

He leaned in closer, his expression morphing from curiosity to disbelief as I pried the box open. Inside lay a collection of old parchment scrolls, their edges frayed and yellowed with age. "This could be what we've been searching for," he breathed, reverently lifting a scroll from the box.

I held my breath as he began to unroll it, revealing intricate drawings and an elaborate script that seemed to pulse with an almost tangible energy. As he read aloud, the words flowed like an incantation, weaving a tale of ancient guardians, dark forces, and a prophecy that hinted at a future entwined with the lake's fate.

"We have to show this to someone," I suggested, my mind racing with possibilities. "We need guidance. If this is as powerful as it seems, we can't take it lightly."

Isaac nodded, but his expression turned grave. "There are people in this town who might not want us to find this. If they know we have it... they could see us as a threat."

A chill settled in the pit of my stomach, the weight of our discovery crashing over me. We were delving into something far greater than ourselves, a force that could alter the very fabric of our lives. "What if we're not the first to uncover this? What if someone else has been looking for it?"

The thought was a thorn in my side, painful and persistent. Isaac's gaze darkened, and he clenched his jaw, his resolve steeling. "Then we need to protect it. We need to find a way to keep this safe until we understand its full implications."

The storm outside raged on, the rain pounding against the chapel like a heartbeat. We could no longer deny the bond between us—the urgency of our mission intertwining with something deeper. As the winds howled, I felt a spark of defiance ignite within me.

"Whatever it takes," I said, determination lacing my voice, "we'll uncover the truth and protect what's ours. Together."

Isaac smiled, a flicker of admiration lighting his features. "Together," he echoed, the promise hanging between us like a spell, binding us to a path laden with uncertainty yet brimming with possibility. And in that moment, I knew we would face whatever darkness lay ahead, armed with nothing but our courage and the unbreakable bond that had formed amidst the shadows of an abandoned chapel.

As the storm raged outside, I couldn't help but marvel at the strange sanctuary we had found ourselves in—a forgotten chapel with secrets etched into its very walls. The air crackled with the anticipation of discovery, yet the shadows felt alive, wrapping around us like specters from a bygone era. I glanced at Isaac, who was meticulously rolling out another parchment from the box, his expression a blend of concentration and something else—a flicker of excitement that mirrored my own.

"Let's hope this one doesn't read like an ancient laundry list," he said with a wry smile, a glimmer of humor cutting through the tension. I could always count on him to find light in the darkest moments. "If it does, I'm holding you responsible for dragging me here in the first place."

"Just think of it as a little adventure," I shot back, feeling my spirits lift as I peered over his shoulder. "You know, a chance to explore our family's dark past. What could possibly go wrong?"

Isaac raised an eyebrow, the corners of his mouth twitching upward. "Famous last words, Ava."

He began to read aloud, and the words flowed like water, painting a vivid picture of ancient guardians tasked with protecting the lake and its secrets. The scroll described the power contained within—an essence so potent it could alter the fabric of reality itself. "It speaks of a 'Veil,'" he murmured, his brow furrowing in concentration. "A boundary that holds back something... something dangerous."

I leaned closer, the urge to unravel every detail consuming me. "What does it say about breaking that Veil?"

He hesitated, the air thick with tension. "It implies that once it's breached, chaos will reign. But it also mentions a key—a specific bloodline destined to either protect the Veil or bring it crashing down."

A cold knot formed in my stomach. "Are you saying our families—our blood—are the key?"

Isaac nodded, the gravity of our situation settling heavily between us. "It seems like it. We have to find out more about this Veil and what exactly it keeps locked away. If it's as dangerous as it sounds, we're not just uncovering history; we're standing at the precipice of something far more consequential."

Suddenly, the wind howled louder, rattling the chapel's structure, and the flickering light of our lantern cast erratic shadows that danced like wraiths along the walls. I felt a chill creep down my spine. "What if someone already knows? What if we're not the only ones looking for this?"

Isaac's gaze darkened. "We have to move quickly then. We can't risk being caught off guard."

Just then, the faint sound of footsteps reached my ears, muffled yet unmistakable against the backdrop of the storm. I turned to Isaac, my heart racing. "Did you hear that?"

He nodded, his expression shifting from curiosity to concern. "We might not be alone after all."

We exchanged a quick glance, the unspoken agreement hanging in the air between us: we needed to hide the scrolls. As if sensing the encroaching danger, adrenaline surged through my veins, fueling my movements. We hurriedly shoved the parchment back into the box, my fingers trembling slightly as I worked.

"Where?" I hissed, glancing around the dimly lit chapel for a suitable hiding place. "We can't just leave it out in the open."

Isaac scanned the area, his brow furrowing in thought. "Behind the altar. It's a long shot, but it might buy us some time."

I nodded, urgency propelling us forward. We slipped behind the weathered altar, a makeshift barrier against the approaching intruder, our hearts pounding in sync as we crouched low, the box pressed tightly against my chest.

The footsteps grew closer, the sound unmistakably deliberate, echoing through the hallowed halls of the chapel. I strained to hear anything beyond the drum of rain on the roof, my pulse racing as a shadow flickered across the threshold.

"Isaac," I whispered, fear clawing at my throat. "What if they're looking for us?"

He held a finger to his lips, his gaze intense and focused. We waited in silence, the storm outside raging on, a symphony of nature's fury drowning out our breaths.

The door creaked open, and a figure stepped inside, silhouetted against the tumultuous backdrop of wind and rain. I squinted to make out the details—dark clothing, a hood pulled low over their face, casting their features into obscurity. My heart raced. This wasn't just anyone; this felt deliberate, almost predatory.

"Come out, come out, wherever you are," the figure called, their voice a chilling sing-song that sent shivers racing down my spine. "I know you're here."

My pulse quickened as I shared a glance with Isaac, his eyes wide with alarm. "This is bad," he muttered under his breath. "We need to make a move. Now."

The figure stepped further inside, scanning the chapel with a predatory grace. "I can sense your presence. You think you're hidden, but I can smell the fear."

I squeezed the box tightly, holding my breath as the figure stepped closer, their movements fluid, almost cat-like. It felt like they were toying with us, savoring the game of hide and seek, and I couldn't shake the feeling that we were the prey.

"Do you want to play a game?" they continued, the tone taunting and dark. "Because I do. And I'm very, very good at it."

Isaac's hand found mine, a comforting pressure amid the rising tension. "We can't stay here. We have to move."

I nodded, summoning every ounce of courage I had. With a swift glance at the figure, I made a split-second decision. "On three, we run for the door," I whispered, my heart pounding in my ears.

"One," Isaac murmured, his grip tightening around mine.

"Two," I counted down, adrenaline flooding my veins.

And then we were off, bursting from our hiding place in a rush, the box clutched tightly against my chest as we sprinted toward the door. But just as we reached the threshold, the figure lunged forward, a blur of motion that sent my heart into a frenzy.

"Stop!" they shouted, and in that moment, the air crackled with a power I couldn't explain.

I skidded to a halt, and Isaac's hand slipped from mine, the box falling to the ground with a thud. The figure stepped into the light, revealing their face—a mask of familiarity twisted into a smirk, a face I thought I'd never see again, a face that turned my world upside down.

"Ava," they purred, "you didn't think you could escape so easily, did you?"

The world around me spun as recognition washed over me like a cold wave, crashing into the realization that everything was about to change. The storm outside faded into insignificance, and in that instant, I understood that the real battle had just begun.

Chapter 12: A Dance with Darkness

The air thrummed with a pulse of excitement as I stepped into the heart of Willow Creek's Lantern Festival. The entire town transformed under a tapestry of twinkling lights, each lantern a tiny beacon of hope against the encroaching darkness of the night. I could smell the sweet scent of caramelized apples mingling with the earthy aroma of the autumn leaves, a sensory feast that tugged at the corners of my mouth. The laughter of children chased the wind, their joy ringing like bells, while couples swayed together in slow dances, lost in their own worlds.

Isaac stood beside me, his presence both a comfort and a challenge. He had a way of making everything seem brighter, as if he carried the sun tucked beneath his shirt. His hair, tousled and wind-kissed, framed a face that was both rugged and boyishly charming. The shadows from the lanterns danced across his skin, highlighting the strong lines of his jaw and the mischievous sparkle in his blue eyes. It was hard to believe he was once just the quiet boy from the back of my history class. Here, surrounded by laughter and light, he transformed into something more, a piece of the festival's enchantment that pulled me closer.

"Can you believe they actually hang all these lanterns up themselves?" he asked, gesturing at the overhead display of colors—gold, red, and soft blues mingling like brushstrokes on an artist's canvas. "I thought for sure they'd hire someone professional to do this."

I chuckled, nudging him playfully. "And miss out on the chance for all this charm? It's like a fairy tale come to life." The moment felt idyllic, yet a subtle tension hung in the air, an echo of the lake's murky depths whispering to me from just beyond the festival's glow.

As we moved through the throngs of festival-goers, I felt the weight of the past pressing in on me. The lake, with its swirling secrets and dark tendrils, loomed just outside the periphery of my thoughts, always lurking, always watching. It had been weeks since I had heard the whispers of its spirit, the chill of its warnings coursing through me. But tonight, I tried to drown those thoughts in laughter and light. I needed this moment. I needed Isaac.

"Dance with me," he said suddenly, his eyes locking onto mine with a fiery intensity that made my heart skip. Without waiting for an answer, he pulled me into the center of a small clearing, where the music flowed like water, sweet and intoxicating. I felt a flutter of nerves but met his gaze, a silent challenge. The air crackled with unspoken words as we began to sway together.

Isaac's hands rested on my waist, firm yet gentle, guiding me through the rhythm of the evening. The world around us blurred into a swirl of color and laughter, the lanterns a warm backdrop to the electric connection sparking between us. I could feel the warmth radiating from his body, and every beat of my heart seemed to echo the pulse of the music. "You're a terrible dancer," I teased, watching as he stepped on my toes with a boyish grin.

"Hey, I'm trying to channel my inner prince charming here!" he shot back, laughing, his eyes sparkling like the stars above. It was a moment so ordinary, yet it felt monumental, the weight of the night hanging in the balance as I let myself get lost in the warmth of his presence.

But then, just as I let my guard down, a cold shiver snaked down my spine, like icy fingers gripping my heart. The music faded momentarily, replaced by an echo of whispers, a distant call that sent dread coursing through me. The lake's spirit had awakened, as if it sensed my defiance, my choice to stand in this moment instead of yielding to its dark embrace. I glanced over my shoulder, half-expecting to see its shadow lurking just beyond the lantern light.

Isaac noticed my sudden stillness, the way my laughter faltered. "What is it?" His brow furrowed, concern etching itself into the lines of his face. "You look like you've seen a ghost."

I forced a smile, shaking my head as if I could dispel the fear with a mere gesture. "It's nothing. Just... the atmosphere, you know? The festival. It's a little overwhelming." But even as I spoke, I felt the words taste bitter on my tongue. I had hoped to leave the lake behind, at least for tonight, but it crept back in with a chilling reminder of its grip on my life.

"Overwhelming in a good way, I hope," he said, a teasing lilt to his voice. He took my hands in his, squeezing them gently as if grounding me back to this moment, this celebration of life. "Let's make a pact. Tonight, we dance like the world outside doesn't exist."

I nodded, the simple warmth of his hands infusing me with strength. "Okay. A pact it is," I agreed, feeling the tension begin to ease as he pulled me back into the music.

As the final notes of the song faded into the night, he leaned in closer, his breath warm against my ear. "And when the night ends, I'll walk you home. Just in case." There was a depth in his voice that hinted at understanding, a recognition of the shadows that lingered just beyond the festival's glow.

I smiled, heart racing with both excitement and trepidation. "Deal." The night stretched out before us, a tantalizing promise of freedom that felt both sacred and doomed, teetering on the edge of something powerful and unknown. For now, though, I chose to dance.

The evening unfurled like the delicate petals of a night-blooming flower, each moment bursting with possibilities that shimmered as brightly as the lanterns surrounding us. Isaac and I swayed to the music, our bodies moving in a rhythm dictated not just by the notes that filled the air but by the unspoken connection that crackled between us. I could feel the warmth of his breath against my cheek, the intoxicating mix of pine and cologne wrapping around me like a soft blanket.

"Do you ever wonder if we're just characters in some whimsical story?" he mused, his voice a soft rumble that felt like home. "You know, like we've stumbled into a fairy tale where everything is supposed to be perfect, but we're really just waiting for the plot twist?"

I chuckled, pulling back slightly to meet his gaze. "Oh, I definitely expect a plot twist, preferably involving dragons or at least a dash of magic. But knowing my luck, it'll probably just be a ghost popping out of the lake to ruin our night." The playful sarcasm felt good, a reprieve from the dark thoughts lurking just beneath my surface.

Isaac laughed, the sound rich and deep. "A ghost? How cliché. I was hoping for something a little more original. Maybe a sea monster?"

"Ah, of course! Something with tentacles that could ruin our dance and drag us both into the depths!" I replied, faking horror as I stumbled back dramatically, earning a laugh from him.

"Now that," he said, stepping forward with a teasing glint in his eye, "would make for an unforgettable first date." His hand found mine again, and with an exaggerated flourish, he pulled me back into the dance, our laughter mingling with the music around us.

But even as we spun and twirled beneath the glowing lanterns, the chill of the lake lingered at the edges of my consciousness, a silent reminder of its ever-present grip on my life. It was like a shadow that stretched and twisted, slipping through the cracks of my joy, threatening to unravel everything I was trying to build in this fleeting moment of happiness.

As we danced, the crowd surged around us, a lively river of colors and laughter, and for a moment, I felt like we were the only two people in the world. I leaned in closer, resting my head on his shoulder, letting the beat of his heart synchronize with my own. "You know, I could get used to this," I said softly, my words wrapped in a warmth I hoped wouldn't shatter too soon.

"Just promise me one thing," he replied, pulling back to look into my eyes, his expression serious yet playful. "If I start to dance like my father at weddings, you have to tell me. No holding back."

"Deal," I said, unable to suppress my laughter. "I'll make sure to guide you back to the realm of the graceful."

Just then, a loud cheer erupted from a nearby booth, where the town's mayor was preparing to light the ceremonial lantern—a ritual believed to ensure the lake remained placid and its spirits benevolent. The excitement in the crowd surged, pulling our attention away momentarily. I glanced up, watching the mayor hold the lantern high, its golden glow illuminating his grinning face. It was a moment that reminded everyone of our shared heritage, our history intertwined with the mysteries of the lake.

But as I turned back to Isaac, the smile slipped from my face. He stood a little too still, his gaze fixed over my shoulder, the lively energy between us suddenly feeling brittle. "What's wrong?" I asked, my heart leaping into my throat as I followed his line of sight.

At the edge of the celebration, where the lanterns' glow waned into the shadows, stood a figure cloaked in darkness. The outline was indistinct, the deep hood casting a veil over the face, but there was something unmistakably foreboding about the presence. It felt as though the air shifted, thickening with an unseen tension that sent shivers crawling down my spine.

"Do you see that?" Isaac's voice was low, barely a whisper as he stepped closer, creating a barrier between me and the unknown.

"Yeah, I see it," I replied, my voice steady despite the pounding of my heart. "But who...?"

Before I could finish my thought, the figure began to move, gliding toward the lanterns as if drawn by their light. The crowd seemed oblivious, laughter and chatter continuing unabated, but an instinctual dread clawed at my gut.

Isaac's grip on my hand tightened, his brow furrowing with concern. "Should we—?"

"Let's just keep moving," I interrupted, my voice gaining strength as I pulled him gently away from the crowd. "We'll find somewhere quieter. It's probably just someone in costume or... well, who knows? This town does love its theatrics."

"Right," he said, still glancing over his shoulder as we wove through the sea of people, my heart racing in time with my thoughts. The figure lingered in my mind, a specter of unease that tainted the vibrant atmosphere of the festival.

We ducked behind a food stall, the scent of fried dough filling the air, and I leaned against the cool wooden structure, willing my heart to slow. Isaac leaned in closer, his expression softening as he took in my flustered state. "Hey, you okay?" His voice was gentle, grounding me amidst the chaos of my swirling thoughts.

"I will be," I replied, forcing a smile that felt more like a mask. "Just... let's focus on the festival. It's supposed to be fun, right?"

"Right," he said, though the concern lingered in his eyes. "How about we grab some food and try that fried dough you mentioned? Nothing chases away shadows like a sugar rush."

I laughed, grateful for his light-heartedness. "Now you're speaking my language."

We stepped back into the crowd, the vibrant lights and laughter pulling me along, but the unease lingered like a dark cloud on the periphery of my joy. As we made our way to the stall, I couldn't shake the feeling that the figure was still watching, that the shadows of the lake had not yet released their hold on our night.

The fried dough stand was a kaleidoscope of color and sound, the scent of cinnamon and sugar wrapping around me like a comforting shawl. I inhaled deeply, savoring the sweetness that momentarily chased away the lingering shadows in my mind. Isaac ordered two heaping servings, the vendor's hands moving deftly as she tossed dough into the bubbling oil.

As the vendor handed us the warm, sugary delights, Isaac turned to me with an exuberant grin. "You know, if I can keep you laughing and full of fried dough, we can face anything—even ghosts or lake monsters."

I took a huge bite, the warmth melting in my mouth, and burst into laughter. "Good to know you've planned for every scenario, including snack emergencies!" I savored the sweetness, letting it distract me from the uncertainty still gnawing at the edges of my mind.

As we leaned against the wooden stall, watching the festivities around us, I noticed a couple nearby, their laughter punctuated by the soft glow of the lanterns. The light danced on their faces, but there was a flicker of unease in the way they kept glancing toward the shadowy edge of the festival. My stomach tightened again, and I quickly turned away, focusing on Isaac instead.

"Okay, I need to know. What's your ultimate comfort food? Because clearly, I'm collecting answers for the inevitable apocalypse," he said, taking a bite of his own dough.

I pretended to think hard, narrowing my eyes in concentration. "That's a tough one. I'd have to say... a cheeseburger. You know, the kind that's greasy enough to make you question your life choices but delicious enough to make you not care?"

He chuckled, his eyes sparkling. "You're speaking my language. Greasy burgers for the win!"

But as we continued to banter, a flicker of movement caught my eye again, that same cloaked figure lingering just outside the festival's joyous chaos. It was a shadow among shadows, indistinct yet unyielding, and my heart raced with a mixture of curiosity and dread.

"Isaac," I said, my voice dropping to a whisper, "look over there."

He followed my gaze, his brow furrowing as he spotted the figure. "What the hell is that?" His playful demeanor vanished, replaced by a seriousness that sent an electric shock of alarm through me.

"I'm not sure," I admitted, trying to keep my voice steady, but the unease rolled over me like a wave. "It's been standing there since we got here."

"Maybe we should—"

Suddenly, a loud crash echoed through the night, cutting through our conversation. A nearby lantern shattered, sending sparks and glass cascading across the ground. The crowd gasped, faces turning toward the sound, excitement rapidly morphing into confusion and concern.

"Stay here," Isaac said, his voice firm as he squeezed my hand briefly before stepping into the crowd, weaving through startled festival-goers. My heart fluttered as I watched him disappear, a mixture of worry and anger twisting in my stomach. He didn't need to play the hero; this was just a festival, a celebration meant to shield us from the darkness.

I took a deep breath, forcing myself to stay put. But the unease inside me festered, a gnawing compulsion to uncover the mystery of the figure that still lurked nearby. With every heartbeat, I could feel the lake's presence inching closer, a phantom tugging at my consciousness.

As I moved cautiously through the crowd, I kept my eyes peeled for Isaac. My heart raced, not just from fear but from an exhilarating sense of purpose. I was no longer merely a spectator; I was becoming an active participant in my own story, ready to face whatever was lurking just beyond the light.

And then I saw it. The figure moved with a grace that was both unnatural and unsettling, gliding past the scattered lanterns with an elegance that sent a chill racing down my spine. I edged closer, drawn by a magnetic pull that made my skin prickle, feeling an urgency I couldn't ignore.

"Isaac!" I called out, but my voice was swallowed by the sudden swell of murmurs and gasps from the crowd, all eyes focused on the flickering lanterns and the chaotic scene unfolding.

Before I could process my next move, the figure turned sharply, revealing a face obscured in shadow yet unmistakably familiar. My heart dropped as recognition settled over me like a heavy shroud. It was someone I knew, someone I'd never expected to see in this haunting context.

The figure raised a hand, pointing directly at me, and in that instant, the air shifted. The laughter faded, the festival dimmed, and a profound silence enveloped us, as if time itself had paused to acknowledge the impending storm.

"Run!" Isaac's voice broke through the haze, pulling me from my trance. He surged back toward me, determination etched on his face, but before I could react, the figure moved again, the tension snapping like a taut string ready to break.

"Don't let it get you!" Isaac shouted, but the warning felt distant as the ground beneath me trembled with a strange energy. The lanterns began to flicker wildly, casting eerie shadows that danced around us, blurring the line between reality and nightmare.

I turned to flee, adrenaline propelling me forward, but the figure was upon us, a dark silhouette framed by the chaos of the festival. My pulse raced as I glanced back at Isaac, who was struggling to reach me through the crowd, his face a mask of concern and urgency.

Just as I felt the cool rush of air behind me, the world exploded into chaos. A deafening roar echoed from the lake, a sound that vibrated through the ground beneath my feet, as if the very spirit of the water was rising in fury. The figure's eyes glinted in the lantern light—was it anger or desperation?

And in that moment, time splintered, the night fracturing into a thousand shards of fear and uncertainty. I was left standing at the precipice of darkness, caught between the light of the festival and the chilling embrace of the unknown, a single question echoing in my mind: What had I awakened beneath the surface?

Chapter 13: Bound to the Shadows

The air felt thick with the scent of damp earth and impending rain, as if the sky itself were holding its breath, waiting for something to break the tension. I stood on the shore of the lake, its surface shimmering under the sullen glow of the overcast sky, the water mirroring the turmoil within me. Each ripple seemed to whisper secrets that I was just beginning to grasp, secrets that held the promise of power and danger, of awakening forces that had lain dormant for too long.

Isaac had always been my anchor, the one steady point in my chaotic world. But lately, he had become an enigma wrapped in shadows, his presence more ghost than flesh. The weight of his secrets pressed down on us like an unyielding fog, and as I gazed into the depths of the lake, I felt the sharp pang of betrayal clawing at my insides. How could he not trust me with this? The betrayal stung deeper than I had anticipated, wrapping around my heart like a vice.

"Is this what you wanted to tell me?" I asked, my voice trembling with a mix of hurt and anger. The words tumbled out before I could rein them in, raw and unfiltered. "That I'm some sort of monster to be contained? That you've been keeping secrets from me while I'm here, standing on the edge of... whatever this is?"

Isaac ran a hand through his tousled hair, the gesture familiar yet foreign. "You don't understand, Kira. This isn't just about us. There are people who will do anything to keep this power from being unleashed." His voice was low, earnest, and laced with a fear that mirrored my own. "They think you've tapped into something ancient, something that could destroy everything."

"Everything? Or just their control over it?" I shot back, taking a step closer, feeling the tension spark between us like electricity. The very air crackled with the weight of unsaid words, and for a fleeting moment, the world faded away until it was just the two of us, suspended in this moment of revelation and accusation.

He looked away, staring out at the swirling mist that danced just above the water's surface. "They're not wrong to be afraid. You have no idea what this place is capable of. I thought I could keep you safe, keep us safe." His gaze turned back to me, intensity etched in his features. "But the more I learn, the more I realize that I might not be able to."

Every word felt like a dagger, each one thrust deeper than the last. "So what? You'll just walk away? You'll let them take me because it's easier?" My voice broke on the last word, a crack that echoed my fraying resolve. The idea of losing him, of losing this connection that had pulled me from the brink of my own darkness, sent a cold shiver through my bones.

"You have to believe me, Kira. I'm trying to protect you. This is bigger than us!" His frustration spilled over, and for a heartbeat, I glimpsed the turmoil that churned beneath his calm facade. His hands flexed at his sides, a sign of his own internal struggle.

I stepped back, the distance between us widening like a chasm I wasn't sure we could bridge again. "What if I don't want to be protected? What if I want to explore this power, figure out what it means?" The challenge hung in the air, a dare cloaked in desperation.

"Then you'd be playing with fire, and I won't let you burn." His voice was a low growl, raw and untamed, sending a shiver down my spine. He was fierce, unyielding, and yet I could see the flicker of doubt in his eyes. I felt it too—a seductive pull toward the dark depths of the lake, a call that resonated in my very bones.

"You don't get to decide that for me," I replied, fighting to keep my voice steady, my heart racing as I felt the pulse of the lake beneath my feet, its heartbeat syncing with my own. "I have to know. If there's something within me, something powerful, I can't just ignore it."

His expression softened for a moment, and I could see the struggle in his gaze, the conflict between wanting to protect me and the undeniable connection we shared. "You're not just anyone, Kira. You're special, and that makes you a target. They won't stop until they have you—or worse."

The thought sent a chill down my spine, an icy tendril of fear wrapping around my heart. I could sense it, the lurking shadows waiting just beyond the treeline, poised to strike. "What do we do then?" The words slipped from my lips, and I realized how much I longed for him to take my hand, to face whatever was coming together.

Isaac took a step closer, the warmth of his presence pulling me back from the precipice of despair. "We need to learn about your abilities. I need to understand what's awakened in you and how to control it. If we can't harness it, we'll be at their mercy."

His willingness to fight alongside me, to explore this uncharted territory, reignited the spark of hope within me. We were bound together, not just by our love but by this newfound knowledge that threatened to upend our lives. I reached for him, our fingers brushing lightly, igniting a current of unspoken promises.

The world felt both fragile and expansive in that moment, an intricate web of possibilities stretching before us. I knew then that whatever shadows lurked in the corners of our lives, we would face them together. And if that meant wading into the depths of the lake, into the very heart of its mystery, then so be it. The journey ahead would be perilous, but for the first time in days, I felt a flicker of determination igniting within me. We would confront the darkness, but not alone. Together, we would uncover the truth, no matter how deep it lay buried beneath the waters.

A chill swept over the lake as the sun dipped below the horizon, casting long shadows that seemed to stretch endlessly toward me. I stood at the water's edge, wrestling with the realization that our lives had irrevocably shifted, each heartbeat echoing with the weight of our choices. The air was electric, charged with possibilities that felt as terrifying as they were exhilarating. Behind me, the trees whispered secrets, their leaves rustling like the hushed conversations of conspirators. I was caught in a maelstrom of emotions, and the turbulent current tugged at me, urging me to dive deeper into this new reality.

Isaac stood close, yet his distance felt insurmountable, a barrier of uncertainty and fear that loomed between us. I could see the internal battle waging in his eyes, and it mirrored my own confusion. "What's next then?" I asked, my voice a blend of frustration and longing. "Do we just wait for them to come and take me? Because I'd prefer not to become the main attraction for some shadowy organization bent on 'containing' me."

He ran a hand over his face, weariness etched in every line of his expression. "No. We prepare. We need to understand what they think I've awakened in you." His tone was resolute, but there was an underlying tremor, a hint that he wasn't entirely sure what that preparation would entail.

"Great. More mystery. Just what I needed today." I crossed my arms, trying to quell the rising tide of anxiety. The last thing I wanted was to step into a shadowy world where I might have to prove my worth—or worse, my innocence.

Isaac's gaze softened as he stepped closer. "Kira, I'm serious. There are rituals and histories tied to this lake. We need to gather information, find out what you're capable of. If there's even a chance that you've tapped into something..." He trailed off, and I could see the flicker of dread in his eyes.

"Then what? We put me in a glass jar and hope they don't notice I'm gone?" I quipped, attempting to lighten the mood, but my voice lacked its usual playfulness, the weight of reality draping over us like a heavy blanket.

He chuckled softly, the sound both soothing and maddeningly infuriating at the same time. "I wouldn't put you in a jar. You'd break it before the day was over." There was a spark of mischief in his eyes that made my heart flutter, but it quickly faded under the somberness of our situation.

"I could always charm the guards," I replied, my voice steadying. "Make them forget I'm even here." The idea was ridiculous, yet there was a truth hidden within the jest. My newfound abilities, whatever they were, could offer me a way out of this predicament.

"Charming them might be a challenge, especially if they have centuries of experience with people like us," Isaac said, his brow furrowing as he regarded the water, the deepening dusk reflecting a world we couldn't quite see. "But it might also be our only option. We need to delve into the lake's lore, see if there are any clues about what you're capable of."

"Let's just hope the local library has more than just dusty old tomes and 'how to bake the perfect pie' recipes," I mused, trying to steer us back to a more hopeful territory. "I don't know about you, but I'm not feeling particularly heroic right now."

"Heroic? No. Desperate? Definitely." His lips quirked up into a smirk, and for a moment, the weight of our conversation lifted. "But desperate can lead to some interesting results. Just think of it as an adventure."

"An adventure. Right. I'm all for that, as long as it doesn't involve running from angry ghosts or trying to summon ancient spirits." I leaned back on a large stone, its surface cool against my skin, and looked out over the water, its depths shrouded in mystery. "What if we fail? What if I can't control whatever it is they think I've awakened?"

Isaac moved to stand beside me, the warmth of his presence soothing some of the tumult within. "Then we'll face it together. No more secrets. We'll learn, adapt, and if we can't find a way through it, we'll figure out how to fight it. You've faced darkness before, Kira. You have strength you don't even know you possess."

The confidence in his voice bolstered my resolve. "So, first step: research." I nodded, determination sparking within me. "How do we start?"

"We'll visit the town's archives tomorrow," he suggested, his voice growing more serious. "I've heard whispers about an old journal that belonged to one of the first settlers. It's said to contain records of the lake's history and the strange occurrences tied to it."

"An old journal? Perfect. If it's anything like the libraries I grew up with, we'll likely find it tucked behind a pile of other forgotten relics."

"Or hidden beneath an ominous layer of dust, perhaps guarded by a formidable librarian," he added, his playful tone making me chuckle despite the anxiety simmering beneath the surface.

"I can handle a librarian. I've read enough books to know their weaknesses," I replied, a teasing lilt in my voice. "But what if it's not just dust we're dealing with? What if the journal is cursed or something?"

"Then we'll find a way to break the curse," he replied, his gaze unwavering. "I'll handle any curses while you charm the librarian."

"Deal," I said, feeling a flicker of excitement return to my chest, pushing aside the fears that had threatened to engulf me moments before.

As the sky deepened into twilight, a fresh wave of determination washed over me. This wasn't just about the lake's power or the shadows that threatened to consume us. It was about reclaiming control over my own life, stepping boldly into the unknown. Whatever waited for us in those dusty archives, I was ready to face it—together with Isaac. The stakes were high, the journey uncertain, but I knew one thing for sure: I wouldn't back down. Not now. Not ever.

The next morning dawned with an oppressive grayness that seeped into every corner of my mind, mirroring the uncertainty that clung to my thoughts like morning fog. As I stood in front of the mirror, I splashed cold water on my face, hoping to wash away the remnants of anxiety. My reflection stared back, eyes wide with a mixture of determination and trepidation. I straightened my shoulders and took a deep breath, reminding myself that this was not just about finding answers; it was about reclaiming my narrative, my power, and my life.

Isaac arrived just as I was lacing up my boots, a small package of fresh pastries in hand, the scent wafting through the air like a beacon of comfort. "You can't face a mysterious past on an empty stomach," he said, flashing a grin that lit up his features despite the shadows that lingered around us.

"Ah, the secret to successful archeological digs: sugar and carbs," I quipped, taking a pastry from his hand. The flaky pastry crumbled as I bit into it, sweetness exploding on my tongue. "Now I feel like I can conquer anything. Even dusty old books."

"Dusty old books can be dangerous," he replied, his voice playful but laced with an undercurrent of seriousness. "They might hold dark secrets or unfathomable power."

"Or just a lot of boring passages about the local flora." I chuckled, but a tremor of apprehension ran through me. We both knew there was more at stake than mere boredom.

The town archives were nestled in an unassuming brick building, its façade worn with age yet radiating an aura of quiet authority. The moment we stepped inside, the familiar scent of aged paper and wood greeted us like an old friend. Dust motes danced in the soft light filtering through the windows, creating an ethereal glow that made the shelves of books and artifacts seem almost magical.

I scanned the room, my heart racing with anticipation. "Okay, let's find that journal before we get lost in the labyrinth of knowledge." The sense of adventure surged within me, momentarily drowning out the fears that had shadowed my thoughts.

"Right. We'll split up—tackle this place like an archaeological dig team," Isaac suggested, his enthusiasm infectious.

"Agreed. But if you start talking about 'fossils' and 'carbon dating,' I might just find an excuse to flee," I teased, nudging him playfully.

He smirked. "I'll keep the paleontology to a minimum."

We dove into our respective searches, the silence of the archive punctuated only by the soft rustling of pages and the distant sound of a clock ticking. I lost myself in the rows of ancient tomes, each one holding the weight of history within its spine. With each book I pulled down, I could feel the pulse of the lake echoing in my mind, a reminder of the power waiting to be unraveled.

After what felt like an eternity, I finally came across a worn leather-bound journal tucked away in a shadowy corner. Its spine was cracked, but the cover held an air of mystery that made my heart race. I brushed the dust away and opened it, revealing a delicate script that danced across the pages.

"Isaac! I think I found it!" I called, excitement bubbling within me. He appeared at my side almost instantly, his eyes widening as he took in the sight of the journal.

"Let's see what secrets it holds." He leaned closer, and together we began to read, the words transporting us to a time long past. The journal detailed the history of the lake, of the settlers who first arrived and their strange encounters with the water. It spoke of rituals, of sacrifices made to appease something ancient lurking just beneath the surface.

"What are they talking about?" I murmured, my brow furrowing. "It sounds almost... alive."

Isaac nodded, his expression growing serious. "This lake has its own heartbeat, its own will. We need to be cautious."

As we read on, the journal revealed a chilling prophecy—one that spoke of a chosen individual awakening the lake's power and drawing the attention of those who wished to control it. My heart sank as I realized the implications. "This could be me," I whispered, dread pooling in my stomach.

"Or it could just be a myth," Isaac offered, but his tone lacked conviction.

"Right. A myth. Like unicorns and the Loch Ness monster," I replied, my sarcasm failing to mask the fear curling around my heart.

Just then, a shuffling sound broke through the silence, drawing our attention. An older man, the town historian, shuffled into the aisle, his glasses perched precariously on his nose. "Ah, I see you've discovered the journal of Gideon Holloway. A fascinating read, isn't it?"

"Fascinating and a little disturbing," I admitted, my voice tight. "It mentions—"

"—the awakening," he interrupted, his eyes narrowing. "You must be careful. The lake is not to be trifled with. Those who seek its power often pay a heavy price."

"Right, noted. But what do you mean by 'awakened'?" I pressed, curiosity overriding my caution. "What exactly happens?"

He hesitated, casting a glance over his shoulder as if expecting someone to appear from the shadows. "It's said that the lake holds memories—of those who have come before and of the choices they made. If you awaken its power, it will draw attention. Not just from the organization you're concerned about, but from others... those who've waited for centuries."

An icy chill gripped my heart. "What kind of others?"

"Those who believe they have a claim over the lake's gifts. You may find yourself hunted." His voice was low and foreboding, each word laced with a warning that sent shivers down my spine.

"Great, just what I need," I muttered under my breath. I exchanged a glance with Isaac, and the unspoken agreement hung heavily in the air between us. We couldn't back down now; we were already in too deep.

"We'll be careful," Isaac assured the historian, his voice steady. "We're not looking for trouble. We just want to understand."

As the old man nodded, I felt the tension in the room shift, an invisible thread tugging at the edges of our fate. "You don't understand yet, do you?" he said, his voice barely above a whisper. "You've already begun to draw them in."

The ground felt as if it were slipping beneath my feet, my heart racing with the realization that our time was running out. I could almost feel the weight of unseen eyes watching us, lurking in the corners of the archive, waiting for the moment to strike.

As we gathered the journal, I felt an unsettling presence wash over me, a chill that coursed through my veins like ice water. The distant sound of a door creaking open echoed through the hall, a subtle warning that set my nerves on edge. "Did you hear that?" I whispered, my heart pounding in my chest.

Isaac's expression hardened, his gaze shifting toward the noise. "Stay close," he instructed, his protective instincts kicking in.

But before I could respond, a figure emerged from the shadows, cloaked in darkness and intent. I took a step back, breath hitching in my throat. This was not just a librarian or historian; this was something else entirely—someone who knew more than they were letting on.

"Looks like the time for secrets is over," the figure said, voice low and smooth, sending a ripple of unease through the room. "And it's time for you to make a choice."

The air crackled with tension, the promise of danger looming just beyond the threshold of our fragile safety. I felt the pull of the lake's secrets tugging at me, a siren call that whispered of power and peril. My heart raced as I took a step forward, determination igniting within me. This was just the beginning, and whatever awaited us, I was ready to face it.

Chapter 14: The Return of the Naiad

The lake shimmers beneath the dying light of the sun, the golden hues bleeding into deep indigo as twilight descends. I stand at its edge, the damp earth beneath my feet cool and inviting, as though it cradles the secrets of ages long past. A soft breeze carries the scent of wet earth and moss, weaving through the trees that border the water, their leaves whispering as if they hold the very breath of the world. But beneath the serene surface, a storm brews, reflecting the chaos in my heart.

It begins subtly—a ripple, a shiver that runs through the lake's depths, unsettling the surface. I've felt its pull for as long as I can remember, a magnetic force that draws me closer, beckoning me to uncover what lies beneath. Just as the sun surrenders to the night, a figure emerges from the depths, rising as though the water itself has given her life. She glides forward, her hair flowing like strands of silver in the moonlight, illuminating the water around her. The Naiad is hauntingly beautiful, her ethereal form shimmering with a light that seems to come from nowhere and everywhere all at once.

"Your heart beats like a drum, echoing through the silence," she murmurs, her voice a melody that resonates within me. "You seek the truth, but truth is not always kind."

Her words wrap around me, cool and suffocating, stirring a cocktail of fear and fascination in my chest. I want to speak, to demand answers about my family's legacy, but the words catch in my throat, heavy with the weight of what I know is coming.

"I know why you've come," she continues, her gaze piercing into mine with an intensity that makes my skin prickle. "The lake reveals what you wish to hide. It knows your blood and the sins of those who walked before you."

My thoughts race, a cacophony of memories and half-formed questions. The stories my grandmother whispered on stormy nights, tales of curses and bonds that entwined our fates with the waters. But those were just stories, weren't they? Just folklore meant to keep children from wandering too far from home.

The Naiad leans closer, her expression shifting from serene to something sharper, more dangerous. "You are bound to me," she declares, her voice a mixture of triumph and threat. "Your family has tethered itself to my realm, and I will not let you go. Your fate is entwined with the tides of this lake, and no force can sever our bond."

Just then, Isaac appears on the path behind me, his presence a grounding force. He halts mid-step, eyes wide with disbelief as he takes in the apparition before us. "What the hell is happening?" he asks, voice laced with concern, but I can see the curiosity glimmering in his gaze, the way he always gets when faced with the unknown.

The Naiad's expression darkens, her beauty twisted into something menacing. "This one thinks he can protect you. How quaint," she laughs softly, the sound chilling. "But he knows nothing of the darkness that festers here. His attempts to intervene will only seal his fate."

"Back off!" I shout, my heart racing as I step between Isaac and the lake. "You don't get to threaten him."

She cocks her head, a strange amusement playing in her features. "Oh, but it's not a threat, child. It's a warning. Your bond with this boy," she gestures at Isaac, "is a candle in a tempest. You will only draw him into the depths of your turmoil."

Isaac takes a step forward, his expression resolute. "I'm not afraid of you, and I'm not going to let you take her away," he declares, voice steady, though I can hear the tremor beneath the surface.

The Naiad's laughter ripples through the air, mocking and cold. "You have no idea what you're standing against," she hisses. "The lake will claim what is rightfully hers. I will not be thwarted."

As her words settle like lead in the pit of my stomach, I feel the world shift. The air grows thick with tension, the lake's surface darkening as if it has taken offense at the confrontation. The once serene evening morphs into a tableau of impending chaos. I reach for Isaac, our fingers brushing for just a moment before he turns back to face the Naiad.

"Leave her alone!" he demands again, a fire igniting in his eyes. "You can't just manipulate her with your mind games."

But the Naiad merely smiles, a slow, eerie curl of her lips that speaks of ancient power. "Ah, but I can, and I will. The bond we share runs deep, and it cannot be undone. Your love will not save you, nor will it shield her from the lake's true nature."

Her gaze flickers between us, and in that moment, I feel the weight of her words like chains clamping around my heart. The pull of the lake is undeniable, an echo of a past I have yet to fully understand. I glance back at Isaac, his features set in determination, and I wonder if he truly grasps the danger that lies ahead.

The Naiad begins to recede, fading back into the water, her voice trailing behind like smoke. "Remember, child, the lake is both sanctuary and prison. Its depths hold the truth, but at a cost. And you will pay dearly for what you wish to uncover."

With that, she disappears into the shimmering surface, leaving us in a silence thick enough to choke on. The water now lies still, an ominous mirror reflecting our troubled expressions. The weight of the Naiad's warning lingers between us, a specter hovering over our uncertain future.

The air is still thick with the Naiad's warnings, her voice echoing in my mind like a forgotten song. Isaac's brow furrows in thought, a shadow passing over his features as he processes the threat we've just faced. The sun dips below the horizon, surrendering the last of its light to a twilight that feels pregnant with portent. I take a deep breath, trying to ground myself, but the taste of fear lingers on my tongue, bitter and metallic.

"Are you okay?" Isaac asks, stepping closer, concern etched in the lines of his face. His usual bravado has dimmed, replaced by a vulnerability that draws me to him like a moth to a flame. I can't help but admire the way he always seems to know when I'm struggling, even without me saying a word.

"Yeah, just peachy," I reply, attempting a lightness that falls flat. "You know, just had a little chat with a lake spirit who thinks we're doomed." I force a smile, but the tremor in my voice betrays my facade.

"Doomed, huh?" he replies, his lips twitching into a half-smile. "I suppose that's one way to start a Friday night. I was thinking more along the lines of takeout and Netflix."

A small laugh escapes me, a fleeting reprieve from the weight of our reality. "Well, if we make it through the night, I'll gladly take you up on that."

Isaac looks out over the lake, his expression shifting as if he can still feel the Naiad's presence lurking beneath the surface. "Do you think she's really gone?" he asks, the uncertainty evident in his voice.

I shrug, feeling a shiver creep down my spine. "I don't know. The way she spoke... it felt like she was toying with us, like we're just pieces on her chessboard."

Isaac's jaw tightens, and he takes my hand, grounding me in the moment. "We'll figure this out together. I promise," he says, his grip warm and reassuring. The sincerity in his eyes makes my heart race, but the thought of the Naiad's warning looms over us like a storm cloud.

As we stand there, the night deepens, and the stars blink to life overhead, each one a pinprick of light against the vast darkness. I pull away from Isaac slightly, my thoughts drifting back to the stories my grandmother used to tell. I had always thought them fanciful tales meant to keep my imagination alive, but now they felt like a map guiding me through this bizarre reality.

"I need to know more," I murmur, half to myself. "About my family, about her. There's something we're missing, something important."

Isaac nods, his gaze unwavering. "Okay, so we dig deeper. Where do we start?"

"The old library in town," I suggest, recalling the dusty shelves and the librarian who seemed to know more than she let on. "They have records—old books, journals. Maybe something about my family's connection to the lake."

"Lead the way," he replies, his tone lightening as he matches my determined stride. Together, we walk the path leading back through the trees, their branches swaying gently in the breeze, almost as if they're whispering secrets of their own.

The library, a relic of another era, stands stoic and proud at the end of the street, its stone façade bathed in the soft glow of streetlamps. Inside, the air is cool and scented with paper and ink, an aroma that feels like home to me. The librarian, a woman with silver hair and sharp spectacles perched on her nose, greets us with a nod.

"Looking for something specific?" she asks, a knowing glint in her eyes that makes me uneasy.

"Just some old records," I reply, my voice steady. "About the lake and its—um, history."

"Ah, the lake," she murmurs, almost to herself. "It holds many tales. Follow me."

As she leads us to a back room, the atmosphere thickens with anticipation. Dust motes dance in the air, illuminated by the light streaming through the windows, casting a nostalgic glow over ancient tomes. I scan the shelves, my heart racing as I imagine what stories might be waiting to be uncovered.

The librarian pulls a hefty volume from a shelf, its spine cracked and worn. "This one contains accounts of the town's legends," she says, her voice a mere whisper. "And of those who've come before you."

Isaac and I exchange glances, our curiosity piqued. She opens the book, the pages brittle beneath her fingers, and points to a passage. "There was once a young girl who wandered too close to the water's edge," she begins, her voice weaving a tapestry of words that pulls us in. "They say she was claimed by the Naiad, bound to the lake for eternity."

My pulse quickens as the librarian continues. "Generations passed, and with them, the stories faded, but the bond remained. Families like yours carry the weight of that history, the choices made echoing through time."

"What kind of choices?" I ask, leaning closer, urgency tinging my voice.

"Sacrifices, mostly. There are tales of bargains made, and of the costs that followed. Those who were too curious found themselves ensnared by the lake's enchantment."

Isaac's hand brushes mine, and I can feel the heat of his concern radiating through me. "This doesn't sound good," he murmurs, his voice low.

"No, it doesn't," I agree, feeling a chill creep down my spine. "But it's the only thread we have to follow."

The librarian closes the book gently, the weight of her knowledge heavy in the air. "You must tread carefully," she advises, her expression grave. "The lake is a fickle mistress, and its depths hold secrets best left undisturbed."

As we step back into the main hall, I can't shake the feeling that the Naiad's warning looms larger than ever. The lake was not just a backdrop to my life—it was a character in my story, one that held the power to unravel everything I thought I knew. With Isaac by my side, I felt a flicker of hope amid the encroaching darkness. Together, we would delve into the past, but I couldn't shake the sense that something sinister was already in motion, ready to ensnare us both.

The library feels both suffocating and liberating, the walls lined with knowledge waiting to be unearthed. Isaac and I linger just outside the thick, wooden doors, our minds racing with the implications of what we've uncovered. The librarian's words echo in my head, and I can't shake the sensation that every tale she shared was a thread, intertwining our destinies with a darkness we were only beginning to grasp.

"I can't believe how deep this goes," I say, shaking my head in disbelief. "I always thought those stories were just legends, you know? I mean, who really believes in water spirits?"

"Apparently, our families do," Isaac replies, a grin playing on his lips despite the grim nature of our discoveries. "And it looks like we've inherited their talent for getting into deep water—pun intended."

I can't help but chuckle, the tension in my chest easing ever so slightly. "Right? But this isn't some whimsical fairy tale. It feels real, Isaac. The Naiad, the curses... it's all connected, and I can't just walk away from it."

"Walking away isn't really an option at this point," he replies, his eyes scanning the street outside as if expecting the Naiad to rise from the shadows. "So what's the plan, fearless leader?"

My heart thumps at the thought. "We need to talk to someone who knows more—someone who can help us navigate this mess."

"Do you have someone in mind?" he asks, his brows raised.

I pause, considering the few people who might hold the keys to our labyrinth of family secrets. "There's Mrs. Alderidge, the old woman who lives by the lake. She was there the night my grandmother told me about the Naiad. Maybe she knows more than she let on."

Isaac nods, determination lighting his features. "Lead the way. I've got your back, and maybe we can convince her to part with some of her secrets."

As we make our way toward the lake, the streets grow quieter, the only sounds the crunch of leaves beneath our feet and the distant croak of frogs settling into the night. The moon casts a silver sheen across the water, a mesmerizing sight that belies the chaos swirling in my heart. Each step feels like a dare, the shadows growing thicker around us as the trees loom overhead, their branches stretching like gnarled fingers.

Mrs. Alderidge's cottage sits just beyond the tree line, its silhouette outlined against the luminous lake. We approach cautiously, the door a weathered frame with peeling paint that speaks of years gone by. I knock, the sound echoing into the stillness, and a moment later, the door creaks open.

The old woman stands there, her hair a wild halo of white, eyes sharp as a hawk's. "Ah, the curious ones," she says, her voice raspy but strong. "I was wondering when you'd come knocking."

"Mrs. Alderidge, we need to talk," I say, urgency threading through my tone. "It's about the lake... and the Naiad."

Her expression shifts, a flicker of something—fear?—crossing her features before she quickly masks it with a stern glare. "You shouldn't be meddling in things beyond your understanding. The lake has its own will, and it doesn't take kindly to intrusions."

"Believe me, we didn't choose this," Isaac interjects, his frustration boiling just beneath the surface. "But it seems like we don't have a choice anymore. We're already in too deep."

Mrs. Alderidge studies us for a long moment, and I can almost see the wheels turning in her mind. Finally, she steps aside, gesturing for us to enter. "Come in, but be warned: once you tread this path, there's no turning back."

Inside, the air is thick with the scent of dried herbs and something smoky, like old wood burning. The walls are lined with shelves crammed with jars and trinkets, each one a testament to her years of collecting the forgotten and the mysterious. A fire crackles in the hearth, casting flickering shadows that dance across the room.

"What do you know about the Naiad?" I ask, barely able to contain my urgency.

She settles into an armchair, her gaze piercing. "The Naiad is no mere spirit. She is a keeper of the lake, and her wrath is as powerful as the water she commands. Your family, child, has a history with her—a bond forged in desperation and sacrifice. She does not forgive easily."

"Sacrifice?" I echo, feeling a chill settle deep within me.

"Yes. The stories speak of those who bargained with her, seeking love, wealth, or power, and the prices they paid. Your ancestors were once among those who sought her favor."

Isaac shifts uneasily beside me, and I can feel the tension radiating from him. "And what does that mean for us?" he presses, his tone urgent.

"It means that the Naiad holds you accountable for the debts of your bloodline," she replies, her voice dropping to a whisper as if the very walls might be listening. "If she claims you, she will not rest until she has what she desires."

"What does she want?" I ask, the question lingering in the air like a storm cloud.

"Ah, therein lies the question," Mrs. Alderidge replies, her eyes narrowing. "Some say she craves companionship, while others believe she seeks revenge for past wrongs. The truth, however, is often far more complex. The lake is alive, a force of nature that feels and thinks as we do, and it guards its secrets closely."

My mind whirls with possibilities, dread coiling in my stomach. "And what if we can't break this bond? What if she comes for us?"

A sly smile crosses her lips, a hint of dark amusement lighting her eyes. "Then you must be prepared to pay your own price. The only way to sever the bond is to confront her directly, to face the spirit that binds you to the lake. But beware—this path is fraught with peril, and many who have ventured it have never returned."

"Great," Isaac mutters under his breath, his frustration bubbling over. "So, we either confront a vengeful water spirit or become her next victims. No pressure."

I can feel the weight of my ancestors pressing down on me, their choices echoing through time, urging me to act. "We have to try," I say, my voice steadying with resolve. "If there's even a chance to break this cycle, we have to take it."

Mrs. Alderidge nods slowly, her expression grave. "If you choose to face the Naiad, you must be prepared for the truth. The lake does not give freely, and it remembers everything."

As the fire crackles, casting shadows that twist like phantoms around us, a sudden chill sweeps through the room. The air grows heavy, as if the very essence of the lake is intruding upon us, and I can't help but glance toward the door.

"Do you hear that?" I whisper, my heart racing as the sound of water slapping against the shore drifts through the cracks.

Mrs. Alderidge's expression turns solemn. "It is the lake, calling you," she says, her voice low. "You must decide now, before it's too late."

The ground beneath us trembles, a low rumble that shakes the very foundations of the cottage. My breath catches in my throat as the walls seem to close in, and I exchange a frantic glance with Isaac.

"Now," I say, adrenaline surging through me. "We have to go—right now!"

But before we can move, the door bursts open, and a wave of cold air sweeps into the room. The Naiad's voice fills the space, dripping with an ethereal menace.

"You cannot hide from me," she sings, her voice a haunting melody that sends chills racing down my spine. "You are mine, bound by blood and fate. Come to the lake, or lose everything you hold dear."

The world spins as dread wraps around my heart like a vise. The lake is calling, and I realize in that instant that running away is not an option. Not now. Not ever.

Chapter 15: A Heart Divided

The air around us crackled with tension as I stood at the edge of the lake, its surface a glassy mirror reflecting the turbulent sky. The water, usually a soothing blue, now shimmered with an ominous hue, as if it held secrets deeper than the depths below. The Naiad's curse coiled around my heart like a vine, tightening its grip each day, suffocating the joy I once found in the world around me. Isaac stood beside me, his presence both a comfort and a torment, his worry palpable, slicing through the twilight air.

"Maybe we should just leave," he said, his voice low, a whisper filled with desperation. "Get out of here, away from this place." His gaze was fixed on the horizon, where the sun dipped low, painting the sky in hues of red and gold, colors that reminded me of both hope and blood.

"Leave?" I echoed, my heart aching at the thought. "And go where? The curse is woven into me, Isaac. I can feel it. It's not just this lake; it's in my blood." I turned to face him, needing him to understand. "It's like an anchor, pulling me down into the depths, and I can't fight it."

He ran a hand through his tousled hair, frustration etched across his handsome features. "I can't just stand here and watch you fade away! I won't lose you to this—this monster." His voice cracked, and for a moment, the brave facade he wore faltered, revealing the boy who was terrified of losing the girl he loved.

"Do you think I want to be here?" I snapped, but my anger was tinged with sadness, a reflection of the turmoil inside me. "This isn't a choice. It's a curse. Every moment I'm here, I can feel it digging deeper, and I don't know how much longer I can resist." My voice trembled as I spoke, the vulnerability I felt slipping through the cracks in my bravado.

He took a step closer, his eyes searching mine for some semblance of hope, but all he found was the truth I had been hiding even from myself. "You don't have to do this alone," he said softly, his hand brushing against my arm, sending a jolt of warmth through my skin. "We can figure this out together."

A shaky breath escaped my lips as I looked down at the lake, its depths swirling with dark shadows that seemed to reach out toward me, beckoning me closer. "Together," I whispered, the word tasting bittersweet. Could we truly unravel this curse that was binding us, or were we simply delaying the inevitable?

In that moment, the air around us shifted, heavy with unspoken words and unshed tears. I could almost hear the lake calling to me, its siren song seductive yet treacherous. "It's not just the lake," I admitted, my voice barely above a whisper. "It's me. The longer I stay, the more I feel like I'm losing myself."

Isaac's face fell, and I could see the weight of my confession sink in, wrapping around his heart like a vice. "Losing yourself how?" he asked, an edge of fear creeping into his tone. "What do you mean?"

"Every time I look at the water," I said, my gaze unwavering, "I see things. Things that aren't real. Memories that don't belong to me. Sometimes, I feel... different, as if I'm not the person I used to be." I shivered as a cool breeze whipped through the trees, brushing against my skin like a ghostly caress.

"Different how?" he pressed, his concern transforming into a fierce protectiveness that made my heart swell and ache simultaneously.

"It's like I'm being pulled in two directions," I admitted. "Part of me wants to dive in, to give in to whatever this curse is, while the other part fights to stay here, to fight for us." The truth hung between us like a fragile thread, quivering under the weight of our fears.

Isaac stepped back, the distance between us suddenly feeling insurmountable. "I can't let you go," he said, his voice cracking, despair creeping into the edges. "I won't let you."

His determination ignited a flicker of hope within me, even as dread settled in my stomach. "But what if this isn't something we can fight?" I countered, my voice shaking. "What if the lake has already claimed me?"

His expression hardened, a mix of anger and fear radiating off him. "You're not a prize for it to take. You're stronger than this. You have to be." His gaze turned back to the lake, and I followed it, watching as the water seemed to ripple in response, a living thing, swirling and undulating with an energy I couldn't comprehend.

"Strength only goes so far," I replied, my voice trembling with the weight of my reality. "What if it's not enough?" The words felt like a confession, a surrender to the darkness that had been lurking just beneath the surface of my consciousness.

He stepped closer again, and this time, I could feel the heat radiating from him, grounding me. "Then we fight together," he said firmly, determination sharpening his features. "Whatever this is, we'll face it. I refuse to let you slip away without a battle."

I wanted to believe him. The intensity in his eyes ignited a spark of courage within me, a flicker of the person I used to be. But as the wind howled around us, I couldn't shake the feeling that time was running out. The curse was growing stronger, and I could almost hear the laughter of the Naiad echoing through the trees, taunting us as we stood on the precipice of the unknown.

"Promise me," I said, clutching his hands, the warmth of his skin soothing against the chill of uncertainty. "Promise me we'll fight, no matter what it takes."

He squeezed my hands tightly, a fierce light igniting in his eyes. "I promise," he said, the words a vow that bound us together against the encroaching darkness. And in that moment, as the sky darkened and the first stars began to twinkle in the vast expanse above, I dared to believe that perhaps, just perhaps, love could be a shield against the curse that threatened to consume me.

The night wore on, a velvet curtain draped over the world, and the lake shimmered like a polished stone, alive with secrets and shadows. I could hear the soft lapping of the water against the shore, a constant whisper that both comforted and unnerved me. It felt as if the lake was trying to communicate, drawing me closer with promises of understanding, yet warning me of the danger that lay beneath its tranquil surface.

Isaac's hand remained in mine, our fingers entwined like the roots of ancient trees that clung desperately to the earth, yet I felt the distance of a chasm growing wider between us. He broke the silence, his voice a husky murmur as he gazed into the inky depths. "What if the lake is alive? Like it has a will of its own?" The thought lingered in the air, heavy and oppressive, as if we were both afraid to move, lest we disturb the delicate balance of our unspoken fears.

"Alive or not, it certainly feels like it has a claim on me," I replied, my tone laced with irony. "Perhaps I should start taking it out to dinner, establish some boundaries." I tried to inject humor into the moment, but it fell flat, swallowed by the weight of our reality.

He chuckled softly, but it was tinged with unease. "Dinner sounds nice. Just you, me, and a side of cursed water. Maybe we can order some calamari on the side." The corners of his mouth turned up, but his eyes betrayed the worry that gnawed at his soul.

I appreciated his attempt at levity, even as a shiver danced along my spine, echoing the warning of the water. "What if we don't make it to dinner? What if this is all we have left?" I let the question hang in the air, the starkness of it settling like a weight on my chest. "What if I become... something else?"

Isaac turned to face me fully, the moonlight casting silver highlights in his hair, illuminating the determination in his gaze.

"Then we'll face it together. If you become something else, I'll find a way to bring you back. Even if I have to wrestle the Naiad herself." His confidence was like a warm blanket against the chill that surrounded us, yet I felt the tug of doubt deep within me, a voice whispering that it might already be too late.

"Do you really think you could take her on?" I teased, trying to lighten the mood, even though a small part of me was terrified at the thought. "She's a water spirit; you'd probably just end up soaked and apologizing."

Isaac laughed, the sound ringing through the stillness, but his laughter faded as quickly as it had come, replaced by a more serious tone. "I'd take the soaking if it meant saving you. We'll find a way to break this curse."

The resolve in his words was reassuring, yet as I searched his eyes, I saw a flicker of fear, a reminder that the Naiad was not a foe to be underestimated. "But at what cost?" I murmured, glancing back at the lake, where the darkness rippled ominously. "What if the price is more than either of us can pay?"

He took a step closer, bridging the gap between us with an intensity that made my heart race. "We can't think about that now. We have to stay focused on what we can do, not what we fear. Fear is a liar, remember?" His voice was firm, the softness of his words wrapping around me like a lifeline.

"Right," I replied, inhaling deeply, attempting to absorb his strength. "Fear is a liar, but it's also a very convincing storyteller." The truth was, the more I fought against the curse, the more I felt it tightening its grip, whispering sweet lies that tempted me to surrender.

Just then, a soft rustling came from the underbrush, pulling our attention away from the lake. I squinted into the darkness, the shadows shifting and twisting as if alive. "Did you hear that?" I asked, my heart rate quickening as instinct kicked in. The woods felt charged, as if the trees themselves were holding their breath.

Isaac nodded, his body tensing beside me. "Yeah. It sounded like—"

Before he could finish, a figure emerged from the trees, stepping into the moonlight. A woman, tall and ethereal, with hair that flowed like liquid silver and eyes that glinted with mischief. "Well, well," she said, a teasing lilt in her voice. "What do we have here? A couple of lovebirds caught in the web of destiny?"

My stomach dropped. "Who are you?" I demanded, instinctively stepping closer to Isaac. He tightened his grip on my hand, a silent promise that he would protect me.

"I'm merely a friend of the lake," she replied, her smile enchanting yet unsettling. "And perhaps a messenger of sorts. The Naiad has been watching you, you know. She's curious about your bond, the way you cling to each other like the last two leaves on a dying tree."

"Curious?" Isaac asked, his voice low and cautious. "Is that why you've come? To deliver some sort of warning?"

The woman's laughter danced in the air like chimes in the breeze. "Warnings are just the whispers of fear, darling. The Naiad doesn't want to harm you. She wants to help."

"Help?" I scoffed, skepticism coating my words. "What kind of help comes from a curse?"

She tilted her head, her expression shifting to something more serious. "The kind that offers a choice. You see, the curse isn't merely a punishment; it's an opportunity. A chance to break free from the binds of your mundane existence."

"Opportunity or not, I'm not interested in trading my life for whatever this is," I retorted, my heart racing. "What's your angle?"

"Ah, but that's the beauty of it," she said, her eyes glimmering with a mixture of mischief and wisdom. "The lake has many layers.

To navigate them, you must first decide what you truly desire. Do you wish to remain tethered to this world, or are you ready to embrace something far more powerful?"

Isaac's grip on my hand tightened as he leaned closer, protectively shielding me from her enigmatic gaze. "What do you want from us?" he asked, his voice a low growl, the protective instinct flooding through him.

"Nothing," she replied, the softness of her voice at odds with the intensity of her gaze. "Just a choice, dear boy. The lake offers paths you've yet to explore. What lies beneath is not just darkness, but also the potential for transformation. Are you brave enough to embrace it?"

The weight of her words settled heavily in the air, filling the space between us with a tension that was both exhilarating and terrifying. My heart raced as I considered her offer, and I caught Isaac's gaze, searching for an answer in the depths of his brown eyes. Would we dare take the plunge into the unknown, or would we retreat back to the safety of the shore? The choice loomed ahead like a darkened path, twisting into the shadows of the night, and I could feel the lake's call echoing within me, urging me to step forward.

The woman's enigmatic smile widened, revealing a hint of something both mischievous and unnerving. "You stand at the crossroads of choice," she said, her voice lilting like the melody of a forgotten song. "The lake does not merely offer curses; it presents paths, each woven with possibilities. Will you seek the familiar, or dare to plunge into the depths of the unknown?"

I exchanged a quick glance with Isaac, his eyes dark pools of uncertainty reflecting the shadows that danced around us. "This is some kind of game to you, isn't it?" I challenged, my voice steadying as anger surged through me. "Toying with our fears? Why should we trust anything you say?"

"Ah, but trust is a fickle thing," she replied, her gaze steady. "What do you know of trust when the very essence of your being is at stake? The curse is merely a reflection of your fears, and to conquer it, you must confront what lies beneath."

"Confront what?" I shot back, a surge of defiance igniting my voice. "You're not making any sense! What do you want from us?"

She tilted her head, as if considering my words, and then a soft laugh bubbled from her lips, enchanting yet hollow. "To discover the truth, darling. The truth of who you really are. The curse is not just a burden; it's a gateway to understanding your deepest desires."

"Understanding?" Isaac's tone turned skeptical, his body tense. "This sounds more like a trap than a revelation."

"Maybe it is," she conceded, her expression shifting, the mischief fading into something more serious. "But every trap holds the potential for freedom. You must decide if you wish to be ensnared by the curse or if you'll seize the opportunity it presents."

I felt the air thickening, charged with anticipation. The night felt heavy with unspoken promises, and the lake shimmered ominously in the background. "If we choose to accept this... opportunity, what will happen to us?" I asked, my heart racing. "What do we risk losing?"

She stepped closer, her gaze penetrating, as if she could peer straight into my soul. "You risk everything. But sometimes, everything is the very thing that frees you. The choice is yours—remain anchored to the shore of certainty, or dive into the depths of possibility. But be warned, the deeper you go, the harder it is to return."

The weight of her words pressed down on me, the gravity of her meaning sinking in. The curse wasn't just a malevolent force; it was an invitation to explore parts of myself I had long buried, desires I had denied. Did I dare step into the unknown, risking everything for a glimpse of the truth?

Isaac's voice broke through my thoughts. "We need time to think," he said, and I could hear the urgency in his tone. "We're not making any decisions now."

"Time is a luxury you may not have," she warned, a hint of steel beneath her silky voice. "The Naiad grows impatient, and with her impatience comes chaos. You have until the first light of dawn to decide."

A chill swept through me at the mention of chaos, and I glanced nervously at the lake. The surface rippled as if in response to her words, and I could almost hear the water sighing, a sound both alluring and foreboding.

"What happens if we don't decide?" I asked, dread creeping into my chest.

"Then the curse will take hold fully, and you will become a part of the lake's tale, lost to the depths forever," she replied, her expression almost sympathetic. "The choice lies in your hands, but know this: the Naiad's will is not to be taken lightly."

As she stepped back, the shadows behind her seemed to lengthen and swell, the darkness absorbing the moonlight until she was little more than a silhouette. "Choose wisely," she said, her voice echoing like a haunting refrain as she faded into the trees.

I stood frozen, the weight of her words pressing against my chest like a boulder. "What do we do?" I asked, my voice trembling slightly as I turned to Isaac. "I don't want to be a part of some fairy tale gone wrong."

Isaac's brow furrowed, his expression thoughtful yet troubled. "We need to think this through. The curse has a grip on you, but it's not you. Whatever this is, we can find a way to break it."

"Break it?" I scoffed, frustration bubbling to the surface. "We can't even understand it! How do you break something when you don't even know what it is?"

"By trying," he said firmly, determination shining in his eyes. "By confronting it together, and if necessary, wrestling with whatever the Naiad throws at us. We can't let fear dictate our choices."

I let out a shaky breath, the conviction in his voice somewhat soothing my panic. "And if this opportunity leads us into a worse nightmare?"

He stepped closer, his warmth wrapping around me like a shield. "Then we face it. I won't let you face it alone."

"Then what do we choose?" The question hung between us, the enormity of our decision threatening to overwhelm me. I could feel the lake's gaze, its dark depths watching and waiting.

As dawn approached, a faint glow began to seep into the sky, the first light illuminating the edges of the trees. We had little time left. "Let's go back," I suggested, needing a moment to gather my thoughts away from the lake's oppressive weight. "We need to think this through, away from... all of this."

Isaac nodded, and we turned, retracing our steps through the dense underbrush. The sounds of the forest waking around us felt oddly comforting, yet I couldn't shake the sense of foreboding that clung to the air.

But as we neared the clearing, a rustling came from behind us, and I glanced back, heart racing. The shadows shifted once more, the darkness gathering as if it had a life of its own.

"What was that?" I whispered, my pulse quickening as I strained to see.

"Probably just an animal," Isaac said, but I could hear the tension in his voice, the way he stepped protectively in front of me.

Then the noise grew louder, branches snapping, and a figure emerged from the underbrush, its silhouette dark against the encroaching light. My breath hitched in my throat as the figure stepped into view. It was a man, drenched in shadows, his features hidden in the gloom, but there was something familiar about him—a haunting reminder of the past I had tried so desperately to forget.

"Hello again," he said, a smirk twisting on his lips. "Miss me?"

I froze, recognition dawning with a jolt of shock. The lake was no longer the only thing threatening to pull me under; the past was rising up like a tide, and I had no idea how to stay afloat.

Chapter 16: The Reckoning

The moon hung low over the lake, its silver light glimmering across the water's surface, turning the undulating waves into a tapestry of diamonds. Each step I took on the well-worn path seemed to echo through the stillness of the night, a rhythmic pulse that matched the quickening of my heart. The familiar scent of damp earth and the faint musk of pine enveloped me, wrapping around my senses like a comforting shawl, though tonight it felt tainted with a sense of foreboding. Isaac's footsteps trailed behind me, a steady reminder of his presence, yet they felt distant, as if the space between us had expanded with every step.

As we reached the clearing that opened to the lake, the shadows began to shift, darkening the edges of my vision. Figures emerged from the trees, their shapes indistinct, yet the energy they radiated was palpable, thickening the air with a tension that made my skin prickle. They were not just any figures; they were the remnants of the organization Isaac had once been a part of, the ones who whispered of power and control, of ancient rituals that thrummed beneath the surface of our world. Their eyes glinted with a hunger I could not comprehend, and I felt a chill creep up my spine, curling around my spine like a serpent.

"What are you doing here?" I managed, my voice steadier than I felt. I looked to Isaac, who stepped forward, a protective stance that instantly ignited a spark of hope within me. His jaw was set, and the lines of his face were taut with tension, a warrior ready to defend, yet I could see the uncertainty flickering in his eyes.

"We've come to put an end to this," one of the figures spoke, a woman with long dark hair that cascaded like a waterfall down her back. Her gaze bore into me, demanding answers I didn't have. "You've awakened something that should have remained dormant, and now the balance is tipping."

"Awakened?" I echoed, glancing at Isaac. "What do you mean?"

They began to close in around us, and I could hear the rustling of their garments, a sound like dead leaves in a bitter wind. Their presence felt suffocating, pressing down on me as they accused us of unleashing forces beyond our understanding. The words swirled in my mind, a storm of confusion and fear. Isaac turned to me, his expression darkening.

"It's about the lake," he said, his voice low. "They think you've done something, that I've somehow led you to this. They want to blame someone."

The truth was I had felt a connection to the lake, a siren call that had beckoned me deeper into its mysteries, but I had never intended to awaken anything. I looked back at the figures, who had begun to chant in a low, rhythmic hum, their voices weaving together like a web of sound that vibrated in the air. The sensation made my skin crawl, the energy pulling at the edges of my consciousness.

"Sacrifices," another figure hissed, his eyes wild with fervor. "Rituals that bind the lake. You've disrupted centuries of balance, and now you must face the consequences."

"Consequences?" I spat, anger flaring within me. "You're the ones who put this place at risk. How could you let it happen?"

The woman with dark hair stepped closer, her eyes narrowing. "You don't understand the power you're toying with. It's not just water; it's a force that can reshape worlds. If we don't rebind it, everything will spill over."

"Rebind?" Isaac challenged, his voice rising, a tremor of fear and defiance lacing through it. "What does that even mean? You can't just seal it away again. It's not a bottle you can cork."

Their eyes shifted, and I felt the weight of their gaze on Isaac, assessing, calculating. The silence stretched between us, taut as a bowstring, before one of the men stepped forward, gesturing towards me. "You are the key. You alone have awakened its power. You must decide, now, if you will help us."

"I don't know what you're talking about!" I cried, but inside, uncertainty gnawed at me. The lake had chosen me somehow; it had drawn me in like a moth to flame, igniting something deep within me. Was I a key or a curse?

The figures exchanged glances, their intentions clouded. I could feel the weight of their expectations pressing down on me, and yet, something in me stirred—an urge to defy them, to stand firm in my truth.

Isaac stepped forward, his voice a protective growl. "You're not taking her. You don't understand her connection to the lake."

"Your loyalty blinds you," the woman snapped, her tone cutting through the tension like a knife. "You think love is enough to protect her from this? You're risking everything, Isaac."

He shook his head, defiance burning in his eyes. "And you think your rituals will save her? They'll only serve to bind her, to suppress what she is meant to be."

In that moment, the atmosphere shifted, electric with potential. I took a breath, feeling the ground beneath my feet, the pulse of the earth resonating with the water's rhythm. This was not just about rituals or accusations; it was about choice, about embracing my role in this tangled web of power.

I stepped forward, pulling away from Isaac, my heart racing. "I'll face this myself. If the lake has chosen me, then I need to understand why." My voice rang with a determination that surprised even me. I wasn't just a pawn in someone else's game. I was more than a threat to their carefully constructed balance.

Isaac's eyes widened in disbelief, and for a moment, a flicker of fear passed between us. But I stood firm, my resolve hardening. I wouldn't let them silence me; I would uncover the truth of my connection to the lake, even if it meant defying everything I thought

I knew. The shadows around us seemed to deepen, wrapping me in their embrace, and in that moment, I felt the weight of destiny settle upon my shoulders.

The tension crackled in the air as I stood before the shadowy figures, their faces obscured but their intent clear. I felt like a marionette caught in a fraying string, swinging between Isaac's protective presence and the relentless pull of the lake. "I'm not afraid of you," I said, my voice trembling only slightly, but the heat of my defiance surged through me like a wild fire.

"Fear is not what we expect from you," the woman with the dark hair replied, a sardonic twist to her lips. "We anticipate clarity, understanding. You've touched something that has always been beyond your grasp, and now you must decide what to do with it."

"Touching something doesn't mean I'm ready to wield it like a weapon," I shot back, feeling an adrenaline rush from the confrontation. Behind me, Isaac shifted uneasily, his eyes darting between the figures and me, searching for an unspoken agreement that I had yet to make.

"Not a weapon, but a choice," the man with wild eyes insisted, stepping closer, his posture both menacing and alluring. "You stand at a precipice. The lake is a doorway to a power that can reshape your very essence, and it is vital to know what you wish to do with it. Do you want to risk it all, or will you bind it like we ask?"

"Risk what?" I demanded, feeling a rising tide of indignation. "You think you can intimidate me into submission? You're the ones who've treated this place like a playground for your machinations."

"You don't understand," the woman interjected, her voice a low hiss. "This is about survival—yours and everyone else's. The lake has been disturbed, and now the balance teeters on a knife's edge. You have an opportunity to right what has been wronged, but you have to choose wisely. Otherwise, it could swallow you whole."

A shiver ran down my spine, resonating with the ominous undertone of her words. I turned to Isaac, searching his face for guidance, but all I found was a tangled mess of concern and determination. "I won't let them take you," he said quietly, the gravity of the situation weighing heavily on his shoulders.

"Taking me? That's not their plan, Isaac. They want me to commit to something, to turn this into a battle for control. I can't just agree to that without knowing what I'm up against," I replied, my gaze steady on the approaching figures.

The man laughed, a sound that was more unsettling than humorous. "You think you have a choice? The lake has already chosen you. You've stepped into a role you cannot escape, whether you embrace it or resist it."

"Then enlighten me," I challenged, folding my arms defiantly. "What role have I been cast in?"

"You're the bridge," the woman said, her expression softening slightly, revealing a flicker of something genuine—perhaps even sympathy. "The lake speaks through you. Your connection is stronger than you realize, and it can be a gift or a curse. We don't wish to take that from you. We want to help you harness it."

A slow realization dawned on me, like the first light of dawn creeping over the horizon. "Help? You think you can help me by invoking some ancient ritual that sounds like it belongs in a horror movie? This isn't some puppet show where I dance on your strings. I want to understand, not be used."

"Understanding is the first step," Isaac interjected, his voice firm yet tinged with concern. "You need to listen to what they're saying, even if their delivery is less than warm. If the lake is as powerful as they say, we can't just walk away."

"I refuse to be part of your little scheme," I shot back, feeling my blood boil. "You're the ones who've created this mess, and now you want me to clean it up? Where's the accountability? Where's the responsibility?"

The woman's lips tightened, a moment of vulnerability eclipsed by her resolve. "You're right to be angry. We've made mistakes. But we're offering a solution. You have the chance to make a difference."

I glanced at the lake, its waters shimmering under the moonlight, a siren luring me closer. The ripples danced invitingly, and in that moment, I felt a swell of energy within me, resonating with the pull of the water. There was something deep within its depths, an understanding that eluded me, but I could sense it beckoning, coaxing me to venture beyond the chaos of this moment.

"Why should I trust you?" I asked, my voice quieter now, the fight momentarily ebbing. "You could just as easily betray me."

"Trust is a fragile thing," the man admitted, his tone shifting to something less aggressive. "But the lake isn't just a physical place; it's a living entity, a nexus of power. We need to work together if we want to keep it—and you—safe."

Isaac stepped closer to me, his warmth an anchor in the storm. "You don't have to decide everything right now. Just listen, explore this connection. We can face this together."

The energy in the air thickened, charged with an unspoken pact. I drew a deep breath, weighing the options laid before me. The lake whispered promises of power and freedom, yet I sensed the weight of responsibility pressing upon me, a mantle that would reshape everything I thought I knew.

"What's the alternative?" I asked finally, the words tasting like steel on my tongue. "If I refuse?"

The woman's eyes flashed with an emotion I couldn't quite decipher—was it fear? Determination? "Then we'll have no choice but to bind you and the lake. It's not just about you anymore. There are forces at play that extend beyond this moment, beyond your understanding."

A chill swept through me as I contemplated her words. The stakes were higher than I had imagined, and I felt the gravity of the decision hanging above me like a sword ready to drop. But I wouldn't be coerced into fear. I would confront whatever darkness lurked beneath the surface of that water, whatever power it held.

"Then let's find out what that means," I said, turning towards the lake. The moonlight danced across the water, and I felt a strange surge of confidence rising within me. "If the lake has chosen me, then I'll embrace that choice, on my own terms."

Isaac's hand found mine, a firm grip that anchored me as we stepped forward together. The air buzzed with anticipation, and the shadowy figures shifted, uncertainty rippling through their ranks. I could sense the tension rising, the power of the lake pulsing in response to my defiance, urging me onward into the unknown.

The lake shimmered beneath the moonlight, its surface a mesmerizing tapestry of light and shadow. My heart raced as I took a tentative step forward, feeling the pull of the water, an ancient call that resonated deep within my soul. The tension among the figures behind me thickened, a palpable reminder of the stakes at hand. I glanced back at Isaac, his brow furrowed with concern, but his grip on my hand was steady, lending me courage.

"Stay close," he whispered, his voice barely more than a breath, but it wrapped around me like a warm embrace. I nodded, though my heart beat wildly in response to the impending confrontation. This was my moment to forge my own destiny, to become more than a pawn in a game I barely understood.

The shadowy figures shifted, their intentions flickering like candle flames caught in a gust of wind. The woman stepped forward, her eyes fierce and unwavering. "You can't just plunge into the depths without knowing what lies beneath. The lake is a mirror reflecting your innermost fears and desires. Are you prepared for what you might find?"

"Prepared? Hardly," I shot back, a spark of defiance igniting in my chest. "But I won't let you dictate my path. If I'm meant to understand this, then let it come."

The man with the wild eyes exchanged glances with the woman, an unspoken communication passing between them. "Very well," he said, a glint of something darker flashing across his face. "But remember, you sought this connection. The consequences are yours to bear."

As he spoke, a sudden wind swept through the clearing, swirling leaves and dust, and for a moment, I felt the breath of the lake on my skin, cool and invigorating. It was as if the water itself was responding to my challenge, rippling with anticipation. The moonlight reflected off the surface, revealing glimpses of shadows darting just beneath. I could almost see the currents of energy that lay coiled beneath the surface, waiting for someone brave enough—or foolish enough—to dive in.

"Together," Isaac said, his voice firm as he stepped beside me, the warmth of his body a reassuring presence against the chilling uncertainty. "Whatever happens, we face it together."

I took a deep breath, summoning the courage that pulsed within me, and then nodded. "Together," I echoed, my voice stronger now, filled with a newfound resolve.

The figures seemed to shift uneasily at our unity, their expressions flickering between disbelief and irritation. "You think solidarity will save you?" the woman spat, her voice laced with a mix of contempt and concern. "You'll need more than that. You'll need to let go of everything you think you know."

Before I could respond, the lake erupted in a sudden surge, sending waves crashing against the shore. The water glowed, a radiant blue light emerging from its depths, illuminating the night with a surreal glow. I staggered back, startled, but the pull was too strong to resist. I felt it beckoning me, urging me to approach, to dive into the unknown.

"Isaac!" I shouted, feeling the rush of adrenaline and fear coursing through me. "What's happening?"

He grasped my arm tightly, his eyes wide with both awe and fear. "I don't know, but we need to be careful. This isn't just a body of water; it's alive. It's reacting to you."

"Then I need to respond." I turned back to the lake, my heart pounding. "I can't just stand here and let it dictate my fate."

The shadows around us seemed to ripple, shifting in response to my determination. The figures whispered among themselves, their voices rising in a crescendo of anxious murmurs. "You have no idea what you're doing," the woman warned, her tone a mixture of fear and anger. "You'll regret this."

I squared my shoulders, defiance coursing through me like wildfire. "Maybe, but I won't regret not trying. I won't let fear dictate my choices any longer."

As I took a step toward the water, the luminous glow intensified, bathing me in an ethereal light. I could feel the energy vibrating through the air, a force that both excited and terrified me. I was drawn closer, unable to resist the magnetic pull of the lake. It was more than water; it felt like an entity, a consciousness that wanted to communicate, to reveal secrets I had yet to grasp.

Suddenly, a deafening roar erupted from the depths of the lake, sending waves crashing against the shore. The ground trembled beneath my feet, and I stumbled, the energy in the air sparking with chaos. "Isaac!" I cried, looking back at him, panic surging as I clung to the moment.

"We have to go!" he shouted, but even as he spoke, I felt the lake's call weaving through my veins, a siren's song that drowned out everything else.

"Wait!" I screamed, torn between the urge to flee and the desire to uncover the truth that lay beneath the shimmering surface. The figures behind us moved, shadows casting ominous shapes as they tried to contain the chaos brewing in the air. "Don't let them take me!"

The lake erupted again, this time with a force that sent water spraying high into the night sky. I felt the cool droplets on my face, and in that moment, the world around me narrowed to a single point of focus—the swirling depths that promised knowledge and danger in equal measure.

I stepped closer, instinctively aware that my choice was becoming clearer, more imperative. "I'm going in!" I declared, the words spilling from my lips before I had time to think.

Isaac lunged forward, panic etched across his features. "No! You can't! You don't know what will happen!"

But it was too late; I was already committed. As my foot touched the water, an electric shock surged through me, coursing from the tips of my toes to the crown of my head. The lake roared in response, the waves rising higher, the light pulsing with an intensity that threatened to engulf me entirely.

The world twisted, the boundaries of reality warping as I plunged into the depths. Water enveloped me, cold and vibrant, and I felt the rush of currents swirling around me, lifting me deeper into the heart of the lake. I could see flashes of light and shadow, fleeting images that danced just out of reach, and I felt a voice calling to me, whispering secrets that stirred my very essence.

But just as the lake embraced me, an explosion of energy erupted from the surface, and I could feel the grip of the shadows pulling back, desperation twisting their features. "No!" I heard them shout, their voices echoing in the depths, but I was already lost in the kaleidoscope of water and light.

As I sank deeper, the world above grew distant, and a new reality unfolded around me—one that promised both revelation and peril, a truth I was unprepared to face. Just when I thought I might grasp it, a dark figure emerged from the shadows, its eyes glowing like coals in the night. It reached for me, and in that heartbeat, I realized the true depth of the lake's power.

And then, in a surge of chaotic energy, everything went black.

Chapter 17: The Curse Unleashed

The air around the lake crackled with an electric tension, a whisper of something ancient awakening beneath its shimmering surface. The once placid waters now roiled, swirling in hues of deep emerald and ominous black, as if the very essence of the lake was rebelling against our meddling. Each ripple seemed to pulse with a life of its own, echoing the growing storm inside me. Isaac stood beside me, his fingers entwined with mine, grounding me against the chaos swirling not just in the water, but also in my heart.

"Are you sure we want to do this?" he asked, his voice low and steady, but I could hear the tremor beneath the surface, a reflection of the turmoil brewing in both our souls. The Naiad had warned us—no, implored us—to reconsider. But there was something insistent about the pull of the lake, as if it were a siren song calling to me, urging me to unlock whatever lay hidden beneath its depths.

I took a deep breath, trying to calm the whirlwind of emotions. "If we don't, who knows what will happen? This curse—it's more than just stories. It's real, and it's tied to me." The words hung in the air between us, heavy with implications. I had never been one to back down from a challenge, but the stakes felt higher than ever.

Isaac's grip tightened, a reassuring squeeze that sent a jolt of warmth through me. "Then we'll face it together," he declared, his gaze unwavering. I admired his courage, his unwavering support, but a flicker of doubt gnawed at me. What if this burden was mine alone to bear? What if in my attempt to protect him, I only drew him deeper into danger?

As if summoned by my thoughts, the Naiad appeared at the water's edge, her form materializing from the fog that clung to the lake like a shroud. Her eyes, deep and sorrowful, reflected centuries of sorrow and fury. "You must understand," she intoned, her voice both melodic and thunderous, "the power within you is not simply a gift. It is a weapon, and if unleashed without caution, it could bring ruin to all that you hold dear."

I swallowed hard, the weight of her words pressing down on me like a stone. "What does that mean?" I asked, my voice barely above a whisper. "What am I meant to protect?"

She hesitated, her ethereal form flickering like a flame caught in the wind. "The lake is a guardian, and you are its keeper. The curse binds you to it, but it also links you to the legacy of your ancestors—a legacy that has long been forgotten, buried beneath the weight of time. The power you possess can either heal or destroy, and it is the choice you make that will determine its fate."

A chill ran down my spine, and I could feel the water's pull intensifying, a magnetic force tugging at the very essence of my being. I glanced at Isaac, seeking solace in his presence, and found his eyes alight with curiosity and fear. "What do we do?" he asked, the vulnerability in his voice making my heart ache.

The Naiad looked between us, her expression softening just a fraction. "You must confront the truth within yourself. Only then will you understand how to wield this power." With that, she turned and submerged herself into the depths, leaving us alone with the tumultuous waters.

In the silence that followed, I could hear the pulse of my own heartbeat, a reminder that the decision loomed over us like a storm cloud ready to break. "Are you ready for this?" Isaac asked, his brow furrowed, the weight of his concern clear.

"Ready or not, we have to try," I replied, determination hardening my voice. I could feel the echoes of my ancestors thrumming in my veins, urging me forward. "Let's see what the lake wants to reveal."

Together, we approached the water's edge, the waves lapping at our feet, their cool touch both inviting and foreboding. As we knelt at the bank, the water surged, rising and swirling around us, forming shapes and shadows that danced like memories just out of reach. I closed my eyes, centering myself, feeling the ancient energy pulsing beneath the surface. It was a rhythm, a heartbeat that resonated with my own, drawing me closer to the truth.

Suddenly, the water began to shimmer, and images emerged—snippets of my lineage: women in flowing gowns, their hands raised toward the sky, calling upon the elements. I gasped as the realization struck me—these were my ancestors, bound to this place, their power echoing through time. I felt their strength, their struggles, as if they were weaving themselves into my very soul.

"Do you see them?" Isaac whispered, his voice tinged with awe.

"Yes," I breathed, tears stinging my eyes. "They're here. They've always been here."

A pulse of energy surged through me, igniting a fire that threatened to consume everything in its path. I opened my eyes, feeling the weight of their legacy resting on my shoulders. This wasn't just a curse; it was a calling, a chance to reclaim what had been lost.

But the thrill of revelation quickly twisted into a sharp pang of fear. What if I couldn't harness this power? What if it broke me instead of liberating me? The storm inside me swelled, and I felt a crack—a fissure forming between my resolve and my uncertainty.

"I don't know if I can do this," I admitted, the honesty raw and unfiltered.

Isaac's expression softened, his blue eyes piercing through the storm clouds of doubt that swirled in my mind. "You're stronger than you think," he said, his voice steady. "Whatever happens, I'm here."

In that moment, I knew he wasn't just my anchor; he was also my beacon. With renewed determination, I took a step closer to the water, my heart racing as I prepared to embrace the truth that lay before me.

The lake continued to churn, the power within it waiting, beckoning me to dive deeper—not just into its waters, but into the very essence of who I was meant to become. The air was thick with the scent of wet earth and something more, something ancient and powerful. I was ready to discover the depths of my inheritance, even if it meant unleashing a curse I could barely comprehend.

The air grew thick with anticipation as I peered into the depths of the lake, its surface shimmering like shattered glass. The Naiad's warnings echoed in my mind, a relentless mantra that fueled my anxiety. "A weapon, a keeper, a legacy." It was as if the words had taken on a life of their own, swirling around us like the restless waters, reminding me of the burden I now carried. As I knelt on the bank, the cool mud squelching beneath my fingers, a flicker of determination ignited within me. I would not let fear dictate my fate.

"Are you ready?" Isaac's voice broke through the tumult of my thoughts. He was still at my side, steady and unwavering, as if he could absorb some of my uncertainty through the warmth of his presence. "We can back out at any time," he added, though I could hear the slight tremor in his tone, a testament to the tension crackling in the air between us.

"No, we can't," I replied, my resolve solidifying like concrete. "I need to know what this is about. If there's a power inside me, I have to understand it."

Isaac nodded, though the shadows in his eyes betrayed his worry. He turned back to the lake, and I followed his gaze, watching as the water began to churn more violently, responding to my rising determination. The Naiad had hinted that the lake was more than a body of water; it was alive, a conduit of energy that bridged the worlds of the seen and unseen. As I concentrated, I felt a pull, a gentle yet insistent tug in my core, urging me to lean closer, to surrender to the depths.

Suddenly, a series of ripples broke the surface, and the Naiad emerged, her hair cascading like dark seaweed, adorned with shimmering droplets that sparkled in the sunlight. "You are not ready," she warned, her tone laced with urgency. "You must tread carefully; the power within you can bring great joy or unimaginable destruction."

"Then help me understand," I pleaded, desperation creeping into my voice. "What does it want? Why me?"

Her gaze softened slightly, though it still held an edge of caution. "The lake chose you, but with that choice comes a price. To wield the power of your ancestors, you must first confront the truth of your lineage—the darkness and the light intertwined within it."

I exchanged a glance with Isaac, who seemed to breathe in the tension hanging in the air. "And how do we do that?" he asked, his voice steady.

"By diving into the waters and surrendering to the depths of your own being," the Naiad instructed, her voice a melody that soothed the wild churning of the lake. "Only then will you unlock the memories that lie buried, the truths that have been kept from you."

"Dive in? Just like that?" I scoffed, feeling a mix of skepticism and trepidation. "What if I drown?"

"Metaphorically or literally?" Isaac quipped, the corner of his mouth lifting in a smirk. I shot him a warning glare, but his humor was a balm against the rising tension, reminding me that even in the face of uncertainty, we could find moments of levity.

"Both," I sighed, feeling the weight of what was being asked of me. The churning water seemed to amplify my heartbeat, each pulse reverberating through my body.

The Naiad stepped closer, her voice dropping to a conspiratorial whisper. "Fear not the depths. Your spirit is more resilient than you know. Just trust in yourself, and the power will reveal itself."

With a deep breath, I glanced at Isaac once more. "We're doing this together, right?"

"Always," he affirmed, his eyes bright with determination.

Taking a step closer to the water, I could feel its coolness beckoning me. I could almost hear the echoes of my ancestors, their voices rising from the depths like a haunting symphony. "Alright then," I said, steeling myself. "Let's find out what's lurking down there."

We exchanged a nod, a silent pact solidifying our shared purpose. As we stepped into the lake, the water enveloped us, cool and strangely invigorating. I felt the rush of adrenaline spike through my veins as we descended, the surface above us fading into a dim shimmer. The world around us transformed into an otherworldly realm, shades of blue and green swirling, wrapping around us like an embrace.

The deeper we went, the more the water sang, a haunting melody that resonated with something deep within me. It was as if the lake itself was alive, sharing its secrets through the currents. I closed my eyes, surrendering to the sensation, allowing myself to drift into the unknown.

And then it happened—the memories unfurled like petals of a blooming flower. I was no longer just me; I was the whispers of generations past, the laughter and the sorrows, the triumphs and the failures. Visions cascaded around me—women in my family, strong and fierce, wielding powers that were both a gift and a curse. I could feel their struggles, the weight of expectations, the battle between light and darkness that raged within each of them.

"Do you see them?" Isaac's voice echoed in the murky depths, his presence grounding me even as the visions swirled around us.

"I do," I gasped, struggling to maintain my focus amid the chaos. "They're showing me... something. I think it's my past."

A flash of pain gripped my heart as a memory emerged—one I had buried deep. I saw my mother, her face twisted in anguish, the power she held spilling over like a tidal wave, overwhelming her.

"You must control it, not let it control you," she had once whispered, her voice tinged with both hope and despair.

I felt tears slip down my cheeks, merging with the water around us, but they weren't just my own. They were a collective grief, a sorrow that had been passed down through generations. The realization struck me: I wasn't just fighting for myself; I was battling for the legacy of all those who had come before me.

"I can't bear this alone," I said, the weight of my ancestors pressing down upon me. "What if I fail?"

"Then we'll fail together," Isaac replied, his voice firm and unwavering, cutting through the storm of doubt that threatened to consume me. "But you won't fail. You're stronger than you realize."

His words wrapped around me like a lifeline, igniting the flicker of strength that resided deep within. I pushed forward, determined to confront whatever darkness awaited me in this realm. The water pulsed with energy, and I felt the connection to my lineage strengthen.

As the visions continued to swirl, I sensed something else lurking in the depths—a shadow that whispered promises of power but dripped with malice. "Beware the lure of the darkness," the Naiad's voice echoed, warning me of the seductive pull of my own potential.

Just as I thought I had a grip on my lineage, the shadow surged, wrapping around my heart like a vise. "Embrace it," it hissed, seductive and dark. "With this power, you can change everything. You can be more than just a keeper; you can be a ruler."

For a heartbeat, I wavered, the temptation palpable. What if I could harness this power and wield it for my own? What if I could bend the currents of fate to my will? But then I glanced at Isaac, his steadfast presence a reminder of what truly mattered. Power without purpose would lead only to ruin.

"Enough," I declared, my voice resonating through the water like a thunderclap. "I choose light."

With that proclamation, the shadow recoiled, the water around us surging in response to my decision. I felt a fierce warmth ignite in my chest, and I reached deep within, summoning the strength of my ancestors. The swirling visions coalesced, and I knew then that I wasn't just a vessel; I was a bridge between worlds.

As the water thrashed and churned, I steadied myself, ready to embrace my legacy—not as a weapon but as a guardian. It was time to reclaim my heritage and confront whatever darkness threatened not just the lake, but everything and everyone I loved.

The moment I declared my allegiance to the light, the atmosphere shifted, the weight of uncertainty cracking like ice beneath our feet. The shadow recoiled, not just in the water but within me, the darkness retreating as if stung by the very essence of my decision. The lake shimmered around us, transforming into a kaleidoscope of colors—blues and greens that spiraled like an artist's palette, vibrant and alive. I could feel my ancestors rallying behind me, their spirits lending strength to my resolve.

"Do you feel that?" Isaac asked, his voice barely rising above the symphony of the water, which had shifted from chaotic to harmonious. "It's like the lake is celebrating or something."

"More like it's relieved," I replied, a laugh bubbling up that I couldn't quite contain. The tension that had gripped me moments before began to loosen its vice-like hold. "I think we just made a friend."

"Let's not get ahead of ourselves," he quipped, glancing cautiously at the swirling depths. "Remember the last time we tried to befriend a powerful being? We ended up with a curse instead."

"True, but this is different. I can feel it," I insisted, my heart racing not just with adrenaline, but with the thrill of connection. I was no longer just a vessel of power; I was part of something grander, a tapestry woven with threads of strength and resilience from those who came before me.

As the last tendrils of darkness faded, the Naiad emerged once more, her form ethereal against the backdrop of the now tranquil waters. "You have chosen wisely," she declared, her voice ringing like a bell, echoing through the water and reverberating in my bones. "But remember, with choice comes responsibility. The darkness may be driven away, but it is never truly gone. It lurks, waiting for a moment of weakness."

"Great," I muttered under my breath, though I couldn't help the smile tugging at my lips. "A friendly reminder to keep my guard up. Just what I needed."

"Humor in the face of danger?" Isaac said, feigning a gasp. "What would your mother say?"

I shot him a playful glare. "Probably that I'm crazy for hanging out with a water spirit while submerged in a lake."

"Touché," he admitted, chuckling softly. "But seriously, what now? Do we go back to our normal lives, or is there some ancient ritual we need to perform?"

The Naiad floated closer, her expression somber. "You must unlock the potential within you before the darkness can return. There are trials ahead, tests of your strength and resolve. You cannot face them unprepared."

"Trials? That sounds ominous," I replied, my heart rate quickening at the thought of yet another challenge. "What kind of trials?"

"They will reveal the truth of your lineage and your worthiness to wield the power of the lake. Trust in the journey, and you will discover your path."

I nodded, knowing the gravity of her words. Deep down, a flicker of fear threatened to resurface. What if I failed? What if I wasn't strong enough to bear the burden of my ancestors?

"Just tell us where to start," Isaac urged, squeezing my hand tighter. "We'll face whatever comes next together."

"Very well," the Naiad replied, a hint of a smile breaking through her stoic demeanor. "Your first trial awaits at the heart of the lake. Follow the currents, and they will lead you there."

With that, she vanished beneath the surface, leaving us alone once more in the magical depths.

"Heart of the lake," I mused aloud. "Sounds like an adventure. And by adventure, I mean terrifying ordeal."

"Adventures are rarely without their moments of terror," Isaac replied with a smirk, his eyes sparkling with mischief. "What's life without a little excitement?"

"Or a lot of heart palpitations," I added, rolling my eyes. "Alright, let's go."

We took a deep breath and dove deeper into the water, the sensation of weightlessness wrapping around us like a second skin. The current pulled us forward, guiding us toward the center of the lake. As we swam, the world around us transformed—sunlight pierced through the depths, casting shimmering beams that danced like fairies in the water. It felt otherworldly, surreal, as if we were swimming through a dream.

As we approached the heart of the lake, a sudden chill washed over me, the warmth of the sunlight fading like a distant memory. The water darkened, and the currents became tumultuous, swirling with a ferocity that took my breath away. I exchanged a glance with Isaac, and in that fleeting moment, we both recognized the shift—something was wrong.

A low growl reverberated through the water, shaking me to my core. It wasn't just the sound that terrified me; it was the overwhelming sense of dread that accompanied it.

"Do you hear that?" I asked, my voice barely a whisper as I felt the fear creep in.

"Yeah," Isaac replied, his expression suddenly serious. "What the hell is that?"

The darkness before us churned, coalescing into a shape—a mass of shadows that twisted and turned, forming into something vaguely humanoid, its eyes glowing like molten gold, piercing through the murky water.

"This isn't good," I breathed, instinctively moving closer to Isaac.

"Can you use your power?" he urged, his voice steady but edged with concern.

"I don't know how," I admitted, feeling the weight of the moment settle heavily upon me. "What if I unleash something I can't control?"

The creature surged forward, and I could feel the darkness enveloping us, thick and suffocating, as it reached for us with elongated limbs that writhed like snakes. The urge to flee clawed at my insides, but I stood my ground, heart racing as I tried to summon the energy that had surged through me moments before.

"Focus," Isaac urged, his eyes never leaving the creature. "You can do this. Remember the warmth, the connection you felt with your ancestors. Channel that."

As I closed my eyes, the memories of the women who had come before me flooded my mind—their strength, their sacrifices, their laughter. I could almost hear their voices, a chorus of encouragement echoing through the depths. I took a deep breath, letting the warmth rise within me, feeling it pool in my chest until it became a blaze of light.

The creature lunged, its jagged form lunging toward us, and I instinctively raised my hands, summoning the power within. Light erupted from my fingertips, casting away the darkness and illuminating the water like a sun breaking through the clouds.

But just as the creature recoiled, howling in rage, the ground beneath us trembled, sending shockwaves through the water. "What's happening?" I gasped, struggling to maintain control.

"Hold on!" Isaac shouted, grabbing my arm as the lake began to boil, the water churning violently around us.

In that moment of chaos, a fissure opened in the depths below, pulling everything into its gaping maw. My heart lurched as we were yanked downward, the creature shrieking in fury above us, the last vestiges of light flickering like a candle in the wind.

As I fell, the world above vanished, swallowed by the darkness, and the last thing I heard was Isaac's voice, a desperate plea cutting through the void. "Fight it! Don't let it take you!"

And then everything went black.

Chapter 18: Beneath the Surface

The water embraced us like a shroud, wrapping around my body in a cool, enveloping caress. Each stroke pulled me deeper into the lake, the surface fading into a shimmering memory above. Isaac's hand clasped mine, a lifeline in this submerged world, where shadows danced like phantoms just beyond the reach of our understanding. As we descended, the pressure of the water became a familiar weight, a reminder that we were moving towards something hidden—something waiting for us beneath the surface.

The sunlight filtered through the water in beams, creating a celestial ballet of light and dark. I focused on Isaac's face, illuminated in fleeting glimmers, his expression a mix of determination and something softer, an unspoken promise that we would emerge from this together. The air was thick with unuttered words, and I could feel the current of fear and hope intertwining in my chest, like vines wrapping around my heart.

As we continued our descent, an ethereal shimmer caught my eye. There, at the bottom of the lake, lay an altar—an ancient stone structure encrusted with barnacles and time itself. It was as if the lake had been waiting for us, holding its breath, concealing this sacred remnant beneath its cool surface. I could hardly comprehend its majesty, the stone carved with intricate symbols that pulsed with a heartbeat of their own. This was not merely an altar; it was a repository of secrets, a vessel of memories from lives long past.

Isaac's grip tightened around my hand as we reached the altar. The moment my fingers brushed against the cold stone, a jolt of energy coursed through me. It was electric, surging through my veins like wildfire, igniting something deep within my soul. The sensations were overwhelming—visions swirled in my mind, fragments of laughter and sorrow, echoes of sacrifices made in desperation. Each heartbeat resonated with the legacy of my bloodline, a lineage intertwined with the very fabric of this lake. The ancient presence that had guided us here felt familiar, like a forgotten lullaby whispered to me in dreams.

Suddenly, it all made sense. I was not just a seeker; I was the last of my bloodline, the final guardian of an age-old curse that hung like a storm cloud over this lake. My fingers traced the symbols on the altar, and with each stroke, I felt the weight of responsibility settle upon my shoulders. I had the power to either free this place or bind it forever, and the gravity of that realization was both exhilarating and terrifying. What if I failed? What if my choice sealed the fate of not just me, but of everyone I loved?

"Are you okay?" Isaac's voice broke through the tumult in my mind, his concern grounding me once more. I glanced at him, his eyes wide with an intensity that made my heart race. It was the kind of look that both terrified and thrilled me, the kind that reminded me of the stakes we were playing for. "You look like you've seen a ghost."

I managed a weak smile, but it didn't reach my eyes. "Just a little overwhelmed, I guess." The words felt flimsy, too light for the heavy truth I was grappling with. "This altar—it's alive, Isaac. I can feel it. It's like a part of me has been waiting for this moment."

Isaac nodded, his expression serious. "We can do this together. Whatever you decide, I'm right here." The reassurance in his tone wrapped around me like a warm blanket, giving me strength I didn't know I had.

The water began to shift around us, a gentle current that felt more like a beckoning than a threat. It urged me to make a choice, to act before the opportunity slipped through my fingers like sand. With each passing second, the energy from the altar grew stronger, thrumming beneath my palm like a heartbeat synced to my own.

I took a deep breath, water filling my lungs, but it was different now. Instead of panic, there was clarity, a focus that anchored me in the swirling chaos of emotion and memory. I could sense the lake's pain, its suffering; I could feel the weight of countless souls, trapped in the grip of the curse that had plagued my family for generations. This was more than a battle for my life; it was a reckoning with my heritage, a chance to break the cycle of despair.

"I think I know what I have to do," I said, determination solidifying my resolve. The weight of my decision loomed large, but beneath it was the undeniable truth that I could not walk away from this altar without doing something. The echoes of my ancestors whispered encouragement, their presence an unyielding force urging me forward.

As I closed my eyes, the water around me dimmed, and I surrendered to the sensation of connection—past and present weaving together into a tapestry of purpose. I felt Isaac's presence beside me, a steady flame against the gathering shadows, and I drew strength from his unwavering support. Together, we were more than just two souls caught in a turbulent tide; we were a force of change, ready to confront whatever awaited us above the surface.

With one final glance at the altar, I felt the energy coalesce around me, ready to be channeled. I opened my eyes, meeting Isaac's gaze, and in that shared moment, a silent agreement formed between us. Whatever lay ahead, we would face it together, hearts aligned against the darkness that had haunted my lineage for far too long. The choice was mine to make, but I was not alone. As we began our ascent back to the surface, I understood the gravity of what was to come—and the hope that glimmered just out of reach.

As we broke through the surface, gasping for air, the sun felt like a blessing on my face, warm and golden, washing over the chill that had seeped into my bones. I clung to Isaac, the water cascading off us like the remnants of a nightmare just fading into daylight. The realization of my lineage settled heavily on my shoulders, each breath a reminder of the power I now wielded and the choices that lay before me.

"First order of business," Isaac said, shaking the water from his hair with the enthusiasm of a puppy, "we need to get you some dry clothes. I can't have you freezing while we plot the downfall of a curse. It's bad for morale." His grin was infectious, and for a moment, the gravity of our discovery lightened, allowing a hint of laughter to escape my lips.

I glanced back at the lake, its surface calm and unassuming, hiding the chaos that churned beneath. "Right. Because nothing says 'epic battle' like a fashion emergency." I couldn't help but tease him, grateful for his ability to weave humor into the tension. "I suppose I could use a new look for my big moment. Something heroic but also stylish."

"Perhaps a cape?" he suggested, raising an eyebrow, his voice dripping with mock seriousness. "Every hero needs a good cape. It's practically in the job description."

"Caped crusader or not, I still need to figure out how to break this curse," I replied, my playful demeanor faltering as I thought of the weight of my heritage. "There's a lot riding on my shoulders now." The truth lingered in the air, heavy and undeniable.

Isaac's expression shifted, his playful banter giving way to genuine concern. "Hey, you're not in this alone. Remember that. We'll find a way to break it together. You're not just the last of your bloodline; you're also the person who can change its fate."

His words stirred something within me, a flicker of courage igniting in the depths of uncertainty. We made our way to the shore, the dampness of my clothes a reminder of our recent plunge into the unknown. The trees surrounding the lake stood sentinel, their leaves rustling gently, as if whispering secrets of old.

We reached my little cottage nestled at the edge of the forest, its warm wooden beams inviting us in like an embrace. Inside, I rummaged through my drawers, the familiar scent of lavender and cedar filling the air. "Okay, what's the strategy?" I asked, pulling on a soft sweater that smelled of home, the fabric comforting against my skin.

Isaac leaned against the doorframe, arms crossed, watching me with an intensity that made my heart flutter. "We need to learn more about that altar. There must be something in the town's history books or the local archives that can give us clues."

"Great idea! Because nothing says 'romantic adventure' like dusty old books and ancient texts," I replied, playfully rolling my eyes. "But I suppose if we're diving into the depths of my family's past, it might as well be together."

With that, we decided to head into town, a quaint place with cobblestone streets and small shops that felt like a cozy embrace. As we walked, I felt the weight of history all around me, the stories hidden in every brick and beam. The townsfolk greeted us with warm smiles, oblivious to the turmoil simmering just beneath the surface.

"Let's start with the library," I suggested, leading Isaac down the narrow path lined with blooming wildflowers. "They have an extensive collection of local history. Who knows what we might find?"

The library was a charming structure, with ivy clinging to its walls and a large oak door that creaked as we entered. The scent of old paper and polished wood enveloped us, creating a sense of reverence. I loved this place; it was a sanctuary of stories waiting to be uncovered.

"Do you think they have a section for cursed artifacts?" Isaac quipped, scanning the rows of shelves. "I bet it's next to the section on 'How to Become a Superhero in Four Easy Steps.'"

"Very funny," I shot back, suppressing a laugh. "I'm sure it's right next to 'Finding the Perfect Cape.'"

We split up, each diving into the stacks, our whispers mingling with the rustle of pages turning. I lost myself in the musty tomes, pages yellowed with age, the stories of my ancestors swirling like ghosts in my mind. There were entries about rituals, legends of the lake, and accounts of my family's history, each line drawing me deeper into a narrative I was only beginning to understand.

Hours slipped by, the sun arching across the sky, casting golden rays through the library's tall windows. I could hear Isaac's occasional exclamations from his corner, the sound of a chair scraping against the floor as he shifted. The tension was palpable, both of us aware that with each word we unearthed, we were edging closer to the truth.

Finally, I stumbled upon a particularly old book, its leather cover cracked and weary. Flipping it open, I was met with handwritten notes in the margins, as if someone had poured their heart into these pages. There, buried within the text, I found references to the altar and the curse, the sacrifices made in its name. "Isaac! Come here! You need to see this!" I called, my heart racing as I pointed to the passage.

He hurried over, eyes widening as he scanned the words. "What does it say?"

"The altar was a site of devotion, but it became tainted over the years," I explained, excitement bubbling within me. "It mentions a guardian—someone chosen to either bind or free the spirit of the lake. It's tied to the bloodline, but there's a ritual, something I need to perform at the next full moon."

Isaac's brows furrowed, a mixture of awe and concern crossing his face. "That's in just a few days. We need to prepare. Do you have everything you need?"

"I'm not even sure what I need," I admitted, a tremor of uncertainty creeping into my voice. "But we have to find out. This curse—it's not just a legend. It's real, and it's part of me now."

His hand found mine, squeezing gently. "Then we'll figure it out. Together." The promise in his eyes was a balm to my frayed nerves, a steady reminder that I didn't have to face this alone.

As we gathered our things to leave, a sense of urgency washed over me, the world outside the library growing darker as night crept in. I knew we were stepping into a realm fraught with danger, but the flicker of hope ignited by our discovery kept me anchored. Whatever awaited us, we would confront it head-on, united in purpose and spirit. And with Isaac by my side, I felt ready to face the darkness that threatened not only my family but the very heart of the lake itself.

The moon hung high in the night sky, casting a silvery glow over the lake that felt almost otherworldly. The water shimmered like a blanket of stars, but beneath its tranquil surface, the remnants of an ancient curse lingered, waiting to be awakened. My heart raced as I stood at the water's edge, the cool breeze wrapping around me like a shroud, bringing with it the whispers of the past. The full moon loomed large, its presence a reminder of the ritual that awaited me.

Isaac stood beside me, his silhouette a reassuring presence in the dark. "You ready for this?" His voice was steady, but I could hear the tension underlying his words. I turned to him, finding comfort in the way his eyes sparkled, even in the moonlight.

"Ready as I'll ever be," I replied, attempting a smile that didn't quite reach my heart. "What's the worst that could happen? Other than unleashing a curse upon the world, of course."

Isaac chuckled softly, the sound easing some of the tightness in my chest. "You know, you make a compelling case for staying home and binging on ice cream instead."

"But where's the fun in that? Besides, if I don't do this, who will?" I took a deep breath, feeling the weight of my ancestors pressing against me. "I can't turn back now. It's time to face this."

The air crackled with energy as we made our way to the altar, now fully revealed under the moon's watchful eye. The stone structure seemed to pulse, as if it were alive, beckoning me closer. The symbols carved into its surface glowed faintly, each mark a testament to the sacrifices made and the power that lay dormant.

"Do you have everything?" Isaac asked, his concern evident. He had insisted on gathering items for the ritual, scouring the library for any clue about what I might need. A small bundle lay in his hands, a collection of herbs, a vial of salt, and a ceremonial knife that felt both intimidating and oddly reassuring.

"I think so," I said, glancing over the items. "At least, I hope this isn't some elaborate joke. What if we get it all wrong? I'd hate to end up binding myself to a spirit for eternity. Talk about awkward dinner parties."

"Just remember to follow your instincts," he replied, his tone earnest. "You're meant to do this, and I'll be right here, no matter what happens."

With his words echoing in my mind, I stepped closer to the altar. The ground beneath my feet felt warm, almost as if the earth itself was alive with anticipation. I placed my hand on the stone, and a surge of energy raced through me, igniting every nerve ending. The whispers of the lake surrounded me, a symphony of voices that echoed with sorrow and longing.

"Spirits of the past, I call upon you," I spoke, my voice steady despite the rapid beating of my heart. "I am here to confront the curse that binds us, to seek your forgiveness and find a path to freedom."

The air grew still, the night wrapped in silence, and I could feel the weight of history pressing against me. It was both exhilarating and terrifying. As I poured my energy into the altar, I felt the connection deepen, a tether between my spirit and the ancient forces at play.

Suddenly, a gust of wind surged through the clearing, lifting my hair from my shoulders and swirling around us. I glanced at Isaac, who looked as startled as I felt. "Is it supposed to do that?" he asked, eyes wide.

"I hope so," I replied, trying to keep the tremor from my voice. "Just part of the plan, right?"

With a deep breath, I continued the ritual, reciting the incantation I had discovered. Each word flowed from my lips, imbued with intent, weaving a tapestry of hope and healing. The symbols on the altar began to glow brighter, pulsating in rhythm with my heartbeat, and I felt the spirits around me, their energy rising to meet mine.

Then, just as the final words slipped from my mouth, the ground shook violently. The water of the lake surged and roiled, reflecting the turmoil above. I stumbled back, my heart racing as the very essence of the curse began to unravel before my eyes.

"What is happening?" Isaac shouted over the roar of the wind, his voice strained. The air crackled with energy, the tension palpable as if the very fabric of reality was being torn apart.

"Stay close!" I yelled, trying to reach him through the chaos. But the wind howled louder, drowning out my words, and the world around me blurred in a whirlwind of shadows and light.

Suddenly, a figure emerged from the depths of the lake, rising like a specter from a dream. I squinted against the brilliance, my breath hitching in my throat as the apparition took form. It was a woman, ethereal and haunting, her eyes filled with an anguish that mirrored my own. The resemblance was striking, her features unmistakably familiar—she looked like me, but older, wiser, and yet deeply sorrowful.

"Why have you come?" her voice echoed, resonating through the chaos, deep and melodic. "What do you seek at this altar of sacrifice?"

"I—I seek to break the curse!" I managed to shout, my heart pounding. "I am here to free you, to free all of us!"

Her gaze pierced through me, searching, judging. "To break the curse is to embrace the truth of your bloodline. Are you prepared to bear the weight of your ancestors?"

A chill ran down my spine as I met her gaze, and for a fleeting moment, I hesitated. What would that mean? To embrace the truth of a lineage steeped in darkness and sacrifice? But then I thought of Isaac standing behind me, of the people in town, of the lives affected by this curse, and I squared my shoulders.

"Yes," I replied, my voice unwavering despite the storm around us. "I am ready."

The woman's expression softened, but before she could respond, the altar erupted with a blinding light. I shielded my eyes, feeling the pull of the lake, as if it wanted to consume me whole. The wind roared like a tempest, and with it came a rush of water that splashed around my ankles, encircling me like a protective barrier.

"Then accept your fate," she intoned, her voice rising above the din. "But know this—once the curse is broken, there is no going back."

And with that, the light enveloped me, and I felt myself being pulled under, the world spinning into darkness. I reached for Isaac, desperate to hold on to something solid, but his voice faded, lost in the cacophony of the lake's awakening.

Just as the darkness threatened to swallow me whole, I glimpsed the reflection of the moon in the water above, a beacon of light in a sea of uncertainty. In that moment, I realized I had stepped beyond the threshold, and there was no turning back now. My destiny awaited me, tangled in the depths of the lake, where the curse and my bloodline intertwined in a dance as old as time itself. The question remained—what would I find when the light faded and the waters settled?

Chapter 19: The Choice of Fate

The sun hung low over the lake, casting a golden sheen on the water's surface, transforming it into a glimmering tapestry of light and shadow. I could feel the cool breeze tugging at my hair, the scent of damp earth mingling with the fresh aroma of pine needles and wildflowers. It was a scene that once brought me peace, but now it held an undercurrent of dread that gnawed at my insides. This place, once a sanctuary, had morphed into a stage for my fate, and the weight of that realization pressed heavily on my shoulders.

Isaac stood beside me, his presence both comforting and agonizing. He was a mix of strength and vulnerability, a man shaped by the trials we had endured together, his dark hair tousled by the wind, and those intense blue eyes—like twin sapphires—studying me with an intensity that made my heart race and my throat tighten. I wished I could convey to him how much I cared, how fiercely I wanted to shield him from the turmoil swirling within me. But words failed, caught in the tangle of emotions I couldn't fully articulate.

"What are you thinking?" His voice broke through my reverie, low and hesitant, as if he feared the answer.

"I'm trying to figure out how to untangle this mess," I replied, forcing a lightness into my tone that felt wholly unnatural. "You know, just your average day by the lake, contemplating a curse."

He chuckled, but it was tinged with an edge of concern. "You don't have to do this alone, you know. Whatever it takes, I'm with you."

His promise wrapped around my heart like a balm, but the truth clawed at me from the inside. Sharing this burden meant sharing the pain, the darkness that had threatened to consume me since the day I discovered my lineage. "Isaac, this isn't just about me. The curse... it's mine to break, and it might take you with me."

The Naiad's voice echoed in my mind, her words laced with ancient wisdom and a haunting urgency. "You alone can break the curse, but it will come at a cost." I had replayed that line over and over, a riddle wrapped in shadows. What was the cost? And could I bear the weight of it?

"I'd rather face the dark with you than live in the light without you," Isaac countered, his resolve crystallizing in the fading sunlight. The sincerity in his eyes stirred something deep within me, a yearning so profound it made my breath hitch.

I turned my gaze to the lake, the surface rippling gently as if responding to my turmoil. It felt alive, imbued with the memories of laughter and tears, of fleeting moments that shaped who I was. But there was more—whispers of the past floated just beneath the surface, the secrets of those who came before me, intertwined with my fate.

"Why did it have to come to this?" I murmured, more to the wind than to him. "I never asked for this curse, this... this burden of choice."

Isaac's hand found mine, his touch grounding me in the chaos. "Maybe it's not just a burden. Maybe it's an opportunity."

"An opportunity for what? To dive into an abyss of uncertainty? To gamble with our lives?" My voice rose, tinged with desperation, but he held my gaze steady, unyielding.

"To take control," he replied softly, as if daring me to see beyond the immediate shadows. "To shape our own destinies, rather than letting the curse dictate our lives."

A shiver coursed through me, both from the chill in the air and from the weight of his words. The possibility he offered shimmered before me like the sun on the lake, a glimmer of hope against the dark tide of despair. But hope came at a price, one I wasn't sure I could pay.

As if sensing my internal struggle, the Naiad emerged from the depths, her form ethereal, water cascading from her skin like liquid silver. "You are stronger than you believe," she said, her voice lilting and melodic. "But strength is not enough; you must decide what you are willing to sacrifice for freedom."

Her presence sent a ripple of dread through me, the reality of my situation crashing down like waves against the shore. The curse had tethered me to this lake, to this moment, and I felt the cold grip of fate tightening around my heart.

"What if the cost is too great?" I whispered, the question escaping my lips before I could reel it back.

The Naiad's gaze was unwavering, piercing through the layers of my doubt. "Life is built on choices, each one leading you closer to your true self or further from it. Only you can decide what is worth fighting for."

I could feel the earth beneath my feet, solid and unyielding, yet it felt as though the ground was shifting, pulling me toward a precipice. In that instant, clarity washed over me, a flood of understanding that cut through the fog of confusion.

"I want to choose," I declared, the conviction in my voice surprising even me. "I want to choose a future where I'm not just a vessel for this curse but the master of my own fate."

Isaac squeezed my hand tighter, his eyes alight with pride and something deeper, something almost palpable between us. "Then let's choose together."

The Naiad watched us, a faint smile gracing her lips as if she knew this was the turning point. My heart raced as I took a step closer to the lake, the water shimmering with promise, reflecting not just my fears but the strength I hadn't realized was there all along.

With each breath, I felt the courage swell within me, the realization that love—true, unwavering love—could be the key to breaking the chains of the past. And in that moment, as I stood at the edge of the unknown, I knew that whatever lay ahead, we would face it together, ready to carve our own destiny amidst the echoes of fate.

The water lapped gently at the shore, each wave whispering secrets that danced on the air. With a deep breath, I stepped closer to the edge, my heart racing in tune with the rhythm of the lake. The sun dipped lower, painting the sky in a riot of oranges and purples, as if the world itself was holding its breath, waiting for my next move. I felt Isaac's hand warm against mine, a tether in this storm of uncertainty, his presence like a lighthouse guiding me through the darkening haze.

"I don't want to lose you," I confessed, the words spilling out before I could catch them. It was a raw admission, the kind that strips bare the soul. I turned to look at him, seeing the flicker of fear in his eyes, but also a determination that ignited a spark of hope within me.

"You won't lose me," he replied firmly, as if saying it would make it true. "You're the strongest person I know. Whatever it takes, I'm in."

That conviction in his voice filled the hollow spaces in my heart, but I couldn't shake the gnawing anxiety. The Naiad watched from the water, her ethereal form shimmering in the twilight, a living reminder of the magic and danger that surrounded us. "The cost is yours to decide," she said, her voice a haunting melody that echoed in my mind. "Every choice you make shapes the future."

My heart clenched at the weight of her words. I had spent my entire life evading the shadows of my heritage, and now I was being thrust into the center of a storm I had never asked to enter. But the truth remained undeniable—I was here, standing on the precipice of fate, and it was time to confront the darkness that lay ahead.

With a deep breath, I stepped forward, the cool water enveloping my ankles like a lover's caress. It felt electric, alive with possibility, and I closed my eyes, allowing the sensations to wash over me.

Memories swirled in my mind—the laughter of friends, the quiet moments shared with Isaac, and the fears that had haunted me since childhood. "If I break the curse," I murmured, more to myself than to anyone else, "what will I have to sacrifice?"

"Your fear," Isaac whispered, stepping closer, his voice a steady anchor in the chaos. "You have to let go of what holds you back."

"Let go of my fear?" I scoffed, a nervous laugh escaping my lips. "Easier said than done. You've seen me jump at shadows. What if I'm too late?"

He stepped beside me, his shoulder brushing against mine, a simple act that radiated warmth. "Then you jump together. We'll figure it out. We always do."

In that moment, the barriers I had built around my heart began to crumble. The thought of facing the unknown with Isaac at my side filled me with a sense of purpose I had never expected. I opened my eyes, locking my gaze with the Naiad. "I want to break the curse. I want to embrace whatever comes next."

"Very well," the Naiad said, her smile a glimmer of approval. "But know that once you step into the water, there is no turning back. You will be tested, and your heart will reveal the truth."

I nodded, the gravity of her words sinking in. Taking one last glance at the fading light, I stepped deeper into the water, the cold liquid enveloping me like a shroud. A rush of energy surged through me, filling every part of my being, awakening something ancient and powerful that lay dormant within.

Suddenly, the lake trembled, ripples expanding outward as a surge of energy crackled through the air. The water churned violently around us, and I felt Isaac grip my hand tighter, the fear etched on his face blending with awe. "What's happening?" he shouted above the cacophony.

"I don't know!" I yelled back, my heart racing as I fought to keep my balance against the shifting tide. The Naiad's form glimmered like a beacon amidst the chaos, her voice a clarion call. "Face your truth! Only then can the curse be undone!"

The words struck a chord deep within me, igniting memories of choices long buried beneath the weight of expectations. I could see glimpses of my past—the fear of failing, the weight of my family's legacy, and the love I'd discovered with Isaac. Each fragment was a piece of the puzzle, but what was the truth that would unlock my freedom?

With a surge of determination, I closed my eyes again, delving into the wellspring of my emotions. I thought of the laughter we shared, the dreams we wove together under the stars, and the fear that had often silenced my voice. "I am more than my curse," I declared, the words echoing through the chaos. "I am a daughter, a friend, a lover. I am brave, and I choose love over fear."

As I spoke, the water around me began to shimmer, transforming into a vortex of swirling light. It pulled me deeper, and I could feel the energy coursing through my veins, igniting a fire within my heart. I opened my eyes to see the Naiad floating before me, her expression one of fierce pride.

"Now, you must confront the shadows," she urged, gesturing toward the depths of the lake. "Face the parts of yourself that you've hidden away."

As if drawn by an invisible force, I submerged into the water, the coldness enveloping me like a second skin. I could see the darkness swirling below, shapes twisting and turning like specters of my own making. Fear clutched at my throat, but I pressed forward, determined to confront the shadows that threatened to drown me.

Visions flickered around me—moments of doubt, memories of feeling unworthy, flashes of every time I had backed down from a challenge. I felt the weight of those moments, the bitterness of regret swirling around me, but then a light pierced through the darkness—a memory of Isaac, smiling at me with unwavering belief.

With a surge of strength, I reached out to the shadows, embracing them, not as enemies but as parts of myself that had long been neglected. "I am not afraid of you!" I shouted, my voice echoing through the depths. "You do not define me!"

The shadows recoiled, and with each word, the darkness began to dissipate, replaced by a shimmering light that spread warmth throughout my being. I emerged from the depths, gasping for air, feeling lighter, freer than I had ever felt before. The lake glimmered, reflecting the brilliance of the twilight sky, and I turned to Isaac, his face a mask of awe.

"You did it," he breathed, his eyes shining with unshed tears. "You broke the curse."

I smiled, a wave of relief and joy washing over me. "I think we both did."

In that moment, standing at the edge of the lake, I understood the true meaning of sacrifice. It wasn't about losing parts of myself but rather embracing all that I was, flaws and all. And with Isaac by my side, I felt ready to face whatever came next, a newfound courage sparking within me like a beacon in the night.

The light shimmered on the lake's surface, a canvas of vibrant colors swirling in the afterglow of dusk, and the air crackled with the energy of my transformation. I felt the weight of the past slipping away, the chains of expectation and fear dissolving in the clarity of my choice. As I stood there, half-submerged, Isaac's gaze anchored me, grounding me in the chaos.

"Are you sure about this?" he asked, his voice a husky murmur, the worry etched across his handsome features tugging at my heart.

"Do I look like I'm about to change my mind?" I quipped, trying to inject some levity into the moment. "This is my big chance to become a legendary heroine or at least a really impressive cautionary tale."

A reluctant smile broke through his tension. "You'd better not just be going for the cautionary tale, because I can't have you dying on me. I need you around to make fun of my terrible fishing skills."

"Deal," I replied, the light banter wrapping us in a fragile cocoon against the dark waters. Yet, beneath my playful facade, a ripple of apprehension surged through me. The Naiad hovered nearby, a shimmering specter of power and mystery, her eyes glinting with an intensity that sent shivers down my spine.

"Remember," she intoned, her voice a haunting echo in the twilight, "your heart will guide you, but your choices will shape the outcome. Embrace what comes, for the true test lies ahead."

With those words lingering in the air, I took a breath deep enough to fill my lungs with courage and plunged into the depths, the cool water enveloping me like a velvet shroud. Instinctively, I let the currents guide me, navigating through the darkness, my body moving with an urgency that pulsed with newfound strength. The shadows of my past loomed around me, flickering like specters, and I reached out to touch them, ready to confront what lay hidden within.

Suddenly, a jolt of fear shot through me as a familiar face emerged from the murky depths—a ghostly reflection of myself, but twisted, her features marred by despair and doubt. "You think you can escape us?" she hissed, her voice a blend of mocking laughter and bitter sorrow. "You think you can change your fate?"

"I'm not here to escape," I replied, my voice steady, even as my heart raced. "I'm here to embrace it."

She laughed, the sound echoing ominously around me, but I pushed forward, channeling every ounce of love and strength I had. "You are not stronger than your fears," she taunted, a smirk twisting her lips. "You will always be shackled by your lineage, by the choices made before you were even born."

"No," I countered, each word a defiant lash against the chains she sought to bind me with. "Those choices shaped my past, but they do not dictate my future. I am not a prisoner of my bloodline. I choose my path."

With that declaration, the darkness surged forward, wrapping around me like a vice. But in the midst of the encroaching shadows, I felt a spark ignite within me—a flicker of light fueled by the love I felt for Isaac and the life I wanted to create. I summoned that energy, allowing it to swell until it burst forth in a brilliant flash, scattering the shadows like autumn leaves caught in a gust of wind.

As I broke through, the water shimmered, and the Naiad appeared beside me, her expression a mix of admiration and intrigue. "You have faced the darkness within," she said, her voice resonating like a distant chime. "But there is one final trial awaiting you on the surface."

I nodded, a flicker of determination igniting my spirit. "What must I do?"

"Return to the shore," she instructed, "but be wary. The true challenge will test your heart, and only by holding onto the light within can you conquer it."

With a deep breath, I propelled myself upwards, breaking through the surface and gasping for air. The night sky sprawled above me, dotted with stars that sparkled like diamonds, but the tranquility was deceptive. A sudden chill swept over the lake, and I felt the air shift, thickening with an unsettling energy that sent a shiver down my spine.

As I stumbled onto the shore, I glanced back at the lake, and my breath caught in my throat. The water had turned an inky black, swirling ominously, as if a tempest brewed beneath its surface. I turned to Isaac, who stood a few paces back, his eyes wide with alarm.

"Did you see that?" he called out, voice taut with concern.

"I did," I admitted, my heart racing. "But it felt... right? I faced my past, Isaac. I confronted the darkness."

Before he could respond, a low rumble vibrated through the ground, and the air crackled with tension. The surface of the lake erupted, sending waves crashing against the shore, and from the depths emerged a figure—a shadowy silhouette, indistinct but radiating an aura of palpable power.

"What is that?" Isaac shouted, stepping closer, instinctively reaching for me.

I could barely reply, my voice lost in the sudden chaos as the figure took form, revealing itself to be a woman, her features strikingly familiar. A reflection of myself, but older, with a fierce expression that combined wisdom and wrath.

"Who are you?" I stammered, my heart pounding against my ribcage.

"I am the Echo," she declared, her voice reverberating with authority. "I am the embodiment of the choices made by your ancestors, the keeper of the curse that binds you."

The wind howled around us, whipping my hair into a frenzy, and I felt the weight of her presence bearing down upon me. "You think you can break free from your lineage?" she continued, her tone a mix of challenge and intrigue. "You are but a child playing with forces beyond your comprehension."

"No!" I shouted, defiance surging within me. "I am not a child. I am ready to forge my own path!"

The Echo's laughter echoed through the night, dark and resonant. "Then prove it. Face me, and show me that your heart is strong enough to withstand the burdens of the past."

In that moment, I felt the pulse of my own heart, a steady rhythm that ignited the courage within me. The shadows of doubt threatened to creep in, but I remembered the love I had discovered, the strength I had unearthed. "I will not back down," I declared, my voice unwavering. "I will not let fear dictate my fate."

"Very well," she replied, the challenge laced in her tone. "Let us see if your heart can truly conquer what lies ahead."

The air thickened with anticipation as the Echo stepped forward, and I knew this was only the beginning of a battle that would test every fiber of my being. The lake roared behind me, its depths swirling with ancient magic and the weight of untold stories. As the confrontation loomed, I braced myself for the reckoning, knowing that the true test of my courage was yet to come.

Chapter 20: A Wound Unhealed

The water glistens under the fading light, a restless expanse that seems to pulse with a life of its own. I can almost hear it humming, a melody of grief and hope that pulls at my heart. My gaze flickers to the horizon, where the sun drowns slowly, bleeding orange and crimson across the sky like a bruise. It's beautiful and tragic all at once, much like my life. I can feel the weight of the moment pressing down on me, a gravity that threatens to crush everything I've ever known. Isaac's grip tightens, grounding me as if I might be swept away by the very magic I've come to understand.

"Lila, you don't have to do this," he insists, his voice rough with desperation. I can see the tension in his jaw, the way his brows knit together as he searches my face for a sign that I'm not lost to this madness. But how can I explain to him that this is the only way? How can I share the visions that plague my nights, the whispers that fill my waking thoughts, without sounding like a fool?

"I do," I say, my voice steadier than I feel. "This lake, it holds answers. It holds power. Power that can change everything."

"Or it could destroy you," he counters, his eyes a stormy mix of worry and anger. "You're not just another sacrifice for whatever ancient being lurks beneath. You're more than this—more than a pawn in some twisted game."

His words wrap around my heart, squeezing it tighter. The truth is, he's right, and yet he's wrong. I am not merely a pawn; I'm the queen moving toward a checkmate that could cost us both our lives. The path I've chosen is fraught with danger, but it's one I must walk, alone if necessary. I want him to understand that there is a part of me that longs to protect him from the darkness that threatens to consume us. I can't let that darkness extend its tendrils into our lives any longer.

I take a deep breath, inhaling the salty tang of the air mixed with the earthy scent of wet sand. "Trust me, Isaac," I whisper, hoping he can feel the sincerity in my words. "This isn't just about me. It's about everyone. About us. If I can confront this, we might have a chance to end the curse for good."

His shoulders slump slightly, the fight in him wavering as he struggles to come to terms with the depth of my resolve. "You think this will fix us? You think facing whatever this is will somehow mend the fractures between us?"

My heart aches at his words, a bittersweet reminder of the love we're fighting to hold onto. "I have to try," I reply, the urgency in my voice rising like the tide. "For us, for everything we've lost. I can't keep running from it."

He swallows hard, and I can see the flicker of doubt cross his features. The lake's surface ripples, reflecting the chaos of our emotions, and suddenly the wind shifts, carrying with it the scent of something ancient, something that calls to me with an intoxicating promise. The water sparkles like a thousand stars trapped beneath the surface, and I feel the magic coursing through me, beckoning, urging me forward. I know I must answer the call, yet part of me longs to stay, to bury my head in Isaac's shoulder and forget the weight of my destiny, if only for a moment.

"I'll be right here," he says finally, his voice thick with emotion. "I'll always be right here, waiting. Just... be careful, okay?"

Those simple words almost unravel me. I want to tell him that there's nothing cautious about the path I've chosen. The truth is, I am terrified. But fear is just another emotion, one I can wield if I must. I nod, my throat tight, and step back from him, breaking the connection that has been both my anchor and my chain. As I move toward the lake, the air grows colder, an unnatural chill that seeps into my bones, and the water rises in a gentle swell, greeting me like an old friend.

The surface churns softly, whispering secrets I'm desperate to uncover. I kneel at the water's edge, feeling the cool liquid lap at my fingers, sending electric shivers up my arm. With each heartbeat, the magic amplifies, resonating deep within me, merging with my essence. I close my eyes and surrender to it, letting the pull of the lake draw me deeper into its embrace.

Images flood my mind—flashes of a time long past, of sacrifices made and promises broken. I see figures draped in shadow, their faces obscured but their intentions clear. They are the architects of the curse, the very beings whose whispers haunt my dreams. I shudder, fighting against the tide of emotions that threaten to overwhelm me. This is the moment I've been waiting for, and yet it feels like stepping off the edge of a precipice into the unknown.

"Show me," I plead, my voice breaking the fragile silence. "Show me what I need to do."

The water churns more violently, a tempest of memories and emotions swirling around me. The whispers grow louder, a cacophony of voices that speaks of loss and redemption, of love that transcends time and pain. I reach out, feeling the energy surge through my fingertips, a binding force that pulls me closer to the truth. With every pulse, I sense Isaac behind me, the weight of his gaze both a comfort and a burden.

"Lila!" he calls, urgency lacing his tone, but I can't turn back now. I've come too far, and there's no going back. The lake is awakening, and I must embrace it, must confront whatever lies beneath the surface. The tension in the air thickens, and I realize that this moment could change everything—or destroy us both.

The water shifts beneath me, its surface now a mirror reflecting not just the deepening twilight but the tumultuous emotions roiling inside. The whispers from the lake rise, swirling around my mind like an intoxicating mist, beckoning me to step into its depths. I can almost hear the echo of my own heartbeat, thrumming in time with the pull of the water, an ancient rhythm I am both drawn to and terrified by. Isaac's presence lingers like a protective shadow, even as the distance between us stretches.

"Lila," he says again, softer this time, his voice breaking through the haze of magic that envelops me. "You don't have to do this alone. Whatever you're facing, I'll be right by your side."

I want nothing more than to turn back to him, to wrap myself in his arms and forget this night ever began. But I know the truth, that there are forces at play far beyond our understanding, shadows lurking in corners we haven't dared to explore. "You can't fight this for me," I reply, my voice steady despite the tempest in my heart. "You have to trust that I know what I'm doing."

The look he gives me is a cocktail of fear and admiration, and I feel a pang of guilt for dragging him into this world of enchantment and danger. "What if this is a mistake?" he asks, his brow furrowing as he searches for a sign, any sign, that this is not the end of everything we've built.

I pause, glancing back at the lake, its surface undulating like a living thing, and in that moment, I see it—the fleeting glimmer of something beneath the water, a flicker of light that promises answers. "Every step we've taken has led us here, Isaac. If I don't do this now, we might never have another chance."

With one last, lingering look, I release his hand, the warmth of his touch fading into the cool night air. I can feel the weight of his gaze on my back as I wade deeper into the water, the cold creeping up my legs, wrapping around me like the embrace of an old lover. The lake welcomes me, its depths mysterious and beckoning.

As I step further in, the water rises to my waist, and I gasp at the shock of the chill. It is invigorating, awakening something deep inside me, something that had been dormant for far too long. The whispers grow louder, a cacophony of voices intertwining, urging me forward into the unknown. I can't fight it; I can't resist the magic any longer. The world above fades away, the air thickening with the scent of earth and moss, intoxicating and heady.

I take another step, and suddenly, the ground beneath me shifts. I'm no longer standing on solid earth but floating, suspended in the lake's embrace. Panic flares briefly before the water cradles me, and I realize that I'm not sinking; I'm being drawn down, down into the depths where secrets lie waiting.

"Lila!" Isaac's voice pierces the murky silence, pulling me back to reality. His worry echoes in my mind, and a flicker of doubt ignites within me. But the pull of the water is relentless, wrapping around me like a silken ribbon. I can't let his fear anchor me now; I have to break free of this curse that binds us both.

Deeper I go, the water thickening, each stroke feeling like a leap into another realm. Colors swirl around me, vivid and alive. Memories flicker, haunting and beautiful, blurring the lines of time. I see images of my childhood, moments shared with my parents, laughter echoing in the air, the warmth of summer days spent on this very shore. And then the darkness begins to seep in—the shrouded figures, the stormy nights filled with screams, the insatiable hunger of a curse that has clung to our family for generations.

My heart races as I remember the tales told in hushed whispers, of sacrifices made to the lake, of the price paid for power. The momentary joy is swept away, replaced by a stark understanding of what is at stake. I must confront it, face the very essence of the curse that has haunted us, and break its hold once and for all.

As I sink deeper, the water shifts, and suddenly I am not alone. Figures swirl around me, faces half-formed, their features twisted with anguish and desperation. They reach for me, their fingers like icy tendrils, beckoning me to join them. "Help us," they whisper, voices entwining in a haunting chorus. "You are the key."

"Who are you?" I manage to choke out, the pressure of the water tightening around my chest. "What do you want from me?"

A murmur ripples through the figures, and one emerges clearer than the rest, a woman with sorrowful eyes and flowing hair that moves like water itself. "You must understand," she says, her voice resonating in the depths of my mind, "the curse binds us all. You are the last of your line, the only one who can set us free. Embrace the magic within you; only then can we be liberated."

Her words wrap around me, binding my fear and hope together, and I realize that this is not just about breaking a curse; it's about acceptance. Acceptance of who I am, of my past, of the tangled threads of fate that have led me here. My heart swells with determination. "I will not abandon you," I promise, feeling the warmth of the magic growing inside me, igniting every fiber of my being.

"Then claim your birthright," she urges, and the figures shift, merging into one another, the light between them growing brighter, illuminating the path before me. The water starts to swirl violently, and I feel the surge of power coursing through me. It's exhilarating and terrifying, but I know I have to harness it.

I close my eyes, allowing the magic to envelop me completely, and then I plunge deeper, diving into the heart of the storm that lies beneath the lake's surface. This is the moment where everything could change, where the past and future collide in a dance of destiny. In this watery embrace, I gather the courage to face whatever darkness awaits, determined to not only uncover the truth but to rewrite the story that has bound us all for far too long.

The world around me fades, the water enveloping me in its cool embrace as I descend further into its depths. The shimmering figures swirl, their anguished faces blurring in and out of focus as I struggle to maintain my composure. "I will not abandon you," I repeat, forcing the words from my lips, a promise to the ghosts of my family and those lost before me. With every heartbeat, I feel their energy intertwining with mine, urging me to unlock the power buried deep within.

"Embrace your birthright, Lila," the spectral woman whispers, her presence radiating warmth amidst the cold. I focus on her, drawing strength from her intensity, a flicker of hope igniting within me. "Only you can sever the chains that bind us."

As I plunge deeper, the light shifts, the water darkening around me, swirling with shadows that pulse with a life of their own. I can feel the weight of the curse pressing against me, a tangible force that seeks to drag me down into oblivion. "You think you can wield power you don't understand?" a voice hisses from the depths, a deep, rumbling sound that sends shivers down my spine.

"Try me," I retort, surprising even myself with the confidence lacing my words. The tension around me thickens, a challenge laid bare in the depths of this ancient lake. I can feel the pull of the darkness, a seductive whisper promising safety in surrender. It would be so easy to give in, to let the tide sweep me away from the turmoil that has been my life, but I refuse to be just another victim.

"Foolish girl," the voice mocks, echoing through the liquid void. "You think you can change what was written long ago? You're nothing but a fleeting moment in the grand tapestry of time."

"Maybe," I say, gritting my teeth against the pull of despair, "but I'm a moment that's ready to fight." The words resonate through the water, a surge of defiance that sparks a reaction. The shadows recoil, flickering away like mist before the dawn, and for a heartbeat, I feel the warmth of power pulsing within me, a raw, unshaped energy that craves release.

I stretch out my hands, feeling the vibrations of the water humming through my fingertips. "I am here," I declare, my voice steady, stronger than I've ever felt. "I will not be your pawn any longer." As the energy builds, I see the swirling figures react, their faces reflecting a mixture of awe and dread.

In that instant, the water around me begins to boil, the surface breaking with a cacophony of sound, and the shadows dissolve into a thousand pinpricks of light. I am no longer afraid; I am the storm. I draw on the ancient magic, channeling the power that flows from the depths of my lineage, harnessing it as if it were an extension of myself. "Together, we can break this curse!" I shout, the energy coalescing into a brilliant orb of light that bursts forth from my hands.

The brilliance illuminates the dark depths, casting the shadowy figures in stark relief. Their faces, once twisted in agony, now radiate hope, urging me on. "Yes! Let it flow!" the spectral woman cries, her voice rising above the tumult, and I feel the connection between us strengthen, the power thrumming through the water like a heartbeat.

The orb expands, pulsating with life, and I channel all my grief, my anger, and my love into it. I think of Isaac, the way his laughter feels like sunshine breaking through storm clouds, and how his eyes hold both the weight of sorrow and the promise of hope. I picture the life we could have, unshackled from the chains of the past. "For us!" I roar, and the orb surges forward, a comet blazing through the darkness.

As it collides with the shadows, there's a moment of silence—a breath held in anticipation—before the water erupts in a blinding explosion of light. The energy radiates outward, a shockwave that sends me spiraling back, crashing against the unseen barrier of the curse. The figures swirl around me, their voices rising to a crescendo, blending into a symphony of power that resonates within my very core.

But then, as the light begins to wane, the voice returns, louder and angrier, reverberating through the water like thunder. "You dare defy the legacy? You will pay for your insolence, child!"

The shadows surge back, more aggressive, clawing at the light that flickers weakly in my grasp. Fear grips my heart as I feel their pull dragging me down into the darkness. I fight against it, my energy waning, and desperation floods through me. "No! I will not be afraid!"

With a final surge of will, I reach for the remaining strength within, feeling it pulse in sync with the figures around me. "Together!" I scream, and they respond, their energy wrapping around me, fueling the flickering light one last time.

But just as it seems the tide is turning, the shadows lash out, a desperate attack from the remnants of a past I had hoped to escape. I feel the energy surge, overwhelming and painful, as it crashes into me, tearing at the seams of my resolve. I am thrust backward, the brilliance of the orb flickering, shadows seeping through the cracks like oil in water, dark and consuming.

"No!" I scream, but my voice is swallowed by the chaos, and just as the shadows begin to close in, the water swirls violently, tossing me like a leaf caught in a tempest. A sharp pain erupts in my chest, a blinding flash that steals my breath, and I realize with horror that the curse is not merely a force I can defeat—it is a part of me.

I struggle against the current, my heart pounding, but the shadows tighten their grip, dragging me down toward the depths where the darkness reigns. And in that terrifying moment, I see Isaac, his figure growing smaller and smaller above me, a desperate plea etched on his face. The weight of my choice crashes down on me as I reach out, knowing that this may be the last time I see him. "Isaac!" I call, my voice fading into the abyss, swallowed by the darkness that now claims me.

As the water closes over my head, the light flickers one last time before extinguishing, leaving me suspended in an overwhelming void. I am lost, trapped in a world where the past and future collide, where the stakes are higher than I ever imagined. And as the shadows wrap around me, I know I must face whatever lies ahead—not just for myself, but for the love I've fought to protect.

Chapter 21: Heart of the Lake

The lake pulls me under, deeper than I have ever gone, the water cold and dark as midnight. I am no longer aware of Isaac's voice calling from the shore, or of the world above. Beneath the surface, the silence envelops me, thick and heavy, wrapping around my limbs like a shroud. My heart pounds in my chest, an insistent drumbeat echoing in the watery void, urging me to fight against the chill that seeps into my bones.

Suddenly, she appears before me—the Naiad. Her figure glides effortlessly through the water, ethereal and haunting, shimmering like moonlight dancing on the lake's surface. Her hair flows around her, a cascade of silver strands that swirl in the currents. I gasp, the cold water filling my mouth, and yet, I feel an inexplicable connection to her. It's as if I am staring into a fractured mirror, my own face twisted in grief and sorrow. I recognize the hollow in her eyes, the weight of regret etched in every feature.

"Do you see now?" she whispers, her voice a soft lilt that reverberates in the water. "You are bound to this place, just as I am. Your blood sings the same lament I once sang."

"What do you mean?" I manage to reply, my words bubbling and twisting in the frigid depths. "What curse? What lament?" The questions tumble out of me, desperate for answers, but she only shakes her head, a flicker of sadness passing across her face.

"They came here long ago, your ancestors. They broke a promise, forsaking the peace of the lake for their own desires. And now, the price must be paid," she explains, her voice weaving through the currents like a haunting melody. "You think you can escape it, but it clings to you, to the very essence of who you are. You are part of this legacy, just as I am."

The weight of her words crushes me, and for a fleeting moment, I wonder if I will ever return to the surface. My lungs scream for air, and panic rises in my chest, yet something keeps me anchored to her gaze. "What is the price?" I ask, my voice a thin thread in the suffocating silence.

Her expression darkens, and a flicker of anger flashes in her eyes. "You want to know the price? It is the hope you cling to. It is the love you so desperately seek. Your heart is a vessel for the pain of those who came before you, and until it is emptied, you cannot be free."

A rush of memories floods my mind—my mother's tear-streaked face, the way she'd smile despite her sorrow, the burden of unspoken words that had hung between us like a dense fog. I realize then that I had thought love could conquer all, could break any curse. But here, in this watery grave, the Naiad is telling me a different story. Love does not conquer. It binds.

"Isaac," I whisper, his name a silent plea against the pressing darkness. "I can't lose him."

"Then you must confront the truth," the Naiad replies, her voice a soft caress that somehow carries the weight of thunder. "He is not what you think. The curse we share runs deeper than you can imagine. It will seek to take everything you cherish, to twist it into something unrecognizable."

I recoil, the thought striking me like a physical blow. Isaac, with his easy smile and comforting presence, how could he be entangled in this? "No, it can't be. He's not like that."

"Isn't he?" she challenges, her expression resolute. "Love is a powerful thing, but it can just as easily become a weapon. It will turn on you when you least expect it, feeding off your fears and insecurities."

Desperation wells up inside me, and I shake my head defiantly. "I won't believe that. Not about him. Not about us."

Her laughter ripples through the water, a sound both beautiful and cruel. "You are young and stubborn. But tell me, what will you do when the truth is laid bare before you? When you discover the darkness lurking beneath the surface of your love?"

Before I can respond, the water shifts around me, and I feel myself being pulled upward, the currents fighting against my desire to linger. The Naiad's gaze holds me captive, and I sense a deep, ancient sorrow behind her eyes, a grief that speaks of countless betrayals. "You are running out of time," she warns, her voice fading as the light from the surface grows brighter. "The heart of the lake beats in time with your own. You must choose, and soon."

Just as I break the surface, gasping for air, Isaac's voice calls my name, urgent and full of fear. The sunlight blinds me momentarily, and I'm blinded by the contrast of warmth against the chill that still clings to my skin. I look back at the lake, its surface calm and unassuming, yet I know it holds secrets darker than I could ever comprehend.

"I'm here!" I cry, my heart racing. The world above feels so foreign, so bright compared to the haunting depths I've just emerged from. Isaac stands at the water's edge, his expression a mixture of relief and worry, but I can't meet his eyes. The Naiad's words echo in my mind, a haunting refrain that threatens to unravel the fabric of my reality.

"Where were you?" he asks, stepping closer, concern etched in his features. "I thought—"

"I know," I cut him off, the urgency in my voice palpable. "But I need you to trust me, Isaac. There's so much we need to talk about."

He opens his mouth, and for a heartbeat, I fear he'll dismiss me, but then he nods slowly, his brows furrowing in determination. "Okay. We'll figure it out together."

But even as I say those words, I can feel the weight of the Naiad's curse hanging over us like a storm cloud, ready to unleash its fury at any moment. I glance back at the lake, the reflection of the sky flickering across its surface, and I know that beneath it lies a truth waiting to be uncovered—a truth that might just destroy everything I hold dear.

The air is thick with tension as I struggle to make sense of the Naiad's words, the weight of them sinking into my chest like stones. Isaac is there, just a few feet away, his eyes wide with concern, but he feels miles away. I pull my thoughts together, the memories of the depths swirling in my mind like murky water. I can't let him see how close I was to being lost forever, nor can I let him know how shaken I truly am.

"Are you okay?" His voice is steady, but there's an edge to it, a thread of urgency that pulls at my heart. I can't help but admire how even in a moment like this, his concern is for me. It feels comforting and terrifying all at once.

"I'm fine," I lie, forcing a smile that I hope masks the turmoil beneath. The truth feels too fragile, too raw, and I don't want him to bear the weight of it. "I just... slipped."

His brow furrows, and I can see the skepticism flickering in his eyes. "You slipped? You were gone for ages. I thought you might have drowned or—"

"I didn't drown," I interrupt, a little more sharply than I intended. "I just had a moment. You know how it is." I try to keep my tone light, but it feels forced, like trying to wear a dress two sizes too small.

"Right. A moment," he says, crossing his arms, his expression a mix of concern and curiosity. "And what exactly did this moment entail? A leisurely chat with the lake?"

"Something like that," I reply, taking a deep breath, the taste of brine still lingering on my tongue. "It's complicated."

"Complicated seems to be our default setting lately," he murmurs, a hint of a smile tugging at his lips, as if trying to lighten the mood. But there's something darker lurking behind his playful tone, a recognition that we're tangled in something neither of us fully understands.

"Can we just... talk about something else?" I suggest, glancing back at the lake, its surface shimmering innocently under the afternoon sun. The beauty of it almost mocks me. "Maybe we could grab a hot chocolate or something? I think I could use a warm drink after all that."

Isaac studies me for a moment, searching for cracks in my facade. "Okay," he finally says, his tone shifting from concerned to slightly teasing. "But if you're hiding some sort of lake monster in your pocket, I'm going to need to know now."

I chuckle, grateful for the reprieve, even if the laughter feels hollow. "No monsters, I promise. Just me and my brilliant self."

We walk in silence for a few moments, my heart thumping in my chest with every step away from the lake. The trees arch overhead, their leaves rustling gently in the breeze, creating a symphony that feels far too serene for what's brewing inside me. I glance sideways at Isaac, the way the sunlight catches his hair, turning it into a halo of gold, and I feel a pang of longing mixed with fear. How can I let him in when I'm still grappling with the darkness myself?

"So, did the lake tell you anything useful?" he asks, breaking the silence, his tone playful but his eyes serious. "Like, do I need to start worrying about how many sacrifices I need to make to appease its wrath?"

"It was more like a life-altering revelation," I reply, trying to inject some humor into my words. "You know, the usual—how I'm tied to a curse that's been festering for generations and how my very existence is at risk."

His brows shoot up, and he stops walking, turning to face me fully. "Wait, what? You can't just drop that like it's casual dinner conversation."

I take a step back, feeling the weight of his gaze. "I didn't want to worry you," I say, my voice dropping. "But the Naiad... she said I'm bound to this curse, and it's not just my fate at stake. It involves our families, our histories. It's all tied together."

Isaac's expression shifts from confusion to concern as the reality of my words sinks in. "Okay, so what do we do? How do we break it?"

"I wish I knew," I admit, my voice trembling. "She didn't give me answers, just cryptic warnings about love and loss and shadows lurking beneath the surface."

He steps closer, the intensity of his gaze anchoring me. "Then we find answers. Together. Whatever it takes."

I nod, feeling a spark of determination ignite within me, but it's quickly overshadowed by the dread of what lies ahead. "But what if the truth is worse than we fear? What if we can't handle it?"

He reaches out, brushing my arm with his fingertips, and the warmth of his touch sends shivers down my spine. "We can handle anything, as long as we're together. Just promise me you won't shut me out again."

"I promise," I whisper, though a part of me wonders if I can keep that vow. The fear of dragging him into the storm brewing inside me is suffocating.

As we resume our walk, I try to focus on the trees surrounding us, the way the sunlight filters through the branches, casting dappled shadows on the ground. The world feels vibrant, almost alive, yet it's marred by the knowledge of the curse that looms over us like a dark cloud.

When we reach the cozy café nestled at the edge of town, the rich aroma of coffee and warm pastries envelops us, a stark contrast to the cold depths of the lake. Isaac holds the door open for me, and I step inside, momentarily lost in the warmth and chatter of the patrons. I glance around, taking in the soft lighting, the mismatched furniture that somehow feels homey, and I feel a flicker of hope that maybe, just maybe, we can carve out a moment of normalcy amid the chaos.

We find a small table near the window, sunlight spilling across the worn wooden surface. Isaac orders for us—two hot chocolates, extra whipped cream, and a slice of their famous chocolate cake. My stomach growls at the mention of cake, but my heart is heavy with the burden of secrets.

"Okay, tell me everything," he says, leaning forward as our drinks arrive, steam curling into the air. "What did the Naiad say? And don't leave out any details this time."

I take a deep breath, steeling myself for the conversation that could change everything. "She spoke of a curse, one that binds us to this lake, to our ancestors. She said it's tied to love, to the choices we make. I think..." I pause, the weight of my next words almost too much to bear. "I think it might have something to do with you."

His brow furrows, confusion flickering across his features. "Me? What do you mean?"

"I don't know, but I can feel it. The moment I came up for air, it was like something shifted. The Naiad's warning echoed in my mind. It made me wonder if our love, this connection we have, is part of something much larger than we realize."

Isaac's expression turns serious, the playful lightness fading away. "What if it is? What do we do then? Do we just walk away, pretend none of this is happening?"

I look into his eyes, searching for answers in the depths of his gaze. "I don't want to walk away. But I can't ignore what's happening either."

He nods slowly, contemplating my words. "Then we'll figure it out. Together."

As we share a piece of cake, the rich, chocolatey flavor a sweet distraction from the storm brewing in my mind, I feel a flicker of hope. Perhaps the Naiad's curse, as dark and foreboding as it seems, could also be the key to uncovering our true strength. And maybe, just maybe, facing the truth together could transform our fears into something powerful—something that could shatter the curse's hold and bring us back to the surface, free from the weight of our past.

Sitting across from Isaac, the rich taste of hot chocolate warming me from the inside, I try to shake off the weight of the Naiad's revelations. The café buzzes with life—laughter, the clinking of cups, and the comforting hiss of the espresso machine—but all I can focus on is the dark water that lingers in my thoughts. With every bite of chocolate cake, I am reminded of the Naiad's words, and a dread coils tighter around my heart.

"So, what's the plan?" Isaac asks, breaking through my spiral of thoughts. His casual tone juxtaposes sharply with the heaviness I feel. "Do we go back to the lake and throw rocks until something magical happens? I mean, I'm game if you are."

"Throwing rocks is definitely one way to make a statement," I reply, forcing a grin as I stir the remaining foam in my cup. "But I was thinking something a bit more strategic. Maybe we could... I don't know, research? Find out more about what happened with my ancestors?"

"Ah, the old-fashioned way," he says, mockingly putting on glasses and pretending to read an imaginary book. "Dare I suggest a library? Or are we talking about digging through dusty old family albums filled with embarrassing baby photos?"

"A library sounds great, but I'm more interested in the family history angle," I respond, unable to suppress a laugh. "If I'm cursed because of my ancestors, I'd like to know what they did to land us here. Plus, you can't tell me you wouldn't be intrigued to find out if there's some long-lost treasure involved."

Isaac raises an eyebrow, leaning back in his chair with a grin. "Treasure, you say? Now you have my attention. And who knows?

Maybe there's a secret map hidden in your grandmother's attic. A treasure hunt could be just the distraction we need."

His playful banter brings a warmth to my chest, momentarily pushing aside the dread that had taken residence there. "Okay, treasure hunt it is! Just promise me if we uncover any family skeletons, you won't freak out. I'm pretty sure they don't appreciate being disturbed."

"I promise, but only if you promise not to scream like a banshee when you see them," he replies, a teasing glint in his eyes.

The lightness of the moment fades as I glance outside. The sun is beginning to dip behind the trees, casting long shadows across the pavement. An uncomfortable thought seeps in—what if the curse isn't just an abstract concept? What if it's already reaching into our lives, affecting us in ways we can't yet understand?

"Hey," I say, trying to shake the unease, "do you think the curse could manifest in other ways? Like, what if something has already happened, and we just don't know it yet?"

Isaac's expression turns serious, and he leans in closer, the laughter fading from his eyes. "I suppose anything is possible. But you're not the kind to just sit back and let it happen, are you?"

"No, but it doesn't mean I won't be worried," I admit, my voice barely above a whisper. "What if it's already changing us? What if..."

Before I can finish, a loud crash reverberates through the café. Everyone turns to see a group of teenagers at a nearby table, one of them having knocked over a stack of plates, sending them clattering to the floor. The sharp noise jolts me out of my thoughts, and I feel a strange sense of foreboding settle in my gut.

"Okay, that was dramatic," Isaac quips, trying to lighten the mood again. "Should we be worried about an impromptu plate-throwing contest next?"

"No," I say, though the distraction hasn't alleviated the tension. "But it did remind me that chaos is lurking just beneath the surface.

It's like the lake; it looks calm, but you never know what's going on below."

"True," he concedes, his brow furrowing in thought. "But sometimes chaos can lead to the best adventures. Maybe we just need to embrace it, right?"

"Embrace the chaos? Sounds like a plan, but I'd prefer a bit of warning first," I reply, letting out a breath I hadn't realized I was holding. "Like a sign or a guide. Preferably something a little more tangible than a watery specter."

As if on cue, a shiver runs down my spine. I glance toward the window, and my heart drops. A figure stands at the edge of the café's patio, half-hidden by the gathering shadows. It's a woman, her hair a wild tangle of dark curls, her clothes tattered and flowing like she's just emerged from the depths of a forest. There's something almost haunting about her, an otherworldly presence that makes my skin prickle.

"Do you see her?" I whisper, my voice trembling slightly.

Isaac follows my gaze, his expression turning serious. "Yeah. Who is she?"

"I... I don't know," I manage to say, but even as the words leave my mouth, an unsettling familiarity grips me. It's as if I've seen her before, in dreams or in the depths of my memories, but I can't quite place it.

The woman steps closer, her gaze locked onto mine, piercing through the noise of the café like a beacon. For a moment, the world outside blurs into the background, and it feels as though time has stopped. There's a depth in her eyes, a swirling darkness that echoes the Naiad's warnings, and I feel an inexplicable pull toward her.

"Call it a gut feeling, but I don't think she's here for hot chocolate," Isaac mutters, his voice low and tense.

Before I can respond, the woman raises a hand, her fingers curling in a way that sends a jolt of recognition through me. It's the same gesture the Naiad made, beckoning me into the depths of the lake, the promise of truth swirling like shadows in the water.

"Lena!" the woman's voice calls, breaking through the café's ambiance like a sharp knife. It is melodic yet filled with a haunting resonance that makes the hairs on the back of my neck stand up. "Lena, it's time. You must come."

"Come where?" I manage to say, though my heart is racing, the urgency in her voice triggering a flight response.

"Lena, listen to me!" She takes another step closer, and the crowd in the café begins to murmur, the atmosphere thick with confusion and apprehension.

"Who are you?" I call out, my voice trembling as I grip the edge of the table, my knuckles white.

"I am the one who knows the truth," she replies, her eyes piercing into mine, unyielding. "You cannot escape your destiny, and the lake awaits you."

A chill races down my spine as her words wrap around me like a vice. I can feel Isaac's presence beside me, his hand moving to touch my arm, grounding me even as the shadows around the woman deepen, closing in on the edges of reality.

"Lena, don't go near her," Isaac warns, a tremor of concern in his voice.

But the woman's gaze holds me captive, and in that moment, everything shifts. I am no longer in the café. I am standing at the edge of the lake once more, the water beckoning me, whispering secrets that I am desperate to uncover. I don't know if I want to run or reach out to the woman who claims to know the truth.

"Lena!" The urgency in her voice heightens, and I feel the weight of destiny pressing down on me, a pull I can't ignore.

With a sudden burst of resolve, I stand, ready to face whatever lies ahead, but before I can take a step, the café door swings open, a gust of wind sweeping through, carrying with it the scent of rain and something else—something sweet yet foreboding. The woman's expression shifts, and in a heartbeat, I can feel the world tilting beneath my feet.

"Lena, wait!" Isaac's voice cuts through the chaos, but I am already moving, compelled by a force I cannot understand, stepping toward the woman whose secrets are intertwined with my own.

Just as my fingers brush against the cool, invisible barrier separating us, the ground trembles, and a crack splits the air. The café erupts into a frenzy of noise, the lights flickering ominously, and I realize—whatever is about to happen will change everything.

And then, as if the universe itself is holding its breath, the world around me dissolves into shadows, and I am plunged into a darkness deeper than the lake itself.

Chapter 22: The Breaking Point

The air hangs heavy around us, thick with unspoken words and bitter regret. I stand there, drenched in more than just water, my heart pounding a frantic rhythm that echoes the turmoil in my mind. Isaac's arms have released me, his gaze a storm of emotions swirling in his chestnut eyes, emotions I can't afford to decipher right now. All I know is that my voice, once a beacon of hope between us, has turned into a jagged weapon, carving deeper into the chasm that has formed since I unearthed the truth.

"Don't you get it?" I shoot back, my voice trembling with indignation, the words spilling out like the icy water that still clings to my skin. "I'm not letting the curse define me. I'm fighting against it!" My pulse races, a furious drumbeat that matches the chaos around us, the lake's surface reflecting the tumult of our hearts. Each ripple feels like an accusation, a reminder of the pact I never wanted to make but found myself ensnared in, all for the sake of a legacy I never chose.

Isaac shakes his head, the dark curls framing his face catching the last glimmers of twilight. "Fighting? This doesn't feel like a fight. It feels like surrender." The words land between us, heavy and unyielding, and I flinch as if he's physically struck me. The hurt in his voice cuts deeper than I expected, and for a moment, I see the flicker of despair in his eyes—an all-too-familiar look that has haunted me since I realized the implications of my discovery. I feel my resolve wavering, but I can't let him see it. I can't let myself crumble beneath the weight of his disappointment.

"Maybe you don't understand," I say, swallowing hard against the bitter taste of vulnerability. "This is more than just me. There are others involved, others who have suffered—who still suffer. The curse is a chain that binds us all, and I'm trying to break it." The cool air brushes against my damp skin, a stark contrast to the heat pooling in my chest, the fire of determination mingling with the chill of fear.

"And what about us?" Isaac counters, his voice rising, jagged with frustration. "What happens to us if you're too busy saving the world? I can't stand here and watch you lose yourself to this... this obsession." Each word is a stone thrown into the water, sending out ripples that clash with the unresolved tension simmering between us. I can feel the unsteady ground beneath me shifting, and it frightens me.

"I can't just stop, Isaac!" I shout, anger and desperation twisting together in my throat. "What do you want me to do? Turn my back on everything I've found? Ignore the people who need my help?" The question hangs in the air, charged with meaning, but he only stares at me, his silence more deafening than any argument.

We stand at the edge of the lake, a haunting place where our dreams once danced like fireflies in the dusk, now transformed into a battleground where every glance is laced with accusation. The moon hangs low in the sky, a watchful eye that sees everything, illuminating the shadows lurking between us. It feels impossibly vast, this space, like an ocean separating our hearts. I want to reach for him, to bridge the gap, but the fear of what I might find stops me.

He takes a step back, breaking the fragile connection we had clung to so desperately, and I feel the sting of loss wash over me like the cold lake water that clings to my skin. "You've become someone I don't recognize," he says quietly, the words wrapping around my heart like a vise. "I don't want to lose you, but you're pushing me away."

My throat tightens, and I can feel the dam within me cracking under the pressure of his words, the ache of truth rushing forth like a flood. "I'm not trying to push you away. I'm trying to save us! This—" I wave my arms wildly, gesturing to the vast lake, the world beyond it, "—this isn't just about me. I need to do this. I have to."

"Have to?" He echoes, incredulous. "Or want to? Because it feels like you're choosing the curse over us." His voice softens, and for a fleeting moment, I see the boy who once laughed with me under these stars, the one who made promises under the canopy of the universe. I want to reach out, to pull him back into my orbit, but the truth looms between us like a wall.

"I don't want to choose!" I cry, the desperation spilling from me like an open wound. "I'm scared, Isaac. I don't want this to define me, but I don't know how to fight it without losing you." My confession hangs in the air, and the weight of it pulls at my insides, a tangible fear that gnaws at the edges of my resolve.

Isaac's expression softens, a flicker of understanding shining through his anger, but it's overshadowed by the hurt that lingers in his eyes. "Then let me help you. We can face this together. But you have to let me in. You have to trust me."

A part of me longs to surrender, to lean into his strength and let him anchor me in the storm. But another part, the part that feels like a wild, untamed creature, wants to break free and claim my destiny on my own terms. The internal battle rages, and the silence stretches like an eternity, the cool night air thick with unresolved tension and longing.

I know that whatever choice I make now will reshape everything. It will carve the path we take, the future we might share or shatter. And as I stand there, caught in the crossroads of desire and duty, the moonlight dances across the lake, reflecting the chaos within me—a battle of light and shadow, love and fear, freedom and connection. I take a deep breath, ready to either fight for us or for myself.

A brittle silence settles between us, thick with unspoken truths and the scent of damp earth. The lake, once a place of dreams and secrets shared under a blanket of stars, now feels like a vast expanse of unforgiving reality, mirroring the rift that has opened between Isaac and me. I wrap my arms around myself, as if I can contain the chaos brewing within, my heart racing like a trapped bird. It's hard to believe that just hours ago, laughter and warmth had been our reality, but now, we're two islands adrift in a storm, each unwilling to navigate the tumultuous waters of the other's heart.

Isaac's expression shifts, the anger in his eyes giving way to something softer, a flicker of understanding tempered by the unmistakable hurt that shadows his features. "I get it, okay? You have this burden. But you don't have to carry it alone." The words hang in the air, imbued with a sincerity that makes my heart ache. I want to believe him, to let go of the fear that has wrapped around me like a vise, but the shadows of doubt loom larger.

"What do you know about this burden?" I retort, a touch sharper than I intended. "You're not the one who feels the weight of generations resting on your shoulders, the pull of something dark lurking just beneath the surface." My voice falters, a slight tremor betraying my resolve, and I turn away, the shimmering lake an unwelcome reminder of everything I stand to lose.

He steps closer, the warmth radiating from him an anchor in the cold night air. "Maybe not, but I know what it's like to fight against something you can't see, to feel like you're losing pieces of yourself. I won't pretend to understand your pain completely, but I do know what it's like to feel powerless."

For a moment, the tension gives way to a fragile thread of connection, and I allow myself to glance back at him, searching for the flicker of the boy who had once captured my heart so effortlessly. The moonlight dances across his skin, casting shadows that highlight the sharp lines of his jaw and the gentleness in his eyes. There's an honesty in his gaze that makes my chest tighten, and I realize how desperately I want to trust him, to let him shoulder this burden with me.

"I just... I don't want to drag you into my darkness," I confess, the words tumbling out as though they've been waiting for the right moment to break free. "What if I lose myself to this? What if it consumes me? I can't bear the thought of losing you too."

His brow furrows, and he reaches for my hand, intertwining our fingers, grounding me in a reality that feels so precarious. "You're not that easy to lose, you know? You're stronger than you think, and together, we can find a way through this." There's a warmth in his voice, a light that cuts through the uncertainty that has hung over us like a cloud.

I take a breath, allowing his words to sink in, the warmth of his touch igniting a flicker of hope in the depths of my soul. "But what if it's not enough?" I whisper, the vulnerability of the question hanging between us like a fragile thread.

"Then we'll make it enough," he replies, a fierce determination lighting up his eyes. "But you have to trust me. I won't let you fight this alone."

Before I can respond, a sudden rustle from the woods at the edge of the lake shatters the moment. My heart races again, adrenaline coursing through my veins as I turn toward the sound. Isaac stiffens beside me, and the momentary warmth between us turns to ice, our shared uncertainty palpable in the sudden chill of the night.

"Did you hear that?" I murmur, peering into the darkness, the trees looming like silent sentinels. "It's probably just an animal."

"Right," Isaac replies, a hint of tension creeping into his voice. "Or it could be something far less friendly."

The woods seem to draw closer, shadows shifting as though alive, and I can't shake the feeling that we're being watched. The curse looms larger than life in my mind, an ominous presence that seems to whisper my name from the depths of the water. "We should go back," I suggest, my voice barely above a whisper. "This place... it doesn't feel safe."

As we begin to retreat, the rustling grows louder, an unrelenting crackle that sends chills down my spine. Just as we reach the edge of the trees, a figure emerges from the shadows, and my breath catches in my throat. It's a girl, her hair a wild halo around her face, eyes wide with fear and urgency.

"Help! You have to help me!" she cries, her voice high and frantic, echoing across the stillness of the lake.

"What's wrong?" I ask, instinctively stepping forward, my heart pounding in rhythm with her panic.

"They're coming!" she gasps, her words tumbling out in a rush. "They're looking for me. You have to hide me!"

Isaac and I exchange a glance, confusion mingling with concern. "Who's coming?" he asks, his voice steady despite the tension crackling around us.

"The ones who are cursed!" The girl looks over her shoulder, eyes darting as though she expects to see dark figures emerging from the trees at any moment. "They want to take me back. I can't go back!"

My heart races, the weight of her words sinking in like a stone. "Cursed?" I echo, glancing at Isaac, whose brow is furrowed in thought.

"Yes! I don't know how long I can keep running. Please, you have to help me!" The girl's desperation resonates in my bones, a chilling reminder of my own struggle against the unseen forces that threaten to consume us all.

"Okay, okay," I say, my mind racing as I try to piece together the sudden twist of fate that has landed this girl in our midst. "We'll help you. But you need to tell us everything you know."

The night swells with uncertainty, the air thick with a sense of foreboding as we draw closer to the depths of a mystery far darker than I had ever imagined. In that moment, I realize that this isn't just about my fight against the curse anymore. It's about so much more—about connection, survival, and the unraveling of secrets that could change everything.

The girl stands before us, a tempest of fear and urgency, her wild hair framing her face like a crown of chaos. There's an unmistakable desperation in her eyes, a rawness that stirs something deep within me, but I can't shake the nagging question: who is she, and what does she know about the curse that seems to twist the very air around us?

"Okay," I say, stepping closer, my voice firm yet gentle. "Breathe. We're here to help you. Just tell us everything." I can feel Isaac's presence beside me, his quiet strength radiating reassurance as he assesses the situation, his eyes scanning the shadows for any sign of danger.

The girl nods, her breaths coming in quick gasps. "My name is Clara. I've been running from them for days—no, weeks. They think I can help them break the curse, but I won't go back. I can't!" Her voice rises, frantic. "They'll make me one of them."

"Who are 'they'?" Isaac asks, stepping forward, his tone serious yet inviting. "What curse are you talking about?"

Clara's gaze darts back toward the woods, her body trembling as if she can feel the threat closing in. "The cursed ones," she whispers, as if saying the words too loudly would summon them from the shadows. "They were once like us, but the curse twisted them into something... something monstrous. They want to drag me into their world, to use me as a pawn."

My heart races at her words. A sense of dread washes over me, mingling with a flicker of curiosity. "What do you mean by 'twisted'? How does this curse work?" I ask, desperate for answers that could untangle the web of fear enveloping us.

Clara's eyes widen, and she takes a step closer, her voice dropping to a conspiratorial whisper. "It's not just a spell. It's a darkness that seeps into your soul. They believe I have the key to reverse it, but the truth is, I don't know anything. I just want to be free."

Isaac glances at me, concern etched across his features. "And what makes you think they'll come for you? Are they here now?"

"I can feel them," Clara breathes, her voice trembling. "They're drawn to me, and I don't know why. I just know I'm running out of time."

As if summoned by her words, a low growl echoes from the depths of the trees, a sound that chills my blood. Clara gasps, her face paling as she stumbles back. "They're close! We need to hide!"

Instinct kicks in, and I grab her arm, pulling her back toward the shoreline. "This way! We can't stay here." Isaac is already scanning the area, his protective instincts kicking in as he looks for a place to conceal us.

"Over there!" he points toward a cluster of large rocks and dense underbrush at the edge of the lake. We move quickly, adrenaline coursing through our veins, the pounding of my heart drowning out the rustling of the leaves behind us.

As we scramble behind the rocks, the growling intensifies, the sound echoing like a thunderstorm rolling in from the horizon. "What are they?" I ask, keeping my voice low as we huddle together, our breaths mingling in the cold night air.

"I don't know," Clara whispers, her eyes wide with terror. "But they're not human anymore. They've lost themselves to the curse, and they'll stop at nothing to reclaim what they think is theirs."

The shadows lengthen around us, and I can feel Isaac's warmth next to me, his presence a calming balm amid the rising panic. "We need a plan," he says, his voice steady. "We can't just hide here forever. If they want Clara, we can't let them have her."

"But how do we fight something like that?" I murmur, a sense of hopelessness creeping in. "What can we do against a curse?"

"Maybe we can turn the tide," Isaac suggests, his mind working rapidly. "Clara, you said you didn't know anything about how to reverse the curse. What if you do have some piece of information that could help us? Something they don't want you to share?"

Clara shakes her head, her fear palpable. "I don't know anything! I'm just a girl caught in the middle of something I didn't ask for."

The growling sounds closer now, the underbrush rustling as if something is pushing through, searching for us. My breath quickens, and I feel the weight of panic pressing down on my chest. "Clara, think!" I urge. "What about the lake? Does it have any connection to the curse? Or to you?"

Her eyes flicker, a moment of realization sparking within the depths of her panic. "The lake," she breathes. "I heard them talking about it... about a ritual that needs to be performed during the full moon to harness its power. They believe it can amplify the curse, make it stronger."

Isaac and I exchange a look, the implications of her words settling in the air between us like a heavy fog. "If they're trying to harness the lake's power, we can't let them complete that ritual," Isaac says, a determined edge creeping into his voice. "But how do we stop it?"

Before Clara can respond, the growling crescendos into a series of guttural snarls, and my heart plummets as dark figures emerge from the treeline, their forms warped and twisted, eyes glowing like embers in the night.

"Hide!" I hiss, pushing Clara back against the rocks, my heart racing as I scan the area for anything we can use. Panic rises, a tight knot in my throat as the cursed ones step into the moonlight, revealing gaunt faces and elongated limbs, their movements jerky and unnatural.

"We can't let them find us," I whisper, fear clenching my stomach. But as they draw closer, their snarls growing more menacing, I realize we may not have the luxury of hiding much longer.

"Don't let them take me!" Clara cries, her voice cracking with terror.

The lead figure pauses, tilting its head as if sensing our presence, and I hold my breath, heart pounding in my chest like a war drum. Just when it seems like we might have a moment to escape, a sudden flash of movement catches my eye—another figure slips through the trees, tall and cloaked in darkness. It strides with an authority that demands attention, and I can't help but wonder if this new presence is friend or foe.

"What is that?" I whisper, feeling a chill creep down my spine. The new figure raises its hand, and I sense a surge of power that feels both alluring and dangerous.

Clara's eyes widen, and I grip her arm tightly. "We need to go now!"

But as I turn to pull her away, a loud growl erupts from the lead cursed figure, and it lunges toward us, its elongated claws reaching out as if to grasp the very air around us. I shove Clara behind me, adrenaline surging as I prepare to confront the threat, only to find the cloaked figure stepping forward with unexpected speed, intercepting the creature in a blur of motion.

"Run!" the cloaked figure commands, its voice deep and resonant, sending chills down my spine. "I'll hold them off!"

My heart races, a fierce desire to protect Clara battling with the instinct to flee. "No! We can't just leave you!" I shout, panic flaring within me.

"Go!" The figure's voice booms, and with a sudden sweep of its arm, it unleashes a burst of energy that lights up the night, illuminating the shadows like a storm breaking at dawn.

In that brief moment of blinding light, I see the horrors we're up against, and I know we don't have a choice. I pull Clara with me, and we take off running, the sound of chaos erupting behind us as the clash of power echoes through the night.

As we race toward the safety of the trees, a final thought echoes in my mind, the realization that this battle is far from over. We are caught in a web of ancient curses and dark forces that threaten to unravel everything we know. And as the growls fade into the distance, a new question arises—who was that figure? And what price will we have to pay to uncover the truth?

Chapter 23: Shadows in the Fog

The mist envelops us like a living thing, curling around our legs and whispering secrets only it can understand. With each step, the world beyond seems to evaporate, leaving us in a dreamlike state where familiarity melts into the uncanny. I can barely make out the silhouettes of the trees lining the path; their gnarled branches stretch toward the sky like desperate fingers, yearning for a light that never breaks through the heavy blanket of fog. The air is thick with moisture, clinging to my skin and filling my lungs with the scent of wet earth and decay, a reminder of the darkness lurking just beyond the edge of my perception.

Isaac's hand finds mine, his grip firm yet gentle. There's an electric charge between us, a connection that feels both exhilarating and terrifying. I glance at him, his features softened by the haze, and I wonder how we ended up here, bound together by secrets and fears that threaten to tear us apart. His eyes—usually so bright and mischievous—hold a shadow of uncertainty, a flicker of doubt that mirrors my own. The Naiad's song echoes in the distance, haunting and beautiful, a siren call that wraps around us, pulling at the edges of my mind.

"I hate this fog," I mutter, trying to inject some levity into the suffocating atmosphere. "It feels like we're in one of those cheesy horror movies where everyone gets picked off one by one."

Isaac chuckles, though the sound is strained, as if he's forcing it through clenched teeth. "As long as I don't end up as the token boyfriend who gets eaten first, I think I can survive a little mist."

I roll my eyes, grateful for his attempt at humor. "Don't worry, I've got a knife, and I'm not afraid to use it." I pat the small blade tucked into my boot, a reassurance in a world gone awry.

As we continue down the path, the trees loom larger, their trunks thick and imposing, shadows creeping in to swallow the light. A flicker catches my eye, a movement just beyond the trees, and my heart skips. "Did you see that?" I whisper, my voice barely breaking the silence.

"What?" Isaac's tone shifts, the playfulness gone, replaced by alertness.

"That—there was something moving. Just over there." I point into the depths of the fog, but it swallows my words, erasing them before they can take root in his mind.

"I don't see anything," he replies, his voice steady, but I can hear the tremor beneath it. "Just keep moving. We're almost to the lake."

I nod, but my pulse races, and I feel the weight of unseen eyes upon us. We quicken our pace, the soft thud of our footsteps muffled by the fog. With each step, the haunting melody rises, wrapping around us, a velvet noose tightening with every note. It's beautiful, yes, but it carries a weight of sorrow that tugs at my heart. Memories of laughter and warmth clash violently with the cold dread creeping into my bones.

When we finally reach the lake, the scene is both breathtaking and terrifying. The water lies still, a mirror reflecting the ghostly silhouettes of the trees, the fog swirling above like a living shroud. It feels wrong, this serenity, a deceptive calm that belies the chaos swirling beneath the surface. I peer into the depths, searching for the source of the song, but the water holds its secrets close, teasing me with glimmers of light that dance just out of reach.

Isaac steps closer, his breath catching as he stares at the lake. "It's like it's calling to us," he murmurs, his voice barely above a whisper.

"Or warning us," I reply, shivering involuntarily. The fog thickens, wrapping around us tighter, a cocoon that feels more like a trap.

Suddenly, a figure emerges from the mist, ethereal and haunting. She glides across the surface of the water, her hair flowing like liquid silver, her eyes reflecting the moonlight with an otherworldly glow.

The Naiad. I recognize her from the tales woven into the fabric of our town, stories passed down like heirlooms, each recounting her beauty and her curse.

"Do you see her?" I breathe, a mix of awe and terror swelling within me.

Isaac doesn't respond, his gaze fixed on the apparition. The song intensifies, wrapping around us, pulling at our hearts like a gentle tide. I can feel the weight of the world shifting, the air thickening with magic and despair.

"Stay back," I warn, instinctively stepping in front of Isaac. "She's not here to help us."

But he takes a step forward, his curiosity igniting a spark of reckless bravery. "She's beautiful," he whispers, captivated.

"Beauty can be dangerous," I say, my voice sharp with urgency. "We don't know what she wants."

The Naiad smiles, a smile that holds both invitation and danger, her eyes glimmering with secrets. "Come to me," she sings, her voice weaving through the fog like a silk thread, delicate yet strong. "I can show you what lies beneath the surface."

Isaac's expression falters, a flicker of conflict crossing his face. I grip his arm, desperate to pull him back, to remind him of the stories we heard as children—the cautionary tales that warned of being lured by a song too sweet to resist. The fog thickens around us, and I can feel the darkness inching closer, the shadows in the corners of my vision whispering promises that should never be kept.

"Isaac, please," I plead, my heart racing as the fog seems to pulse with the rhythm of the Naiad's song. "We need to leave. Now."

Isaac hesitates, torn between the enchanting figure gliding across the water and the tugging instincts urging him to retreat. The Naiad's voice drips like honey, each note stirring something deep within him, something I can't quite fathom but fear nonetheless. "Look at her," he murmurs, and in that moment, I sense the weight of his fascination battling against the heavy tide of danger.

"Yeah, and what's looking at us?" I shoot back, my heart pounding in my chest like a trapped bird. "She's beautiful, sure, but beauty isn't everything. It can be a mask, a lure."

"Not every beautiful thing is dangerous," he counters, his voice strained, caught in the delicate balance of awe and caution.

"True, but this isn't a bouquet of flowers, Isaac. This is a siren," I say, my eyes never leaving the Naiad. "And we're not sailors. We're just... us."

The fog swirls, heavy with unspoken threats, wrapping around us like a lover's embrace turned sinister. The Naiad steps forward, her silhouette shimmering with ethereal light, her eyes locking onto mine with an intensity that makes my stomach twist. "You are drawn to the lake, aren't you?" she calls, her voice a soothing balm that cuts through the chilling air. "I can show you its depths, the truths hidden beneath the surface. You seek answers, do you not?"

"Answers?" I echo, feeling the hair on my arms rise as if the very air crackles with energy. "You mean the kind that leads to drowning?"

Her laughter dances across the water, light and airy yet laced with an undercurrent of sorrow. "To drown is not to perish but to be reborn. Think of the possibilities! Imagine what lies beneath the weight of your fears."

Isaac steps closer, captivated, and I feel a surge of panic. "Isaac, don't—"

But it's too late. He's entranced, the pull of the Naiad's voice rendering him motionless, his eyes glazed over as if a spell had wrapped around him, binding him to this moment. I reach out, grabbing his arm, trying to pull him back into the safety of our reality. "We can't trust her! Remember the stories?"

He blinks, as if shaking off a dream, his brow furrowing. "I know, but... can't you feel it? There's something here, something calling to us."

"Or to you," I retort, my frustration bubbling to the surface. "Look at her! She's not some gentle spirit; she's a predator in disguise."

The Naiad's gaze sharpens, her smile faltering for just a moment. "You fear me, yet I am here to help. To reveal what has been hidden from you."

"Help? Or hinder?" I challenge, my voice gaining strength even as my heart races. "You're offering something you can't possibly give. We didn't come here to be lured by a song. We came to understand what's happening to our town, to stop whatever darkness is creeping in."

"Then you must trust me," she replies, her voice shifting from honey to something more seductive, more beguiling. "The lake has secrets that only I can unveil."

I grit my teeth, the weight of her words pressing down like a heavy stone. I know this is a trap, a seductive dance meant to ensnare. "And what would those secrets cost us?"

"Everything." The word hangs in the air, heavy with implication, sending a chill through me that goes deeper than the cold fog.

I glance at Isaac, searching for a sign of who he is beneath the spell of her allure. "Don't you see? We can't play her game."

His brow knits together, confusion clouding his features. "I... I want to understand. We can't turn our backs on the truth."

"Truth?" I scoff, anger rising like bile. "What truth is worth risking your life for? This isn't just curiosity; it's madness! Look at the fog—it's alive. It's warning us!"

The Naiad tilts her head, a glimmer of amusement in her eyes. "So passionate, so protective. But what if the truth is the very thing that saves you both?"

"I'd rather take my chances outside this fog than be devoured by it," I declare, pulling Isaac closer, grounding him. "We're leaving. Now."

He hesitates, the internal struggle clear in his eyes. The Naiad's song grows louder, each note wrapping around him like a silken thread, tempting and entrancing. "Why are you fighting this, Sam?" he asks, his voice strained. "You're scared of what you don't understand."

"I'm scared of what I do understand," I reply fiercely, my heart pounding as I tug him back. "This fog, this lake—it's a curse. And curses don't grant wishes. They take everything."

Isaac's gaze darts between the Naiad and me, confusion swirling like the mist around us. "But she—"

"No," I interrupt, my voice rising, the urgency spilling out of me like a tidal wave. "You're better than this! You're stronger than a fairy tale!"

The Naiad's expression shifts, annoyance sparking in her eyes. "You will regret this refusal," she warns, her voice turning cold. "You are turning away from destiny."

"Destiny?" I scoff, taking a step back as the fog closes in, creeping toward us like the fingers of the night. "Destiny is what you make it, and I refuse to let it be dictated by an ancient spirit."

The fog thickens, swirling violently, and I can sense the Naiad's anger rippling through the air. "You think you can escape?" she hisses, her beauty fading into something more sinister, her voice laced with venom. "You have no idea what lies in wait for you."

With that, the fog begins to rise, swirling into a whirlwind around us. Panic surges through me as I tighten my grip on Isaac, trying to shield him from the chaos. "Run!" I shout, urgency fueling my voice as I turn to face the path behind us.

But as we turn, I realize the way we came is shrouded in a thick veil of white, the landscape morphing into an unfamiliar maze.

"What the hell?" I exclaim, disorientation clawing at me as the fog shifts, swallowing the path, and a realization dawns—this isn't just fog; it's a barrier.

"Sam!" Isaac's voice cuts through the haze, panic threading through his words. "What do we do?"

My heart races as I take a step back, desperation creeping in. "We find another way! We can't let her keep us here."

As I scan the edges of the lake, the trees loom taller, their gnarled branches reaching out as if they're alive. Shadows flicker just beyond my vision, shapes shifting and coiling, and I know we're running out of time. "This way!" I shout, pointing toward a sliver of darker space just beyond the nearest cluster of trees. "We'll go around!"

Isaac nods, determination flickering in his eyes as we break into a sprint, the fog clawing at our backs. Each step feels like we're racing against a tide, the Naiad's laughter echoing in our ears, a haunting melody that taunts our escape. The world around us distorts, branches twisting like fingers grasping at the air, and I can't shake the feeling that something is watching, waiting, just beyond our reach.

"Stay close!" I shout over the din, my breath quickening as we push through the thick mist. I can feel Isaac's warmth beside me, his presence a beacon in the ever-deepening gloom. We weave between trees, adrenaline propelling us forward, and as we run, the Naiad's voice echoes like a distant bell, warning us of the danger we can't see.

The forest closes in around us, branches clawing at the air like desperate hands as we race forward. Each step feels heavy, as though the very ground beneath us is reluctant to let go. The fog churns and shifts, wrapping around our ankles, pulling us back with every ounce of its insidious strength. Behind us, the Naiad's laughter rings out, a melody that sends shivers down my spine. It's not just a sound; it's a promise of danger, a reminder that we're not alone in this wretched place.

"Keep moving!" I shout to Isaac, who stumbles slightly as he keeps pace with me. His eyes dart around, searching for any sign of an escape. "We can't let her trap us."

"I can't believe this is happening," he mutters, breathless. "I thought we were coming here for answers, not... this!"

"Yeah, well, apparently the answers come with a side of chaos." I push through the thick underbrush, the foliage pulling at my clothes as if trying to detain me, to keep me here forever. "Just remember: we're in control here. Not her."

The fog thickens, swirling like a tempest, distorting the world around us. I squint, trying to catch a glimpse of the path, but it feels like it's disappearing before my eyes. "There has to be a way out," I mumble, panic bubbling beneath my determination. "If we can just reach the edge of the woods..."

Isaac gasps suddenly, causing me to turn. "Look!" He points toward a flicker of light through the mist, a warm glow that seems impossibly inviting amidst the darkness. "What if that's a way out?"

My heart races, hope igniting within me. "Let's go!" We sprint toward the light, each footfall a desperate plea for safety. The closer we get, the more the fog seems to cling to us, almost as if it's trying to suffocate our escape. The light dances tantalizingly ahead, flickering like a distant star, urging us on.

As we break through the last line of trees, I squint against the brightness, my breath catching in my throat. We stumble into a clearing, and before us lies an ancient stone archway, half-covered in moss and vines. The light emanates from within the arch, bathing the area in a golden glow that cuts through the fog like a knife.

"Is this...?" Isaac begins, but I can already sense the gravity of what we've found.

"A gateway?" I finish, my voice barely above a whisper. The air hums with energy, a vibration that resonates deep within my bones. I step closer, heart pounding as I examine the arch. The stones are etched with symbols, intricate and mesmerizing, each one telling a story I can't quite grasp. "This is incredible."

"Do you think it leads to safety?" Isaac asks, his eyes wide, reflecting the glow.

"Or to more trouble," I reply, my instincts screaming at me to be cautious. "We can't just walk through without knowing what's on the other side."

The light pulses, beckoning, and I can feel the magnetic pull of the unknown drawing me closer. But as I step forward, a shadow slips from the periphery of my vision, dark and unsettling. I whirl around just in time to see the Naiad emerging from the fog, her expression shifting from enchanting to something far more menacing.

"You cannot leave," she says, her voice laced with an unsettling calmness that sends chills down my spine. "You belong to the lake now. You've come too far to turn back."

I feel Isaac's presence beside me, his breath hitching as he processes the situation. "What do you mean we belong to the lake?" he asks, incredulous. "We don't belong anywhere except back home!"

"Home?" The Naiad laughs, a sound devoid of warmth, echoing through the clearing. "You think you can escape the destiny that awaits you? This place has marked you. The lake has chosen you."

"Chosen us for what?" I demand, my voice rising. "To become one of your victims? We won't be part of your twisted game!"

The fog roils, swirling violently, and I feel the air shift, charged with a new, foreboding energy. Shadows dart through the trees, shapes more tangible now, more sinister. I can see them coalescing, figures cloaked in mist and darkness, drawn to the sound of our defiance.

Isaac tenses beside me, his hand gripping mine tightly. "Sam, we need to go," he urges, fear lacing his tone. "Now."

But the Naiad steps forward, her gaze piercing. "You cannot run from what is already within you." Her voice carries an otherworldly resonance, each word dripping with a hypnotic allure. "The lake's power flows through your veins. You are connected to its magic, its darkness. Embrace it."

"Embrace it?" I scoff, unwilling to yield to her manipulations. "Why would I want to be a pawn in your game?"

"Because you are already a part of it," she replies, her smile a serpent's coil, both charming and deadly. "Your fears, your desires—they are entwined with the lake's fate. You cannot deny what you truly are."

"What are we?" Isaac asks, uncertainty flickering across his face.

"Potential," she answers, and the word hangs in the air, weighty and foreboding. "You can wield this power. Together, you can become more than mere mortals. You can reshape the very fabric of this world."

"Yeah, right," I mutter, stepping back as I pull Isaac with me. "I'd rather be a mere mortal than a puppet on your strings."

"Sam, wait!" Isaac says, but my instincts scream for me to retreat. I can't allow myself to be lured into her web, to let her words wrap around me like chains.

But as we back away, the shadows surge forward, coiling around us like tendrils of smoke, constricting and tightening. "You will see," the Naiad says, her voice echoing with an unsettling finality. "You will all see."

Suddenly, the archway flares with light, illuminating the clearing in a blinding glow. The shadows writhe, pushing against the radiance, but I can feel the weight of their malevolence pressing in on all sides. My heart races as the archway beckons, a portal to something beyond, a chance for escape—or a deeper entrapment.

"Isaac, we have to choose now!" I shout, the panic threading through my voice. "We can either run into the light or face whatever horror she's unleashing!"

Just then, a scream erupts from the depths of the fog, piercing through the tension, chilling my blood. "Run!" I cry, adrenaline surging as I drag Isaac toward the archway, desperate for safety, desperate for freedom. But as we reach the threshold, the ground beneath us trembles, and the shadows lurch forward, hungry and relentless.

"Sam!" Isaac's voice rises above the chaos, full of fear and determination. "What do we do?"

But before I can answer, the shadows engulf us, swirling around like a storm, the light from the archway flickering as the Naiad's laughter dances in the air—a haunting reminder that we are far from safe.

Chapter 24: The Bound Souls

The air around me crackles with an energy I can't quite name, an electric pulse that tugs at my consciousness as I stand on the edge of the lake, the water a murky mirror reflecting the chaos of the sky above. Dark clouds swirl overhead, casting shadows that dance like specters on the surface, each ripple and wave whispering secrets of sorrow and longing. The voices are there again, rising like a swell from the depths, each one a thread pulling me deeper into their tragic tale. I squeeze Isaac's hand tighter, feeling the warmth of his skin juxtaposed against the chill of the wind that bites at my cheeks.

"I can't hear them like you do," he says, his voice a soothing balm amidst the turmoil, "but I can see it in your eyes. You're fighting something. Let me in, Rachel. Let me help you."

His presence is a lifeline, a flicker of hope amidst the suffocating dread that clings to my heart. Yet, I know the path laid before me is mine to tread, a journey entwined with sacrifice and shadows. It's an unspeakable burden, and the thought of dragging him down with me makes my chest tighten with despair. I turn my gaze back to the lake, its surface now churning as if in response to my internal conflict.

"Isaac, this isn't just about us. It's about the souls trapped here," I whisper, my voice trembling. "They've been forgotten, their cries swallowed by the very darkness we're trying to keep at bay. If I don't do this, they'll never be free. And neither will we."

His brow furrows, the familiar line forming between his eyes, a sign that he's grappling with the enormity of what I'm proposing. "I understand, but what if—"

"No," I interject, firming my resolve despite the flutter of doubt in my chest. "I won't let fear dictate our choices. This pact—the first one—was forged out of desperation, but we can change its course. We can break the chains of this darkness."

The wind whips around us, tugging at my hair as if urging me to step closer to the edge, to embrace the abyss. It feels like a call, a summons from the very souls that haunt this lake, their agony resonating within me, echoing through the corridors of time. I shut my eyes, allowing their pain to wash over me like a tide, a bittersweet reminder of my purpose. The taste of salt lingers on my lips, the kind that can only come from tears shed long ago.

I can almost see them—the figures trapped beneath the surface, their faces twisted in anguish, eyes wide with a pleading I can't ignore. Each spirit represents a story left unfinished, a life cut short by the darkness that lurks at the fringes of our world. And in that moment, I realize that I am not just Rachel anymore; I am a vessel for their stories, a bridge between the past and the present.

"Okay," Isaac breathes, a reluctant acceptance woven into his words. "If you're going to do this, I'll be right here with you. We face it together."

His unwavering support is my anchor as I step closer to the water, the edge now slick with algae and the remnants of lost hopes. I can feel the energy pulsing beneath the surface, the heartbeat of a lake filled with sorrow and shadows. As I look into the depths, I see more than darkness; I see flickers of light, small and stubborn, fighting to break free. It ignites a fire within me, a determination that burns brighter than my fears.

"Listen to me," I call out, my voice steady despite the tremors in my heart. "If you can hear me, I want to help. I'm here to break the chains binding you to this place. Let me be the light in your darkness."

The waters roil in response, a whirlpool of emotions swirling around my feet, pulling at me as if to say, "Will you risk everything for us?" A ripple of energy dances up my spine, and I close my eyes, reaching deep within myself, searching for the strength that has lain dormant for so long. I draw in a deep breath, summoning the memories of the first pact, the desperation that birthed it.

In my mind's eye, I see the figures from the past—the ancient guardians standing on the shores of this very lake, their hands raised in supplication as they made their fateful bargain. I can feel their fear, their hope, mingling with the present. They were seeking salvation, not knowing they were planting the seeds of their own doom. My heart races, a thunderous drum against the silence of the approaching storm.

"Together," I whisper to Isaac, knowing we're teetering on the precipice of something monumental. "We can rewrite this story."

As I speak, I feel a surge of power gathering around us, the air thick with magic and intention. The voices rise in a crescendo, weaving together their desperate pleas into a singular harmony that resonates deep within my bones. I can feel Isaac's presence beside me, his heartbeat syncing with my own, creating a rhythm that defies the chaos surrounding us.

"On three," I say, my voice steady, echoing the resolve blooming within me. "One... two... three!"

And as we plunge into the water, the darkness envelops us, a chilling embrace that stirs something primal within my soul. I have no idea what lies ahead, but as I grip Isaac's hand tightly, I know that whatever comes next, we will face it together. The lake's depths beckon, and with them, the promise of release—both for the souls ensnared in its grasp and for us, bound by a love that transcends even the fiercest shadows.

As we plunged into the depths, the water engulfed us in a cold embrace that stole the breath from my lungs. Panic threatened to rise, but the sensation was quickly replaced by an intoxicating rush of clarity. I could feel the weight of the lake around me, an ancient force pulsing in tandem with the chaotic symphony of voices swirling in my mind. Each whisper, each cry, melded into a singular purpose, calling me to the very heart of the darkness.

I opened my eyes, the murky water distorting my view, but I could still make out Isaac beside me, his determination radiating like a beacon. He moved effortlessly, an anchor amidst the chaos, his focus unwavering. "Rachel, focus!" he shouted, his voice muffled by the water but crystal clear in my mind. "What do we need to do?"

It was a question that resonated deeply, unlocking memories I hadn't known I possessed. I could see them now, the spectral figures of those lost souls, flitting just beyond reach, their forms like mist, curling and weaving in the darkness. They hovered around us, drawn to the heat of our living bodies, but still held captive by the pact forged long ago. I felt their longing, their desperate hope for release, and a chill ran through me.

"We have to bind the old pact," I realized, the words spilling from my lips as understanding washed over me like a wave. "But to do that, we need to confront the guardians—the spirits that hold the contract."

With each breath, I felt my resolve deepen. There was a legend in town about the guardians, protectors of the lake who had once walked among the living. Their forms were said to be ethereal, glowing with an inner light, but bound to the lake by the pact that had saved the town generations ago. It was a bittersweet salvation, one that had condemned them to this endless twilight.

"Then let's find them," Isaac said, his eyes bright with determination. "Together."

I nodded, propelled by his unwavering spirit. We moved deeper, the water darkening around us, yet the voices grew louder, more insistent, as if they sensed our purpose. The chill of the lake was no longer just cold; it was an embrace of sorrow, each degree a reminder of the lives caught in this limbo. I felt the shadows swirling around us, the past and present merging, and with every heartbeat, the urgency grew stronger.

Suddenly, a flicker of light caught my eye, illuminating the water like fireflies in the night. I darted toward it, Isaac following closely behind. As we approached, the glow intensified, revealing a shimmering figure draped in flowing robes, the essence of the guardians materializing before us in haunting beauty. Their features were soft yet resolute, eyes filled with the weight of untold stories and endless longing.

"Who dares disturb our rest?" the lead guardian intoned, voice echoing like the tolling of a bell. The words wrapped around me, soothing yet filled with an undercurrent of danger. "The pact is sacred; your presence here is a breach."

I felt the pull of fear, but the desire to help the trapped souls surged within me. "We seek to break the chains that bind you," I called out, my voice steady despite the circumstances. "You sacrificed everything for the town, but it's time to find peace. We're here to set you free."

The guardians exchanged glances, a flicker of uncertainty rippling through their ethereal forms. "Free?" one whispered, the word laced with a desperate hope that tugged at my heart. "But what of the darkness? If we are released, it will return."

"Not if we take the light with us," Isaac interjected, his voice firm and resolute. "We can create a new pact, one that protects the town without binding your souls to this lake. Let us help you."

The lead guardian stepped forward, and I could see the layers of pain etched into their translucent skin. "Such an act requires sacrifice. You must be willing to give up something of great value—your bond, your light."

The enormity of the choice loomed like a dark cloud, pressing down on my chest. I glanced at Isaac, our fingers still intertwined, grounding me in the uncertainty swirling around us. "What would we lose?" I asked, my voice barely above a whisper, the weight of the question settling like a stone in my stomach.

"Your connection to each other," the guardian said, their eyes glimmering with the knowledge of countless choices made before us. "To save us, you would have to sever the bond that brought you here."

I swallowed hard, the words tasting bitter on my tongue. Could I truly risk our love for the sake of souls I had never known? But then the voices rose again, a chorus of lament echoing in my mind, reminding me of their pain, their suffering. It was a tapestry of lives woven with sorrow, and I could feel their yearning for release, each thread binding me tighter to my decision.

"I'm not afraid," I said, each word strengthening my resolve. "If it means freeing you, then so be it. Isaac, I—"

"Don't say it," he interrupted, his voice thick with emotion. "We'll find another way."

But the truth was there, unspoken yet palpable between us, a bittersweet acceptance of the potential sacrifice we both understood. I searched his gaze, and in that moment, I saw the flicker of understanding. The bond we shared was profound, but so was the pain of the souls before us.

"Together," I said softly, letting the words hang in the water between us like a promise, "we can change the course of this darkness."

As the guardians stepped closer, their forms shimmering with an intensity that threatened to overwhelm me, I felt the weight of the decision settle over us. The air thickened, heavy with anticipation, and the voices merged into a singular note of hope, a bridge connecting our worlds.

"Then let it be so," the lead guardian said, their voice echoing through the depths. "We will bind the new pact. But know this:

every light has its shadow, and the darkness will always seek a way back. Are you willing to face it?"

The question hung in the water, a challenge wrapped in promise, and with our hearts racing, we nodded as one. A spark ignited between us, a luminous bond of intention that would change everything. We were ready to confront the darkness, together—bound by love, but unafraid of the shadows looming ahead.

As the guardians' ethereal forms shimmered around us, the air crackled with the gravity of our impending choice. Their expressions reflected centuries of longing, a hope tinged with the melancholy of past betrayals and lost opportunities. I felt the urgency surge within me, like a tide rushing to meet the shore. "We'll do it," I stated firmly, glancing at Isaac, whose eyes burned with determination. "We'll make the new pact, and we'll face whatever comes together."

The lead guardian inclined their head, a gesture that felt heavy with consequence. "Understand this, brave souls: the binding of a new pact requires not only your promise but the energy of your spirits. We will be freed, yes, but in doing so, the darkness that feeds on despair will awaken. It will seek to reclaim what it has lost."

"Sounds like an overdramatic villain in a bad movie," Isaac quipped, attempting to lighten the weight in the air. "What's the worst that could happen? We save some ghosts, make a few more enemies, and call it a day?"

His humor pierced through my anxiety, the warmth of his laughter wrapping around me like a blanket against the cold depths of the lake. Yet, beneath the surface, I sensed the truth of the guardians' words. The darkness was a relentless tide, always lurking, always hungry. "We're ready," I said, my voice steadier than I felt. "Let's rewrite this story."

With a nod from the guardian, a circle of luminescence formed around us, pulsing with energy as if the very essence of the lake was responding to our intent. "Then speak your oath, and let it resonate through the water, the earth, and the air," the guardian intoned, their voice reverberating like thunder in the depths. "Your words will bind us, for better or worse."

I took a deep breath, gathering the strength I felt from Isaac's hand. "I vow to break the chains that bind your souls, to free you from this torment." The words felt heavy on my tongue, laden with centuries of sorrow. "In return, I ask for your protection over our town, a shield against the darkness that seeks to return."

Isaac squeezed my hand, his voice ringing out clear and unwavering. "And I vow to stand by Rachel, to ensure that our bond is the light that guides us through the shadows." His sincerity resonated in the space between us, filling the void with hope.

The guardians moved closer, their forms merging with the light surrounding us. "With your vows, the pact is sealed. But heed this: the darkness will not yield easily. You will face trials, and the bond you cherish will be tested."

A tremor ran through the water, and I could feel the very fabric of the lake shifting. The glowing figures enveloped us, their energies intertwining with ours, creating a tapestry of light and intent. I closed my eyes, focusing on the warmth of Isaac's hand and the brightness blooming within my chest.

As the guardians began to chant, their voices layered in haunting harmony, I felt a surge of energy coursing through me. The lake trembled in response, sending ripples across its surface, a response to the merging of our spirits with theirs.

Suddenly, the waters darkened, and a chilling wave swept over us, snatching the warmth from the air. I could feel the darkness awakening, its presence pressing in like a suffocating fog. The guardians faltered, their light flickering as if caught in a fierce wind. "It comes!" one of them cried, urgency breaking through their melodic chant. "You must finish the binding!"

Instinctively, I grasped Isaac's hand tighter, the desperation fueling my resolve. "We can do this!" I shouted, the words bursting forth like a lifeline. "Together, we're stronger than this darkness!"

The guardian's voices rose higher, blending with the echoing cries of the souls beneath us. "Call upon your light!" they urged, and I felt the energy swell within me, a flickering flame in the overwhelming void.

"Light!" I called out, pouring every ounce of hope and love I felt for Isaac, the town, and the souls we sought to free into those words. "We are the light that will not be extinguished!"

The waters erupted around us, a surge of brilliant light bursting forth from our joined hands. I could feel the very essence of the lake responding, a powerful wave of energy cascading through the depths. The guardian figures solidified around us, forming a barrier of light against the encroaching darkness.

But then, in the midst of our rising hope, a sinister laugh echoed from the shadows. It reverberated through the water, chilling me to the core. "Foolish children," a voice taunted, dripping with malice. "You think you can sever the bond I have with this lake? The pact you forge will only feed my strength!"

I felt the ground shift beneath me, the water roiling as tendrils of shadow slithered closer, wrapping around my ankles like cold fingers. Panic surged in my chest, but Isaac's grip held firm. "Rachel, don't let go!" he shouted, his voice a beacon amid the encroaching dread.

"Keep calling the light!" one of the guardians urged, but their glow dimmed, flickering as if struggling against the tide of darkness. "It's feeding on your fear!"

I clenched my jaw, rallying against the suffocating grip of despair. "You are not my fear," I proclaimed, my voice rising against the tide. "You are not the master of my fate!"

With those words, I focused on the light within, summoning the warmth that ignited with every heartbeat, every breath. "We are the light!" I shouted again, feeling the truth of those words reverberate through the depths, pushing back against the shadows.

The darkness recoiled, hissing like steam against the fierce light erupting from our hands. I could feel the souls behind me stirring, their presence invigorating, each whisper a chorus of support. "Yes! Free us!" they cried, their voices intertwining with our own.

But then, from the depths, a figure began to rise, cloaked in darkness, its eyes glinting with a malicious hunger. "You think you can defy me? You are nothing without your bonds!" it roared, a whirlwind of shadows swirling around it.

Isaac's grip tightened, his resolve unwavering as he stood beside me. "We are everything!" he countered, his voice strong and defiant. The light pulsed brighter, an explosion of energy that resonated with the very fabric of the lake.

And then, just as the shadowy figure lunged toward us, the ground beneath shifted violently, sending waves crashing as reality trembled. "Rachel!" Isaac yelled, his voice swallowed by the chaos, and I felt the world begin to unravel around us.

In that moment of uncertainty, the light flared, pushing against the encroaching darkness, but the abyss was relentless. The last thing I saw before the wave consumed us was the glimmer of the guardians, their faces resolute as they prepared to confront the ancient evil rising from the depths. And then, everything went black.

Chapter 25: The Last Promise

The lake stretches before me, its surface a mirror reflecting the twilight sky, where bruised purples and fiery oranges collide in a dramatic farewell to the day. I can almost hear the water whispering secrets, ancient tales woven into its depths. Each lapping wave seems to beckon, calling me to cross the threshold into a realm where the mundane laws of the world cease to exist. With every heartbeat, I feel the weight of the promise I made, not just to Isaac but to myself—a vow to confront the shadows that have loomed over my life for far too long.

Isaac stands at the edge, a statue of conflicted emotion, his brow furrowed and lips pressed tightly together. He's beautiful in a way that makes the air around us vibrate with tension, his dark hair tousled by the evening breeze, eyes shimmering with unshed tears that could drown the very earth. "Don't do this," he pleads, his voice trembling like the last notes of a song on the wind. "Please. There has to be another way."

Each word he utters is a blade cutting through the fog of my resolve. I wish with all my heart that he were right, that there existed a path less fraught with peril, less steeped in sacrifice. But I know, deep down, that this is the only way. I've spent years being shaped by the world around me, molded by pain and sorrow, but now it's my turn to reclaim that power, to be the architect of my own destiny.

"I have to do this, Isaac," I reply, my voice steady but soft. "You know I can't live like this anymore. I won't let the darkness win." I can see his hands clench into fists at his sides, the muscles in his jaw taut with frustration. He's always been my anchor, a steady presence that grounds me in a reality where everything else feels ephemeral. But this time, I must be the one to navigate the storm.

"Then let me come with you. You don't have to face it alone." His eyes search mine, desperate and imploring. The sincerity in his gaze nearly unravels me. The thought of him standing beside me, fighting the darkness hand in hand, is tempting, but the risk is too great.

"Isaac," I whisper, stepping closer, my heart racing with the gravity of what I'm about to do. "If you come with me, you might not come back. I can't lose you." The air is thick with unsaid words, our breaths mingling, creating a fog of longing that envelops us. I can feel the electric charge between us, the way our souls seem to dance in a language only we understand. But this moment, like all others, is fleeting.

His fingers brush against my cheek, and the warmth of his touch ignites a flame within me. "You won't lose me," he insists, but his voice wavers, betraying the fear lurking beneath his bravado. "I promise I'll find you. I'll always find you." I want to believe him, but the weight of my choices presses down like an anchor, threatening to pull me into the depths of despair.

"Then wait for me," I say, summoning every ounce of courage I possess. "I'll come back, I swear it." Our lips meet in a kiss that holds the weight of our shared history—every stolen moment, every whispered secret, every promise made under starlit skies. It's a kiss that conveys everything we cannot put into words, a silent acknowledgment of the love that binds us even as I prepare to step into the unknown.

As I turn away, the air feels charged with expectation. The lake shimmers with a siren's allure, its surface rippling like a silken veil that beckons me closer. With each step I take, I can feel the energy swirling around me, a pulsating force that seems to resonate with the very core of my being. I wade into the shallows, the cool water lapping at my ankles, sending a shiver of anticipation coursing through my veins.

The moment I dive beneath the surface, the world transforms. Light fractures into a kaleidoscope of colors, illuminating the depths like a living painting. The water embraces me, wrapping around me like a cocoon, and I'm flooded with a sense of purpose that surges through my veins, invigorating and terrifying in equal measure. I push deeper, seeking the heart of the lake, where the whispers of the ancients swirl like a storm.

As I descend, memories play like shadows around me—images of laughter and tears, moments of bliss that seem so far away now. But they drive me forward, reminding me of what I stand to lose if I don't confront the darkness. The water grows colder, the light fading until all I can see is the faint glow emanating from a distant source. It's the pulse of the lake, the heartbeat of the magic that courses through its depths.

I reach out, fingers brushing against something solid—an altar of stone, etched with symbols that thrum with energy. The moment my skin touches the surface, a jolt courses through me, and I'm overwhelmed by visions of a time long past: battles fought, sacrifices made, and the legacy of those who came before me. Their strength fills me, infusing my spirit with a fire I thought I'd lost.

But with it comes a warning, a whisper that echoes in the recesses of my mind. I am not alone in this place. Something stirs in the shadows, a presence lurking just beyond the fringes of my perception, hungry and malevolent. My heart races, fear clawing at my throat, but I push it down. I have come too far to turn back now. I will face whatever waits in the dark, armed with the love I carry and the promise I made to return.

As I plunge deeper into the lake's embrace, the world above fades into a distant memory, replaced by the surreal beauty of the underwater realm. Silvery beams of light pierce through the water, dancing around me like the laughter of long-lost friends, urging me onward. The air in my lungs feels lighter, my worries dissipating like mist in the morning sun, replaced by a fierce determination that pulses through my veins.

I touch the stone altar, its surface cool and oddly textured, and the moment I make contact, a surge of energy rushes through me, a tidal wave of magic that thrums in my bones. The symbols etched into the stone pulse with an ethereal glow, each one whispering forgotten secrets. My heart races as I try to decipher the patterns, the stories they hold. It feels as if I am standing at the precipice of something monumental, the weight of the world resting on my shoulders.

Then, a shadow flickers at the edge of my vision, dark and formless, slithering through the water like a snake. My pulse quickens, a thrill of fear igniting the spark of resolve within me. I spin around, the murky depths obscuring whatever lurks just out of sight. "Show yourself!" I command, the words tumbling from my lips with more bravado than I feel. The water feels thick, like molasses, and for a moment, I wonder if the magic has indeed cloaked me in its embrace or if I am merely a trespasser in a world that does not wish to be disturbed.

Suddenly, the water ripples violently, and a figure emerges—a tall, ethereal woman draped in flowing robes that shimmer like fish scales, her hair a cascading waterfall of dark tendrils that frame a face both beautiful and haunting. "You should not have come here, child," she intones, her voice resonating like a haunting melody that reverberates through the water. "The lake protects its secrets fiercely."

"Secrets that I intend to uncover," I respond defiantly, my voice steady despite the chill of dread creeping up my spine. "I've come to confront the darkness that has plagued my life for far too long. I won't be afraid anymore."

A glimmer of something akin to amusement flickers in her deep-set eyes. "Brave words, but bravery alone will not suffice. What do you seek?" Her gaze pierces through me, as if she can see every fear I've ever harbored, every tear I've shed in silence.

"I seek the truth," I declare, determination igniting my spirit. "The truth about my past, my family, and the darkness that has haunted me." I take a step closer, feeling the water swirl around me like a living thing, urging me on. "I will not be a victim of fate."

She regards me with an expression that is hard to read—sympathy mingled with something darker, something foreboding. "The truth you seek may not be the truth you desire," she warns. "The lake is a keeper of memories, of choices made and paths taken. Are you ready to bear the weight of what you might discover?"

The question hangs in the water like a stone, heavy and laden with meaning. I think of Isaac, of the love we share and the future I've fought so hard to envision. Would the truth tear that asunder? "I am ready," I reply, my voice firmer now, even as my heart stutters in my chest. "I will bear whatever burden is required. I owe it to myself."

"Very well," she concedes, a slight nod of her head signifying her acceptance of my resolve. "But know this: the past can be a treacherous guide. Follow closely, and do not stray from the path."

With a wave of her hand, the water shimmers and twists, the lake's surface swirling as if caught in a tempest. Images emerge from the depths, swirling around us like a kaleidoscope—fragments of memories, half-formed thoughts, and dreams long buried.

I'm drawn into the current, and as I'm swept along, a new scene materializes before me. I stand in a sun-drenched glade, surrounded by towering trees that stretch toward the sky, their leaves rustling like whispers of old friends. In the center, a small gathering of people—my family—huddled close together, their faces illuminated by the golden light filtering through the branches. My heart aches at the sight, a bittersweet pang of longing for the connections I've lost.

"Mom?" I call out, though I know she can't hear me. She appears vibrant and alive, her laughter a melody I've only known in faded memories. I watch as she cradles a tiny infant in her arms, a baby that looks strikingly like me. The realization hits me like a slap; this is the moment my life pivoted into darkness.

As if sensing my presence, my mother turns, her eyes searching the shadows. "What are you hiding from me?" she asks, her voice low, filled with a knowing that sends shivers down my spine. "You must not let the darkness consume you, dear one."

"Mom!" I reach out, desperate to bridge the chasm that time and circumstance have carved between us. But as I do, the scene ripples and blurs, dissolving into the murky depths once more. The lake swirls around me, its depths unfurling like the pages of a story, revealing the chapters of my life I never understood.

Suddenly, I am thrust into another memory, one laced with shadows and heartache. I stand before an imposing figure cloaked in darkness, his eyes glinting with malice. "You think you can escape your fate?" he taunts, his voice echoing through the void. "You are bound to me, child. Your blood flows with my power."

My heart races as realization dawns. This is the specter of the past I have run from, the darkness that has taunted me through the years. "No!" I shout, pushing against the weight of the memory. "You do not define me!"

With that declaration, a rush of energy surges through me, a wave of light igniting the shadows. The figure recoils, the darkness wavering like smoke in the wind. I feel my strength swell as the lake's magic intertwines with my resolve, creating a force strong enough to confront the very essence of my fear.

"Fate is not a chain, but a tapestry," I declare, my voice echoing with newfound conviction. "And I will weave my own story." As the shadows begin to recede, I know that I am no longer just a victim of my circumstances; I am the author of my destiny, and I will not be silenced.

The darkness shrinks back as I embrace the power coursing through me, every breath igniting the magic that wraps around my spirit like an old friend. With the memory of the cloaked figure still vivid in my mind, I stand resolute, ready to confront the fragments of my past that have haunted me for so long. The lake's depths are alive with energy, swirling around me like a living tapestry of stories waiting to be unraveled.

Before I can take another step, the woman who first emerged from the shadows appears again, her features sharper now, her expression a mix of intrigue and caution. "You are bolder than I anticipated," she remarks, a hint of amusement threading through her voice. "But know that courage does not guarantee safety. The lake has its own will, and it may not take kindly to your intrusion."

"Then I'll just have to prove it wrong," I reply, my voice firm and unwavering. I can feel the strength of my convictions radiating from me, a light that even the darkest depths cannot extinguish. "I'm here to break the cycle of fear, to reclaim what is rightfully mine."

Her eyes narrow, assessing me with a scrutiny that sends a shiver down my spine. "What you seek may come at a steep price. The truth is a double-edged sword."

"Life has never come cheap," I counter, stepping forward, emboldened. "I'm prepared to face whatever it takes." Each word spills from my lips like a promise, binding me to my resolve. The woman nods slowly, a grudging respect forming in her gaze.

"Then prepare yourself," she warns, raising her hands as the water begins to swirl violently, forming a vortex of shimmering light and shadow. The currents tug at my body, pulling me deeper into the whirlpool of memories. "The lake will show you what you need to see, but it will not hold your hand."

With a fierce determination, I plunge into the maelstrom. Colors swirl around me, bright and dark, blending into an iridescent haze that seems to pulse with life. The sensation is both dizzying and exhilarating, like a rollercoaster ride through the very essence of my soul. I brace myself, knowing the revelations awaiting me might shatter the fragile semblance of peace I've fought so hard to build.

I am suddenly thrust into another scene, this time standing in a dimly lit room filled with swirling smoke and flickering shadows. A table lies before me, littered with strange artifacts—crystal balls, ancient scrolls, and a grimoire that hums with an energy that resonates in my bones.

"This is where it began," a voice murmurs, echoing through the air. I whirl around, recognizing the source: my mother, radiant yet fragile, her silhouette illuminated by a ghostly glow. "This is where we made our choices, where the lines between love and sacrifice blurred."

"Mom!" I reach for her, desperate to connect, but she is just out of reach, a shimmering mirage. "Please, tell me how to break free from this curse!"

Her expression shifts, sadness washing over her features like a tide. "The darkness you face is born of our lineage, a weight we all carry. But it is not insurmountable." She gestures to the grimoire, her voice growing stronger, laced with urgency. "You must confront the past to forge your future. Use the truth as your weapon, and do not fear the choices that lie ahead."

As her words fade, the room around me begins to shift, the walls melting away to reveal a vast expanse—a battlefield scarred by time, the air thick with the stench of smoke and ash. Figures clash in the distance, their cries echoing in a cacophony of anguish. I feel a pull toward the chaos, a compulsion to understand what transpired here, to grasp the threads of history that have woven themselves into my existence.

I race forward, the ground beneath me trembling as shadows of warriors flicker past. A flash of silver catches my eye; it's the same cloak I saw on the figure that haunted my dreams. My heart pounds as I approach, the air crackling with anticipation. "Who are you?" I shout, my voice barely cutting through the noise.

The figure turns, revealing a face twisted in malice, eyes glinting with a wicked light. "You dare to challenge what has always been?" he hisses, the shadows swirling around him like a storm. "You are merely a pawn in a game far greater than you understand."

"I'm not a pawn," I retort, defiance igniting within me. "I am the one who will break this cycle!" I summon the energy of the lake, feeling its magic surge through me like a river, coursing into my fingertips. "You will not control me!"

The figure's laughter echoes ominously, chilling my blood. "Control is but an illusion. You will discover that the chains of destiny are not so easily broken." He steps closer, and the shadows writhe around him, hungry and waiting. "Are you prepared to face the truth of your lineage? To unearth the darkness buried deep within?"

Before I can respond, he lunges forward, a shadowy arm outstretched. I brace myself, instinctively channeling the lake's energy into a shield. A wave of power erupts from me, crashing against him like a tidal wave. The force sends him staggering back, but I know this is only the beginning.

"Face me!" I cry, the lake's magic pulsating through me, guiding my actions. The battlefield begins to tremble as the spirits of those who fought before me gather, their energy merging with mine, bolstering my resolve.

But just as I think I've gained the upper hand, the air shifts, and the ground beneath me erupts, fissures cracking open like the maw of a great beast. I stagger, trying to maintain my footing, but the chaos threatens to consume me. The figure smirks, his form melting back into the shadows, taunting me as he disappears. "You cannot escape what is meant to be. The darkness will always find you."

And in that moment of uncertainty, just as the void threatens to swallow me whole, I hear Isaac's voice echoing in my mind, filled with love and unwavering faith. "You are not alone. I will find you."

With that thought igniting a spark within me, I push against the chaos, drawing strength from my connection to him. I refuse to let the shadows win. As I focus on the lake, its energy surging through me, I am ready to confront whatever waits beyond the precipice of this fractured reality.

But the ground shatters beneath me, and as I fall into the depths, the last thing I see is a shimmering reflection of the lake's surface above, my heartbeat echoing in my ears as the darkness closes in around me, an ominous promise of what is yet to come.

Chapter 26: The Rite of Silence

At the water's edge, I stand poised, the damp earth yielding slightly beneath my bare feet, a reminder of the weight I carry. The air is thick with the scent of damp earth and decaying leaves, a fragrance both intoxicating and melancholic, mingling with the cool breath of the lake. Here, the twilight casts long shadows, the sun a reluctant traveler slipping beneath the horizon, leaving behind a tapestry of deep purples and fiery oranges reflected in the water's glassy surface. I can almost taste the change in the air, a salty tang that whispers promises and warnings in equal measure.

My heart thrums with an urgency that echoes against the fading light, a wild rhythm that seems to harmonize with the gentle lapping of the waves. Each pulse reminds me why I am here, why I am about to undertake a ritual steeped in both dread and hope. I have spent years preparing for this moment, unearthing the stories of my ancestors, piecing together the fragments of their fates, unraveling the strands that bind our bloodline to this cursed lake. It has claimed too much already: laughter lost, futures forgotten, and dreams drowned in its depths. This time, I will not stand by and watch.

As I step closer, the water shimmers, revealing the surface of a different world beneath, and with it, the haunting echoes of those lost to its depths. I close my eyes, feeling the pull of the Naiad, her presence a silken thread weaving through my mind. The memories swirl around me, fragments of joy and sorrow, and I hear them—their pleas, their warnings. They tug at my heart, and I grip the small talisman around my neck, a token of my resolve, crafted from a shard of my mother's necklace, the last remnant of her life before she surrendered to the lake's call.

The chant I have memorized flows from my lips, a melody both ancient and achingly familiar. The words are steeped in longing, each syllable a step deeper into the lake's embrace. I watch as the water stirs, undulating like a living creature, a gentle beckoning. "By the blood of my kin and the whispers of the forgotten, I call upon you," I murmur, my voice trembling as it threads through the air. The wind dances around me, carrying my words to the depths, where they slip between the fingers of the Naiad.

She rises from the water like a dream coalescing into form, her skin glistening with droplets that refract the dying light into a thousand colors. She is both beautiful and terrible, her hair a cascade of dark tendrils swirling like ink in water, her eyes holding the weight of countless stories. "You tread a dangerous path, child," she warns, her voice smooth like the surface of the lake, yet laced with an undercurrent of menace. "The cost of this ritual is steep. You must be prepared to pay."

"Whatever it takes," I reply, my determination burning bright against the chill of her words. I feel the strength of my ancestors behind me, a whispering tide of courage urging me on. "I will break this cycle. No more will our family be bound to your depths." My heart pounds, a steady cadence that drowns out my doubt.

The Naiad's laughter is like the sound of breaking glass, sharp and beautiful. "You think it simple? To sever the ties of fate? The lake has its own will, and it may not be so easily swayed." She glances back at the water, and for a moment, I see shadows twisting beneath the surface—faces that haunt my dreams. I shake my head, unwilling to let fear seep into my resolve. "I am ready," I insist, even as my voice quivers.

With a flick of her wrist, the water churns, spiraling upwards in a spiraling vortex, illuminating the gathering darkness. I reach deep within myself, feeling the pulse of magic thrumming in time with my heartbeat. This is my chance, the moment when the past and present collide. I thrust my hand forward, feeling the energy swell within me, coiling like a serpent ready to strike. "I release you," I chant, my voice rising in strength. "You are free from this bondage!"

The lake responds violently, the surface erupting into a cascade of light that blinds me for a moment. As I push my will into the depths, the shadows twist and writhe, breaking apart like shards of glass, freed from their watery prison. Each face that emerges is a reminder of the lives snuffed out too soon, their sorrow mingling with my own as they drift away into the ether, unshackled from their fate.

But even as hope blooms within me, the Naiad's expression darkens. "Foolish girl," she hisses, her voice now a low growl that reverberates through the air. "You seek to undo what was meant to be. The lake will claim its due." I feel it then, a pull at the very center of my being, an ancient hunger that seeks to drag me down, to consume me in the same way it had taken my mother, my grandmother—every woman who had stood at this shore before me.

I stumble back, my resolve faltering as the weight of the lake presses in on me. "No!" I shout, the desperation spilling from my lips. "I will not be another sacrifice!" With that, I dig deep within myself, channeling the strength of all the women who came before me. I push back against the darkness, the shadows that threaten to envelop me, igniting a fierce fire in my chest. I am not merely a vessel; I am a warrior, born from the ashes of my ancestors' pain.

In that moment, I feel a shift within the very fabric of the lake, a crack that allows a sliver of light to seep through. I am not alone in this fight. Their spirits swirl around me, each one whispering encouragement, each voice bolstering my strength. The Naiad shrieks in fury, but I stand firm, the weight of my lineage grounding me. "You will not take me!" I cry, feeling the magic surge, igniting my soul with a brilliant flame that threatens to consume us all. The battle has only just begun.

The lake's silence hangs thick in the air, an oppressive shroud that wraps around me, stealing my breath and stealing my resolve. I can feel the power of the Naiad thrumming in the water, an angry heartbeat, and I realize that in my fervor to free the lost souls, I may have awakened something far more vengeful than I had anticipated. I stumble back, my feet slipping in the mud, my heart racing as shadows pulse beneath the surface. The once tranquil lake now roils with fury, each wave a promise of retribution.

"Foolish girl," the Naiad snarls, her voice a low, haunting melody that reverberates through the trees, curling like smoke in the still air. "You think you can challenge the tide of fate? This is my domain, and every choice has a price." Her form shimmers, twisting into a monstrous visage, her beauty turned grotesque, revealing the true depths of her power. I want to run, to escape this waking nightmare, but my feet remain anchored to the earth, as if the very soil beneath me has chosen to stand in solidarity against the tide of despair.

"I know what you've done," I reply, my voice steadier than I feel. "I've seen the pain you've inflicted on my family. You may have claimed their lives, but you will not claim me!" The words taste bitter on my tongue, but I swallow hard, summoning every ounce of courage that has been passed down through generations of women who have fought for their freedom. I remember my grandmother's laughter, bright and vibrant, echoing in my mind—a reminder that the light still flickers, even in the darkest of waters.

The Naiad's laughter cuts through the air like a shard of glass. "Ah, such spirit! But spirit alone will not save you." She gestures to the lake, and suddenly the water seems to surge, forming serpentine shapes that writhe and coil, eager to pull me under. "You think you can break a bond forged in blood? The souls you sought to free are bound to this place, and their longing to return will be your undoing."

I can see the faces of the lost—my mother's gentle smile, my grandmother's wise eyes, and countless others who had succumbed to the lure of the lake. They hover just beneath the surface, shimmering like fading memories, and my heart aches at the sight. "They are not yours to control!" I shout, the fire within me igniting into a blaze. "I will not let you use them as pawns in your twisted game."

With that, I draw a deep breath and call upon the energy thrumming in my veins, a legacy woven through generations. I can feel the warmth of it, the memories of those who came before me fueling my resolve. "By the bonds of blood and spirit," I recite, my voice rising above the tempestuous waves. "I command you to release them!"

The water convulses, and the Naiad's eyes widen, a flicker of uncertainty crossing her ethereal features. "You think to challenge me? This is madness!" Her voice rises with the winds, but I sense a shift, a crack in her facade of invulnerability.

"I think it's time someone stood up to you," I retort, channeling my strength, willing the currents to bend to my will. "You may have power over the depths, but I have the strength of those who loved and lost, who fought and died!" I can feel the magic coiling around me, twisting like a vine, drawing from the very earth and water that she believes belongs to her.

As I thrust my hands into the air, a blinding light erupts from my fingertips, illuminating the darkened corners of the lake. The Naiad shrieks, a piercing sound that echoes across the water, and the waves begin to recede. The faces of the lost swirl above me, their expressions shifting from sorrow to hope, and I feel a surge of energy as they respond to my call.

"Join me!" I cry, desperation tinged with determination. "We can break this curse together!" The light intensifies, radiating outward, and the water begins to bubble and churn as if it is alive, fighting against the pull of the Naiad's will. In that moment, I feel an overwhelming connection to the souls trapped within, their anguish mingling with my own.

The Naiad roars, a sound that rattles the very foundation of the world around us, and with a swift motion, she reaches for me, her fingers extending like claws, her beauty morphing into a grotesque mask of fury. "You will regret this!" she bellows, but her voice trembles, a sign that I am breaking through the wall she has built around her heart.

"Not if I can help it!" I declare, my voice ringing with newfound strength. I focus on the light, on the hope swirling within it, willing it to expand. The spirits surge forward, their combined energy creating a force that pushes back against the darkness. "Be free!" I command, my words echoing through the trees, reaching out to the very essence of the lake itself.

The waters boil and twist, the air crackling with magic as the Naiad struggles against the tide of my will. "No! You cannot take them!" she cries, but I can see the desperation in her eyes, the fear of losing control. It ignites something within me—a spark of triumph, a glimmer of hope that we might actually succeed.

And then, with a final, defiant roar, the light bursts forth, illuminating the entire lake in a blinding radiance. The faces of the lost swirl around me, their energy intertwining with my own, and as the light engulfs us, I feel the weight of their suffering lifting, their spirits rising like balloons released into the sky.

But the Naiad isn't done yet. In a final attempt to reclaim her power, she lunges forward, her hands reaching for me with a desperation I have never seen. I brace myself, but instead of fear, I feel a rush of compassion. "You don't have to be this way," I whisper, and for a moment, I see a flicker of something softer in her eyes, a memory of who she once was before she was twisted by bitterness and loss.

In that fleeting instant, the world hangs suspended in time. The light swells, and I make one last push, fueled by the love of those who have come before me. "Let go!" I command, not just for the spirits trapped within but for the Naiad herself. The water erupts in a final, magnificent display of brilliance, and in that moment, everything changes.

The radiant light explodes around me, a torrent of energy that feels both liberating and perilous. I am swept up in a current of magic that wraps around my body like a warm embrace, lifting me above the chaos as the Naiad howls in protest. Her scream echoes off the water and reverberates through my bones, each note laced with fury and desperation. In the midst of this blinding brilliance, I catch fleeting glimpses of the souls swirling around me—faces illuminated by the light, their eyes wide with hope, yearning for freedom.

"Let go of your anger!" I shout, my voice barely cutting through the din. "You don't have to be the warden of this place! You can join them!" The words spill from my lips, raw and honest, propelled by an urge to reach not only the spirits but the Naiad herself. She freezes for a heartbeat, caught in the tumult between fury and longing. In that moment, I see the flicker of a different existence behind her defiance—a life before the lake had twisted her essence into something dark and vengeful.

The waves surge higher, crashing against the shore like a chorus of freedom-seeking spirits. The lake shimmers with an intensity I never thought possible, a brilliant kaleidoscope of light and energy merging into a single pulse. As the Naiad hurls herself toward me, her fingers outstretched like a dark cloud blotting out the sun, I brace for impact. "You will never escape!" she bellows, her voice like thunder, and I can almost taste the salt of her tears mingling with the lake's water.

But just as her grasp nears, the light flares even brighter, an explosion of colors that bursts forth like fireworks against the night sky. It envelops us both, and suddenly, everything shifts. I feel the ground beneath me give way as I am pulled deeper into the water, the Naiad's presence looming above me like a tempest. I reach for the light, my heart racing, urging myself to focus on the warmth of the spirits around me.

"Remember who you are!" I implore, my voice a whisper in the chaos. "You were loved once! You can still be free!"

With those words, the light intensifies, flooding the lake with brilliance. The spirits whirl in a dazzling dance around me, their laughter intertwining with the Naiad's fury. "Stop it!" she shrieks, but it's not anger I sense anymore; it's fear—fear of losing control, of being consumed by the very power she once wielded.

The waters churn violently, but in the depths of the chaos, I feel something shift. The Naiad falters, her features softening for the first time, the darkness in her eyes flickering like a candle in the wind. "What... what do you know of love?" she gasps, her voice trembling as the magic swirls around us, intertwining our fates.

"I know it's what keeps us alive," I reply, my heart racing as I seize the moment. "It's what binds us, not just to this place but to each other. You've lost that connection, but it can be found again!"

As I speak, I realize the brilliance is reaching its zenith, a crescendo of power that thrums through the air and reverberates in my bones. The Naiad hesitates, her monstrous form shifting back to something softer, her expression a tapestry of emotions—confusion, yearning, and a flicker of hope. I stretch out my hand toward her, feeling the warmth of the light spilling from me.

"Let me show you," I plead, taking a step forward. "Let me show you what it means to be free!"

Just as my fingers brush the surface of the water, the light surges again, and I'm engulfed in a blinding white flash that consumes everything around me. I lose sight of the Naiad, lose my grip on reality, and feel myself slipping beneath the surface, the magic pulling me deeper into the water. It wraps around me like a cocoon, the world above fading into a distant memory.

For a moment, I am suspended in darkness, weightless and free, and I hear the soft echoes of the spirits calling to me, their voices a soothing balm to my frayed nerves. They guide me deeper, and I can almost see the outlines of their forms, glowing softly against the abyss. Together, we swirl through the depths, searching for something—some way to bind our fates together in this tangled mess of magic and loss.

Then, with a violent rush, I break through the surface of the water, gasping for air as I emerge into a twilight world, where colors bleed into one another and the sky is a riot of purples and blues. I blink against the brilliance, trying to regain my bearings, but the lake has transformed around me. It shimmers like a thousand diamonds scattered across a silken sheet, alive with energy and power.

And there she is—the Naiad—standing at the water's edge, her form no longer twisted with rage but softened by a vulnerability that tugs at my heart. "You..." she begins, her voice fragile and almost lost in the gentle lapping of the waves. "You have no idea what you are asking."

"I know what it feels like to be lost," I reply, my heart pounding as I approach her. "But it doesn't have to end this way."

The tension in the air thickens, palpable and charged. The spirits swirl around us, their whispers urging her to embrace the truth I've offered. "What if I can't?" she murmurs, her eyes searching mine, a glimmer of the woman she once was shining through the storm.

The ground trembles beneath us, and for a heartbeat, it feels as if the very earth is holding its breath. The lake bubbles ominously, and I can sense the tumult of emotions within it—grief, anger, longing—an orchestra of feelings begging to be released. "You can," I whisper fiercely, a fierce determination igniting in my chest. "We all can."

But as I reach for her, the lake roars with sudden ferocity, dark waves crashing against the shore, and I feel a chilling wind sweep through, a herald of something darker approaching. The Naiad's eyes widen in fear, and I turn to see shadows rising from the depths, twisting and writhing like nightmares taking form, their intentions clear and threatening.

"I cannot protect you from what's coming," she gasps, and I can see it in her eyes—the encroaching darkness that seeks to swallow us both whole. My heart races, the gravity of the moment dawning on me. There's no time left to plead for her transformation; the battle is upon us, and the stakes are higher than ever.

"Then let's fight together," I declare, my voice a battle cry against the looming shadows. But as I stand, ready to face whatever emerges from the depths, the ground beneath us splits, a gaping chasm threatening to swallow the lake whole, and I realize—this is only the beginning.

Chapter 27: The Return of the Light

The warmth of the sun spills over my skin, golden rays breaking through the remnants of morning mist that cling to the lake like a memory refusing to fade. As I take in my surroundings, the world appears more vibrant than I recall—each blade of grass, every shimmering pebble, seems to pulse with life. It's a stark contrast to the darkness I've known, where shadows whispered promises of despair. But now, surrounded by nature's symphony, I feel the tentative stirrings of hope alongside the deep ache of loss that still clings to my heart.

Isaac's arms are strong around me, his familiar scent—a mix of pine and something distinctly him—anchors me in this moment. I nestle against his shoulder, allowing myself a few stolen breaths, relishing the solidity of his presence. Yet, the tremor in his embrace betrays the turmoil beneath his composed exterior. When I pull back to look into his eyes, the depths reveal a tempest of emotions, swirling beneath the surface like the waters that once threatened to consume us.

"Are we... free?" I manage, my voice barely a whisper, as if uttering the words might summon the darkness back.

He searches my face, his brows knitting together in thought. "I think so," he replies, his voice low and steady, though the flicker of uncertainty lingers in his gaze. "But freedom comes with its own set of challenges."

I nod, knowing all too well the weight of our history—the sacrifices made, the choices that brought us here, and the lives intertwined with our fate. The lake may be calm now, but I sense the echoes of what it held, the stories of those lost in its depths. A shiver runs through me at the thought of Lila, her laughter once dancing on the wind, now silenced. I can't shake the feeling that her spirit still wanders, tethered to the water that took her away.

"Lila..." I murmur, the name tasting bittersweet on my tongue.

Isaac's expression darkens, shadows crossing his features. "We can't forget her, but we also can't let her memory chain us to the past."

I understand his words, yet the struggle to reconcile the two—honoring Lila while forging a path forward—feels monumental. The air is heavy with unspoken fears, and I feel a knot tightening in my chest. "What do we do now?"

His gaze hardens with determination, as if he's drawing strength from the very earth beneath us. "We rebuild. Not just our lives, but everything that was broken."

I smile, though it feels fragile, like glass in a storm. "Rebuilding sounds ambitious."

"Ambitious is my middle name," he replies with a lopsided grin that softens the tension. "We start small. One day at a time."

The idea of building something new is daunting, yet the spark of possibility ignites a flicker of excitement within me. The thought of a future not dictated by darkness makes my heart race, and I wonder if it's possible to reshape our lives amidst the remnants of our pain.

We rise together, the ground cool beneath my bare feet, and survey our surroundings. The lake lies before us, its surface smooth as glass, reflecting the clear blue sky. Wildflowers sway gently in the breeze, a riot of colors that beckon us to draw closer. Each bloom seems to whisper secrets of resilience, their vibrant petals a reminder that beauty often grows in the most unexpected places.

"Let's go for a walk," Isaac suggests, taking my hand and leading me along the shoreline. The sensation of his skin against mine sends a jolt of energy through me, a connection that reminds me of the warmth of summer days spent laughing together, before the weight of our burdens eclipsed everything.

As we walk, the rhythm of the water lapping against the shore harmonizes with our footsteps, a soothing melody that seems to chase away the shadows lingering in my mind. "You know, I used to think the lake was magical," I say, letting memories spill from my lips like the water beside us. "I thought it could grant wishes or heal wounds. But now, I realize it was just a facade, a cruel trick that lured people into its depths."

Isaac stops, turning to face me, his expression thoughtful. "Magic can be a double-edged sword. It can create beauty, but it can also destroy."

"Like us," I murmur, the weight of my words hanging between us.

A brief silence stretches, filled only by the soft rustle of leaves in the breeze. "We're not defined by what happened," he finally says, his voice firm. "We're defined by how we choose to move forward."

The conviction in his words ignites something within me, a determination that I thought had faded with my old life. "So, we choose to live."

His smile is radiant, a spark of light that dispels the remaining darkness. "Exactly. Together."

With that, we resume our walk, the promise of the future guiding our steps. The sun continues to rise, casting a warm glow over everything, as if nature itself rejoices in our newfound freedom.

As we stroll along the water's edge, I catch sight of something glimmering among the stones. Curiosity piqued, I bend down to investigate, brushing away the dirt and debris. My fingers graze a smooth, polished surface, and I pull it free from its confines—a small, intricately carved amulet, its design swirling like the currents of the lake.

"Look at this," I call out, holding it up for Isaac to see.

He approaches, his brow furrowing in concentration. "Where did you find that?"

"Right here, buried in the sand."

Taking the amulet from my hands, he examines it closely. "It's beautiful," he says softly, a hint of wonder in his voice. "It must have belonged to someone who loved this place."

As I watch him turn the piece over in his fingers, I feel an unexpected connection to the artifact. It carries with it a history, a story I can't quite grasp. "Maybe it's a sign," I say, my mind racing with possibilities. "A token of hope, perhaps?"

"Or a reminder that our past isn't gone; it's simply waiting for us to uncover it," Isaac muses, his eyes sparkling with a light I hadn't seen before.

With the amulet resting in my palm, I realize that this could be the first step in our journey—a symbol of the path we're about to forge, a blend of the past we honor and the future we will build. I smile, heart swelling with a mixture of nostalgia and hope, ready to embrace whatever comes next.

As the sun climbs higher, casting a warm glow across the lake, I find myself caught between the thrill of liberation and the heavy cloak of uncertainty that still clings to me. Isaac's presence is a balm against the emotional storm, and yet the depths of his eyes hint at a shared grief that neither of us knows how to articulate. We drift along the shore, hands intertwined, as if the simple gesture can bridge the chasm created by our past.

"Do you ever think about what comes next?" I ask, trying to pierce the thick veil of silence that wraps around us. "What do we do with our freedom now that we have it?"

Isaac glances at me, his brow furrowing. "I think about it all the time. But it's a bit like standing on the edge of the lake, staring into the water and trying to predict how deep it goes. We can't know until we take the plunge."

I chuckle softly, the sound surprising me. "Well, I've had enough of plunging into depths for a lifetime."

His laughter is infectious, echoing against the stillness of the water. "Fair point. Maybe we should test the shallows first."

We continue walking, our conversation flowing easily, a refreshing change from the weighty discussions that have dominated our lives. The lake, once a harbinger of despair, now feels like a canvas of possibilities. I glance at the horizon, where the sky meets the water, and imagine a world untainted by darkness, a place where laughter and love flourish.

Suddenly, a rustle in the underbrush catches my attention. I stop, squinting into the dense thicket that fringes the shore. "Did you hear that?" I whisper, my pulse quickening.

Isaac shifts closer, his body tensing beside mine. "Yeah, it sounded like... something."

We exchange a wary glance, the earlier lightness in our conversation replaced by a cautious curiosity. As I move to investigate, my heart beats a staccato rhythm in my chest. The branches part with ease, revealing a small clearing, where a solitary figure crouches, seemingly oblivious to our presence.

"Hello?" I call out, my voice echoing slightly in the hushed space.

The figure freezes, then slowly rises. A young woman steps into the dappled sunlight, her wild curls framing a face that radiates both confusion and defiance. "Who are you?" she demands, her voice sharp and wary.

"I'm... um, I'm just a visitor." I stammer, glancing at Isaac, who looks equally taken aback. "And you?"

She narrows her eyes, taking a step closer, her stance defensive. "This is my home. You shouldn't be here."

"Home?" I echo, glancing at the sprawling woods behind her. "You mean this place? But it's—"

"Dead," she interrupts, her expression darkening. "This place was supposed to be alive. We all felt it, but then..." She trails off, her gaze turning distant as she stares into the past, the hurt evident in her expression.

Isaac takes a step forward, his voice gentle but firm. "We're not here to hurt anything. We just... we just broke the lake's curse. We thought it might help."

The girl's expression shifts, a flicker of hope dancing in her eyes before she wrestles it back down. "Help? You think you can just waltz in here and fix everything? You don't know what you're talking about."

"Actually," I interject, trying to find common ground, "we do. We've experienced the darkness that this place holds."

For a moment, uncertainty dances across her face. "What do you mean? You've been cursed?"

Isaac nods. "In a way, yes. But now we're free. We want to share that with others, if there's still time."

"Time for what?" The girl's voice softens, curiosity seeping through her earlier hostility. "To save the land? To bring back the light?"

I step closer, my heart aching for the hope I see flickering in her eyes. "Yes. We can't undo the past, but we can start to build something new. Together."

She hesitates, clearly torn. "You don't know the price of what you're asking. It's not just about willpower or desire; it's about sacrifice."

I feel a knot tightening in my stomach. "We know about sacrifice."

She regards me for a moment longer before she takes a deep breath, visibly weighing her options. "Alright, I'll listen. But if I don't like what I hear, I won't hesitate to kick you out."

Her bravado is admirable, and I can't help but smile at her spirit. "Fair enough," I say, allowing the tension to dissipate slightly. "I'm Kira, and this is Isaac."

"Ember," she replies, the tension in her shoulders easing just a fraction. "And if you're serious about wanting to help, you should come with me. There's a group of us, and we've been trying to hold on to the remnants of what was once here. We could use the strength."

Isaac and I exchange glances, a silent agreement forming between us. "Lead the way," Isaac says, the determination in his voice echoing my own resolve.

As we follow Ember through the trees, I feel the weight of hope settling on my shoulders, a comfortable heaviness that drives away the lingering fear. The forest buzzes with life—chirping birds, rustling leaves, the soft crunch of twigs beneath our feet—and it feels as though the world is awakening around us.

We emerge into a clearing, where a small community has begun to take root. Tents made of colorful fabric dot the landscape, each one filled with laughter and the sweet scent of cooking food. The air hums with energy, a palpable sense of camaraderie that makes my heart swell.

Ember gestures toward the gathering, her expression softening. "This is what's left of us. We're trying to rebuild."

I catch glimpses of the faces—some familiar, some new—each one marked by stories untold and battles fought. "You've done well," I say, genuinely impressed.

"It's not enough," she replies quietly, her gaze fixed on the horizon where the sun begins to dip. "But we're not ready to give up yet."

As I look around at the people working together, their laughter and shouts rising in a beautiful cacophony, I feel an unfamiliar warmth flooding through me. Here, amidst the echoes of laughter and the determination of a community, perhaps we can find the strength to reclaim our future. Perhaps, together, we can weave a new story from the remnants of the past.

The atmosphere buzzes with an energy that is both exhilarating and terrifying as Ember leads us through the makeshift community. Every step is a reminder that life continues to pulse in the wake of despair, but as I take in the faces around me—some weary, others ignited with hope—I can't help but feel a surge of determination. This is a space where we can rebuild, where we can write a new chapter in our lives, one that echoes with laughter rather than sorrow.

Ember gestures toward a gathering of people surrounding a fire pit, their faces illuminated by the flickering flames. "This is where we hold our meetings. It's where we plan our next steps," she explains, her voice barely audible over the lively chatter.

I can see a mix of personalities within the group: some animatedly discussing ideas while others sit back, listening intently, their expressions serious yet engaged. It's a snapshot of resilience—a testament to the fact that even in the darkest of times, the human spirit finds a way to thrive.

"Are they... like us?" I ask, unsure how to frame my question. "Did they experience the lake's curse?"

Ember's eyes darken momentarily. "Everyone here has been touched by its darkness in some way. We're survivors, just trying to make sense of what's left."

Isaac squeezes my hand, and I feel a surge of resolve. "We can help," he says, his voice steady. "We want to share what we've learned."

"Then you're welcome to join us," Ember replies, a flicker of hope igniting in her gaze. "We could use more hands, and perhaps, more ideas."

As we approach the fire pit, I can't shake the sensation that we've stepped into a new world, one where our past mistakes don't define us, and the possibilities stretch out like the night sky above us. Ember introduces us to a few key figures—a wiry man with spectacles who is scribbling furiously in a notebook, a woman with sharp features and an infectious laugh, and a pair of teenagers, their energy contagious as they weave in and out of conversations.

"Meet Finn," Ember says, motioning to the bespectacled man. "He's our planner. If it involves organization, he's your guy."

Finn looks up from his notes, adjusting his glasses with a bemused expression. "Planning is an art, my dear," he says, his voice dripping with mock seriousness. "And this community is a masterpiece in progress."

I grin, appreciating his quick wit. "A masterpiece, huh? What's the canvas made of? Scraps and hope?"

"Exactly!" Finn beams, his enthusiasm infectious. "The best art often is. We're working on a plan to restore what we can of the lake and its surrounding lands. With your help, perhaps we can revive the very spirit that this place has lost."

The excitement in the air is palpable, and as the fire crackles, casting shadows that dance around us, I feel the stirrings of something I thought I had lost: a sense of purpose. But beneath the thrill of planning, I can't ignore the gnawing anxiety in the pit of my stomach.

"What about the others?" I venture, glancing around at the faces. "There are stories of loss and sacrifice. Are there... still dangers lurking?"

The laughter dims as Ember's expression turns grave. "There are always dangers. The curse of the lake may be lifted, but that doesn't mean the dark forces have vanished. There are those who thrived on the chaos, who might not take kindly to our attempts to rebuild."

Isaac tenses beside me, his jaw tightening. "We can handle whatever comes our way. We faced the lake's darkness together; this will be nothing in comparison."

The tension in the air shifts slightly, the resolve palpable. Ember nods, her expression steely. "That's the spirit. We need that strength. The more united we are, the stronger we'll become."

As the night deepens, our plans take shape, mingling with laughter and the crackling fire. We share stories, laughter threading through the discussions as we find a rhythm in the chaos. Finn leads us through logistical challenges, suggesting we map out areas in need of restoration, while the others weigh in with ideas for sustainable living.

"I suggest we start with the garden," the sharp-featured woman says, her voice confident. "We need to bring back the greenery, something that can provide food and beauty. It will lift spirits and nourish our bodies."

"That's a brilliant idea!" I exclaim, the thought igniting something within me. "We could plant herbs, vegetables, and flowers—everything that thrives in this soil. And we could involve everyone, especially the kids. It'll give them a sense of purpose."

Laughter ripples through the group, and as we brainstorm, the atmosphere becomes electric. Ideas tumble over one another, our shared energy fueling the discussions.

But amid the laughter, a weight presses down on me. I can't shake the feeling that we are riding on a wave of optimism that could just as easily crash into the rocks of reality. My eyes wander to the dark edges of the clearing, where the trees stand like silent sentinels, cloaked in shadows. What if our efforts were in vain? What if the darkness still lurked, waiting for the perfect moment to strike?

As the night wears on, the air grows thick with camaraderie and purpose, but I can't help but feel the tension tightening like a coiled spring. Just as the discussion turns to logistics, a distant sound pierces through the night—the unmistakable crack of a branch snapping.

The laughter dies, silence enveloping us as everyone turns their heads toward the sound. "Did anyone else hear that?" I whisper, a chill running down my spine.

Isaac's grip tightens on my hand, and I can see the worry etched on his face. "It came from the woods," he murmurs.

Ember steps forward, her expression transforming from determination to something more primal, instinctual. "Everyone, stay close," she commands, her voice low but urgent. "We may not be alone."

A knot of fear gathers in my stomach as we all inch closer together, the warmth of the fire flickering against the encroaching darkness. I can feel my heart racing, pounding in time with the sudden tension in the air. The shadows deepen, and just as the last words of caution are uttered, a figure emerges from the darkness—a silhouette against the dim light, shifting and uncertain.

"Who's there?" Ember calls, her voice steady but laced with concern.

A response hangs in the air, thick with anticipation, and the world seems to hold its breath. Just as the figure steps into the firelight, I feel a sense of dread unfurling within me. The person's face is obscured, but the glint of something metallic in their hand catches the firelight, sending a jolt of panic through the group.

"Run!" someone shouts, and chaos erupts as we all turn, hearts pounding in our chests, unsure of what comes next. The night, once filled with hope and laughter, now trembles with the looming threat of danger, and I realize that our fight for survival has only just begun.

Chapter 28: A New Dawn

Morning light spills across the lake, a golden brushstroke spreading wide to awaken the world. The water shimmers, reflecting the pastel colors of dawn like a soft, welcoming embrace. It's a scene that might be plucked from the pages of a dream, yet here I stand, awash in the beauty of it all, heart fluttering with an uncertain hope. Isaac walks beside me, his presence both grounding and electrifying. We've journeyed through shadows together, our souls woven with threads of hardship and triumph, but this moment feels different—lighter, almost as if the air itself has shed its weight.

We don't speak for a while, allowing the tranquility of the lake to envelop us. The distant call of a loon punctuates the silence, its haunting song echoing across the water, and I find myself lost in thought. I remember the days when the lake was a source of dread, an ever-watchful predator lurking beneath the surface. It feels absurd to think that just weeks ago, I was consumed by fear, bound by the grip of a curse that threatened not only my life but the very essence of our town. Yet here I am, the curse broken, the town beginning to heal. It's surreal, like waking from a long nightmare into a dawn that smells of fresh earth and blooming flowers.

"Do you ever think about what comes next?" Isaac's voice cuts through my reverie, his tone casual, yet I can sense the weight of his question. He glances at me, his dark eyes searching mine for answers, or perhaps reassurance.

"What do you mean?" I ask, though I know exactly what he means. The future looms before us, an expanse of possibilities.

"Us," he replies simply, his gaze returning to the horizon, where the sun begins to crest over the treetops. "What happens now that we're free?"

A smile plays on my lips, one that feels both foreign and familiar. I've spent so much time navigating the labyrinth of fear and sorrow that the idea of a future feels like an uncharted map. "I suppose we figure it out," I say, trying to sound nonchalant. "One day at a time."

He chuckles softly, the sound warm and inviting, yet laced with a hint of trepidation. "That sounds terrifying."

"It is." I can't help but laugh, a light, tinkling sound that dances above the gentle lapping of the water against the shore. "But maybe a little terrifying is good for us. It keeps things interesting."

Isaac shakes his head, a bemused expression on his face. "Interesting is one word for it. I'd prefer a life where 'interesting' doesn't involve curses or dark magic."

"Point taken," I concede, my heart swelling with affection for this man who stood by me through the chaos. "But we can't forget what we learned. That we're stronger together. That even in the darkest moments, there's always a glimmer of hope."

As the first rays of sunlight pierce the morning mist, casting long shadows across the ground, a sense of urgency tugs at me. I glance at the town in the distance, where wooden houses cling to the hillside like old friends. The scars of the past still linger—the cracked paint, the overgrown gardens—but beneath the surface, there's a vibrancy waiting to emerge, a potential waiting to bloom.

"Isaac," I say, my voice steady now, "we need to help them. We can't let them forget the darkness, but we also can't let them drown in it. They need to see that there's a future worth fighting for."

His brow furrows, and I can see the wheels turning in his mind. "What do you have in mind?"

"We'll start small. Community gatherings, sharing stories of what we faced and how we overcame it. Reminding them of the strength that lies within this town. We'll plant seeds of hope and watch them grow."

His smile widens, the spark of determination igniting in his eyes. "I like that. We can't change the past, but we can shape the future."

And just like that, a new purpose takes root in my heart, intertwining with the love and respect I hold for Isaac. Together, we'll navigate this new terrain, a landscape littered with echoes of our struggles but also brightened by the promise of what could be.

As the sun rises higher, the light spills like molten gold across the lake, glistening in a way that feels like an affirmation. My thoughts drift to my friends—Lila, with her relentless optimism; Ben, whose laughter could shatter the darkest clouds; and Sarah, always ready with a comforting word. They've been my anchors, and now, it's time for me to be theirs.

"Let's do this," I declare, feeling a swell of courage. "Let's rebuild our town."

Isaac nods, and I catch the fierce determination in his gaze. "Together," he affirms, and the word hangs between us, heavy with promise and possibility. The air crackles with unspoken understanding, the kind that springs from shared trials.

The sun continues its ascent, illuminating the path ahead, and I can't shake the feeling that this is just the beginning. Yes, there will be challenges, moments that might test our resolve, but standing here with Isaac, I feel invincible. The curse may have cast a long shadow, but we are stepping into the light, ready to embrace whatever comes next. Together.

The sun spills over the horizon, painting the sky in hues of orange and pink, a gentle reminder of the day's promise. Isaac and I stand at the water's edge, letting the cool breeze tangle with our hair, teasing us with the scent of damp earth and awakening life. Every ripple on the lake's surface seems to echo the laughter of long-lost joy, a melody that softly reminds us of all that has been reclaimed. Yet, beneath this serene façade lies an undercurrent of uncertainty, a tide of emotions that threatens to pull us under if we're not careful.

"Okay, so if we're going to start rebuilding, where do we begin?" Isaac asks, turning to face me, his expression shifting from playful to contemplative. There's a spark of excitement in his eyes, mingled with the shadows of the past.

"First, we need to gather everyone," I suggest, tapping my chin in mock seriousness. "I think a potluck would do wonders. Nothing brings people together like food—especially when it involves Grandma Edna's famous blueberry pie. That could unite even the most reluctant townsfolk."

Isaac chuckles, a rich sound that warms the air between us. "Ah yes, the magical power of pie. The ultimate peace treaty."

"Exactly! We can set up in the town square, maybe hang some fairy lights. It'll feel like a celebration, a chance for everyone to breathe and reconnect." The idea takes root in my mind, branching out like the trees surrounding us, a vision that fills me with purpose.

As I speak, the thought of the town gathering for something other than a funeral or a memorial lifts my spirits. I can picture it clearly: laughter bubbling over the clinking of plates, stories shared amidst the glow of string lights, the community knitting itself back together one bite at a time.

"Sounds like a plan," Isaac agrees, his voice tinged with enthusiasm. "But we'll need more than just pie to mend these wounds. We should also talk about what we went through, give them a chance to share their own stories."

He's right, of course. The weight of silence has lingered too long, a heavy shroud that suffocated any chance of healing. The shared trauma of the curse was something we could no longer ignore, and the prospect of revisiting those memories made my heart flutter with anxiety. Still, it was necessary.

"I can lead the discussion," I suggest, though doubt flickers in my mind like a candle threatened by the wind. "Maybe if I share my experience first, it'll open the floor for others to follow."

Isaac nods, though a hint of concern flashes across his face. "You sure you're ready for that? It's not easy reliving those moments."

"I know," I reply, the words catching in my throat. "But if I can't be brave now, when can I be? We need to face the past together. It's the only way to truly move on."

We both stand in silence for a moment, letting the weight of my words sink in. It feels like a pact, an unspoken agreement to confront what lies beneath the surface, much like the lake we admire. I take a deep breath, feeling the cool air fill my lungs, and then I glance up at Isaac. His presence is a balm, steady and reassuring.

As we turn to leave, a sudden rustle from the underbrush catches my attention. We stop, eyes darting toward the movement, hearts racing slightly at the unexpected interruption. A figure emerges, and as the sunlight breaks through the trees, I recognize Sarah, her usually vibrant hair damp from the morning dew. She's holding a basket, her face lit with that trademark mischievous grin.

"Don't mind me," she chirps, approaching with an air of casual confidence. "I thought I'd gather some wildflowers for the potluck. You know, just in case the pie wasn't enough to brighten everyone's spirits."

Her lightheartedness is infectious, and I can't help but smile. "We were just discussing how to bring the town together again. You're on board, right?"

"Of course! Count me in. I've got a few ideas for games we can play to lighten the mood." She glances back at the basket and then at us, her expression shifting to something more serious. "But we need to talk about what happened. I know we all want to move on, but we have to face it first."

"Exactly," I say, grateful for her alignment with our shared vision. "We can't just sweep it under the rug. It's important that we acknowledge the pain and then allow everyone to heal."

Isaac looks from me to Sarah, the three of us united in purpose. "Then let's do it. Together."

As we walk back toward town, the three of us discussing details and possibilities, I can feel the energy shifting around us. The townsfolk would need guidance, an anchor in the swirling sea of emotions. And we, all of us, had already survived the storm.

The path before us twists and turns, a metaphorical journey laden with uncertainty, yet I find solace in the knowledge that we would navigate it together. Each step brings me closer to the heart of my community, to the people who had unknowingly rooted for me during my darkest moments.

When we reach the town square, the atmosphere is charged with anticipation. The streets still bear the scars of what we've endured, but there's a budding sense of resilience in the air, a collective yearning for renewal.

I can envision the gatherings, the faces of my friends lighting up as we share our stories—some triumphant, others heartbreakingly raw. As the sun rises higher, casting a warm glow on everything it touches, I realize that this moment marks a turning point.

We are no longer just survivors of a curse; we are the architects of our own future, each of us bearing the tools to build something beautiful from the remnants of our shared past.

With laughter, tears, and pie—so much pie—the healing can begin. And as Isaac squeezes my hand gently, I feel a spark of hope igniting within me, promising that together, we can forge a new beginning, one filled with light and love.

The square buzzes with anticipation as the sun climbs higher, casting warm light across the cobblestone streets. Banners flutter overhead, strung between lamp posts, vibrant colors dancing in the gentle breeze. I stand at the center, my heart thrumming with excitement and nerves, watching as friends and neighbors begin to gather. Lila is already in motion, organizing tables laden with dishes, while Ben playfully debates the merits of his famous chili against Grandma Edna's blueberry pie. It feels like the town is breathing again, shaking off the cobwebs of the past, and I can't help but smile at the sight.

"Look at them," I say to Isaac, who stands beside me, arms crossed, a bemused smile on his face. "It's like we've unleashed a bunch of overly caffeinated squirrels."

"True, but you've got to admit it's an adorable chaos," he replies, leaning in closer. "Especially Lila. I half expect her to start directing traffic at this point."

I laugh, watching as Lila attempts to juggle two platters of food while gesturing wildly with her free hand. She's a whirlwind of enthusiasm, and her laughter rings out like a bell, drawing others in. People are starting to congregate, drawn by the delicious scents wafting through the air, a mix of spices and sweetness that heralds a new beginning.

But as the gathering grows, so does the tension gnawing at the edges of my mind. The shared trauma still lingers beneath the surface, an unspoken fear that perhaps this moment of levity is fragile, that it could shatter with the mere mention of the curse. I take a deep breath, trying to center myself. We've chosen to confront our past, and part of me worries about how those memories will surface.

Isaac catches my eye, his expression shifting from playful to earnest. "You ready for this?" His voice drops to a whisper, though the concern in his gaze is anything but subtle.

"As ready as I'll ever be," I reply, forcing a smile that I hope conveys more confidence than I feel. "It's time for us all to step into the light."

As we move toward the makeshift stage, I feel a wave of emotion wash over me—nervousness, determination, and an undeniable sense of solidarity. I take my place at the front, glancing out at the sea of familiar faces. There's Sarah, her expression encouraging, and Ben, who gives me an enthusiastic thumbs up.

"Hey everyone!" I call out, my voice steady despite the fluttering in my stomach. "Thank you all for coming today. This gathering isn't just about food; it's about healing and connection. We've faced something unimaginable together, and today, we're here to celebrate our resilience."

A gentle murmur ripples through the crowd, and I sense a shared understanding, a collective sigh of relief as we embrace the atmosphere of camaraderie.

I look at Isaac, who stands a step behind me, radiating support. "I want to start by sharing my story," I say, feeling the warmth of his presence like a shield against my vulnerability. "It's not easy to relive those moments, but I believe it's important. We need to acknowledge what we've endured to truly move forward."

As I speak, memories flood back—dark nights filled with fear, moments of desperation, and the weight of a curse that hung over us like a storm cloud. But woven through those memories are also threads of hope, the strength we found in one another, the unwavering support of friends who never let me falter.

When I finish, the square feels charged with a new energy, as if we've collectively turned a page. The crowd is silent, processing the weight of my words, and for a brief moment, I wonder if perhaps I've said too much. But then Lila steps forward, her voice ringing clear as she shares her own experiences, and suddenly, the dam breaks.

One by one, stories emerge from the crowd—some filled with laughter, others tinged with tears. Each tale is a testament to the strength of our community, the resilience forged in the fires of adversity.

As I stand there, listening to my friends recount their battles against the curse, I feel the atmosphere shift. What was once a gathering of survivors transforms into a celebration of triumph. There are moments of levity—a funny story about the time Ben accidentally sent a fireball flying during a spell, and bursts of laughter erupt like fireworks, cutting through the tension that had clung to us like fog.

But just as the mood begins to lift, a chill sweeps through the crowd. The temperature drops abruptly, and a heavy silence falls, the laughter faltering as if someone has pressed a pause button on joy. My heart races as I scan the faces around me, a nagging sense of dread creeping up my spine.

"What's wrong?" Isaac's voice breaks through the quiet, his eyes narrowing as he surveys the square.

And then I see it—a figure emerging from the edge of the gathering, shrouded in shadow. My breath catches in my throat as recognition hits me like a punch. It's the same figure I glimpsed in the woods, a silhouette that seems to embody the darkness we fought so hard to escape.

"Who are you?" I call out, my voice shaky but firm. "What do you want?"

The figure steps into the light, revealing a face I never thought I'd see again, a face that sends a rush of conflicting emotions through me. My mind races, trying to grasp how this person could be here, how they could possibly have returned after everything we went through.

"Did you really think it was over?" the figure sneers, a cold smile curling on their lips. "You've only scratched the surface of what's to come."

Gasps ripple through the crowd, and the joyous atmosphere fractures into uncertainty. Fear hangs thick in the air, palpable and suffocating. I can see it in Isaac's eyes, the same mix of shock and determination that must be reflected in mine.

"Stay back!" I shout, instinctively stepping in front of Isaac, a surge of protective instinct rising within me. The town has only just begun to heal, and I refuse to let it be torn apart again.

But as the figure raises a hand, dark energy crackling at their fingertips, I realize that our fight is far from over. The dawning of a new beginning is met with the looming specter of an old enemy, and as the crowd erupts in panic, I know that this moment will change everything.

"Get ready," I whisper to Isaac, the determination in my voice battling against the fear. "It's about to get interesting."

Chapter 29: The Eternal Echo

The air was tinged with the scent of pine and damp earth, a fresh canvas upon which the afternoon sun painted shadows across the forest floor. Each step felt like a silent whisper, my footfalls barely disturbing the fallen leaves that carpeted the trail. Isaac's hand, warm and reassuring, enveloped mine as we navigated the narrow path winding through the trees. His presence was a balm, soothing the remnants of chaos that still flickered at the edges of my consciousness. The haunting echoes of our past adventure, the shadows of the Naiad and the weight of the curse, receded like the tide, leaving behind a tranquil shore upon which we could build something new.

We emerged from the trees, the expansive lake opening up before us like a secret revealed, its surface shimmering under the gentle caress of the sun. Each ripple seemed to reflect the myriad of emotions that had churned within me—fear, hope, love, and the bittersweet taste of loss. I took a deep breath, inhaling the crisp, cool air, and felt the weight of our shared past lift just a little. The water, once a site of turmoil, now cradled the light in its depths, promising renewal and peace.

"Do you remember how it felt when we first saw this place?" Isaac asked, breaking the comfortable silence that had settled around us. His voice, rich and melodic, wrapped around me like a favorite blanket, grounding me in the present.

I smiled, the memory flashing vividly in my mind—a mixture of fear and exhilaration, our hearts racing as we faced the unknown together. "How could I forget? We thought we were stepping into a fairytale, but it turned out to be more like a nightmare with all those twists and turns."

He chuckled softly, the sound mingling with the rustle of leaves above us. "A fairytale gone wrong, maybe. But look at us now." He gestured broadly, as if to encompass the beauty of the scene before us. "We made it through the storm, and we're standing here, together."

My heart swelled at the truth of his words. The journey had been fraught with danger, but every moment had led us to this serene oasis. "Together," I echoed, squeezing his hand tightly. It was a promise, a vow that no matter what came next, we would face it side by side.

The sunlight danced on the water, creating a mosaic of sparkles that beckoned me closer. As we approached the shoreline, I could hear the soft lapping of the waves, a rhythmic pulse that seemed to sync with the beating of my heart. I knelt at the edge, letting my fingers trail through the cool water, sending ripples across the surface. Each disturbance felt like a tiny liberation, releasing the tension that had built up inside me over the past months.

"What are you thinking?" Isaac asked, his tone playful yet laced with curiosity.

"Just... how much has changed," I mused, my gaze fixed on the horizon where the sky met the water. "I used to see this place as a reminder of everything we lost, but now it feels like a beginning."

He moved closer, settling beside me, his shoulder brushing against mine. "That's the beauty of it, isn't it? It's not the place that defines our experiences, but how we choose to remember them."

A comfortable silence enveloped us, and I let the tranquility seep into my bones. Yet, beneath the surface, I felt an undercurrent of uncertainty. Our victory over the Naiad had been hard-won, but there were remnants of that dark period that still clung to me like shadows at dusk. I turned to Isaac, searching his face for any hint of the worries that danced in the back of my mind.

"Do you ever think about the Naiad? About what she said?"

Isaac frowned slightly, a shadow passing over his features. "Sometimes. It's hard not to." He paused, collecting his thoughts.

"But we can't let her haunt us. We took back what was ours. We broke her curse. We have each other now."

I nodded, but the unease lingered. What if there were more echoes of the past waiting to resurface? The world was unpredictable, and while I longed for a life free of turmoil, I also recognized the fragility of our happiness.

As if sensing my turmoil, Isaac shifted closer, his arm slipping around my shoulders. "You're thinking too much, you know. It's okay to leave some questions unanswered."

I leaned into him, finding solace in his warmth. "Maybe you're right. Maybe I just need to focus on the present."

The sun dipped lower, casting golden rays across the water and illuminating the tiny motes of dust that danced in the light. It was mesmerizing, and for a moment, I let myself be swept away by the beauty surrounding us. The lake was no longer a reminder of sorrow but a testament to our strength, a mirror reflecting our resilience.

With a sudden spark of mischief, I turned to Isaac. "Okay, let's make a pact. No more dwelling on the past for the rest of the day. Let's celebrate our survival instead."

His face broke into a grin, the playful spark returning to his eyes. "I'm all for that! What's the plan, oh wise one?"

I stood, arms akimbo, a mock seriousness overtaking my features. "We shall feast like royalty! I have snacks stashed in the car, and we can claim the picnic table over there."

He raised an eyebrow, clearly amused. "Snacks? Is that your grand celebration?"

"Not just any snacks! These are the finest offerings of granola bars and fruit snacks that a day at the lake can provide," I declared, my voice dripping with mock gravitas.

"Then let's not keep our kingdom waiting," he replied, rising to his feet with exaggerated flair.

As we made our way back to the car, I felt a lightness in my step, a sense of purpose in the air. The shadows of the past would always linger, but they were no longer a weight dragging me down. With Isaac by my side, I felt ready to face whatever new challenges awaited us. Together, we were carving out our own story, one filled with laughter, love, and perhaps a few more unexpected twists along the way.

The sun hung low in the sky, casting long, playful shadows that danced across the picnic table where I had laid out our spread. The vibrancy of the day turned every leaf and petal into a splash of color, each hue more vivid than the last. The lighthearted banter between Isaac and me filled the air with laughter, as if we were weaving a tapestry of joy against the backdrop of our recent trials. I had taken the liberty of assembling an assortment of snacks, each one more ridiculous than the last, a reflection of my delight in the moment.

"Granola bars and fruit snacks, huh?" Isaac mused, holding up a bright packaging of gummy bears with an exaggerated raise of his eyebrow. "What's next, cheese puffs and cola? You know how to treat a guy, don't you?"

I tossed a handful of gummy bears at him, the little candies scattering like confetti across the table. "Hey, a celebration isn't about extravagance; it's about spirit! Besides, these are organic!"

He chuckled, popping a gummy bear into his mouth. "Organic or not, it's like you're trying to win the title of 'Most Adorable Picnic Ever.' You're going to need a banner for that."

I feigned shock, placing a hand over my heart. "You dare question my gourmet expertise? This is top-tier lake cuisine, my friend. Besides, I didn't see you bringing anything better."

"Touché." He smiled, his eyes sparkling with mischief. "But I was thinking a little more along the lines of fried chicken and homemade pie, you know, the classics. You can't call this a proper feast without at least one questionable decision involving grease."

I leaned back on my hands, taking in his casual charm. "And ruin this delightful zen moment? Never. This is a sacred space for joy and, if I may add, nostalgia for our glorious snack days."

As we settled into a comfortable rhythm of snacking and teasing, the atmosphere became a cocoon of warmth, where the outside world felt like a distant murmur. But soon, the tranquility was interrupted by the soft, unmistakable sound of footsteps approaching from behind.

Turning, I saw an older couple walking hand in hand, their expressions radiating warmth. The woman had a shock of silver hair that glinted in the sunlight, while the man sported a wide-brimmed hat that shielded his twinkling eyes. They ambled closer, drawn in by the laughter and the scent of snacks.

"Ah, the sweet sounds of young love," the woman called, a hint of laughter in her voice. "It's wonderful to see the youth enjoying life by the lake. Mind if we join you?"

"Please do!" I said, motioning to the empty spot at the table. "We have plenty of snacks, though I can't guarantee they'll rival your favorites."

The couple settled in, their presence adding a different kind of energy to our little gathering. The man introduced himself as Harold, and the woman, with a twinkle in her eye, was Margaret. Their easy banter was charming, filled with playful jabs and loving nicknames that spoke of years spent in each other's company.

"So, what's the occasion?" Margaret asked, eyeing the spread of snacks with a discerning gaze. "A first date? An anniversary?"

"Just celebrating life after a bit of a storm," Isaac replied, his voice warm and open.

"Ah, storms can be tricky," Harold nodded knowingly. "But it's the calm after that's worth savoring. I always say, the best moments come after you weather a few tempests."

I couldn't help but smile at the wisdom they exuded, the kind that only comes from experience. "That's true. We've had our share of... turbulence, but we're determined to enjoy the calm."

Margaret leaned in, her expression serious but her eyes bright. "Good for you. It's easy to get lost in what's happened. You have to hold on to what you've got now. Make the most of it."

I glanced at Isaac, feeling the weight of her words settle between us. "Absolutely," I said softly, knowing the depth of our journey. "We've learned that holding on tightly to love is what gets you through."

"Love and snacks," Isaac added, a playful grin breaking the momentary seriousness. "Can't forget the snacks."

Laughter bubbled up again, and I felt lighter, buoyed by the cheerful camaraderie we had unexpectedly created. As we shared stories—Harold regaling us with tales of their own adventures and misadventures—a comfortable bond began to weave itself among us, one that felt both intimate and grounding.

Yet as the conversation flowed, I felt an odd flutter of awareness, as though I were being observed from a distance. I turned slightly, scanning the shoreline, and my heart sank at the sight of a figure emerging from the tree line. It was a woman, her posture tense, her gaze fixed intently on us. A flicker of recognition danced through my mind, bringing with it a wave of anxiety.

"Everything okay?" Isaac asked, noticing my shift in demeanor.

"Uh, yeah, I just—" I faltered, trying to shake off the unease. "I think I know her."

"Know who?" he asked, his voice low, attention caught.

Before I could answer, the woman stepped closer, her features coming into sharper focus. She was familiar, a ghost from my past, and I couldn't quite place her until the pieces clicked together. It was Lila, a friend from my childhood, her presence both a comfort and a puzzle. The last time I'd seen her, we had been inseparable, lost in laughter, until life's currents pulled us apart.

"Is it really you?" she called out, a mixture of disbelief and excitement in her voice. "I thought I recognized you!"

"Lila?" I stood, the word escaping my lips in surprise. "It's been ages!"

She rushed forward, her arms open wide. I met her in an embrace, the warmth of familiarity washing over me. "I can't believe it! I thought I'd lost you in the world," she exclaimed, pulling back to look at me.

"What are you doing here?"

"Oh, just visiting family nearby. But I had no idea you'd be here." She looked at Isaac, her eyes dancing with curiosity. "And who's this handsome fellow?"

"This is Isaac, my... well, my partner," I said, glancing at him, a smile tugging at my lips.

"Partner, huh? Nice to meet you, Isaac. She's always been quite the treasure," Lila teased, her laughter bright and infectious.

As introductions were made and laughter resumed, I couldn't shake the sensation that Lila's sudden appearance was more than just a coincidence. The air around us shimmered with possibilities, and as I settled back into the comfort of our newfound reunion, I sensed an unexpected twist lurking just beneath the surface, ready to unveil itself when the time was right. The lake, with its serene waters and vibrant life, held secrets yet to be discovered, and I was eager to see what lay ahead.

The laughter of our impromptu gathering filled the air, a buoyant melody that mingled with the gentle rustle of leaves and the distant calls of birds. Lila's return had stirred something deep within me, a nostalgic warmth intertwined with an unsettling recognition of how quickly time could shift the landscape of our lives. As we all shared stories, our words flowed like the water before us, effortless and light, yet beneath it lay the undercurrents of unspoken truths and unresolved questions.

"Remember that summer we spent building that ridiculous fort by the old oak tree?" Lila said, her eyes sparkling with the glimmer of cherished memories. "You were convinced it would withstand a hurricane!"

"Of course! And it did—until your brother decided it would be the perfect launchpad for a flying leap into the lake," I replied, a grin stretching across my face. "The fort was a casualty of his 'bravery.'"

Harold and Margaret laughed, enjoying the familiarity of our stories. Isaac leaned in, a playful glint in his eyes. "And I thought my childhood adventures were something special. You've got to let me in on the secrets of fort-building!"

"Oh, there were many secrets," I teased. "Mostly about how to cover your mistakes with more leaves."

As the sun dipped lower in the sky, casting a golden hue over everything, the atmosphere felt alive with energy, as if the very earth beneath us was celebrating our reunion. But just as I was settling into this cozy warmth, an unsettling feeling crept back in, prickling at the back of my mind.

"So, what have you been up to?" I asked Lila, genuinely curious but also aware of the silence that had settled on her, a thin veil over her usually animated demeanor.

"Oh, you know, just life," she said, her voice cheerful but her eyes drifting away momentarily, as if she were searching for something just out of reach. "Moving around a lot, exploring new places. It's been... interesting."

"Interesting can mean many things," Isaac interjected, his tone light, but I could see the concern flickering in his gaze. "Are you okay?"

Lila's smile faltered for a fraction of a second before she regained her composure. "Of course! It's just, you know how it is—life has its ups and downs. But I'm here now, and that's what matters."

I nodded, but her words lingered in the air, heavy with meaning. I wanted to probe deeper, to understand the shadows that clouded her smile, but before I could voice my concerns, the wind shifted, and a sudden chill swept over us, as if nature itself had sensed the tension.

"Maybe we should go for a walk," Margaret suggested, her voice breaking the moment. "A change of scenery always helps clear the mind."

"That sounds perfect," I agreed, eager for any distraction that would lift the weight of uncertainty.

As we stood up, I noticed Lila's eyes dart toward the water's edge, where the sun had begun to set, painting the lake in shades of crimson and gold. "I'll catch up in a moment," she said, her tone casual but her expression far from it.

Isaac and I exchanged glances, the flicker of concern passing silently between us, but I nodded, allowing Lila her moment. I knew that whatever was brewing beneath the surface of her cheerful façade was not ready to surface yet.

As we wandered along the shoreline, Harold regaled us with tales of his youth, his voice animated as he spun stories of mischief and adventure. "I once tried to catch a fish with my bare hands," he laughed, his eyes twinkling. "Let's just say it didn't end well for me or the fish."

"You must have looked quite ridiculous," I chimed in, envisioning the scene.

"Ridiculous? I'd say more like a beached whale flopping around!" He howled with laughter, and soon, we all joined in, the lightness of his humor washing over us.

Yet, despite the levity, I couldn't shake the unease that had settled over me like a thick fog. Where was Lila? I glanced back over my shoulder, but she was nowhere in sight.

"Excuse me, I need to check on Lila," I said, my heart quickening.

"Sure, we'll keep walking," Isaac replied, concern etched across his face. "Let us know if she's okay."

I retraced my steps along the path, calling out softly, "Lila?" The trees loomed overhead, their branches swaying gently, casting intricate patterns on the ground. "Lila, where are you?"

As I approached the water's edge, my breath caught in my throat. There she stood, her silhouette framed by the fiery sunset, but something in her posture was off. She was bent over, her fingers splayed on the ground, as if she were searching for something.

"Lila?" I called again, my voice sharper now, edged with concern.

She turned, and the expression on her face sent a chill racing down my spine. It was a mixture of fear and determination, eyes wide and unblinking. "I—I think I found something," she said slowly, her voice trembling.

"What do you mean?" I stepped closer, my heart pounding as she knelt beside a large, flat stone half-submerged in the water.

"This stone... it looks familiar. I think I've seen it before." Her fingers brushed against the surface, and for a brief moment, I caught a glimpse of a symbol etched into the stone—a swirling design that felt eerily familiar.

"Where have you seen it?" I asked, dread pooling in my stomach.

She looked up at me, her face pale, and whispered, "In a dream. It was always in a dream."

Before I could process her words, the ground beneath us trembled, a low rumble echoing from the depths of the lake. The water began to churn violently, and the sky above darkened, the vibrant sunset fading into ominous gray.

"Lila!" I shouted, reaching for her, but the air crackled with an energy that seemed to push us apart.

"What's happening?" she gasped, panic flickering across her features as the lake erupted, sending waves crashing toward us.

I staggered back, heart racing, instinctively pulling her to her feet. "We need to go! Now!"

But as we turned to flee, a figure emerged from the depths of the water, a dark silhouette that sent a jolt of terror through me. My breath caught as recognition dawned—this was no mere illusion; this was a specter from our past, rising from the depths, and the echoes of our journey had just begun to resound with a chilling intensity.

With a desperate glance at Lila, I realized we were standing on the precipice of something far greater than our previous trials, and as the figure loomed closer, I understood—this was just the beginning.

9 798227 417640